Last Train to Midnight

Alex Baldock

Bloomington, IN  Milton Keynes, UK

AuthorHouse™
1663 Liberty Drive, Suite 200
Bloomington, IN 47403
www.authorhouse.com
Phone: 1-800-839-8640

AuthorHouse™ UK Ltd.
500 Avebury Boulevard
Central Milton Keynes, MK9 2BE
www.authorhouse.co.uk
Phone: 08001974150

This book is a work of fiction. People, places, events, and situations are the product of the author's imagination. Any resemblance to actual persons, living or dead, or historical events, is purely coincidental.

© 2007 Alex Baldock. All rights reserved.

No part of this book may be reproduced, stored in a retrieval system, or transmitted by any means without the written permission of the author.

First published by AuthorHouse 5/10/2007

ISBN: 1-4259-4827-8 (sc)

Printed in the United States of America
Bloomington, Indiana

This book is printed on acid-free paper.

For PG, Mum, Kate and Nick for love and support and all the furry ones who improve my sense of well being.

Bread and Butter.

A rogue pinhead-width ray of bright, untamed sunlight pierced the tiniest gap in the heavy curtains that hung across the dirty window, and reached, like a laser in its accuracy, into the inner corner of my eye, the corner that always remains ever so slightly open, even in the deepest of slumbers. I struggled to pull my eyelid up from its sticky haven and finally having done so jerked my head away to escape the torturous interrogation of the sun. The sudden movement made my head swirl and a wave of nausea threatened, briefly, to overcome my feeling of fragility, but having recovered for a second or two I lay back down, gently resting my aching head and feeling the soft feather filled pillow mould itself around me.

It was much later that a couple of irate tourists woke me next by shouting outside my partially opened window. The curtains, thankfully, had stopped the beams of sun from entering further into my dark world of night, which I had hoped would last longer than it apparently had, and they now did neither allow the stale air to escape nor the fresh, clean air from outside to permeate through the room.

The terrible thumping and aching in my head was no longer confined to that particular area, but seemingly it had spread to my neck, my shoulders, and my grumbling stomach, which begged for the sustenance I was too wary to give it. Moving any part of my body was again a struggle. At first I began by flexing my toes, wiggling them gently within the confines of the socks that covered them. I could tell they were desperate for air and relief from those sweaty parameters, but that release would have to wait until other more important areas decreed it.

Next were my fingers, always the least fragile and safest part to move, and often, with the arms, the most useful in terms of paralytic crises. They worked happily and seemed pleased to do so, as if they had been static and stuck for too long.

My ankle, at first reluctant to move without pain, soon shrugged off its lethargy and twirled freely, encouraging the toes to wiggle more strenuously and excitedly as they felt their day close to beginning.

Any other movements required greater muscular action, so they had to proceed with care and caution in order to maintain the current state of grace.

The knee was next and bending forwards and backwards only served to convince the toes that use was imminent.

No trauma yet.

The arms were equally responsive and it was here that I found the cause for my aching shoulders; my suspenders. I flicked them off from my shoulders, feeling the release that afforded me. I had to lie back and savour the moment as the blood rushed back in quantity to fill the previously restricted area.

I reached up, slowly, carefully, and gently rubbed where they had pulled across my collarbone, touching the warm smooth skin as if it were a new experience of sex, in wonderment and delighting in every slight movement, every touch of a new patch of skin. I scrunched my face up in pleasure and then in pain as my headache reminded me it was still there. How could I forget?

The effort of rediscovering my shoulders wore me out for a minute, or maybe it was nearer five, so I waited until my heart had returned to its normal, well almost normal, pace before attempting my next daredevil movement.

I had to shrug my elbow underneath me and lever myself up onto it. I pulled my elbow into my side and with an almighty effort, just manoeuvring my torso high enough slipped it underneath against my ribs.

That done I had to get up and then to a sitting position.

I slowly lifted my head, pushing down with my trapped hand and with my free hand in order to force my weight upwards. At first it seemed like there was no effort, no energy, but soon I moved and holding my breath and swinging my legs down so my toes finally touched the cold wooden floor, I found myself sitting gingerly on the edge of the bed.

I sat still, listening to the birds twittering, the cars honking and the people rushing by, not daring to open my mouth in case something other than noise came out. I sat for an eternity, hearing my watch tick round. I couldn't move my head to see what time it was. Frankly I didn't really care at that precise moment. My primary concern was to keep from splattering the floorboards with the churning contents of my unhappy gut. Not an easy task, especially as I now had to try and stand up. Bend my body forward, push up and straighten my legs, then straighten my torso, uncurling the tired muscles as they screamed to be left in peace and finally look in the big rectangular mirror that hung precariously over my aging battered oak chest of drawers.

I leaned steadily forward, clutching the side of the bed as it cracked under the movement. My arms shook. My legs wanted to, but by strength of what little will I had left, I held them relatively steady as they tensed and pushed up. I rose, perhaps too quickly, and stood bent double, hands clinging hard to my thighs, steadying themselves against my legs.

Holding my breath again and clenching my teeth together I walked my hands up my thighs, up to the top of my legs, straightening up as I went, eyes closed, teeth gritted, face contorted with the effort, and then there I was, shoulders hunched maybe, unsteady certainly, but upright.

I exhaled, opened my eyes, tried to focus on my swimming reflection and hurled.

Shit, I thought, as I forgot all sense of moving slowly and staggered as quickly as I could to the bathroom where I wretched and hurled last nights revelries into any receptacle I could see for the next ten minutes.

After I could bring up no more, froth and bile didn't seem to count, I sat back against the bathtub, rubbing my eyes, pushing my sticky hands under the cold running water, lifting them to my mouth and slurping gratefully, anxious to alleviate the sickening taste within my mouth.

I flushed, rinsed the sink and tub, pushing what few solid remnants there were down the plug and went back to the bedroom.

It already smelled vile.

I threw open the curtains, with my eyes closed, and thrust open the window, breathing in the clean air from outside, feeling the coldness of it rush over my face and body. I staggered down the rickety staircase, collected the mop and staggered back up, cleaned up the mess, shrugged on some clothes and staggered to the store below for milk and bread.

The store man laughed as I entered, hunched up like an old man, looking as white as a black man can get.

"Too much Midnight?," he laughed at the obviousness of his statement. I curled my mouth into a quarter of a smile. "You wanna take it reeeal easy. I don' like the look o you when you comin' in here looking like you do. You scare aways my customers." He laughed again. Irritating son of a bitch.

"Tab?," I said.

"Sure Midnight. I don' s'pose you'd find no money anyway. You take care, y'hear." I offered a grumble of thanks and took my leave, wincing at the door chime that signalled my exit, the storeman's deep belly laugh reverberating in my ears. My cousin was rarely sympathetic, just laughing it off as a normal occurrence, which I have to say recently it had been.

I took my meagre provisions back into my three-very-small-room apartment, which my well to do cousin below also owned and allowed me a little lee-way on rent, thanks Daniel, and sat down to eat them with the little butter I had left. Fortunately, they stayed down, digesting uncomfortably.

I didn't feel well at all though and creaking my forty-feeling-eighty year old body back into the bedroom, pulled the drapes tightly together, put some of my clothes on the chair where for the most time they lived, and took a breath.

I had to go back to bed.

A Job.

Fortunately it was a Sunday, and although, of course, if I had a client I would work 24 hours a day, seven days a week, 52 weeks a year, it was a day off. Daniel woke me later by hammering on the door and when I didn't answer, unlocking it himself and finding me covered by innumerable sheets snoring contentedly.

He then, kindly, threw water over my face and I spluttered into consciousness.

"Hey, Midnight man, I have warn you about evils of alcohol. You gotta take a break man, get out less man. I mean you dun nuthin' for weeks now, I mean it, you gotta get sumthin' hap'nin', an' fast, you know, man. I's not gonna bail your ass out forever. You gotta do sumthin' Midnight man."

I think I grunted and shrugged.

It wasn't really my sort of thing, working. I guess I knew he was right though, in a way, but I could be damned if I was going to agree with him now. That would have been too easy and I was never one for making things easy for myself or nobody else; family or no family.

I staggered, still slightly wobbly after my excesses in everything over the last twenty-four hours, to the bathroom, across the cold wooden floor.

A quick piece of advice. Wooden floors look great, but get mats, rugs, put your damn clothes on the floor. They are cold.

I was tempted to glance in the mirror above the sink, but remembering what had happened last time I thought better of it and flicked some water on my stubble, rubbed some toothpaste over plaque, flossed halfheartedly, and dusted a cobweb off my hair. I wiped my hands on my graying Calvin Kleins and wandered, slightly straighter, but still obviously hunched, back to talk, well maybe, to Daniel.

"So, then Midnight, man, whatchagonnado'boutit?," he rolled into one. I looked at him from under the heavy hoods of my eyelids.

"Hey, Daniel, I don' know, alright. Just quit it. I think I gotta get me sorted, you know, 'fore I start on my life. These things gotta take time man, an' time is one thing I got, you know." I pulled on my shirt, foul smelling thought it was, hitched my suspenders back to my shoulders and slipped my feet into the old, but-oh-so-comfortable brogues. "I need space, an' I think you gotta give me some."

"Man, you got it, but you gotta promise me man, you gotta get sorted man. Other you gonna be strugglin' here, an' I ain't frighten' o kickin' your black ass outta here, you dig? Jus' cos yous ma cousin man, you not carryin' on dickin' yo way aroun'. You not messin' me aroun' neither man." I raised my hands in submission. I had to get rid of him. I took a letter from my pocket and waved it at him.

"This arrived, so I'm outta here. I gotta go."

"Sure man, but I mean it man. Catch you later man."

I high-fived him and followed him down the stairs, which creaked unhealthily under both our weights.

"Hey, you gonna wash first?"

I picked up a shirt from the shelf beside him and slipped it out of its plastic packet. Daniel smiled and slapped my back, shaking his head as I retreated out of the door, the chimes clanking bitchily.

I broke into sunlight, slipped on my shirt and shades and got in my car, an old, unreliable, but drop dead gorgeous Ford Mustang 1964 given to me by my first wealthy and thankful clients too many years previously. I had found their errant son playing Don Juan in Florida on his parents credit rating. Not hard to trace, but I wasn't arguing. I took the letter out and read it again.

'Dear Mister Seyle,

I need to see you about a problem I have. Would it be possible for you to come to the following address on Sunday of this week?

Yours

John T Barclay

The address followed and that was where I was now headed.

A problem? John T. Barclay? The name rang several bells, but none of which I could fully put a time, place or face to. John T. Barclay was not a name I would usually have taken notice of, but the man had a fancy address, nice personalised paper and, if a man of that standing, financially I mean, took the time to actually sign his own letter, even if he didn't write the damn thing, then he meant business and business was what he was getting.

John T. Barclay? That's right, it hit me as I drove cautiously, actually showing off the wheels. It wasn't very often that members of the public got to see such a fine example of the automobile as mine undoubtedly was.

Barclay was a multi-millionaire businessman who had blitzed Wall Street in the mid-eighties, managed to hold it all through the crash when all around were failing to hold onto theirs and losing fortunes in minutes. It was a good job my shirt was clean, even if I felt like shit. He had picked up a trophy wife who was in on the Hollywood MAW scene, and was now on the verge of becoming very big.

No cracks about silicone at this point.

Her name was...Cat...Kyle...Cale...Cale Kline? Cale Kline, better known for her recent acting, but modelling and whatever had been part of her trade for a few years before that. For a while, as I worked my way towards his part of town, I wondered how and why he had contacted me. How had he found me? I was not exactly well known in the investigative world. Not recently at least.

I turned off the main road and found myself in an extremely salubrious suburb, tree lined streets, sheltered gardens, slate and chimney only peering over the tall fir trees that grew behind tall gates, fences and walls which enclosed the vast homes setback away from prying eyes.

I glanced at the address again.

Leaving Home.

"Ashes to ashes, dust to dust…"

Other words paled and faded into the bright sunlit background as the terracotta coloured earth was dropped handful by mournful handful onto the wooden box that lay the obligatory six feet below. The mouths murmured words of sympathy and condolence as they passed the tall red haired woman who stood by the grave, crying silently, letting the steady trickle of tears creep out from beneath the blackest of shades that covered her striking blue eyes.

The crowd drifted away leaving the solitary, almost lonely figure watching over the grave diggers as they began the arduous and thankless task of shifting the earth back into the hole from where they had dug it just hours before.

The woman cried new tears with each falling of soil and after the two men finished she remained, standing, contemplating.

It shouldn't have been a shock, but when these things happened there was no telling how the human emotions began to handle such events, and in this case the experience was harrowing.

Her mother, God rest her soul, had been ill for a long time. Years. Since she was fourteen or fifteen. She had been too ill to recognise her since she was seventeen. She had basically been kept alive for the last eighteen months. And now, now when she was twenty-one, the tired woman had passed away, herself only just fifty, though the body in the ground looked nearer to seventy.

She shook her red waves and squinted into the sun, feeling the paper in her pocket.

She bent down to the earth, touched her fingers to her lips and placed them on the red soil, holding them there for a few seconds before standing and finally turning away and walking back towards the outback house which had been her home for all of her young life.

She passed the 'SOLD' sign, giving it a cursory glance, and her car, packed lightly with the few belongings she had wanted to take to the City with her. Doug could torch the rest.

The house was buzzing with conversation which simmered, then stopped altogether as she hovered on the threshold, eyes turning and focusing on her slender figure as she removed the shades to reveal red rimmed piercing blue eyes which strangely hadn't the energy to tear into each and every body standing in the room. Unlike normal. She took a step forward and fixed her eyes on the far corner of the room, then the ceiling, then one by one she managed to draw every guest in towards her, making them wait before she spoke.

Her sharp Australian accent was still in evidence though her voice was softer.

"Thanks for coming. Mum would have loved it; loved you being here, so feel free to stay as long as you want. I can't. I'm sorry, but I have to leave this place as soon as possible, for my sanity rather than any burning desire to leave you people. You have been my life." She paused for a moment, on the verge of more tears. " Many of you know that Roy Grant has bought this place and he and Doug are going to run it however they see fit. The only proviso being that they leave Mum alone." A murmur of approval moved round the room. "Thanks again." She slipped her shades back on. "I have to go."

She turned and walked out, leaving the door to swing shut behind her.

Through the mesh the guests could see her black clad figure slip away from the house, pausing briefly for one last goodbye at the freshly dug earth, then revving the engine of her black pick up and disappearing in a dusty red cloud.

John T. Barclay.

I still shivered despite the ending warmth to the day as the sun just dipped below the horizon. My mind wandered and wondered what Mister John T Barclay could want? I hoped for something easy to get me back on track. Get me working again. But my professional curiosity hoped for something more difficult to stretch my resources and brain cells. The old gray matter was in need of an urgent overhaul having lain idle for too long.

Walking past the gates and walls I could not see a thing, just the greenery of trees and shrubs which led up to hidden brickwork. I was envious of the money that was invested in these areas of residence, the wealth that was created and generated by these areas, by these people. I only hoped they were happy with it. There was nothing more pathetic than someone with the assets to buy anything and who still remained unhappy with their lot. Made me sick.

I finally found the gate and pressed the impersonal buzzer that was situated by the vast wrought iron gates, flicking my eyes at the camera that peered down at me from the summit of the gatepost. I gave a hint of a smile and immediately heard the heavy bark of a guard dog. A German Shepherd, a Pincher, a Rottweiler? I wasn't too anxious to find out.

A disembodied voice crackled through the speaker.

"Am I able to help you?"

"Mister Seyle for Mister Barclay."

"Please enter at the buzzer and close the gate behind you."

The strained tones of an Englishman had welcomed me and I did as I was told. The strained Englishman himself met me at the door.

"Would you come this way."

I followed the smartly attired butler through the vast, opulent hallway. I found myself staring at the porcelain artifacts that were scattered around the black and white tiled floor. Huge vases, the odd statue of Greek or Roman influence. Once upon a time I had known the difference, but now a vague recollection of specific anatomy was the only distinction that sprang to mind as anything like a possibility. Above my head was an ornate, glittering crystal chandelier. I dodged away. I'd never trusted physics with keeping such heavy objects hanging from ceilings. I had only just convinced myself to put a proper shade on my light.

The staircase was carpeted, but at either side there was a gap where the tiles beneath were openly visible.

My rubber soled shoes squeaked poorly. I wished for some proper shoes that clicked magnificently. I straighted my back and pulled myself up to my medical height, around 185cms, and felt better for it.

The butler did a rapid double take as he turned round to make sure I was following and not dawdling. I had only been around 180cms when I first met him. A stoop brought on by time and effort and alcohol.

We passed through a narrow dark channel which opened up into a sober, sombre room, one side of which was covered with what I imagined John T. Barclay proudly claimed as his extensive library.

Indeed the wall was just books, hidden behind a bank of glass doors. I noticed a step stool to one side which again I imagined the esteemed Mister Barclay used, infrequently, to climb to the highest shelf.

In front of this magnificent view sat a sturdy oak desk, the weight of which I could only guess at and then with a level of inaccuracy which would prohibit me from verbalising it. The top was sparsely decorated. A computer at one end, one of the up to date G3 Series laptop, powerbook things which worked as well as, if not better than many desktops. A lamp sat beside and an inkwell occupied the opposite corner. In the age of Biro I found this strangely reassuring.

On a small wheeled table to the back right of this desk sat a more standard desktop computer, its screen flickering blue.

A large window gave light to the room from my right as I stood in the doorway, and more greenery threatened to overwhelm the view. The window, I saw, was actually a door which probably opened onto the seven or eight acres of yard at the back, possibly grassed, probably landscaped.

The rug that I sank into threatened to swallow my feet it was so thick. It was a creamy-brown colour which didn't really go, but if you had the cash, then taste was an optional extra which many chose not to afford. However, it struck me as odd. John T didn't strike me as a tasteless man.

He struck me as a confident man, as a busy man, or at least as a man trying to look busy. His hair was dark with a hint of silver over his ears and flecked throughout. His face was dark and tanned, but smooth, showing no ageing from the obvious sun he enjoyed. He hadn't looked up from tapping into his keyboard since we entered his room and only when the besuited mourner in front of me cleared his throat did he acknowledge us.

"Gates?"

"A Mister Seyle to see you."

Then he looked up.

Gates left as quietly as he had arrived.

The 1991 Businessman of the Year came round from behind his desk and greeted me with an outstretched hand. I returned the shake, feeling the grip of a confident man.

"May I offer you a drink?"

My stomach churned at the prospect.

"You may, but I'd have to decline."

He shrugged and poured himself a finger of Jack Daniels, throwing in a couple of rocks.

"How are you?" He didn't care, just being polite.

"I'm good thankyou. Enjoying the weather."

"Yes, why the hell not? I'm glad you could fit me in to your schedule."

No problem at all, I thought.

"I know you must be busy."

He obviously knew I wasn't.

"Well, I won't waste your time."

Or your money.

"I know this must be mundane, but I've received some extremely disturbing mail recently. I wonder if you'd take a look at it."

"Sure. Why the hell not? S'what I'm here for."

He offered a hint of a smile, but returned to his serious face as he dug in the drawer beside him and produced three pieces of paper, three rather scrappy pieces of paper and handed them to me.

"Your fee is not a problem, charge whatever you normally do. If I'm not satisfied, I'll tell you."

I took the letters and sat down. I needed to. My head was thumping like a heavy metal act was jamming inside of it. I didn't let it show. Years of practice.

'Mister John T. You have something we want. Get ready to pay.'

It didn't really qualify as a letter. A sentence. Two. Not a letter.

'John. Money. Assets. A beautiful wife. Which shall we take first?'

Not really a letter. Why 'we'? Not just a psychotic individual, but a whole disturbed group.

'Barclay. No cops. You will take notice and you will comply. There are no half measures in business. Take everything and answer questions later.'

Not that malicious. Just warnings. Maybe someone who my newly married would be client had upset in one of his many business dealings. Maybe.

"Do you have any idea who it is?"

Barclay shook his head and then broke into a rueful smile.

"Could be anybody. I am a wealthy man, with money in stocks, shares, a restaurant chain, a couple of properties here in the States, one in England, one in Antigua. I have many enemies who simply covet my...trappings. This country is full of whackjobs who would probably be as willing to put a bullet in their own mother, and in some cases already have done, as soon as make an attempt on someone who they think they know because I appear on TIME once a year. Mister Seyle, I am afraid it could be anybody."

"Is this place protected?"

"State of the art."

I had so many questions to ask and essentially they were trivial matters, when did the notes, sentences arrive? Last week.

Hand delivered? No.

Did he have the envelopes? Yes.

Smells? No.

Who had opened them? Gates, but he never read them.

Has anyone else seen them? Cale? No.

Any groups he could think of? Again, could be anybody.

Where were his properties? Houses, here in New Jersey, offices of course on Wall Street, a place in LA, London England, and on the beach in Antigua. Restaurants stretched across the country. LA, New York, Chicago, Toronto, DC, Dallas, Las Vegas. A couple of options in other franchise.

I may have to talk to Gates and Cale? Cale won't know anything. She's too busy schmoozing. Gates won't say anything. Apparently John T would trust his butler with his life.

"That, Mister Barclay, is what I'm trying to protect."

As I turned to go, ushered out by the ever reliable Gates, I stopped and asked one final question. Knowing my dormant reputation....

"How did you find me?"

He sighed and fixed me with an amused, yet stern look.

"You don't remember?"

I tried, but it had been a long and interesting day, chasing hard on the back of a long and interesting night.

"No. No, I don't."

"You found me in Florida, what, twenty years ago. You made quite an impression. And your name is unforgettable." He reached into his wallet and pulled out a dog-eared card. "You gave me that as my parents drove me away, and told me to hang on to it, just in case."

"Just in case." I followed, nodding slowly.

We shook hands.

"This is the 'in case'."

I promised to keep him informed.

My Mustang. A gift from Mister John Barclay's parents. I didn't know what to say really and I just smiled a warm grin of a smile to myself as I slouched back towards its gleaming body as it lay in the evening sun waiting to be gunned into life once more.

It was conspicuous, but that was part of the reason I liked it. No, I loved it. More than anything I had ever possessed, any woman I had ever known, I loved my Mustang more than anything. I could be just so cool, so noticed, so money, when I was in the wheels, on the street, cruising around not doing anything. Just cruising. The engine started second time, not bad really, and grumbled into roaring life as I revved up and pulled away.

For trailing and secretive work I had to borrow my cousin's nondescript black sedan. The bright red sports car was too obvious, too noticeable. Although in New York, anything other than a Yellow was noticeable.

My mind took in the change from high class money, wealthy homes, to the gradual middle class suburbia and then the sweep of blocks filled with apartments, broken windows, burnt out cars, trashy neighborhoods of the inner city. The junkyard slums with a hooker and a dealer on every corner. Every city had them, fortunately this place had fewer than most.

The letters were bothering me.

The New York mark was too easy, but it was the only tiny little clue I had. There was no content, no name, no initial. My client had a problem. John Barclay was a target and as anybody with anybody less important than the President, and on occasion even him if God or the CIA decreed it, defense was not possible. If you were wanted then you could be got. Easy.

Until I had something else, then there was little else I could do. I had a few contacts in NYC who may be able to give me a tidbit of information from which I could expand a theory, but until something decisive happened, then my money would be easy.

The word kept repeating.

Easy, easy, easy.

Everything had been too easy.

Identity.

Sydney was bathed in the warmest pink glow from the winter sun and the Opera House had never looked more spectacular, except maybe on those tourist trap postcards, filtered heavily and coloured to perfection in order to appeal to the homesick who had, just had to send a goodwill message home saying that although it had rained everyday and Dad had to be rushed to hospital after he was bitten by a spider, well how were we to know it wasn't poisonous, but we're having a lovely time and look at this wonderful picture cause it looks like this all the time, you know?

The hostel was basic, but warm, and air conditioned. The proprietress, a Mrs Hallows, was warm, tanned, with a beaming smile, and it was cheap.

The meal had been well appreciated and as soon as her red hair hit the pillow, her eyes closed and she fell asleep.

The following day she was able to walk freely around the town, nobody recognised her as the Silverton Pin-Up of the Year and 'July' on the town's calender, nobody noticed her as Miss Broken Hill and Surrounds.

The Silverton girl had left home and now she was determined to leave her past behind. Her mother gone now in body although long before in mind, Mama Anna went home leaving her when she was eighteen, now she had left her town, her friends, her life. She went through the glass doors and the open plan office greeted her with the buzz of administrative duties being done.

A vacant blonde greeted her with a vacant smile.

"G'day. C'n I help you?"

"Sure. I'd like to change my name."

"Certainly. Do you have..."

"I have no family, no legal guardians, no passport, only this." She plucked a charred piece of paper and handed it over. The blonde looked at the document and recognised it as what was left of a birth certificate. She saw the hurt and distressed look on the receptionists face. "Everything was lost in a fire when I was very young. This was all I have from my mother and she has just been buried, so I have no idea about anything else. Sorry."

"Oh, I'm so sorry. About your mother, I mean." She took the scrap between two long manicured nails. "If you'd just like to take a seat."

The blonde tottered away on her heels, flicking her nails with habit as she approached a man with a sharp crewcut, bent down to talk to him, revealing the colour and extent of her knickers to anyone behind her, and then returned with him in tow.

The man picked up several forms and handed them to the receptionist, who took them and gave him an admiring glance, fluttering her eyelashes as he half smiled and returned to his seat.

"If you could fill in these, and if you don't mind two of us acting as witnesses then we can get Derek, our legal representative to finalise the details for you."

"Thanks."

The forms were mind numbing, but she spent as little time on them as she could, handing them back after fifteen minutes.

"Okay, if you'd just like to take a seat, can I get you a coffee, tea, OJ, water, then I'll get these checked and signed."

"Coffee would be good. Thanks."

Another twenty minutes passed before the totterer returned brandishing the legal documents, smiling excitedly.

"Here you go," she gushed with way too much enthusiasm, obviously thoroughly over excited by the whole event, actually helping someone change their name. She held them out as if she was awarding the Melbourne Cup to the winning owner.

"Congratulations Miss...er...Mercer."

Miss Mercer took the papers, smiled benignly, was forced into an impromptu A-frame hug, and then allowed to leave.

She walked out into the bright sunlight, breathed in deeply and was knocked to the ground by an errant youth on rollerblades.

"Jesus, I'm sorry, shit, man, God, are you, like, hurt? Jesus. Don't I know you? Nancy, right?"

"Nancy Wright?"

"No, wait, man, like, Nan O'Neill? Isn't it? You work at The Cherry Stone? Nan O'Neill? Christ my mate fancies you rotten. Like, man, wait till I tell him. It is Nan O'Neill, isn't it?"

She shook her head.

"No. I'm Alix. Alix Mercer."

The youth looked puzzled.

"Sure...Alex...cool. C'n I shout you an OJ?"

Real Threats.

I was woken by Daniel, again, hammering on the door as if an earthquake was about to hit and I'd had no warning.

"Midnight, you wasted sonuvabitch, get up man. Midnight, call. Get your black wasted ass outta there and git down here man."

I crawled out of bed. Daniel looked disgustingly healthy, and awake, for such an early hour.

"What the fuck is wrong with you? It's like..." I had no idea of what time it was like.

"Midnight it's ten a.m, and there's a white man on hold. Get!"

I got. More slowly than Daniel would have liked me to get, but I got soon enough. I cleared my throat and tried to sound awake.

"Midnight Seyle?"

"Midnight, sorry to get you out of bed..." I couldn't fail to miss the sarcasm...or irony? I never knew which to be truthful. "...but I received another letter this morning. Signed."

I was awake in an instant. My case. My only fucking case.

"I'll be right there, Mister Barclay. Right there." I almost slammed the phone down, but Daniel grabbed my hand as I thrust it downwards and I replaced it slowly.

"Sorry cuz."

"Sure man. Like, shit, you gotta case or sum'in?"

"Sure man."

Daniel shook his head and laughed. He laughed a deep belly laugh. One of those made famous by James Earl Jones.

"Midnight, you kill me man, you kill me." He trundled off, laughing to himself. Bastard.

John Barclay was actually looking slightly paler through his year round tan. He also wore the expression of a worried man.

"Midnight, good of you to come."

"S'ma job, man."

He acknowledged this fact with a good natured smile and wave of his arm, dismissing the remainder of any formalities.

"Here."

He thrust an A4 size sheet at me. A4? I took it.

'Mister Barclay,

As you may have gathered, there are a few concerns that we have with you. In fact there are some major concerns we hold. Anyway, to the point of the matter.

Many years ago you made a bid for a whole block of stores. A successful bid. This became the eponymous, and very English and hugely profitable, Barclay Square.

The sad fact, for you, is that this land was stolen, by you from me and my family, and now we would like it back.

We want to spare any, how shall I put it, mishaps, but if you don't comply, then they certainly will.

We will be in touch.

Gini Firetti.'

"You said it was signed?"

"Did I? It has a name. What more do you want?"

I shrugged. A name was good. Frightening, but good. 'Me and my family' had turned John's blood cold. Gini Firetti.

I knew why it was easy. They made it look so easy. No evidence, but clinical. The Mob had come for John Barclay.

Need to Know.

Barclay had realised this too, which is why he was pale this morning. Nobody messed with them and came out alive, even in this day and age. Corruption, bribery, extortion, all still existed, or so it was rumoured, behind the facade of their many legitimate enterprises. They remained wealthy despite recent problems with some of their bosses being convicted of murder, bribery, fraud, amongst other offences, and they remained powerful. Powerful enough to scare. Powerful enough to make me think twice about continuing with the case.

But I needed the money, and at least the work would be exciting.

Did I really want it to be exciting?

"When exactly did this takeover occur?"

"It wasn't a takeover," he snapped. Boy, it had gotten to him. "It wasn't a takeover, it was a deal, a business deal."

"A business deal?"

"Yes," he snapped again. His cool exterior giving way as a few beads of sweat appeared on his face. He felt me looking and raised his sleeve to them, wiping quickly in a gesture of frustration more than anything. He sat down and pinched his forehead, the skin pudging up between his fingers, small furrows creased across in dark lines. More sweat appeared.

"It was a business deal?," I prompted. He looked up and then away, wincing as he did so. Maybe it was, maybe it wasn't. He sure wasn't giving anything away.

"Mister Barclay, I..."

"I know and I don't care."

"But I..."

"I'm sure you do."

"You have no idea what..."

"Get out and leave me alone. I need time to think. Stay if you want, it'll save you coming back later."

I reeled away, shocked and staggered by his tone. He didn't say it loud, but he meant it and he made sure I knew he meant it. But I had to stand firm.

"If I'm going to be coming back later then why can't you just tell me whatever it is you have to tell me now. It would save us both a lot of time and anguish and you some money." I bargained on his thrift. And failed.

"Because I have to sort some stuff out, some of which you don't need to see or be told." He had stood and as he was talking he walked and I found myself outside the room looking at the closing side of a heavy wooden door. The silent Gates was instantly at my side.

"Drink, sir?"

He rolled his r's and widened his eyes as he did so. It was an unnerving experience.

I took a JD heavy with water, I suspected tap, but it could have been one of the brand names. Most of the time I couldn't tell water from wine from whisky I was that far gone, but in my sober periods the origin of the water mattered least of all. Still, it tasted like JD so that was the important part.

Last Train to Midnight

I sat and waited. For thirty seconds. I wasn't a very good waiter, in any sense of the word. When I was sixteen I spent a small part of the summer working in a burger joint. Not one of the high class places, the ones that everyone knows and sponsor big events, but one of the home brand, independent places which still exist in these days of free market monopoly.

I hated it and I was bad at it. In fact I hated it probably because I was bad at it. The customers were short with me, so I was short back, so they raised their voice, so I raised mine, so they called my boss who raised his...at me and then gave them their meal for half price, or some other deal he dreamt up on the spot to make it look like he was doing something, not aware that everyone else was taking note of how easy it was to get cheap food; bait the waiter.

I mean what can you do? I had my respect and a rep to protect, and I couldn't let nobody diss me and get away with it, cheap, greasy job or no cheap, greasy job. I lasted a whole three weeks before I was told to stay away during opening hours. He was very specific. I went back after closing and bricked his window. I have to say he deserved it.

Waiting, drink in hand, in Mister Barclay's mansion, I was no better. I had to get up and walk around, looking at books on shelves, ornaments on the mantle, pictures, photos, portraits, on the walls and in frames around the place. I suppose I was naturally nosy, which was partly the reason I was a successful (successful?) private detective.

In fact it was my cousin's fault that I was always coinless. It had been he, after I had located the boy who had nicked an armful of candy from under his nose, who had suggested I get up off my worthless black butt and do something proper. I was still, just, a teenager, but the kick had been well placed and a career move like that piqued my interest. Interviews and license later I had my first case - a nice holiday, involving work, in Florida. As I wandered the sun drenched streets before they became popular I thought I had found the perfect life.

A couple of decades and several more jobs in windy Chicago and wet New York and I had begun to wonder. Still, now it was getting a bit late to decide I should have been...a contender.

For what I don't know.

There were many framed photographs of John T with the great and the good and the now not so good. Di Maggio, Ali, Pacino, Reagen, OJ, and of course his beautiful lady wife, Cale Kline.

Cale was a stunningly beautiful woman. In twenty years time she would have the figure and the sharpness of features to maintain her jaw dropping quality when many other twentysomething beauties had lost theirs. A lot of women, successful, famous women managed it. Jane Seymour, Lauren Bacall, Victoria Countess Spencer. Cale Kline would be another.

She was only twenty-two and had only just burst onto the Hollywood acting scene after five years of modelling, whatevering and taking bit parts in forgettable TVM's, DTV's, indie and mainstream movies. There had been the unfortunate and almost these days necessary flirtation with soft-core cinema, but her pelvic plunge had been shortlived and only designed to pay the rent, or so she and her agent told the media. Her latest film had turned the corner for her by taking over $100million in just over ten weeks and already she was being talked about in the same breath as Kidman, Bullock and Witherspoon in terms of her fee for her next big screen appearance. The press had been warned off from camping outside her home, John's home, and threatened with heavy lawsuits if they ignored his, her, their demands. At first they had ignored John and Cale and quickly suits had been filed and the cameras and microphones disappeared round the corner. Neither of the householders were naive enough to imagine it would last forever, but they would deal with it when the time came.

Barclay had met and married Kline inside of six months during the previous year, and the talk was of it being about as long a married life. They were approaching their first anniversary with the knives being sharpened in the background.

First Meeting.

The occasion was a production company party. IBP was five years old, John T Barclay was an investor with clout, Cale Kline was the up-and-comer in one of their new movies. In a restaurant hired for the evening the seating plans placed singles with singles and marrieds with marrieds, in an attempt to keep flirtatious partners on the straight and narrow. It didn't always work. In fact it rarely worked, but the sentiment was there and some of the more paranoid individuals gleaned some comfort from the fact.

Cale was sitting next to Turan Uriely, a German male model who was hoping to become the Next Arnold Schwarzenegger. As Cale understood one word in ten she was optimistic of his chances.

On her other side was Dane Wren who was potentially the Official Next Big Thing and was certainly behaving as if he was. Moody glances all around him as he smoked sulkily, flashing a smile at only the prettiest of the waitresses and paying monosyllabic-so-cool attention to Cale. He was desperately thin, but the hollows of his cheeks as he inhaled highlighted the dark pools of his eyes, the square jaw, the wonderful arc of his eyebrows and the length of his black eyelashes. His hair was short, but unruly, sticking up on top, weaving and lying this way and that. He was, in short, stunning, especially in the dimly lit restaurant which gave mellow tones and dark shadows. Cale found herself staring, and fleetingly he stared back, but recognising she was a something, cause she was sat at the table, but not something-enough cause he didn't know her, he made play after play for the waitresses, knowing they knew him and would be only too glad to join him later. Only near the end of the evening when he was completely stoned did he talk at length, asking his neighbour if she'd like to make his threesome a foursome.

Cale heard, but declined as she was now mesmerised by the more thick set, but still athletically fit figure at the end of her table.

He was so brown, his hair was black, but the flickering lights picked out the gray in his hair. His shirt was powder blue and he wore a geometrically patterned yellow and blue tie. He was also smoking, but a cigar, which made Dane's spliff look like a matchstick. He puffed and laughed, a charming agreeable laugh, and his smile radiated across his face. He must smile a lot, thought Cale, as his looked so at ease with the features around it. She half smiled to herself and took a sip of wine. She had known a boy who looked like a puppet when he smiled, it was so forced.

The man leant forward and talked across the table. Cale stretched back over her chair to see who it was and was dismayed to see Georgina Lovat, a voracious red head with a delicate laugh and an ample cleavage, gazing across the table at the dark haired stranger. Her cheeks were flushed and she was playing with the tendrils of her hair which dangled invitingly by her ear.

Cale felt a wave of jealousy creep angrily over her. Why? Why? She had no claim on a man she had never seen before, let alone spoken to, let alone...

For all she knew George and The Stranger were old acquaintances - they were never friends, never - and were just catching up on old, older, times.

Georgina giggled seductively and the Stranger leaned in closer. Cale groaned inwardly and felt a drink being thrust into her hand. She didn't even look at it, but threw it down her throat, feeling the burning of the tequila as it hit and ran.

"Man, hot, baby," came the surprisingly deep voice to her left. Dane was sitting, his eyes half closed, joint hanging loosely from his lips (oh my God), arm draped across the back of her chair (more for support than lechery). Cale caught her breath as she fell, entranced into his gaze. He held up another glass to her. She took it, chinked it against his and threw it back. Dane lazily held his to his lips then jerked his head back and exhaled noisily with a hint of a groan as the alcohol slipped, burning, down his throat. Dane stood, winked and left, heading for the bathroom. Cale was experienced enough to know when to follow and when not to.

She followed.

In the men's room Dane was hanging loosely off another emaciated boy who was bending over the sinktop, tapping busily. The white line was divided into two, then with a nudge from Dane into three.

SkinnyBoy went first, vacuuming half of the line with his left, then the other half with his right, slumping down in an ecstatic, relieved, satisfied heap. Dane, half asleep from all the joints, had trouble holding himself steady as he lowered his nose over the powder, then shuddered as, with a huge effort, it disappeared. He staggered, then collapsed onto SkinnyBoy, who grunted with the weight that hit him.

Cale, ignoring the 'tut's and whispers of disapproval as other men entered the room, bent her head to the coke and followed the same ritual. As she finished she didn't collapse, but shook her head, gave Dane a kick and left, walking with a new jauntiness that gave away her recreational activities.

The party was breaking up and for a second she panicked as PowderBlue had gone from his seat.

So had Georgina.

"Shit," she murmured and kicked a chair. It fell over and almost tripped an unsteady Dane.

"Man, watch out baby. Less stress, more coke, baby. Coming to paaarrtaay?"

Cale felt Dane's arm creep round her waist, but again she thought it was probably as much for support as anything else. When she felt another arm snake round from the other side she knew it was sexual and a frisson of excitement jumped through her, even before she turned and saw SkinnyBoy smiling inanely up at her.

He was verging on the anorexic, but his eyes were the palest blue she had ever seen and they froze her to the spot.

"Oh, man yeeeessss," she screeched, laughing with delight as Dane's eyes lit up as the coke kicked in. He leaned across to her and kissed her. She responded and felt SkinnyBoy's hand slide over her buttocks, testing, seeing how good she was. She reached round and pushed her hand into his groin. She shivered as his erection pulsed through his khakis, her hand moving against it as Dane kept kissing her.

"So, who's the fourth?"

"Nicky."

Cale's eyes flickered at the thought of three boys, so when Nicky turned out to be a fellow blonde with a chest bigger than hers, she was mildly disappointed. Still, she thought cheerfully, there's Dane. Gorgeous, sexy Dane.

John saw the four of them leave from the rear of his limousine, the black windows shielding him from unwanted observers.

"John?" He continued watching, trying to ignore the whispering that was going on very close to his face.

"John?" This time he turned as the group across the street climbed into a longer, darker limo than his. The flame haired Georgina smiled at him, a seductive smile as she traced her finger across his lips, drawing it away with her as she sat back against the door. The zipper on the front of her dress had slipped a couple of inches, showing off more of the pale chest that John had spent most of the evening trying hard not to look at as he was talking to her.

His mouth went dry as he pulled off his tie and slid over to sit beside her.

He rested his hand gently on her knee, watching his own movements as he did so, his eyes drifting with his hand as it slid up and down the length of her slender, toned thigh. For a woman in her mid forties she still had a fantastic figure, and she knew it.

As his hand reached the edge of her skirt she parted her legs slightly. The fabric curved and his fingertips couldn't resist from creeping underneath, touching the flesh above the stocking tops.

"Georgina…?"

"Gina."

"Gina. Is this going…?"

"Oh, I think so."

John actually blushed and looked down at what his hand was doing, running under the lacy fabric of her stocking, brushing his knuckles over the softer flesh of her inner thigh.

Gina leaned forward and drew him into a kiss, pulling him down on top of her as she wriggled her way along the seat.

The partition between passengers and driver closed silently.

Cale climbed into the back of the limo and thought she was in an apartment. The seats were leather, the mini-bar was full and the four of them fitted in comfortably. Even before the valet had closed the door SkinnyBoy had one of Nicky's nipples in his mouth and was sucking away like it was a tournament. As Cale sat down she almost went through the roof as Dane slid his hand under her and pulled the back of her skirt up around her waist. Cale calmed immediately and fell into an embrace which felt like Dane was falling asleep halfway through. She opened her eyes, aware that the pressure from his hand on her leg had gone limp. He had his eyes open and was watching Nicky go down on SkinnyBoy, her mouth sliding up and down, tongue twirling, licking, her eyes pinned to Dane as SkinnyBoy moaned and groaned under her.

Nicky lay back, legs apart so Dane could see the moistness beneath her skirt. Then she licked her finger and slid it down to touch herself, sliding it in so smoothly that Dane almost came just watching. A trickle of semen dripped from one corner of her mouth.

Cale was repulsed and excited.

SkinnyBoy saw her face and leaned over to her, an encouraging, if slightly dopey smile on his face. He gently touched her just above the knee, then with one hand on each leg pushed them up slowly, fingers barely touching her skin, until he found her knickers and began moving his hands back down to her knees, his fingers teasing the elastic down her legs.

Cale slid with him so she was slumped in her seat, her groin on a level with his face as he slipped the thong over her shoes, his mouth open with earnest concentration as he performed.

The moment Cale felt his hands drop away she reached forward and pulled his head down to her. She held him there as he held her open and started to move his huge soft lips over her, his tongue searching for the the erect nub of her clitoris.

Cale caught Nicky's eye and flicked the top button of her shirt undone. Nicky was there in a flash and flipped the next one open, then the next, then the next, her eyes not leaving Cale's until the fabric parted leaving her midriff exposed and her black bra barely holding her breasts in place.

This was remedied by Dane who casually flicked his fingers behind her back and Nicky took Cale in her fingers and teased and caressed her until her nipples throbbed.

As Nicky did this Dane reached round and drove his fingers into Nicky from behind. Cale felt the other girl tense as he did this, then relax as his fingers got to work, sliding in and out, occasionally drifting an idle thumb over her clitoris. Nicky rocked with him, her hands, then her mouth working overtime on Cale.

SkinnyBoy had taken to little cat licks at Cale, then thrusting his tongue inside her. Cale felt herself shake into a climax, just as Dane brought Nicky off to her right.

SkinnyBoy appeared, his penis still visible, and Cale pushed him back and took him in her mouth.

Nicky unzipped Dane and climbed on top of him, breathing hard, narrowly missing crashing her head on the roof of the limo.

Dane pushed her off, buzzed open the sunroof and stuck his head out, the wind whistling through his hair as the driver raced, charged through the New York night. Nicky stayed inside, returning her mouth to Dane's manhood. SkinnyBoy saw an invitation and pushed Cale away, positioning his mouth on Nicky as she squatted down. Cale for a moment felt horribly left out as Dane howled into the night. Then she slipped SkinnyBoy inside her, reached round and grabbed Nicky's breasts and howled along with him.

John lifted his head to see what the noise was as a car raced past. He recognised the dishevelled head that was baying to the moon from the sunroof and grimaced. The remarkably sexual woman he was inside at the moment had nothing on the blonde at that party.

Cale Kline.

The photographs certainly showed off Mrs Barclay at her best, laughing and smiling and jaw-droppingly sexy. I was amazed she had lasted so long as a well kept secret in acting circles. I suppose she could pick and choose when money wasn't a problem. Gates had reappeared and offered to freshen up my drink. I shrugged and handed him the glass.

"Just a splash more water. Thanks."

He tried to keep the disdain off his face, but as he put three to one water in my tumbler he couldn't quite manage it. I'm not sure whether it was because I was having anything to drink, or because I ruined it with so much water... I hoped the latter. Gates struck me as a man of taste, probably more so than me who was often lucky to get to the tasting stage. Falling over, hurling, sleeping it off, but tasting was a formality that could be swiftly overcome.

This time, in company, in a flash house, my client's house, I sipped. I screwed my face up at the taste. Too much water to whisky. I hoped that Gates hadn't noticed. I turned to see. He wasn't there. He was so silent it was scary. Eerie. Maybe he was Batman?

I sat down again and picked up a magazine. I flicked restlessly and then stood and paced. What was he doing?

I looked at the wall where a huge picture of Cale was hung. She was in her wedding dress, a long sequined affair that showed off her long, smooth, slender arms, her incredible figure and the teasing quality she had in her face.

Her eyes were staring straight through the picture, smouldering with...something. Desire? Wanton desire? They were jade green, enhanced maybe, but startling nonetheless, and they challenged you with every look. No matter where I went in the room, they followed. They taunted me to come closer. Begging me to touch, warning me to stay away.

Her skin was pale, but under the summer sun, or maybe 'touched' for the picture, it had taken on a golden tan, highlighting the blondness of her hair, the greenness of her eyes, the whiteness of her teeth, the coral of her lips.

I took another sip. I had to. Just looking at her, being so close to her. An inanimate object with a vision of her on it. I shook my head and looked away. But I turned back.

Her mouth was set, lips slightly apart, a hint of a smile. Together with the half raised eyebrow, the smouldering eyes and the figure hugging white dress, veil falling to the floor behind her, I was amazed the cameraman had avoided camera shake. But all the best cameras had anti-shake devices on them, and I suppose if you are a pro then you get used to photographing beautiful women.

What a job.

She was sensational. There was no other word for it.

John looked at the stain on his shirt, and then at the apologetic face of the Dog-guy.

"Sorry man."

"Shit. Fucking mustard. I don't even like the stuff."

"Sorry man."

John waved him away and continued on his way.

"Forget about it."

"Man, hey, free dog?"

John was seething and stormed back to the office.

"Jenna, get Brooks Brothers and try and put Gerry off till half past."

The interviewer had had enough. They were all alike. They were all experienced out their ass, all had diplomas, all were dressed smart, and all were clean, smooth skin. Not a pimple in sight. The only goddam problem with modern day living was that everyone was doing it. There was little or no variety.

"Dreen, how many more?"

"One, Mister Franklin. Shall I send..."

"No. Get me a coffee and get me a doughnut. No don't. Get me a coffee and a half melon." Christ even he was doing it.

Ten years ago doughnuts were the staple diet. Now, together with smoking they had almost been outlawed in some areas. Not in The Simpsons though.

Dreen brought them in and Leonard Franklin devoured the melon with relish, still wanting more after he had dragged his teeth along the skin, fighting and tugging for every last mouthful. Juice dripped onto his desk and he wiped it off with the napkin that Dreen had thoughtfully provided. God, when would she do something wrong. Robots, all of them. Every one was turning into an effing robot.

He took a slurp of his coffee and wanted a cigarette. Nah, later.

"Okay Dreen, send it in," he strained, knowing whoever it was would have heard. The door opened, Dreen shot him a nasty look and 'it' waltzed in. She looked like she should have been starring in a remake of Cabaret. Her hot pants were hot, her fingers tweaked a smoke out of her mouth and as she threw her jacket over the chair and sat down Leonard sat open mouthed.

"Mister Franklin, call on line two."

"Tha...thankyou." He fumbled with the numbers in front of him before pressing the wrong one. "Dreen?"

"Line two."

"Thanks." This time he concentrated. She had rested her cigarette on his golfing statue he had on his desk, balancing precariously.

"Hello, Leonard Franklin, Brooks Brothers?"

"Len, hi. John Barclay. Look, I need a favour. Could you get a shirt up to me now? I'd send Jenna, but I've got Gerry Krakewski coming in and I need her."

"Other minions?"

"Len, come on. Please. I need it now. If I sent a body down there it would take half an hour for them to get in to see you..."

"They could just buy you a shirt?"

"Len, I plug you so often. I tip you off about deals. I risk my neck for your bank balance. All I need is a shirt."

Leonard sighed. It was true. He was a wealthy man because of John Barclay, and not just because he was a Personnel Manager for one of the most highly regarded firms in the city.

"Okay, I'll send someone. Lunch?"

"Call you. Thanks Len."

Len shook his head, glanced at the girl who had crossed her legs again, then scribbled something on his pad, tore it off and handed it to her.

"You're hired. Take this, get the shirt, take it uptown, then come back here. You not back by three, you're fired." He stood and offered her his hand. "Welcome to the firm."

She ignored it and flicked her jacket over her shoulder.

"You can keep the cigarette."

Gates had come and gone again, offering me afternoon tea. Which fucking country? I had declined. He promised that Mister Barclay wouldn't be much longer. Than what? I inquired, but the quip was lost on the humourless suit. Although I'm sure I heard a rumble of laughter from the direction of the kitchen just after. Perhaps just my stomach. Lunch had been missed. Afternoon tea would have been good, but I just couldn't bring myself to do it. I know I'd moderated my Southern accent to fit in a bit more, unlike Daniel who couldn't have cared less, but afternoon tea was going a bridge too far. Don't think they'd have made a movie out of it though... Having said that, with the trash that Hollywood, laughingly, thought up... Never say never.

"Brooks Brothers," she sighed wearily. "How many more times? Should I write it?"

"Can you?"

"Sure." She grabbed a pen.

"No, can you write?"

She scribbled on the pad and held it up. Jenna read it.

" 'Fuck you'. Imaginative. Security to Mister Barclays office, thankyou."

The last message reverberated around the building and Jenna thought she could already hear the thunder of size thirteens as Marlon and Ditrek pounded along. The girl rolled her eyes and insolently took off her bag and removed a shirt from it, holding it, sneering.

"Thanks, security, just testing. Not bad. I almost heard you." Jenna had gone red and took a second to find her bearings. "Mister Barclay, a young lady to see you. She says she's from Brooks..."

"I know, I know. Send her in."

Jenna stood and walked prettily and efficiently to the door, holding it open so the girl could slouch in. As she passed, Jenna received a sharp kick on her ankle.

"Owwww."

John looked up, Jenna hastily closed the door swearing to herself and the girl flung the shirt onto John's desk.

Need to Know - 2.

"Mister Barclay will see you now."

Gates had returned, once more, but this time bringing good news. I stood and creaked a bit as I did so. My knees grated, my shoulder clicked and I popped my ankle. Air in the joint and it made a sharp cracking noise as I flexed it. Gates had the wit to look slightly startled at the sound. I bet he oiled himself every day to stop hisself creaking. I shuddered. The thought didn't really warrant thinking about.

John was sitting behind his desk, thumbs raised together, pinching his lower lip. A bizarre sight.

"Midnight, I have to apologise for shouting, but some things are better left alone, and this was one of them. Still, I realise that you are only doing this for my benefit and therefore you have a right to know some things about the deal." He took a breath and swivelled his chair round so his elbows rested on the desk, he leaned forward and he faced me.

"The deal was done between myself and Michaelangelo Marello. We bought it together, planned it together, built it together. Then I bought him out and made both of us very wealthy men, although my wealth from that deal was longer in coming as I had sunk millions into the development, so it took time to pay off and realise a profit."

"How long?"

"Eighteen months, two years."

I whistled. Nothing for something that size. Absolutely nothing.

"How much did you buy him out for?"

"An agreed price."

"How much?"

"You don't need to know that."

"I do. Where can I find him?"

"You can't. He's dead."

There was something in the way he said it that I knew I shouldn't press him any further, but being the PI, and naturally inquisitive/stupid? I asked.

"How?"

"How what?"

"How did he die?"

John took a flicker of a second, but he took that flicker.

"Natural causes."

"He is dead?"

"I was at the reading of the will. Yes, he's dead."

"How much did you get from him?"

He took longer this time, coming to terms with the facts.

"Nothing. I got nothing."

I managed to keep the smile off my face.

"Were you disappointed?"

"A little. I'd be lying if I said otherwise. But he said he'd given me enough from the deal. He had family, friends. We had done a major deal, perhaps *the* major deal of the decade. He had every right to do whatever he wanted with his money, but we had sort of agreed to split any money from the deal down the middle, fifty-fifty, so I was a little hurt, yes. But as I said, he did what he wanted in the end."

I pondered this. He seemed right on, sincere. I left it at that.

"I should know how much?"

"You don't need to. It was millions though. Exact amounts are hard to pinpoint as there were deals going on, money coming in, going out, but it was millions. Is that good enough?"

I nodded. "Sure, that's good enough."

Powder Blue.

John looked open mouthed. The girl slumped in one of the few chairs and sat twirling in it. Fortunately the chair twirled with her and she spun for a moment before stopping and finally looking up at the man behind the desk. Her eyes fizzed for a moment then settled back into their dull expression as she chewed monotonously on gum.

John suddenly found it hard to speak. Cale's eyes had only returned to normal because she was sure he wouldn't remember her. After all the party had been over a month ago.

"There's your shirt."

"I see that. Thanks," he managed, picking up the shirt and sliding it back onto the desk. He started to undo his shirt. Cale got up to leave.

"Where are you going?," John asked, startled, anxiously hoping she didn't have to go. Not yet.

"I gotta go back."

"Why?"

"Cause I gotta job to do. Don' wanna be late."

John winced. From the look of her it wouldn't matter if she was late or not, she wouldn't last five minutes at Brooks Brothers, such were their high standards.

"Sit down."

"Look, buddy, I gotta go, alright?"

"Sit down." His tone was firm, and Cale thought twice, sat down sulkily and mangled her gum more menacingly.

John peeled off his stained shirt. Cale watched him and John watched her. Both knew he had a good physique. Cale just by looking, John by the fact he spent hours and hundreds of dollars at the gym. If he didn't look good he'd want to know why. His shoulders were just broad enough, and he had a hint of definition that Cale just wanted to touch. He was tan; dark and smooth. Enticing.

"I didn't think you needed a job. You're an actress aren't you?"

Cale almost screeched with delight. He remembered, or at least recognised her.

"Sure," she answered coolly. "But I've got nothing and rent's due and you gotta make things work. I need money from somewhere."

"Family?"

"Got none."

"Friends?"

"Same as me. Few of 'em anyway." She pulled her gum out and let it snap back against her chin, sucking and biting it back into her mouth noisily as she watched him button up his shirt.

"PowderBlue," she whispered.

"Excuse me?"

"I gotta go." She stood and turned.

"Stay?"

"What for? I need money. I gotta job, I need money, what do I stay for?"

"Look, I can give you money, I can give you whatever you want, just stay until I've had this meeting, then I'll buy you lunch. Deal?"

Cale had to consider this. Why would he offer something like that if he wasn't on the level? Men, strangers, didn't do that unless they wanted something. And as yet she wasn't a hooker.

Her sad eyes gave her away as she put a hand on the door.

Then she hesitated. She could feel him close to her, although he was still behind his desk in front of the window on the other side of the room. She could feel him looking. Her hot pants were suddenly very hot.

"It'll have to be dinner."

Dinner ended up as a pizza on the floor of his office which stretched long into the night. He told her about his business, she told him about her aspirations. He wrote her a cheque for the rent. She tore it up. He wrote another for two months rent. She folded it neatly and tucked it into her bra.

They laughed a lot as they analysed and criticised everyone they could think of who was at the party, especially SkinnyBoy and Georgina. Dane got off lightly because he was still her get out clause. John didn't really notice. It had been a while since he had female company for longer than the contracted time, not counting Georgina, and he found himself entirely absorbed by the woman stretched out in front of him.

Time ticked by. The lights of the city outside the window burned all night, bright neon mixing with the lamps from streets and cabs. The distant glow from Liberty herself just visible on the horizon if you screwed your eyes up and blocked out all the others from nearby buildings. The Empire State and the Chrysler shone out as the famous landmarks they were, fading slowly in their luminescence as the illuminated night gave way to the natural colours of day.

They walked out to the street and got coffee and bagels at five thirty, drinking and eating in the fresh morning air, the city already beginning to rush by in a noisy cacophony of calls and horns.

When Cale left him two hours later she kissed his cheek making him colour slightly, made a promise to drop in later and wandered away, swinging her hips, and drawing whistles from every quarter as she walked down the street. John broke into a laugh and went back to his office.

Jenna caught up with him at the elevator and raised her eyebrows at his unshaven appearance in yesterday's suit. John clocked her look. Neither said anything. They didn't have to.

Questions.

My client had made a deal with a guy, now deceased, made a fortune for himself, made his partner a very rich man, and now certain people wanted the land back because they thought John had stolen it from them.

It seemed so straightforward.

There would have been no way, no way on earth that they would have allowed John to take the real estate if they had had the choice. No way they would have waited so long to get it back if they could have done so before. Why had they got rid of it, for I was sure John wouldn't have been allowed to steal it from under their noses.

And if that, as my best and possibly my only theory at the moment, was true then the partner, the dead partner, Mister Michaelangelo Marello had a lot to answer for. Except he couldn't.

I drove away with a few further details in my pocket.

I had the address of the lawyer where the will had been read. I had the numbers to all of John's phone lines, e-mail included, so I could get hold of him whenever and wherever he was, and I had a sheet full of figures, which I had taken on trust because there was no way I could have found out about them, concerning the deal itself.

John had caved eventually and thought that if I knew it involved millions then I might as well know the ins and outs of the transaction.

I pulled through a drive-thru, then sat in the car reading and eating, trying to decide what to do next.

In 1987 John T. Barclay had invested a huge amount of money and capital in the joint acquisition of a block of real estate in central New York City with a written and signed partner, Mike Marello.

The deal had cost, give or take, $30million, of which John had supplied $20million. Mike had supplied $7.5million, with the remainder being taken up by smaller investors.

The land had been bought, many of the buildings had been gutted, all had been refurbished and then rented out to the major players who now sat alongside the established names of the city. The new players had been the up and comers, spotted by John as they were making their first real steps and invited, then persuaded to make an initial investment that would make them very rich in the future if they were any good and could stand the competition.

Restaurants, boutiques, fashion houses, had all sprung up almost overnight and as soon as three-quarters of the units were rented John had paid a further $15million to Marello who had then walked away from the project. John had not said why, whether there had been differences of opinion or fights or what, but Marello seemingly walked away with double his initial investment.

Twelve months later, the rents and initial outlay from the rent holders had paid off John Barclay and he began to show profit from his total $35million investment. From then on his own personal profits from the project grew steadily. With a

75% controlling interest, the smaller investors had remained to recoup and profit from their investments, John was able to accrue huge amounts and in 1990 it was at the Barclay Square site that he opened his first restaurant, expanding his chain and his assets by five by the end of the following year.

His earnings were high, but his capital and his real estate and his investments made him an incredibly wealthy man.

The question was, then, why had Marello walked away so easily, or had he been pushed? Why, or how, had he stolen the real estate? Why had Firetti waited so long to come and approach John, especially if they knew about it? And why did you never get what you wanted from a drive-thru?

Closer and yet Further Away.

Jenna looked up as the office in front of her came to a standstill. Well, she should have clarified, the male part of the office came to a standstill, with one or two exceptions which didn't surprise her in the least, as the Brooks Brothers girl walked across the floor towards her.

Cale stopped at the desk and asked if John was in, dropping her cigarette into the ashtray as Jenna nodded and pointed. Both women offered half smiles and Jenna stuck her tongue out as Cale walked away.

John was on the phone, looking intently into the screen in front of him, tapping occasionally, waving and smiling as Cale walked in, then returned to his serious face as he continued with his business.

Cale helped herself to a drink, then slumped into a chair, her floaty lilac skirt falling up her thighs, and the matching t-shirt creasing as she folded into her seat. She drank and watched as John conducted his work with an air of a man on the verge of making a deal which could make or break him. Cale didn't really know any different, she didn't really know how much he was worth, but she thought that any one deal probably wouldn't make that much of a difference to him.

She glanced at him as he sighed and puffed out his cheeks, catching her look and raising his eyes in mock boredom with what he was doing. Cale smiled. It made her feel better to think he wanted to be with her rather than on the other end of a telephone.

Five minutes later he put the phone down and came round to greet the woman, the incredible woman, scrunched so sweetly into his chair.

"Hi." He held out his hand. She took it and shook it.

"Hi," she returned, secretly hoping he'd kiss her hello.

"Glad you could come."

"So am I."

"I squared it with Len...Mister Franklin."

"Sure."

"No, I did. You can do what you want now."

Cale looked a bit confused.

"I still have no money. So how can I..."

"I mean, you don't have to work for him. You can come and work for me, with me." He noticed the skeptical look on her face. "If you'd like?"

"Sure, but what would I..."

"Look, I can find you something. You don't have to do anything, you can do auditions all day, or take classes, or whatever you need, want to do for your career, all you told me about last night, go to Hollywood. Just say the word and I'll write you a cheque, give you some cash, transfer some to you. Whatever."

Cale was speechless and for a few seconds failed to say anything at all. She struggled out of the chair and faced her benefactor.

"I couldn't, I don't know what to say. I mean that is wonderful, but I can't take all your money."

"Sure, you can. I've got more than enough, take some. If you don't feel right about it, fine, don't take any, but I can give enough so that you can do whatever you want. If you want to retire and live in a trailer park in Texas, fine. I'll give you enough so you can do that. Cale...I...I'm not very good at... things...but I think I love you, and I hope that if I can do for you whatever you want, then you might feel an obligation to stay with me."

Cale was stunned. She waved her arms frantically as she twirled around the room, opening and closing her mouth, making little squeaks before crashing out of the door and slamming it behind her.

John stood for a second then made his way over to the door and was on the point of opening it when she burst back in.

"Obligation? You can't just spring something like that on me and then talk of obligation. I hardly know you, you hardly know me. Obligation?," she squealed again. "Love me? I don't...I...I...oh God." She whirled about, flinging her arms, then slammed the door again. John reached it this time and Cale collapsed inside.

"Listen, I'm a business man, I've been getting my way for years, and I do things when I have a feeling for them. And I have a feeling for you. Is it so different? Cale?"

"Yes, it's goddam fucking different. You're talking about my life, you're talking as if you own my life and you can buy my life and you can buy me and I don't like it. I don't want to feel obligated to you, I want to love you."

"Do you?"

"No, I don't know."

John's face fell and he watched her through hurt eyes as she struggled for the words.

"I hardly know you, John? I barely know your name, I don't know what you do and I'm only twenty-one years old.

I don't necessarily want my life planned and designed for me from now until I die."

"Don't you? Really? You said last night that all you wanted to do was to be rich and famous. I can make that happen. I can make that happen, Cale."

"So can I and you can watch me do it." Her voice had changed to anger rather than frustration and she stalked out of the office, head held high, eyes blazing as she slammed the door, colliding with Jenna and sending coffee flying all over everywhere.

John stood in the doorway as Jenna struggled to her feet, desperately wiping coffee from her clothes and the carpet.

John looked at the mess and returned to subdued business mode.

"Mop it up then get the cleaning people in."

Little Italy.

I had headed home at first, but then I thought to strike while John's words were ringing in my ears so I turned towards the county lines and headed into the city. I stopped on the outskirts and found a cab which pulled up outside a building of red brick with a plinth by the door which was covered in gold, brass or silver plaques, each advertising a service in a particular part of the building.

It was situated in Little Italy which made me shiver slightly as I thought of who I was dealing with, but I had had worse and this one, so far was proving okay. Any deeper or more intimate contact with certain sections of the Italian population and I wouldn't just be shivering, but for now I was able to put it down to a slight breeze blowing through the city and I pressed the buzzer.

"Tony Graziani's office?"

"Hi, my name is Midnight Seyle and I was hoping to talk to Mister Graziani?"

"Were you now? Well, he's here, but he ain't talking till I say so. Do you have an appointment?"

"No, I don't."

"You'll have to get an appointment."

"Can I make an appointment?"
"Now?"
"Sure."
"Okay Mister. I'll put you down for..."
"No, no. I need an appointment right now."
"Oh. Oh. One moment."

The line went quiet for a minute while, I presume, the girl was away asking Tony for his permission to let me in. As I was waiting the door buzzed and another man, at least I assumed it was another man, pushed past me on his way out. I caught the door and walked in.

Tony's office was on the third floor and the stairs creaked a little as I walked heavily up them. In my younger days I may have had the energy to bound up them two at a time, but I haven't done that for a good few years. I pulled myself along by holding the rails and finally came to the door.

A dark girl was waiting for me at the door.

"Mister Seyle?" Her voice was clearer, smoother than on the intercom. She was mid-thirties perhaps, maybe a little older, her hair, tied back in a ponytail made her look younger than she was, I thought.

"Yes, Miss...?"

The gentle greeting didn't work and didn't receive a smile either. Instead she ushered me through into the inner sanctum and just one door away from Tony Graziani.

"Mister Graziani won't be a minute. He was just busy with something." Her face gave way to a coy little smile, and for a second I wondered what she meant, then as Tony himself bustled out of his office smoothing his hair back into place I knew. At least I thought I knew.

"Mister Seyle?" He greeted me warmly and was all business.

"Mister Graziani? Good of you to see me at such short notice."

"Forget about it. I need a little distraction every so often. Sara here does everything else, so I have to do something, right?" We all smiled, and Sara slipped behind her impeccably neat desk. "Come in, come in. What is it that I can do for you?" I sat, refused coffee, admired his cramped little room and tried to tell him what I was here for.

"I need some help."

"Sure, 'tswat I'm here for."

"I have some information which I could really do with clarifying."

At once his eyes had become shaded and he was more standoffish than his effusive self of just minutes before.

Still, he had to ask.

"What sort of information?"

"I'm a private investigator, I need a little background, and I need to see a will."

He gestured for me to continue, but he crossed his legs and his arms were folded.

"I need to see the will of Mike Marello."

He shook his head.

"Who?"

"Michaelangelo Marello."

"Nice name, but I don't think I know it."

"Sure you do. I have your name as the man who dealt with his will. Now I know you have a large number of clients here, but Mike Marello is a very important person to me and I would appreciate it if you could show me his will."

"I'm sorry, but I don't know the man." He stood and held the door open for me. "I'm sorry."

It was my turn to shake my head as I stood and made my way into the outer office, where Sara looked up over the top of her glasses at us as Tony showed me the door and hustled me out of it.

"Mister Graziani, I really..."

"You don't and I don't. I'm sorry, but I really have no idea of who you are talking about, so if you don't mind I'd like to get back to what I was doing before you interrupted."

I left quietly.

He was good at moving people, I'll give him that. I had followed his every move and found myself on the doorstep before I had been in the building for more than fifteen minutes, with nothing to show for my, albeit, minimal efforts.

I assumed John was right in his paperwork, after all a man who had so many millions could easily lose track of a scrap of paper with an address on, but I doubted it. He was an organised man with an organised life. He didn't lose things.

I sat and watched the building for a while. Few people came and went. I found a vendor and got a dog and a beer and sat and watched from across the street for a while longer.

Breaking and entering was an option, but maybe not just yet. I don't know why I didn't trust the word of a man who was paying my bills, but when he said Marello was dead something didn't quite ring true. I had to confirm it first before I went anywhere else.

But not tonight.

I finished my beer, found a cab and got a ride out to pick up my wheels.

From there to a bar, and from there to bed.

Well, that's where I woke up.

I started drinking when I was eleven. Well, that's not strictly true. I had my first drink when I was eleven, but I actually started, really started drinking when I was thirteen. It had been an avuncular friend of the family had introduced me to scotch, and I hated it. It didn't taste nice in my mouth, it didn't leave a nice aftertaste and I threw up very soon afterwards, although I swore this to be due to the tub of ice-cream I had eaten and not the mouthful of liquor I had swallowed.

However, practice and perseverance and many blurred nights later I was a fully fledged drinker and on my twelfth birthday I was rushed to hospital to have my stomach pumped. I gave up for a few months after that, but my appetite had been given a taste it really actually liked and it was inevitable that I found my way back to my Pop's liquor cabinet sooner rather than later. An occurrence, I must add, that my hide would regret for days every time I sat down. But that, as they say, was it. I was hooked, lined and sunk without trace. I always claimed, still do, that I'm not addicted. That I can stop whenever I want. I just don't want. And I probably couldn't. But I only really drink at night. I mean *really* drink. The kind of drinking that costs a fortune in cash, friends and lost hours. I only do that at night. And not every night. Once a week, maybe. Maybe not even that. I can't afford it.

John and Cale.

The next time John saw Cale was when she walked back into his office three days later, eyeballed him every inch as she stalked across the room to him sat behind his imposing desk, and punched him. Hard. And not an open palm slap, but a proper clenched fist, full force, extended arm punch which drove him backwards out of his chair and into a cowering heap on the floor, peering back over his desktop at her blazing eyes.

"I'm not and never will be obligated to you, John, I want, I am going to do it my way, make my own choices, make my own mistakes and come out of it where I want to be. But... but..." She faltered and dropped her gaze for the first time since crashing through the door a minute earlier. "...but I can't stop thinking about you and that's never happened to me. I just want to be with you..." She caught his astonished look once again. "...and...and that's never happened to me before either. So I figured that these things can't be like coincidence, so, what I think is that, is that, I think I,...is what I think is...I love you. And I know this may seem like really cold and whatever, but I'm not a businessman and I don't know how you do things and if it comes across as that then I'm sorry...it...it didn't mean to, but it's true and please say something otherwise I'm going to go round in circles and end up marching out of here again having talked myself out of it."

"No," John burst into life, suddenly alarmed. "No, no, don't."

He stood, his hand feeling his cheek and the bruise that had already formed, discolouring his face with a darker mark against the deep ingrained tan.

Cale looked embarrassed and looked at the floor, that back up at his face as she reached forward to touch the mark, pulling her hand away just as her finger touched his skin.

"I'm sorry."

"Forget it. Here, sit down."

She sat. She slumped and began biting her nails. John perched on the edge of his desk and took her fingers away from her mouth.

"Don't."

She began rubbing her fingers together, working them hard against each other in her lap. John slipped off and knelt at her feet, pulling her hands apart and holding them in his.

"Don't."

She caught his amused look and half smiled back at him.

"Well, what the fuck can I do?"

John hesitated and thought for a second about any possible repercussions of anything he might say, considering what had just been said in this more normally sober, quiet, restrained environment of his office.

"Kiss me."

Leaning forward, clutching their hands together as their chests moulded into one, Cale's mouth met John's, lips touching, tongues gently searching, exploring.

"Mister Barclay, Mister Larcow's here?"

John pulled away. Cale sat back on her heels as they faced each other.

"I have to..."

"I know." She touched her finger to her lips and reached out and placed it softly on his. "But I'll see you later?"

"Sure." She stood and at the instant Jenna opened the door Cale swished out, offering the merest hint of a wink as she passed.

The wedding rivalled New Year in Time Square for the event of the year in New York, with the great and the good of the city coming out to meet, greet and celebrate with wizard financier John T. Barclay and his beautiful, stunningly gorgeous in fact, young bride Cale Kline. The society papers were out in force telling the story with varying degrees of exaggeration from the truth. Only one was accurate, due to an exclusive deal John and Cale had signed for interview rights, and even they dressed it up beyond recognition in swoons and missed heartbeats. Love at first sight was voted as the most overused phrase of the day.

The mayor, deputy-mayor, corporate chairmen, directors, executive and non, board members, bored onlookers, secretaries, P.A's, personal trainers, lesser spotted acting talents and a handful of celebrity faces from Hollywood mingled together, exchanging anecdotes and cigarettes over endless glasses of Moet. All agreed that Cale would benefit the most from the partnership in terms of John's wealth and contacts, although no-one dared to call her a gold-digger.

The couple honeymooned in Paris and Antigua before returning to The Big Apple to carry on with their lives as husband and wife.

The only black spot was when Cale refused point blank to become Cale Barclay, but John relented after being faced with another row hard on the heels of their first one. It was only a name, after all.

Contacts.

You would think that I'd get used to hangovers. No way. Every time I slip closer and closer to that unconscious oblivion I warn myself that the night and the day after will be painful and make me feel like death, but usually by then I am too far gone to care that much and far too bombed to stop drinking. They get easier to cope with, once you've discovered what works and what is likely to make you feel like starting again just to stop the cure from working. I guess these days sleep is all I need. When I was younger it was getting up and getting on. A good solid, greasy start to the day and that would set me up. But now I find sleeping it off works just as well. Takes longer and screws more with your life, but it is less expensive and ultimately works probably better for me.

So, I slept.

When I finally struggled out of bed it was getting dark again. In years gone by at this point I would have grabbed my jacket and gone and done it all over, but I remembered that I actually had a job for once in my life and decided that I should go and do some work on it. I didn't know what I was going to do. There was nothing I could do really. Graziani would have long since gone home, John hadn't been in contact all day and so there was obviously nothing new from his angle. I knew this because Daniel would have moved heaven and earth to tell me if he had called. Cale was away in L.A and as much as I wanted to talk to her that would have to wait. So, the only thing I had left was a bunch of bedraggled sentences all screwed up in a pocket, somewhere in amongst my many discarded clothes. I shook my head at the sight I had created and knew I couldn't face it. Work beckoned and in the past if in any doubt I had always gone to see Olivia.

Her place was down the steps down a back alley down the darkest street in Harlem. But she was an angel. Really. I had known her from way back when a mate of mine whose name I can't recall to this day had given me her number and told me to go and get laid. I had, but apart from the obvious gratification she had helped me on a case I had at the time. She knew everybody. And plus she knew everybody. I gave her a name and she told me where they hung out, and who they were close with, what they drank, who they saw. She must have had a phenomenal memory and from the way she worked she must have been a wealthy woman, but she was an angel. In disguise if you like, but an angel. She might just as well have had wings on her back.

Her place, as I described it, was actually her work place. She had an apartment she lived in uptown, the address of which she gave to few people. I was one of them, but I'd never been there.

Her place of work was neat, clean and sparse. It had three rooms. A small room with a stove and a sink, an even smaller john and a huge bedroom.

I guess it was the sitting room for most other people who would have lived there, but for Olivia it was a bedroom. It had to be.

She varied her work between here and one or two clubs she danced at. She loved the dancing. She was a hooker to pay the bills.

I slipped down the wet steps and knocked.

She answered, all long eyelashes and smoky aura, her silk thigh length black robe slightly open to reveal the shimmering black negligee beneath and the smooth chocolate skin beneath that.

"Midnight, honey, whatja doin' here sweetheart? Whatja outta here for then? Oh my God, it's bin a while, ain't it? Sure it has. Oh my, come on in."

I followed her in, watching the silk move over her buttocks, trying to stay focused. On work.

"I came to wish you a happy birthday, sugar."

"Aw, Midnight, you sent a card, but thanks anyway. Whatja really here for?" She stretched up and kissed me warmly, hugging me close, running her hands up and down my back. She had been twenty-eight recently. A good few years younger than me, but so much wiser.

"What is it ever, Olly?"

"Sex?"

I smiled. Maybe later.

"A place."

"Coffee?" She wandered out to the stove without waiting for my reply.

"Sure."

"So whatja up to then? I here yous got a job?"

My eyebrows rose quietly in surprise. How did she know these things? I shouldn't be surprised though, she's done it loads of times. I mean known what I'm doing before I do. Actually that was the case once. I went to see her about another job and she gave me the the lowdown on a case I hadn't even been offered yet. Sure enough, this guy calls me the next day. Amazing. Contacts everywhere.

"Yep."

"John Barclay. Big client. Was at his wedding last year with a guy from Wall Street. Oh, beautiful wife. What's he want?"

She handed me the coffee and I took a sip. Instant as ever. She ushered me to sit. I sat.

"He wants help. He's been getting these threatening notes..."

"Letters?"

"No, notes, and the last one came with a name."

I could see by the look in her face that she wanted the name. That was after all the reason I was here, and she knew it. I took a sip from the coffee and swallowed it down, pursing my lips at the bitter taste. "Gini Firetti."

"Gini Firetti? The Guy? *The* Guy? Wow. I mean, I know some of his friends, but the man himself don't need the like of me, you know? He can get whomever he wants." She dared to look impressed for a second as she drank and thought. She knew what I wanted. Somewhere where he was. Somewhere public so I don't get whacked too easy, but somewhere quiet so we can talk.

Like I need to talk to this guy. He says and I jump. No talking involved. Easy.

"You sure you want this? I mean he's not a man to be messed with, ya know? I know people who don't come back looking too good. I know people who don't come back period." She tried to outstare me, force me to back off a little. But I didn't. I had to do something, go somewhere. Even if it wasn't now, then at some point I felt I'd end up in the company of Mister Firetti and I knew I wanted it to be on as many of my terms as possible.

"No, but thanks. I gotta see the guy sometime, maybe. I won't use it if I don't need it, okay? I won't."

She shrugged, knowing that was probably the best she was going to get.

"So, how you doin'?" I had to ask.

"I'm good thanks. Still up at Jerry's place, still down here, still uptown. My three safe havens. Bars and beds in between."

"Cool, Olly, cool."

We talked for about an hour until a knock interrupted us and I had to make like a client as she hustled me out of the door to make way for her next one. She tipped me a wink as I shuffled out the door. I flicked my eyebrows in thanks. Not a word. Not a word.

Finding a Break.

Sydney was steaming after the storm as the sun beat down on the rivers running down the streets. Alix Mercer was dancing half naked on a boat in the middle of the harbour with the Opera House glinting away in the background as the camera clicked and whirred through spool after spool of film. Modelling had always come naturally to her, but acting was proving harder to get into. Auditions were few and far between for movies and she had to go straight in otherwise she would end up languishing in TV hell for too many years and by then it could be too late. She gritted her teeth as she smiled and moved for the camera. One day, she thought to herself, as she tucked her fingers under her waistband, making them crease as though she were pulling them down, one day she would be able to pick and choose what she did. She would be in a position of security whereby that would happen and she wouldn't have to worry about doing poxy magazine shoots to pay her escalating bills.

"Okay, that's it. Thanks sweetie."

At the instant her smile dropped from her face her mobile began playing Waltzing Matilda, signalling an incoming call.

"Hello, Alix Mercer?"

"Hi, Alix, Karen."

"Hey Karen, what's new?"

"You are sweetie, you are. We showed your picture to Damian Cross and he's excited. Can we meet later? I know you've got that audition thing, but sweetie Damian is the hottest thing, you have to meet him. He's putting this movie together and he's got Tom Daly already, but they couldn't find a girl, and I think you are it. Whaddya say? I mean this could be big, and that tonight is a multi, just looking at faces really, whaddya say?"

"Karen, you got me tonight...?"

"I know, I know, but this could be so much better, please come, please, my place, whenever, but no later than ten, right? See ya."

Alix held the phone to her drying clothes that clung to her body. If Karen Michaelson was right, then Damian Cross, the most exciting young director working in Australia currently and Tom Daly, the hottest young actor still left in Australia and he was tipped to leave for the States as soon as. Decision time.

It was dark when Karen rushed out to meet her as the cab pulled across the gravel driveway.

"Ali, darling, where have you been? I've almost had to tie Damian to the chair to keep him here."

"Why, what have you told him?"

"Nothing sweetie, nothing. Just go in and dazzle."

Karen moved ahead and Alix noticed Damian Cross flick his stubbly face in her direction before turning back to his conversation with... With the undeniably gorgeous, handsome as hell, fair haired Adonis that was Tom Daly. Alix felt her knees quiver for a fraction of a second.

"Damian, this is Alix Mercer."

Damian waved his hand and continued talking to Tom. Alix ignored them both and poured herself a drink, vodka with ice, then sat down facing Damian. He was the one she had to impress, no matter how good looking Tom was.

Damian didn't bat an eyelid or miss a beat at all, but continued talking. Karen perched on the edge of her seat, smoking rapidly and looking as if she'd been wired all evening. She was more excited than Alix about meeting Damian Cross.

"So this girl comes in, can't have been more than sixteen, and Inchy gives her the script and she looks at it once, takes her top off and launches into something I've never heard in my life, but she was convinced this would work. We laughed. Anyway, since then, nothing. Terri Mar, who I wanted, is tied up with Steven Beech and Debbie Grayham is in the States reading for the Coen's. So nothing."

Now he looked at Alix, and not even a full look. He just looked into her eyes.

"I like the look, but I don't want a model, Karen, I told you that, no models. They think cause they stand in front of a camera they can do the whole acting thing like falling out of a plane, but they can't. Sorry, Tom, waste of time."

Cross stood up and stubbed his cigarette out, blowing smoke over Alix's head.

"Damian, darling, wait, can't you even..."

"I said no models."

Tom jumped up and was about to say something, but a raised finger from Damian and a look that would have killed at a hundred paces told him all he needed to know, and as he slipped past Alix he gave a small shrug in apology. Alix looked away.

The two men had been gone a full five minutes before either of the two women spoke.

"Karen, you said..."

"Honey, I know what I said, and if I had told him before he got here then he wouldn't...have got here." She looked confused as she said it, but waved it away. "Still, he looked at you. If you can get an acting part..."

"How can I do that when you pull me off readings to visit with a two-bit schmuck who can't be bothered?"

Karen bristled.

"Damian Cross is not a two-bit schmuck. He is the hottest..."

"No. He is a two-bit schmuck."

Alix jumped up and stormed out of the room. Karen hesitated and then stormed after her.

"Alix, Alix, hey."

"What? What pearl of wisdom can I have now?"

"Hey, wooah. I said he was excited and he was..."

"Hmm, really. Did I miss that part? Cause he left pretty damn quick."

"He liked your look. He loved your look." Karen emphasised the point loudly, before fading to a mumble which Alix barely heard. "He just doesn't like models."

Alix shot her a thunderous look and was about to march away when she realised she didn't have her car.

"Shit."

Karen stood in the doorway smoking, watching the smoke drift away on the gentle breeze.

"Alix, darling come back inside. You might as well stay here. Come and have a drink. Cigarette?"

"You're drunk enough already."

"So what? I can get drunker."

"Really." Alix really didn't care.

"Oh yes. Much drunker." She finished the rest of her drink and turned back inside. Alix watched her sway back through the house and wanted to leave, but knew she couldn't. She kicked the gravel and heard it skitter away, went inside and slammed the door.

By the time she got back home the following day Alix was thoroughly unthrilled and nursing a huge hangover. Used to drinking lager when she lived on the farm she couldn't handle spirits and her head pounded as a reminder. She threw the clothes she had worn to impress Damian 'Dickhead' Cross on the floor and crawled under the sheets. If this was how it was going to be then....then...

Booze and Broads.

The bar Olivia had given me wasn't a bar. It was a door. A doorway guarded by two other doors who had knuckle dusters the size of the Capitol glinting under the neon lights of the street. I sat in the window opposite, sipping a beer, not my normal, I know, but I had to make some sense of what I was doing, sitting watching...two goons guard an inanimate piece of wood. I had to laugh. I should have laughed. But I was still nervous about being just this close to Firetti. More beer. And more beer.

By the time the table looked as though it was full of bottles and my pockets were beginning to feel the draught of space when there had been money much earlier on, I had totally lost my nerve about approaching the three doors on the other side of the street. Again not usual after I've been drinking, but who can say what happens in these situations.

I'm a great believer in fate. So, as I climbed in my car and eyeballed one of the doors as I drove by, I believed that if Mister Firetti and I were going to come together at any point, then it would happen without me trying to pluck up the courage to do so.

I've worked in this game for the better part of my life and I still get the jitters about some jobs, some people.

All the top sports stars say nerves are there to help you, they get you buzzing, focused, on the job in hand.

They make me run away.

Okay, that's not true. Mixed with alcohol they make me run away, so generally, for me, I leave them alone. I go with Fate.

Anyway, I had seen where the place was, and that was not where I wanted to meet him. It was obviously his place and getting in would be hard enough, without actually getting in to see him, shadowy, mysterious figure that he really wasn't.

The second place I had managed to drag out of my sensational source was only a couple of blocks from where I had been drinking and I stopped to check it out. It was a dancing club, not too sleazy, enough dry ice and neon to start your own dry ice and neon company, but there were tables rather than a floor show, an obvious backroom entrance/exit for privacy, a number of more secluded booths, and a top floor which overlooked the catwalk style dancefloor below. I slipped upstairs and was met by another door, in a tux, who politely asked me who I was with, was I a member, and as I bluffed my way through both questions he took a step towards me. I backed off, raised my hands and shrugged as I tripped back down the stairs.

Warned off, big time.

I obviously needed a reason to be up there. Maybe that was where Firetti went, though I figured him for more of a hands on approach.

This joint would have to be examined closer.

I stayed for an hour or two, had a lap dance, just to pass the time. Roxanne was a sexy brunette who told me I couldn't touch her as she wriggled and writhed all over me, making it virtually impossible for me not to touch her. I stroked my fingers along her thigh which she didn't seem to mind, but as soon as I flicked idly at the thin strap of her g-string she moved position so I was faced with her chest, not her ass. I don't even remember the song.

The bar was only half full, mostly regulars I guessed, and most were watching the dancers, occasionally offering dollar bills to each girl as they swayed provocatively in front of their beer goggled eyes. Casual relaxation seemed to be the way of things. Once I noticed a girl lead the way into the back and privately wondered what went on through the curtain. I left that particular pleasure for another time and left the bar about 2am.

A Star is Born.

"Tom?"

A curl of longish fair hair flopped down over his left eye. He looked at her out from under the curl.

"Hi." They stood looking at each other for a few seconds, neither really knowing why he was there, both wondering what should happen.

"Can I come in?"

Alix held the door open and stepped away.

"Sure."

He slipped inside the room, brushing by her, his smock top and his arm just touching her upper arm as he immediately began looking around the small, homely room.

"It's nice."

"Yeah, right."

She closed the door and offered him a seat. He declined and glanced out of the dirty window. Alix sat down.

"Tom, why are you here?"

He spun round and had to drop his gaze down to her.

"I came to ask you something, but I have a choice about what it is." He saw the puzzled look that crossed her face. "Maybe you could choose?"

"No, maybe you could. You came here, you choose the topic for discussion."

"It's not like that."

He sat and looked at her, watching her watching him.

"Last night, I, well, we both liked the look of you. It's just that...that Damian has this thing....about models. People do. I have it about control freaks. Can't stand them, don't know why they are like they are." He shook his head, waving his arms frantically. "That's beside the point. He has this thing, and well, it clouds his otherwise excellent judgment."

"Really?"

"Oh yeah. He's awesome." Alix arched an eyebrow. "But it clouds his judgment. So I want you to do a screen test with me."

Alix held her breath, waiting for him to continue. When he didn't she reminded herself to breathe out.

"Why? I mean, why? Does Damian know? I've never really acted. Does Damian know?"

"No he doesn't. He can't until he sees it. He won't even remember you."

"Huh, thanks."

"He won't, but he will. I think you'd be great. I don't care if you've never acted. It's not hard, and if you've modelled then at least you're used to cameras being in your face. You'll do it?"

"I'd like the job, I'd like Damian to know about it, but I realise that he wouldn't even look at it if he knew it was me, especially after the way he reacted last night, so yes, I'll do it. Does Karen know?"

"No. D'you want to tell her?"

Alix thought for a minute. Karen would probably kill her, but after messing her about she could sweat it.

"No." They smiled at their little secret. "When d'you want me?"

"This afternoon. Now."

"Fine." She stood, grabbed her jacket and held the door open. "Let's go."

Tom had a copy of the script and had cobbled together a cameraman to shoot the three scenes they had picked.

The first was the initial meeting between the two characters.

Tom looked strangely serene as he sat on a chair (doubling for a seat in a car). Alix swallowed and approached, leaning on the imaginary car.

"Get out the car, get out of the car, now!" She waved her arms around, gesturing for him to react and get out. Tom never moved.

"Hey! Hey, get out of the car."

"No."

"No? What do you mean no? You nearly run me over, I want to talk to you, and you saying no? You ain't too bright are you mister?"

"I guess I ain't."

"So get out here."

"Look honey, I'm really sorry, but there's no harm done, I didn't hit you, so just let me get out of your way." Alix pretended to pull a gun and thrust her hands into Tom's face.

"No, you'll be out of my way permanently if you don't get out of the car right now." She had dropped her voice to a whisper as she threatened him.

"You have beautiful eyes." The air crackled between them as Alix released the pressure of her hands for a second, unsure of what to do. "And I'd hate to see such pretty eyes in trouble.

So, I'll just get out of your way." He made a move to leave, but Alix jerked him back into place.

"You are gonna stay right here while I get your plates and licence, and if you don't I'll shoot you first." She warned the suddenly wary Tom.

"No you won't, cause then you'll be in for murder as well as assault, violent assault at that. And that means life, not just Christmas."

"Fuck you, fuck you, fuck you" She hit the 'car' with the 'gun' as she screamed at him, then collapsed onto the floor (having no car to lean on), crying.

Tom knelt down and pushed his hands through her hair. Alix fought for a second, but Tom was obviously stronger and held her down, stroking her hair away from her face, looking at her intently.

"Beautiful, captivating eyes."

Alix looked up, her face telling the story of how scared she was, her vulnerability, her need to be cared for, loved, her desire to control being lost with her aggression.

"Okay, people, that was great. Hot stuff." Nobody responded. "People, Tom, Alix?" Tom and Alix pulled away and looked everywhere until there eyes met again.

"Okay?"

"Fine. You?"

"Good. Nick?"

"A-okay Tom man, A-okay."

"Next..."

Damian was sitting in between Karen and Tom as the projector started rolling. Karen was still wondering why she was there, but Tom had said he had a new talent to show her, so she pulled on a cigarette and waited as the pictures crackled into life in front of her.

Damian sighed at the pale, small room that was shown on the screen, with nobody in view.

"Tom?"

"Patience Damian. Wait a second."

At that moment Tom strode into view and took up his position, sideways to the camera, shrugging and exhaling as he waited. On the cue he began pretending to drive and stop.

Off screen came the first shout, then Alix came into shot.

"What the... Tom, is this it?"

"Damian, just watch, okay?"

"Tom?"

"It's okay Karen, just watch."

"So get out here."

"Look honey, I'm really sorry, but there's no harm done, I didn't hit you, so just let me get out of your way."

"No, you'll be out of my way permanently if you don't get out of the car right now."

Both the screen and the room had gone quiet.

"You have beautiful eyes. And I'd hate to see such pretty eyes in trouble, so I'll just get out of your way."

"You're gonna stay right here until I get your plates and licence, and if you don't then I'll shoot you first."

"No you won't, cause then you'll be in for murder and assault, armed assault at that. And that means life, not just Christmas."

"Fuck you, fuck you, fuck you."

Karen sat open mouthed, Damian moved his lips with the words he knew so well, Tom alternately watched the screen and the astounded reactions of the two people on his right. As the scene finished Damian and Karen looked at Tom who beamed broadly.

"Tell me that wasn't just you?" Karen quizzed, breathing smoke into the air.

"Karen, baby, did you not see how she sparkled up there. Not only is she sensational to look at, but she sets the celluloid on fire. Tom is good, but he is not God. She has the raw talent, the natural energy, the stunning looks and the roughness to pull off that part. She is intense, she makes you believe, she is great, he is great, I am great, this film is great, we are involved in making greatness." He paused for breath, clearly excited by the prospects. "Show me more. You shot more, right? Roll it, Howie."

"He loved it, he absolutely loved it," enthused Karen as she and Alix entered the restaurant, Karen seeking out the black and blonde heads of Damian and Tom. "Damian Cross," she said to the hovering host.

They crossed the room, a couple of heads turned to see who they were with as they sat down with the unmistakable figures of Damian and Tom.

"Darling, you are wonderful and you have to come and make this movie. Tom was just saying that it has to be a reality check, not over the top Hollywood stylee, but like Pretty Woman, but darker, dirtier. It will be good, but if you come on board it can be great."

Alix played with her napkin and turned the cloth round in her fingers, making them wait.

"I thought you didn't like models?"

"Honey, I don't."

"Then I can't do it."

"But you are an actress, not a model. You could never be that good as a model, and I've never heard of you as one so you obviously aren't. But an actress. Alix, you are going to be very, very big as an actress."

Alix sat, stunned. She hadn't expected him to say he still disliked models, but she hadn't expected him to say that she was an actress either. She knew that her performance had been good, cause Tom and Nick had both loved it, but impressing Damian hadn't crossed her mind. Now it had happened she wanted to grasp it with both hands.

"Then I would love to do it."

Twilight.

The old man shuffled his way to the wheelchair and slumped down heavily into it. It creaked and clanked as he shifted his weight to get comfortable, then he flipped the foot rests up and they moved off.

The corridor was empty, strangely, it's sharp, sickly antiseptic smell making the care assistants hold their breath for a while. The man didn't bother. He had grown so used to it that if it smelled any other way he'd wonder what was wrong. They passed an open door and he looked in. A nurse was changing the sheets, her face red and her eyes sore. The man signalled to stop and he stared at the nurse until she looked up at him.

"Harry?" he mumbled, already knowing the answer.

The nurse tried to hold it together as she nodded, but broke down and sobbed silently on the bed. She was relatively new and death was something she would get used to, but Harry had been a natural charmer and she had been taken in so simply that getting out was that much harder. "Come and see me later," he said.

She looked up. "I..."

"Nine?"

She smiled, trying to make herself feel better as well as an encouragement to him, and nodded. He nodded back having seen it all before, and signalled to go again.

He adjusted his bathrobe over his knees as they reached the elevator, in case they met Miss Daisy again. She was only seventy-five and still had a good head of hair.

The ride down was as bumpy as ever. For all the money that had gone on building this place as state of the art as they could get it, they had scrimped on the elevator. It was cold and metallic inside, no carpet, no music, no small boy in an oversize uniform saying 'Going up' or 'Going down'.

They only had to drop one floor, but each day it seemed longer and longer. Except when it was raining of course and then it just fell down to the ground floor.

Today it was sunny, as it was normally in Florida, and the sun made the joints a little freer and the demeanour a little lighter. The staff were happier when they could be outside away from the smell of antisepticised death and decay that filled the rooms and corridors inside, away from the soiled beds, the bedsores, the bedbaths. He wondered what they slept on at home cause if he was them he'd be fed up of beds. Maybe they all tried hammocks, or futons.

He picked up his stick and walked into the sunshine. He could walk, but only short distances, and he got a chair down because of the elevator. Balance never had been his strong point.

The bench was empty. He smiled. He liked the time to himself before she arrived. It was just to the right of the terraced area, a few meters onto the landscaped lawn, just enough so the blades of grass could curl their way round the edge of his carpet slippers and tickle the pale skin on his foot. Sometimes he walked barefoot, but only when he wasn't being watched. He loved the feel as his feet sank into the lush greenery, the cool grass against the relative warmth of his feet. He had always wanted to be an outdoor type, and his brief flirtation with baseball had given him that chance, but injury and other factors had curtailed his major league career, so the smell of the game had been lost in his past.

He sat down heavily, the bench creaked a little under him as he adjusted his position, putting his feet flat on the lawn, lying his arm on the rest to his left, resting the stick between the bench and his left knee. He breathed in the smells of summer, the flowers which were packed tightly and deeply in the borders all over the swell of green acres that surrounded the main building. The insects swarmed all over the colourful petals, zipping busily between pockets of pollen, avoiding each other as they buzzed through the hot, scented air, dive bombing and irritating some of the human obstacles in their path.

Scanning the view, searching for familiar faces, walks, coughs, the man breathed heavily, savouring the fresh air, the slow breeze that flitted through, across the open compound.

Ronald was there, flirting with Carmen, again. He chuckled as he watched Ronald playfully tap the Hispanic girl on her ass as she got up to leave. Carmen skipped away, her laugh catching the breeze and bringing a moment of lightness and well being to the assorted characters within earshot.

The man smiled. Laughter, like yawning, was infectious, especially when it came from a beautiful young woman, and Carmen was certainly that.

"Son of a bitch."

The man turned to see Scott shaking his head in disbelief. Walter had once more picked him carefully apart on the chessboard. Walter sat back, pipe chugging away in his mouth, rubbing his hands over his substantial stomach, laughing a deep croaky laugh, almost to himself.

"83-63 I make it."

"Yeah. Whatever." Scott paused for a second then began placing his pieces back on the board, Walter mirroring him. They would play until dark descended.

He watched as Dana came out and handed Julio his drugs. Must be three o'clock.

His eyes became sharper, more focused as he looked now, watching for her, but pretending not to. He didn't like her seeing him as he was, but he couldn't help that now. She had been his for so long and she had known no different, so for her not to see him would be harder on them both. He was fortunate to be in good enough health to be able to meet her outside, or sitting in a day room, rather than lying in a darkened room with tubes attached to everywhere. He could still appreciate her and convince himself that he was still able to care for her. She brought him pleasure and stories and he gave her strength and experience.

And there she was.

He watched as she sauntered across to him, her slender body, her wonderful legs, her stunning face which broke into a beaming smile as she saw him watching. Then she was there, arms thrown around his neck, face buried in his graying, thinning hair.

For a moment they just held each other, such was the bond, each valuing and loving the other, both knowing that every visit came closer to being the last.

Making A Move.

As he ran his fingers through her luscious red hair, Alix shivered slightly. His hard, well muscled, naked body lay behind hers, warm and smooth as his mouth nibbled her earlobe. She pushed her head into the pillow, allowing him more access to her neck, which he took, moving his lips down, softly, tickling gently, making the tiny hairs on her skin stand on end. His mouth found the muscle on the top of her shoulder and he bit down hard. Alix couldn't move as Tom held her tightly round the waist, but the sensation was impossible to ignore. Trying to wriggle away Tom held her more firmly, already feeling his erection growing as her breath came harder, little moans escaping from her lips as he bit down again. Alix reached round and pulled him against her. Tom adjusted his position, tilting his pelvis, reaching down and parting her legs guided himself into her. The sensation from his teeth on her neck had already aroused her to the point of frenzy, but as Tom slipped inside her she felt herself on the verge of climaxing. As soon as he moved inside her her muscles exploded, releasing the pressure and pent up energy she had been storing since the day of the funeral in an ear shattering scream of violent pleasure.

Tom followed seconds later, squeezing her breast so hard Alix thought he'd tear it off.

As they fell asleep, wrapped around each other, the same thought occupied both their minds; even if the film was shit, the extra curricular performances would be great.

The first week had gone smoothly on the set of 'Making a Move'. Damian had shouted orders all week and the squillions of minions had jumped and run to meet his every desire, all hoping he might notice them and give them a line, a walk on, something else, as his reputation and past form suggested he might. But so far he had disappointed.

Alix felt instantly at home. The set looked like chaos. Not even organised chaos until Damian clicked his fingers and the cameras rolled into action. She and Tom hadn't managed to keep their burgeoning affair secret for longer than a couple of days as they succumbed to every moment of tender pleasure they could in between, before and after takes. Some of the cast and crew tutted, muttering about how unprofessional it was to display it so openly. Others were delighted at having some sensational gossip to discuss. Alix Mercer, hitherto unknown and Tom Daly, Aussie hunk and hero. There would be a story to tell.

'Making a Move' told the story of a budding bank robber, Jack Scully, and how he thwarted a larger, better organised group of thieves by robbing the Pacific Bank just minutes before they were due to. He then has to flee with the money as the big black jeeps of the bad guys chase him and hunt him down. He escapes as far as Adelaide, then meets up with the obligatory love interest, a beautiful red head who he narrowly misses running over as he looks for a suitable hiding place. Unfortunately, the red headed stunner is hot on the heels of the guys who are hot on his heels, and as her contacts tell her the story, it dawns on her that she is now sleeping with a wanted criminal. She leaves and comes back the next morning with armed police to find him gone without a trace.

So begins the manhunt through Australia's premier cities.

No-one gets close to the man running for his freedom as he keeps just about one step ahead of everybody until finally at Sydney airport he can't run anywhere else as he waits, frustrated, for his flight.

In walks the red head, scans the crowd, sees him, grabs his sleeve....

"Hey!"

She looked at the face and saw no recognition. "Sorry, my mistake."

Raelee pulled away and scanned the heads of the crowd once more. "Shit." She clambered onto a seat and looked, but couldn't see anyone she thought looked even vaguely like the man she was chasing; the man she had, literally in her grasp, but let go; the man she perhaps wanted to see just one more time. Once more.

"Sir?"

She spun round. "Don't call me that."

"Excuse me, ma'am?"

She looked exasperated, willing her deputy to actually say something without putting his hand up to ask permission.

"What, Jenkins?"

"Any sign, ma'am?"

She shook her head, checking hair colour again, staring at the exits. "No." She jumped off the seat. "Check outside again."

"Sure thing."

Last Train to Midnight

He wasn't here. He wasn't here. She felt it in her soul, deep down inside, at the very heart of her being. She slumped in a seat, feeling the nervous tension seep out of her. For so long she'd been fighting a double front, chasing two wanted men, and now she had the one she didn't want. Her mind cast back to when his car had skidded past her ankles in Adelaide, how he'd looked at her with those blazing eyes, not quite sure whose fault it was, but damn sure it wasn't his. He'd been so calm with her, until she'd pulled her gun on him.

"Could Miss Raelee Kole please make her way to the check-in number 15 please. Miss Raelee Kole to check-in 15."

She took a second to realise it was her, then she was running.

"Fifteen, fifteen, fifteen, fifteen..." Her heart pounded as she ran, dodging the public and their enormous bags of luggage. Then she saw it and skidded to a halt just short of sending a man onto the conveyor with his suitcase.

"Raelee Kole, I'm Raelee Kole, a message?"

"Ah Miss Kole. This was left for you."

The man behind the desk handed her an envelope which she tore at, ripping at the paper, anxious to see what it was.

"When?"

"I'm sorry?"

"When? When was it left?"

The man looked at his watch and then, inexplicably, at the clock behind him.

"Ten minutes ago."

"Who by? Who left it?"

"Man, tall, blond hair. Mister Kean. Jason Kean, I think. Leslie, what was that bloke's name who you went all drippy for?" Leslie shot him daggers and stuck her tongue out. Raelee rolled her eyes. It didn't matter.

The note. The note.

Darling Raelee, Sorry to have missed you, but things were getting a little hot. Unfortunately, I have to go. There can be no words to describe the feelings of meeting you then losing you. You made a good day perfect and a bad time better. I almost came back, but I know you'd do your job, so I have to move again. This time I know I'll never see you, so this is the end of a beautiful relationship.
Take care, Raelee and know that I love you
Jack.

She crumpled the note and turned her face away from the desk, tears pricking her eyes, then walked slowly across the concourse, unaware of the hundreds of holidaymakers streaming about around her.

CUT TO: RAELEE'S HOUSE. INT. DAY. (Raelee is looking through her mail, picks one out, looking puzzled. She opens it. As she reads, so does the camera, picking up a Box number and one line of writing. Raelee whispers it as camera pans up to her smiling face.)
"Meet me in Paris?"
Credits roll.
It was certainly not especially original, but with the vision of Damian Cross and the talent of the two leads, plus solid support from the rest of the cast and crew, then they were all hoping for a big success not only in Australia, but also around the world. With it being made on a small budget of $AUS 25 million hopefully the arthouse circuit, along with competition at Cannes and Sundance, would provide a springboard to profit and calls from the big players in the States. But that was a while in the future, with post-production a distant blip

on the horizon as Alix and Tom set up for their first scene together.

"Nervous?" enquired Tom as Alix slipped out of her towel and dived under the sheets next to him.

Alix laughed and looked round the twenty-odd people she had just been naked in front of.

"No. You?"

"Because it's you, no."

He kissed her gently on the mouth.

"Okay, you lot, gate, quiet please, ready, camera rolling, and action."

Tom had climbed on top of Alix and kissed her firmly on the neck, using his teeth slightly. Alix was instantly lost and felt herself becoming aroused, moaning into Tom's hair.

Damian muttered directions to himself as his actors moved together under an opaque sheet.

"Move your hand up, to her shoulder, roll off a bit, in her hair, pull her head back, good..."

Alix was already moving on instinct, as Tom made her squirm with lust.

"More, move now..."

Tom did on cue and Alix's eyes shot open. "Tom," she whispered in his ear away from the sound mic.

A couple of the crew saw her reaction and looked at each other, with wondering expressions.

"Okay, pause, kiss her mouth, Tom, Tom, kiss her Tom." At this point the crew knew something was up. Tom had only now pulled up and kissed her hard on the mouth, his hand feeling for her. Alix moaned into him, feeling herself redden round her neck, knowing her body was betraying her, loving the idea of what was happening.

"Okay, move towards it, feel the climax."

They were already way ahead of him as Tom pushed into Alix harder. Alix pushed her head back and Tom descended on her neck as she liked.

As he did so he felt her muscles grip him tightly and they were swept into an orgasm of a force neither had experienced before.

"And there we have it. Cut it there. Print it, check the gate." He paused as Tom and Alix caught their breaths, gazing into each others eyes, questioning, excited. "Great, both of you. You can get out. We don't need to do that again."

No Success.

Okay, I confess, I hadn't been getting anywhere. It had been over a month since I first saw John Barclay and I had had nothing to report. I sensed he was a little impatient, but willing to indulge me, which was fortunate. I still hadn't met with the elusive Mrs Barclay, but John promised she'd be home within a couple of weeks, God knows where she'd been, and so I had to be content with that. Essentially I was waiting until something happened.

Gini Firetti was not a man to make threats and then not carry them out. He would get round to it, I was sure, but until that time I was marking time.

I didn't want to push him into doing anything, for I was sure he wouldn't let me down on that score anyway, so I didn't need to hurry things along. After all, time was and indeed is money.

The lawyer, Mister Graziani, had again been less than helpful.

I'd gone to see him again and found that this time he had gone out. Miss Baumann, as I discovered her name was, let me in and I sat for a while before asking if she could help me. Of course she couldn't and was about to send me on my way when the Boss arrived back, licking his lips with the sugar from his donut.

"Mister Graziani, good to catch up with you."

"Mister...?"

"Seyle." He knew me alright.

"Sure, sure, Mister Seyle. I told you before I don't think I can help you?"

"Are you sure? Couldn't you check. I mean I have..."

"I know, a source, we all do. I can't help you." He gestured with his arms. "I'm sorry."

I looked crestfallen and got no sympathy from an impassive Miss Sara Baumann as I left the office of Mister Graziani for the second time without any success.

Maybe he really didn't know anything....

Falling.

"What's he like? I mean, you know, what's he like?"

Alix laughed and sent a sly look across the courtyard at Tom who was sitting, laughing in his annoyingly sexy way with Damian. There had been no denying their relationship after the first couple of weeks had made it obvious to those cast and crew who were around day after day, take after take. The little shared looks, the secret little glances, the snatched moments in and behind trailers and the fact that on screen they were falling head over heels, chemically, smoulderingly in love. Their screen-time crackled, so Damian told them, and they couldn't help it. Even during the scenes of fear and anger there was something unmistakable about the way they looked at each other, something in the way their eyes locked, their movements always suggesting at touch, at intimacy, at sex. As they reached out to each other, forcing themselves to pull their hands away, knowing that the signals were intense, feeling so close, so desperately close, having to keep the shackles on until Damian cut the action. And you could cut the action with a knife.

The first meeting, the first love scene, the escape, the airport. All the big set-ups had sparkled with raw passion, a dark, slightly seedy, yet typically sun-drenched Australia had played its mouthwatering, landscaped part as the two protagonists chased their way across the red earthed outback. The camera lapped up the dark, lengthening shadows as though it had been made specifically for that purpose. Damian Cross made his cinematographer, Peter Maher, turn away time and again from the scene to get footage of the silhouetted blackness of a tree or a cluster of boulders against the smooth, seductive purply-blue evening sky as the orange sun blazed with the last molten embers of its daily climatic spectacle.

Alix and Tom spent nights under the stars, wrapped in each others arms under a blanket watching the stars twinkle and shoot in the black curtain above, watching the ash spark and die in one of the many campfires lit around the set.

Tom looked at Alix's strands of red, twirling his fingers amongst them, gently tugging and stroking his way over her head, massaging gently, making her shiver as he inched his ticklish way over her body, warm beneath the blanket. Her body responded and arched against him, leaning back and pushing her head into his shoulder, her hair rubbing against the hardness of his body.

"Tom?"

He was half asleep, dazed and doped with feelings he had never experienced before for the beautiful woman he was next to. His grunt was a real answer.

"Which star is ours?"

He breathed deeply and leaned back, examining the sky, searching for one, special glint of light that perhaps, just maybe, meant something. He pointed, reaching out over her head.

"That one."

Alix followed the finger and fixed on a point that could or could not have been the exact one he had on his mind. She smiled to herself and hugged his arm a little tighter across her chest. It felt good just to have him there, next to her, against her, with her. She had been swept along as much as he had. Damian hadn't shown them any rushes, it wasn't his way, he liked to do things with his own autocratic style, but from the way he had eased up slightly on his directions, they sensed that he was giving them a little rope to play with, happy with what they were producing on screen, hoping they wouldn't hang themselves with it.

The day dawned early, bright, clear and already a haze shimmered over the ground. Wildlife was alert and hunting before any human stirred, snakes slithering between rocks and shrubs, silently stalking, ambushing swiftly, birds and lizards making the most of the cool air, knowing the scorching day would once more be prohibitively hot for exploration later on. Spiders hung on their dewy strands, waiting patiently.

Alix turned and curled her arm over Tom, reaching her fingers to his. Tom didn't move, but let her hand slip into his, squeezing slightly, unconsciously, making her feel secure, letting her know he was there, glad she was there. His mind was working overtime, and had been for an hour or so. He had watched her sleep for a while, feeling her back push gently against his chest as she breathed in, her mouth twitching as she dreamed, but had to turn away and allow his thoughts to drift away. He hadn't meant to fall in love. He felt dazed and confused that it had happened, that he had let it happen. That this incredibly beautiful woman had made it happen.

But ever since yesterday, after he spoke to his agent, his fears had been confirmed. How could he tell her he was going to America? Would she care? Would she go with him? He had never been so nervous in his life before he knew, and now he did he was scared. He didn't know how....he didn't know how hurt....he hadn't thought...not really....I mean you don't like to....you just don't....not before you know.

It would have to end. It would all have to end.

Alix felt his body tense as his fingers tightened their grip on hers. She smiled to herself as she imagined what he was dreaming about. They hadn't had sex for almost two weeks now, but still the frission, the electric connection was there and they didn't need to take it any further than they had. Often they were just too exhausted after filming, and just lay around in a bath or in bed, naked together. That was enough.

He twitched and turned over. He smiled. Alix smiled back sleepily. So this is what it felt like.

Sweet Rosie.

For a day or so I had been convinced. The call, the day, time, place. I wrote them all down to make sure. I couldn't always rely on my pickled brain. I was going to meet one of the most beautiful women in the world. In my opinion. Nicole Kidman was achingly beautiful, Lauren Bacall in her Big Sleep days was sexy as they come, the serene, ageless, almost plain beauty of Julie Christie, the cute, come hither look of Halle Berry, Whitney Houston's voice. Oh god Whitney Houston's voice.

Cale Kline, if her photographs were anything to go by, could certainly match them. If she could act as well, then she would be on millions of bedroom walls before she had time to get a no nudity clause in her contract.

And I was going to meet her.

Or I thought I was.

I should have known better, should have realised that nothing was going to be quite that simple.

The meeting was all set up, but then I got a call.

"Hey John. What can I do for you?"

He sounded apologetic immediately, but businesslike enough to have cancelled meetings before.

"Midnight, I'm sorry, but I have to postpone Cale for a while. She jetted off to LA last night. Big audition or something. Look, we'll rearrange. Gotta go."

The phone clicked and I slumped. Snatched from the jaws of...something.

This left me with another afternoon spare, kicking my heels, flipping cards into a cap, watching Jerry Springer, Ricki Lake, Oprah. I was tempted to start drinking earlier than usual, but managed to hold off until it went dark at least.

I had also managed to get off the scotch and had begun on beer. I wasn't keen, but I stayed sober longer, which wasn't necessarily a good thing you understand, but gave me more time to think. Although this came to be of no use either, as I still found my way to the club, you know the club, his club, the lap dance place, Gini's joint, and walked in around midnight. Ironic, huh?

It was almost deserted. I recognised one or two faces. They nodded in my direction, perhaps anxious to feel they weren't alone, perhaps wanting affirmation they weren't the only ones there, perhaps they recognised me.

I took a seat at the bar, took a drink and watched a latino girl twirl and writhe up against a metal pole in what passed for a G-string, accepting the dollars the stage-flies tucked under the string bit of the G.

My eyes wandered to the balcony. It was bathed in a cloudy pink shroud. Figures moved around, moving back and forth, exiting right, then returning with a tray of drinks, a coat, a bag. Seconds after the girl with the coat walked past, a man jogged down the stairs and left the club. I sighed with relief. One less heavy to worry about. I had a feeling this could be the night I met Gini Firetti.

As I watched no one came or went for several minutes. In fact the music stopped pumping and settled into a slower, steady beat. Less up front, more subtle.

I smiled to myself at how anything in such a place could pass for subtle.

The girl on the stage had changed and now a blonde weaved to the rhythm. Looking up a girl was leaning on the balcony rail. Her skirt was short and shiny. Silvery-blue. She had the thinnest of straps going across her back, and three inch heels on her shoes. She appeared to be talking, although I couldn't really tell. At one point she turned and looked over the rail, scanning the floor below, turning back to whoever, laughing. Her face looked happy when she did that.

Then there was someone else. A man. He was obviously standing very close to her as she leaned away slightly, arching back over the rail. His big hand reached round and pulled her head back towards him. Again she laughed. His hand was under her skirt now at the back. From where I was sitting at the bar I could see as he knelt down, peeling her shiny panties down her legs. Silvery-blue.

She had stopped moving and he stepped in between her legs. Her hands were on his chest, her head squirming away from his, then....

He had hit her and in an instant turned her round so she faced me, and was now probably pounding into her.

I had to....

"No one comes in here, buddy. Back off."

"Look Mister Firetti knows me. I just wanna say hi. Come on." I offered him a twenty. He took it and ripped it in half.

"Fuck off."

"Come on, buddy. Look Gini and I go way back. His grandfather knew mine, and so on. I just wanna say hi."

Over the music, as a morbid and desperate backbeat, I could hear muffled screams.

"Look, no guns, no knives, just wanna say hi. You can throw me out if he says no, okay?" He hesitated. "Okay?"

"Stay there."

He went, I moved up a step and almost collapsed as I saw the guy stop mid-fuck and look over at me. The girl half turned, and I saw her face.

The chump was back.

"Sure." He poked a thick finger in the direction of the only group up there. I followed, swallowing hard as I approached.

I had to think and carefully. The grandfather thing wasn't going to hold longer than a few seconds, but I had to persuade him to talk to me. If not for my sake...

"Do I know you?"

Maybe not even a few seconds.

"Cause if I don't know you, then you are taking a very big risk, my friend, coming up here and disturbing my social life." He paused and puffed on his enormous cigar. "So? Do I know you?"

"We have a mutual friend."

"Get this schmuck out of here." He waved a hand dismissively and I felt a huge meathook of a hand try and crush my shoulder as it persuaded me to get up.

"John Barclay. I know John Barclay." Nothing happened. "He asked me to come and talk with you." A gesture and the meathook's grip loosed off a little. I could feel the purple bruise already swelling. "I, he wanted to try and cut some sort of a deal. He bought the land in good faith and if he'd known it was yours then of course he wouldn't have been interested.

Well, not without consulting with you first off." Another gesture and the meathook departed altogether, along with all the other assembled company.

"Can the girl stay?" I blurted hastily. She whimpered slightly and shook her head which only convinced Gini to keep her in sight. "I like her," I added as way of mitigation for wanting her there. Not just so I could keep an eye on her.

She stayed and Gini made sure he was settled before he spoke again.

"So what's the deal. I don't do deals, you should know that."

"Sure, sure. John bought the land in a deal with..."

"With Marello, yeh, I know all that shit. But where's Marello now? Six feet down in some concrete if he's anywhere. I know all that, Marello, Barclay, the deal. But that land was mine and Marello took advantage of me to get it. He stole it, he's dead, so the debt passes to his partner, who is our friend." He looked at me. "Does this make any sense to you?"

He thought I was a moron.

"A little. I don't tend to get involved in his deals, but it makes some sense, sure it does. But I'm a little confused as to why you want the land back now? I mean why wait so long to get it, if you knew that Barclay had it?"

"Time passes, things change, circumstances change. I just happen to have time and inclination and need right now. Plus all the paperwork hadn't been investigated and I don't like going off under prepared, know what I mean?"

I tried not to laugh. The number of times the Mafia had been associated with a hit which had no apparent motive, I found it faintly ridiculous that they had always been totally, legally prepared before putting a bullet in the back of a victim's head. Still, if that's the way he wanted to play it, I wasn't in a position to disagree. Me against the world. His world.

"So, with Marello dead, you think you're out of pocket in some way, and you want John to bail you out?"

"No. No, no, no. There is no bailing out. What is this? There is no bailing out. He owes us. He owes me. I am claiming what is rightfully mine, and I will get it, either in land or dollar bills." He paused and took another a few rapid mouthfuls of smoke. "We are done. This meeting is over. You know the way."

I got up to go, stopped short of saying thanks for his time, and caught a glimpse of the girl.

"Hey, look, I'm going back downstairs. Can I buy the girl for an hour?"

"Sure, take her, take her, but go the back way. I don't want her scaring them down there." He sneered at her blood spattered, mascara smeared, bruised face, then we were shown the back staircase that led directly into the part of the ground floor which I presumed must be where you ended up when you went through the curtains.

Well, I had promised myself.

It was impressively lit; dark, yet light to see, blackness everywhere, underlit booths, private, seedy, a stench of sex.

I sat in the first one.

"What you want?" She smiled, or tried to, but the dried blood cracked as she did so.

"I don't want anything."

She stared at me. Quizzical, bemused, disappointed? Perhaps she didn't know what to do now. A rookie.

"Sure. You pays your money."

She sat opposite, legs crossed tightly, pointed away from me as she lit a cigarette and blew smoke upwards to join the heavy cloud that sat there already, stagnant, repugnant, choking the life from all those who entered.

She swung her hair loose, shielding one side of her face, the other side. She couldn't escape the business of showing. She had to show herself, to me, to the club. To herself.

I had known hookers, whores, dancers, strippers since forever. In my line it was often where you ended up, and if you were in any one place for a time then you got to know people. She was not exceptional, but her hand shook as she smoked and she blew harder than she need, exhaling the smoke, the job, her life. I had only ever asked Olly this question. I had known her for a few years before I felt we'd got to that stage and for all the others I knew by name, those who said hello as I passed even occasionally when they were performing, I had never felt like that.

But now it was just right.

"Why d'you do it?"

She coughed and almost laughed. Almost. Her look wasn't humorous, but piteous and desperate.

"Whaddya do?"

I shrugged.

"I'm a private detective."

"Sure y'are. Who you following, dick? Me?" She let out a hollow, dry, heard it all before laugh and took a long drag.

I reached into my pocket. As I did so she flicked her head towards me, her eyes anxious.

I held out a card to her and she relaxed again seeing it was not a piece.

"Here."

She took it, letting the heat from the fag-end drift threateningly over my knuckles. She looked, smiled and threw the card on the table.

"I c'n get one o'those. Dollar down the drugstore. Print your own."

"Sure you can. But why would you? Who wants to be a dick, huh? Who? You don't, I don't really, but you gotta do something. You dance, I detect."

The smoke escaped her lips as she spoke.

"So what you detecting? You following me for real?"

Wary again. Nervous of my job, not me.

"I want your boss."

She tensed and shivered slightly despite the heat of the club. I wiped the sweat from my head to highlight I noticed.

"What you want with Luca?"

"Luca? Who the fuck's Luca? I don't know any fucking Luca?"

"You want my boss? You want Luca, right? He's a bastard. A class-A, fucked in the head son of a bitch, but he treats me good."

"Treats you good? Like what? Like what is that? Feeds you coke and gets you laid. Real good."

"He looks after me, so fuck you. You said so, you don't know him, you don't know shit, man. Fuck you. Fuck you."

"Bullshit, missy. He was the one giving it to you upstairs right? Right?" We had begun shouting and I wasn't surprised when a big black bastard put his head through the curtain shot us a look, told us to shut the fuck up and withdrew his big bowling ball skull. Asshole. Since when were people quiet when they got laid.

She nodded at my question.

"He hit you. He hits you regular. He fucks you so you curl up in a corner, then he feeds you coke so you get high and forget, then he fucks you when you're high, and it's so gentle, so sweet, so you fucking remember, you stupid ...stupid..." I tailed off. I shouldn't have called her stupid. It just came out. She was on the point of screaming at me, but I leapt across and firmly slapped my hand over over her mouth. "Why d'you do it? Why? What's your name, baby, what's your name?"

At that point, when she broke down in tears, she looked so young, so fragile, so lost.

Then she pushed my hand away.

"You wanna fuck?"

"No, I, no what's yo..."

"Come on baby, let's go, let's go screw like you wanna, how you like it, on top, underneath, from behind?"

She slid her fingers under my collar and pulled me after her. As we headed down a corridor, I looked back and caught a glimpse of a face watching us.

Not so stupid.

Down the blackest of corridors was a door which opened into a room. A sex room. There was a bed, a couch, a table. Handcuffs, scarves, whips were gathered on the table. She sat on the edge of the bed, legs apart, back on auto.

"I don't want to fuck you. Not here, not now. No, I mean.... Look, sugar, what's going on? How old are you? Why you do this, what's your name, where you from? Let me help you?"

At this she looked up, but her eyes glazed instantly, thinking I was playing her.

"I mean it. What can I do for you?"

"You can fuck me, you bastard. They come in here and find us talking like a couple of middle aged therapists then I'm fired or beaten half dead anyway, so the best thing you can do is fuck me."

I was mad. She didn't want my help fine. She didn't want my money fine. Then I was leaving.

"I'll be back in the bar if you change your mind." I looked back at her swollen face, although she'd managed to wipe most of the blood away with some of her tears. I turned the handle. "I mean it. I'll help you."

I left.

In the half hour it took her to find the courage, the nerve, the humanity to save herself and come and find me I had got fairly well plastered. The bar kept the shots coming and I kept slugging 'em down. She looked a darn sight better when I couldn't focus on her.

"Honey, you made it. Can I get ya a drink? Bartender, two more right here. Siddown, sit, sit."

She sat and held out her hand.

"I'm Rosie."

"Sure are sugar. Rosy in every way, rosy cheeks, rosy clothes, rosy ass I'll bet." The drinks were there. She looked miserable. I clinked mine against hers. "Cheers then Rosy, bottoms up." My loud self indulgent laughter wasn't helped by the fact I did most of it on the floor as I slipped gracelessly off my barstool.

I didn't remember being helped to the cab, but I noticed the girl, Rosy talking as she tried to shut the door.

"I'm taking him home, Luca, now back off. No, no he's not. He's in no fit state, he probably won't even get to his place, so I'll take him to mine. Yes, I'll get paid. I'll fuckin' rob the fucker." I heard a kiss. "Tomorrow, sure."

I was virtually passed out as we pulled away, but was kept awake by Rosy as she rummaged through my pockets. I couldn't be bothered if she was going through my wallet, I was unconscious.

Rosie found what she was looking for and handed it to the driver then settled back, biting her lip anxiously, occasionally checking out the back window, satisfying herself no-one was there who shouldn't have been.

She looked at the dark, friendly, snoring face slumped uncomfortably against the door and hoped he was good as his word.

She'd taken the word of one man since arriving in the city and had ended up in 'showbusiness'. Her half hour of thinking had involved some decisions she had forced herself to make. Leaving the club was easy, leaving Luca was harder, leaving the coke...well, one day at a time. Her possessions, the few she had brought from her home in Buffalo, were in her apartment and would stay there. Her photos, the clothes, letters unbearably cheerful from her mother anxious to know how she had settled in, how she enjoyed her wonderful opportunity that she had landed. Had she met anyone famous? Yeh, Mom, I wiggled my ass in front of that daytime soap actor til he came in his pants.

She didn't want to know. She would never know. Rosie didn't mind leaving the letters.

But trusting another man was the hardest decision. She had trusted her father when he had promised to always be there for her. He had left when she was six.

She had trusted her Mom's new husband when he had said that her Mom didn't mind him touching her. Anyway, if she knew then we didn't have to tell her. She was fourteen.

She had trusted Luca when he had promised to get her a job in the theater when she had arrived six months ago. When she was sixteen.

Now she was trusting an African-American private dick because...because he hadn't wanted to fuck her.

On one level her body was aching for what she was used to - sex and drugs, fearing without them she couldn't justify herself as an attractive teenager. On another her mind still worked and she felt safe and strong because she had made a difficult decision that she felt was right. Maybe she would be dead by the morning, but the man on her right had made her feel both repulsive and human in the same instantaneous second and his reward was to make good on a promise.

The cab headed into Jersey City and hunted down the address that the young lady had given him on the card from the guy's pocket. They had seemed an odd couple, but you never could tell these days, especially at two in the morning outside a downtown club.

Someone's watch alarm was beeping loudly not far from my inner ear, the sound magnified by the gentle thump that played across my eyes as I opened them, squinting at the early morning sun. I flicked my head in the direction of the bleeps and looked at the brightly coloured Swatch on the pale white wrist that lazed over my left shoulder and rested in pasty contrast against my head.

The night before was a bit of a blur, but I remembered meeting a girl, a dancer and drinking a great deal very quickly. I reached over and found my pants, my wallet. Empty. Again. Shit. Daniel would have to spot me five bucks for breakfast.

I couldn't recall bringing anyone home though. I never usually did that. Bring anyone home I mean. I'm forty for God's sake, not a teenager. Bringing women home was not something I wanted to get back into. I found once that they cluttered up my life and I didn't intend to let it happen over.

She was white, pale white at that, dark hair, tousled on my pillow, pale blue T-shirt loose, hiding her body, but I could feel the smooth skin of her legs on mine. She looked young. Too young.

I didn't jump out of bed, but I moved quickly enough to wake her. She turned and looked at her watch, then at me. For a second fear crept across her eyes, but my question soothed her.

"Did we have sex?"

She laughed. It was a relief to get that reaction. I think.

"No way man. You were like unconscious. I thought I'd have to get the Paramedics you were so gone. The cab driver had to haul you up here." Her eyes flicked to the floor. Mine followed and I noticed a sheet and an untidy pile of clothes heaped along beside the bed.

"I was just cold. Sorry."

I waved her apology away. I couldn't remember.

"No problem sugar. You okay?" Bits and pieces came back to me as I saw her bruised cheek and her badly cut and swollen lip. "Shit." She saw me look and hid her head under her t-shirt. "No, no I mean I know what went on...at the club at Gini's."

She looked blank. I didn't bother. Explanations, recriminations, whatever, could come later. I was surprisingly hungry.

"Food?"

She nodded and half crawled out of bed before she realised her legs were bare. I smiled. It was sweet to know she still had a little shyness, a little dignity left. I threw her a pair of jogging pants which she put on and followed me down, barefoot on the creaky stairs.

"Midnight, I got your usual..." He stopped as...she followed me in. "And you got a friend. What she want?"

"Honey..." I couldn't remember her name. "...This is my cousin Daniel. Daniel this is...?"

"Rosie."

"Well Rosie, I don't know what Midnight told you, but he owes me millions for what he takes on credit." He gave up. He didn't have the heart. "Ah shit, take what you want and get out of here." Rosie followed my lead and picked up a pack of bagels, some soft cheese and a bottle of 7Up, before scooting back upstairs. Daniel called me back.

"You doin' her man? You doin' her cause she too young, and I don't tolerate no shit like that. You fuckin' gone too far if that true, Midnight. You stupid dumb fuckin' asshole. You know how old she is? Do ya?"

"I ain't doin' her Daniel, I don't know how old she is, but I can't explain now. I'll talk later when she's in the shower. Don't worry, it's a good deed, trust me."

"The day I trust you is the day that Ella Fitzgerald walk in here and start singing to me, my man. Trust you? Huh."

I left. I'd explain later, then he wouldn't be able to do enough. I knew him better than he thought I did. She ate like it was going out of fashion, hurling chunks of bagel piled high with cheese into her already full mouth, swallowing 7Up around them. She wiped her face when there was just a couple of bagels left in the torn wrapper. She fixed me with an earnest stare.

"You not eating?"

I swallowed the remainder of my coffee and picked up a cigarette, indicating that was my kick start.

She shrugged and proceeded to polish off the rest of the food. I'd have to get more.

I finished the cig and was about to go to the shower.

"You wanna shower?" I'd stood and made to take my shirt off. She curled up a little, balling herself into the chair, hugging her knees tightly against her chest, thinking I wanted to shower with her. "No, no. You go. I'm gonna go and talk to my cousin." I threw her a vaguely clean towel. "Here. Knock yourself out."

She caught it, having to let go of herself as she did so, involuntarily unfurling and slipping easily off the chair. She offered a smile as she slid round me and locked the bathroom door quickly.

I went down and explained to Daniel who, as I thought, was anxious to help and let me take more provisions back with me; chocolate, coke, chips, all essential kid food. I even persuaded a t-shirt out of him which had the holidaying 'I love New Jersey' across the front. Red on black.

When I got back she was sitting reading on my bed, waif like as she looked paler and younger now the make up had gone and she gently rubbed her wet hair.

"Hey. Got you a t-shirt." I threw it and she went nuts. I mean she squealed in delight at getting a lousy t-shirt with a lousy message on it. I wouldn't have worn it if you'd paid me. She dashed into the bathroom once more and came out resplendent, the grubby pale blue having been replaced by the jet black. She even looked proud.

"I had a New York one." She stopped, though I sensed there was more. Perhaps it was too obvious. She didn't heart NY.

She clambered back onto the bed and I left her there as I went to shower and shave.

She was still there when I came out, eyes glued to the page, not wavering to look out of the window, not rifling my pockets, my desk. Just another kid who had got it wrong somewhere along the line. But you couldn't save 'em all.

"How old are you?"

She stopped reading and slowly placed the book in her lap. Her eyes didn't quite meet mine as she decided to tell me the truth or not. I think she did.

"Sixteen."

I left it at that. Now she'd told me one thing it would be up to her to tell me the next. If she wanted. I figured she would.

"I gotta go out." She slumped back against the wall, curling up again to protect herself from being left alone. I opened the door and took a step down the staircase, then stopped. "You comin'?"

Golden Gloom.

The final day of filming had been completed and the cast and crew were, virtually to a man and woman, propping up the bar in a packed place in the middle of Perth. Damian Cross was hoisted up on the shoulders of a couple of the crew who weaved unsteadily as they held him skyward. The beer had been flowing freely for a few hours already.

"People, people..." the bar quietened and Damian cleared his throat. "...this has been, without doubt, without comparison, the most fun I have had on a film...ever."

A resounding cheer went up and those not involved scurried away to a dark corner to escape. "I say this because, and those of you who know me will back me up here, because I am not renowned for having fun behind a camera. I love it intensely, I am heavily devoted to it, and I will go on doing it until, hopefully, I die. Assuming I die that is."

Ironical groans circulated. "Being a creator, I know how God felt. If I was a director and a surgeon, then I would be the Great Almighty. But I'm not and as a director, as a man who loves film and as a guy who is usually so taken up with producing something sensational, to say that I have enjoyed myself, is a testament to you all for being so crap that I knew it wouldn't be a success very early on."

Jeers and boos mixed with hurled orange and lemon slices and beer mats, which Damian tried in vain to dodge and rocked uncertainly on the broad shoulders below him. "I'm only kidding, I'm only kidding, hey stop it. Jerry, put the chair down. Down, Jerry, leave it, walk away. Okay, no, I'm only kidding. It is a testament to all of you for making my job easier and allowing me to really enjoy it, so thankyou, thankyou all and the bottles now on the bar are from me, thankyou"

He was lowered into a mass of handshakes and kisses and friendly punching that when he finally managed to rediscover the bar there was just a couple of bottles of champagne left. He took one and poured himself a glass, scouting over the tops of heads for his two leads. If anyone had to be personally thanked it was Tom and Alix.

The sun glinted slowly down over the horizon, blinking orange amongst silhouetted shapes. Alix held Tom round the waist, her head resting on his shoulder as she looked over the city from their balcony. He had been strangely quiet this evening, not filled with the exuberance of the end, not excited to have finished and able to spend more time with her, not even exhausted at coming to the end of a hectically short shoot. Just quiet. Withdrawn. Not here, there or anywhere. Certainly not with her.

"Hey you?"

He leaned back without speaking. He wasn't sure how to say it.

"Tom? What's up?" She tried to make it sound light, casual enquiry, not a desperate plea for communicational assistance.

"What?"

"What's up?"

This time he turned and pushed her shoulders so she had to sit. Alix paled as she was manoeuvred with gravity.

"Honey, there's this...thing and I don't know how to tell you." Alix sighed and sat back.

"Just tell me."

Tom sat back on the floor and looked at his feet, pathetically bare with blisters from his new shoes glaring back at him.

"I'm going to America."

"Tom, oh my god, that's wonderful, that's fantastic, when when, can I come with you, oh hell I'm going with you, Tom aren't you excited, that's fantastic....that's not what you had to tell me, is it?"

His face had barely slipped from misery, only to break into a smidge of a smile at the excitement Alix showed.

"No, it's not." As he looked up his eyes were red and he let go of her hand as he opened his mouth to speak. "We have to break up." Alix sat back and was at a loss for how to react. Immediately she felt empty and lost, but as she examined the detail on Tom's face she knew there had to be a reason. He had to give her a reason. He owed her that. But she didn't have time to ask why. "And you have to get an Aids test."

"What?"

He almost jumped towards her, anxious to take her in his arms and tell her everything would be alright, when he knew that it wasn't, when he knew that it couldn't be.

Alix let him hug her, and she hugged him back. Her initial shock was tempered by the realisation that for her to have to get a test, Tom must have already had one.

"You're HIV? The sex, the no sex for the last three weeks, that's w..." She tailed off and held him tighter. "I'm here Tom, I'm here. When did you find out?"

"Three weeks ago. I got a call from my agent saying I was wanted in America for a movie, you and I had a wonderful half hour in the trailer, then I got a call from my doctor. He didn't want to tell me over the phone, but I made him. I would have told you then, but I didn't know how, I didn't want to spoil it, I couldn't hurt you like that in the middle of the shoot."

"But what about you? You've been amazing from then until now, you've never been better, we've never been better?"

"We haven't been close."

"We have, we have." She cradled his face in her hands.

"We haven't had sex, and the acting. Well, I guess I had something which focused me a little more intensely than I've had before."

"The sex doesn't matter." Although they both knew it did.

"It does, Ali, you know it and I know it."

There was a knock on the door which threatened to interrupt, but neither took any notice and carried on just holding each other, the darkness enveloping the sobbing couple as they cried against each other.

"I only have the virus, it's not full blown and may take years to get there, if at all, what with the current drug regimes that you get these days, so don't waste all your efforts tonight. There may be many more to come." He tried a smile, and for a second it flickered, then died as a cascade of tears descended once more.

A further knock resonated through the apartment, the suddenly ethereal, wistful Faure lingering on the night air as the final embers of daylight took their richly coloured bow.

Tom stood.

"I should answer it." He shuffled off, wiping an already grubby sleeve across his face.

Alix pushed her fingers through her hair and for a moment wallowed in her own mortality.

"Tom, great to see you, where's Alix? I had a feeling she might be hiding up here." Damian marched across the room, arms awaiting Alix. But she didn't stand and fly into them. She peered out from under her hair and offered the briefest, weakest smile.

Damian stopped and was about to launch into some chastisery spiel when he caught himself and appeared to recall something from seconds earlier.

"What's going on? Are you two okay? Broken up and hate each other?" he laughed. It stung. "Tom? Alix?" He turned to them alternately. Neither wanted to say anything without the other's consent and support. Alix stood and went over to Tom, taking his hand and rubbing his arm as he braced himself.

"Damian..."

"What, what? You guys are killing me here. It's a party. Let's party."

"Damian, shut up."

"Alix I..."

"Shut up."

Damian zipped his mouth and hurled the key over his shoulder.

"I've got HIV, so might Alix, we're a little upset, okay?"

Damian stepped forward and hugged them both, setting them both off crying again.

"I'm so sorry. When did you know? I mean, was it like today, or a week ago, or before we started, or when? I'm so so sorry, you guys. If there's anything, I mean anything, let me know, don't hesitate, I mean it." He looked at the bottle in his hand. "I guess I don't need this anymore." He threw it on the couch.

Alix thought otherwise and opened it quickly.

"Alix, honey, I think that's a little insensitive."

"Damian, I always intended to enjoy my life, to do what I want so I can get out of it what I want. If God, or Fate, or whatever has handed me a short fuse then fine, but I'm still breathing and until I stop..." she popped the cork dramatically, sending it soaring over the now brightly lit city, "...I plan to enjoy myself."

She poured three glasses, watching the bubbles spill over making a pool on the table then watching as at dripped into a dark patch on the carpet.

"Tom? Damian?" They both took a glass and waited somewhat nervously.

"This is not the end. We all die eventually and when you're numbers up then there's not a lot you can do about it..."

"Alix, seriously...."

"It's alright Damian. Carry on Ali."

"So, until such time, may I propose that we are friends and continue to support and love each other with impunity no matter what and more so now than ever."

Tom and Damian looked at each other then raised their glasses as Alix did.

"To Damian..." she drank, "...to me..." she drank more, "...and especially to Tom." She drained her glass, pirouetted beautifully and flung the crystal over the balcony, rushing over to watch it fall onwards, racing to it's ear-pleasing tinkling end in a million tiny little crystal fragments on the concrete twenty-one storeys below.

"Alix, shit, oh my God." Tom leaned over and peered into the blackness. "You could have kil..."

He stopped as a closer shattering sound broke his apparent consternation.

Spinning, they saw Damian grinning broadly, pointing to the fireplace.

"Thomas?"

"Oh no. No." They stared at him, knowing he'd have to give in. Finally he gave in and a smile creased his face up. "Where?"

"Wherever you want."

He looked out over the city, then into the blackened fireplace, alive with sparkling glass, then around the room.

He pointed to a picture, a dully pale pastel effort which hung on the wall, insipidly waiting for life. Pulling his arm back he coiled himself up like a baseball pitcher and released the spring he had created, parting with the glass and watching it cartwheel across the room, hitting the picture dead center, shattering on impact, and spidering the glass in the frame, the cracks shooting outwards, creating depth, giving structure and meaning, offering purpose.

For a moment he was open mouthed, then he grinned at his allies in vandalism and picked up the bottle. He went to the door, knowing they'd follow.

"Party?"

A Regular Day.

I had to go out although I didn't have anywhere to go. I asked Rosie, I presumed that was her real name and didn't go any further, if she wanted to pick up any of her stuff. She just shook her head and curled up in the passenger seat.

Daniel had been kind enough to give me his credit card. I have been able to forge his signature since I was eight and it bugs the hell out of him, but Rosie needed clothes.

"You go to Maxx or K-mart, none of this Ralph Lauren bullshit, Midnight." I had been warned.

She wore her shades to hide her eyes, the bruises, herself from the world, but she still ducked down every time she thought she saw someone who might recognise her. I told her that it was unlikely. We weren't in New York now, so she was going to be fine. She wasn't ready to believe me.

We shopped like I hadn't shopped in a long time. Not that I shop often you understand. Don't confuse me with a fashion victim. I like my clothes...to cover me, and that's about it. Charity or Gucci I'm not fussed.

Rosie, I got the feeling, was a little let down by the stores we went to, probably more used to Luca's gold card and

Bloomingdales and Saks than the cheaper end of the market that I took her to.

But she was happy enough and found some 'named' stuff at a reasonable price which I couldn't refuse. Sorry, Daniel couldn't refuse. We left and headed home.

Rosie was quiet, and had been most of the day, despite a couple of excitable moments in the stores. I wasn't sure how she was feeling. She was probably shocked, had no money, or very little. She had none of her gear which she hadn't wanted to pick up so she had no reminders, momentos of her previous life. I realised she may not want any of her immediate past, but I had thought, naively, that she may want something from her home life. I was positive Luca wasn't anything to do with her family.

But until she talked or gave me something to work from I had no way of helping her. Other than being here with her, beside her. Making her feel really wanted. I know I said that women had often cluttered up my life in the past, but Rosie wasn't there in that way. She was around without making any demands. She seemed happy enough to come out with me; equally happy to stay in and read, snacking on junk, taking her time with whatever was going through her mind.

Again I felt that there had to be issues unresolved and the only way for her to deal with them was in her own time. She had been strong enough, courageous enough, scared enough to leave, now she had to be all those things and more in order to stay away. I could make things as easy as I felt was right, keeping her doing things, letting her do things, but as with all things it was up to her as an individual to get through it. If she didn't want it, then she would relapse and probably disappear on me. If she did want it, then I'd probably have to get used to having her around.

Apart from her, I'd seen Gini Firetti and, so far, lived to tell. It hadn't gone totally as planned, I'd accomplished nothing, but I'd met him and that was a start as far as I was concerned.

I had to tell John and toyed with the idea of taking Rosie with me, but I called him instead. Easier, quicker, cheaper.

He was happy with the outcome, more pleased I'd actually done something a tiny bit constructive I should imagine, but he seemed pleased. I guess this could have been as a result of a good trading day rather than anything to do with his current problems elsewhere, but it cheered me up and focused my mind a little.

The day ended as we ate ice-cream watching cars roll by on the freeway, heading here, there and everywhere, not noticing, not caring about the black guy and the pale white chick swapping flavours in silence.

Lost Loves.

Suddenly it was pandemonium as they entered the bar and were engulfed by all and sundry, cheering and shouting and not noticing in their alcoholic haze the red rimmed eyes of the trio who had just arrived. The driving forces behind the movie; the writer/director and the two stars, ambling in clutching a bottle, looking like being mobbed was something they were very used to.

Tom immediately headed to the bar as Alix was dragged to dance and Damian forced into a corner and asked a million questions at once.

The evening had been in full swing for some time and many of those in the room were lucky to be still in the room, having consumed more alcohol than was good for anybody. Many of the hulking drivers and mechanics were still looking relatively sober on ten pints of cold Australian lager, but some lesser mortals were leaning precariously against pillars, doors, walls and each other, looking distinctly green, eyelids closing as the liquor continued and the hours flew by.

From the dancefloor Alix tried to keep an eye on Tom, but soon lost herself to the music, occasionally noticing people dashing out to the bathroom or the car park, some trying both with none too successful results. As the night wore on she naturally got more and more drunk and ended up on Damian's lap as the first shaft of daylight crept in through the windows.

An ambulance hurried by, lights flashing, but no sirens, leaving the pretty few who were left almost standing to more gentle melodies as they swayed around the floor against each other, a few enjoying an end of party smooch just for the hell of it. All the couples had left much earlier, either serious or desperate, hopelessly, drunkenly infatuated, or in need of a session of wonderfully uninhibited, drunken sex.

Alix glanced blearily round the room, seeing who was left, vaguely wondering if she actually knew any of them.

"Daimyun, Daimyun..." She pinched his cheek and he came to, blinking his eyes at her to let her know he was still asleep really. "...Daimyun, c'n I come to...Amrrrica with you... wh'n you go? C'n I?"

"Alix, of course. Of course you can. So long as I can go back to sleep. Now fuck off and drink some coffee."

"Huh." She slipped off and sank slowly to the floor, crawled to the bar and pulled herself up. She tried to focus on the barman, failed miserably, but was pleasantly surprised when a coffee was placed in front of her.

"Oh, cheers mate." She looked at him from one eye, keeping the other one closed as the room spun less when she did. "Leetle coffee for breaky, hee, hee, hee." She giggled to herself then became very straight and serious as she lifted the cup with a shaky hand and put it to her lips, sipping some of the liquid and feeling its warm trickle inside.

Damian joined her, carefully turning a stool back the right way up before sitting on it heavily, leaning his head against the bar, surprised to find his forehead in a small puddle.

"Shit," he exclaimed quietly and to no-one in particular as he also received a welcome cup of coffee. "Ta."

For a few minutes they just sat, listening to the small bouts of conversation that were springing up around the room as others awoke and greeted their surroundings with headache induced moans and yawned g'days. More and more people struggled out of uncomfortable night-time embraces, moving out of dark corners to meet and greet at the bar. All found a cup of very strong, very black coffee in front of them a minute or so later. Subdued chatter continued and slowly the stragglers left one by one, clattering out into the virtually empty early morning street, squinting as the shards of sun tore down, locking arms for stability in twos and threes before deciding on a direction and heading out of sight.

Alix and Damian soon found themselves alone with the bar staff.

"I gotta go."

"Where did Tom go?"

Damian shrugged. "Dunno."

"Oh."

"Share a cab?"

"Sure."

They set out into the daylight, found a cab and slumped next to each other on the back seat, one trying to stay awake while the other caught surreal, unconnected clips of the day starting. A paper boy hurling rolled up copies onto dewy lawns, street cleaners bustling along the kerbs, occasional cars carrying the early birds to breakfast meetings. Curtains remained tightly closed as the last vestiges of sleep were dragged out for as long as they could be without bedside alarms buzzing and bleeping annoyingly to life, followed by the alarm sensitive TV's and radio's which zipped into full swing, following the news stories of the morning so far.

The cab remained quiet until it arrived at Damian's hotel where it was stopped at a police cordon.

Damian paid the driver and half dragged Alix onto the cold concrete, her shoes crunching on some shattered glass. For a second she thought of who could possibly be so irresponsible before recalling a hazy memory of earlier in the night. She didn't have the energy to laugh, but her eye caught Damian's and they shared a knowing smile.

"Sir, ma'am, I'm sorry, but are you staying in this hotel?"

Damian took it upon himself to answer for the both of them.

"We are. Why?"

"Are you Damian Cross of Brent Gardens, Sydney, owner of a blue BMW, licence...."

"Yes, yes. I haven't driven anywhere, as you can see. I've been out all night and just got back via a cab."

"No sir, but someone has been driving your car. If you'd just like to step this way, we have an incident area set aside."

Alix was struggling to understand within the foggy confines of semi-consciousness, but Damian was suddenly wide awake, his first thought being of his precious import.

The incident area was a single desk manned by a pretty brunette in uniform and a murderous looking plain clothes officer.

The officer sat forward as soon as Damian and Alix were shown in, the brunette stood and offered coffee, tea and a chair before her superior had time to bark any questions at the fragile looking couple. Their hangover wasn't about to get any better.

After refusing any refreshment Damian sat wearily, by now having to clutch Alix close to keep her upright.

"Damian Cross?"

"Yes." Damian replied with as much interest as he could muster. His initial feeling had been replaced by 'oh it's only a car and I won't need it anyway if I'm in America'.

"And this is...?"

"Alix Mercer."

"Ah." He seemed surprised and turned to his female colleague to make a note of the name. The woman did so, looking sympathetically at Damian and Alix who now had her eyes firmly closed, her head resting against Damian's shoulder.

"Mister Cross, have you had a good party?"

"Thanks, yes. What is this..."

"You've been there all night?"

"Yes. Many, many people will tell you exactly the same. All night."

"Okay. You are under no suspicion of anything. In fact if you were, by the state I imagine you are in just by looking at you this morning we'd probably be questioning you pretty severely by now, so don't worry on that score." He offered a hint of a smile, but he was clearly not happy about spending all night waiting for these two to arrive.

"Detective..."

"The point, Mister Cross, concerns your car."

"I gathered that."

"At a time between one and two a.m it was removed from the parking lot underneath this hotel, driven towards the outskirts of the city and then no further. The car was found with its front end against a tree, no sign of tyre marks which could have been caused by a severe braking manoeuvre, and the driver was..." Even the hardened officer paused as he came to the real news. "...found dead at the scene."

Damian knew what was coming next. Alix was awake and scared.

"Tom?" Damian nodded slightly and pulled her closer to him as she thrust her hand to her mouth, just failing to stop herself being sick.

Instantly there was someone at her side, helping her away, someone else cleaning already, handing a cloth to Damian who sat stunned by her reaction. Only then did he realise just how close they had been.

"You know the driver?"

"I think so."

"There was some identification." He passed a driving licence and a couple of credit cards over the desk, but Damian didn't need to look at the man in the picture or the adjoining name. Only one other person had ever been allowed to drive his car. Only one other person knew where the keys were. Only one other person knew the ignition code.

"Was it...an accident?"

"We don't think so. We also found this in your room." He handed over a sealed envelope with two names on the front, written untidily, underlined, a big broken heart by one of them.

Damian tore at the envelope, slicing his finger as he did so.

He barely took in the first line, but concentrated and read on down the page.

Dear Damo and Ali,

You may never know how much you mean to me, but hopefully this will go some way to telling you.

I have done all I want. Apart from marry, have kids, which now I can't do, but movies, this one especially, fallen in love, Alix - forever, had the closest personal friendship I could ever wish for, Damian, and seen so many sunsets and sunrises I have the colours emblazoned across my memory. I can never forget them.

But this has come as a shock. A big, overwhelming, horrific, terrifying shock and one which despite having you two beside me, I cannot deal with. I have had three weeks to tell myself to fight it, three weeks doing something I love, being with people I love, and I know that it will not ever be as wonderful again. So I'm going out on a high, believe me.

It won't seem like that, I know, and I can only hope that you don't take it too hard. But Alix, when your numbers up and all that..........

I'm sorry Damian about the car, but it wasn't your colour.

I'm sorry Alix for ruining your life, if that's what I've done. You literally mean the world to me, the earth, the sun, the stars, our star.... I cannot live with you like this, so I will die with you in my heart.

Love always
'Making a Move'
Tom.

Damian slid the page back onto the desk and took it in. The state of mind he must have been in, the despair he felt through the laughter in that very room earlier on, perhaps the alcohol had pushed him to a level of morbidity from where he just couldn't get back, but maybe he'd been planning the whole thing for three weeks, since he knew. Perhaps he'd thought about it and decided he couldn't live with it, no matter what the circumstances were, no matter who was there to help him.

For a second a wave of anger burst through Damian. If he and Alix weren't good enough friends that Tom thought the only way out was to commit suicide, then perhaps he didn't deserve any of their sympathy.

The thought lasted only a second to be replaced with horror at how Tom must have been feeling over the final weeks of the shoot, then amazement at how he had performed with these destructive thoughts whirling around his mind, clouding his life with uncertainty. Yet he had been faultless. He had sparkled, he had worked so well with everyone around the set. He had an electricity with Alix, he had grown into a presence that even Damian had to admire from behind the camera. He would be a star.

He would have been a star.

The past tense sent a bolt of icy cold through his body and he shivered slightly.

"Could I have a drink?"

A drink was brought and he scalded his mouth as he drank it too fast.

A policewoman came and whispered in the detectives ear. He nodded and stood.

"Your friend has been sedated and put to bed."

"Is she...?"

"She's fine." He paused again, knowing part two was more harrowing still. "Sadly, and I know its early, but we could really do with an ID on the body?" He left the question hanging. Damian simply nodded and stood, following the detective as he went outside, staring blankly as they drove to the morgue, not noticing the stench of the place as the cover was pulled back.

Then he looked.

The beautiful golden hair was matted with blood, the skin pale, the forehead and nose smashed almost beyond recognition. Yet there was an overall feeling of peace to the man on the slab. There was no sense that this man had died frustrated, angry, but willingly and on a level with himself, with what he had and what he was leaving.

Damian looked for a few moments, resisting the temptation to wipe his hand through his hair, to touch the face of his friend one last time. He nodded, happy that his final memory was of Tom laughing, amongst a crowd on his way to the bar.

Alix slept through the day and awoke only briefly, popped two more sleeping pills and placed her head back on the pillow. Neither when Damian returned and sat next to her, stroking her hair, nor when the telephone rang early the following morning did she wake. It was lunchtime when she finally came to and dismissed the nurse who had been watching her, saying she was fine and Damian was all she needed right now.

The two of them talked and talked until it was dark, then until it was light again, mainly about Tom, but eventually about what they were planning to do next.

"I have to get away."

"Me too."

"Where are you going to go? America I suppose."

"No. You?"

"America. I know Tom was going, but I was as well. Life does go on, Ali."

"I know, I know. I'll end up there eventually, but I'm going somewhere else first. What will you do in LA?"

"Sell the movie, make it the success that it deserves to be. For all of us. For Tom. Then see what comes up." He waited as he wanted to be told not to. But Alix felt it was instinctively right so smiled a weakly encouraging smile and hugged him harder.

"For Tom."

"Where are you going? Really?"

Alix looked up, looked out of the window, felt the breeze drift in, the warmth of it brushing against her skin.

"When I was a little girl my Mum became very friendly with just one particular woman, who after my Mum got sick basically brought me up, as best she could with a headstrong teenager anxious to do other things than study on the radio all day. Mama Anna. When Mum died, well just before actually, Anna returned home to what was left of her own family who she had left to come to Australia with her husband. I kept in touch, so I'm going to see her." She paused, but spoke just as Damian was on the point of asking again. "In Greece."

Thrown Together.

Rosie had still not talked to me at length, but I was being incredibly, and for me somewhat unbelievably, patient. Usually by this stage, almost a week into our relationship, I would have been holding her down and demanding she tell me. But I wasn't. I couldn't. For some reason she had to tell me. She had to want to tell me. And so far she didn't.

However, the seven days had been rather busier than I expected they would be. Alarmingly I had a call from a woman wanting her husband, her suspected unfaithful husband, followed to see if he was having an affair.

Rosie had been more excited than I was at getting another job and insisted that I take her with me. I didn't have a choice.

The man in question was easy to pick out, his wide black framed glasses making him an easy spot once we located him hurrying out of his office block. We followed him to a run down hotel opposite a run down park, followed him in, got in the same elevator and watched him go into a room. Number 20. Rosie and I held hands. She chewed gum and waggled her hips. I tried to look guilty, but Rosie told me afterwards I was crap at it. The man did give me a knowing smile though, so I figured I'd done enough to suggest what I hoped to suggest.

We waited and watched the door. Nobody else went in, so we had to wait until he came out.

Eventually, about an hour later, he did materialise, flustered and frantically clutching his case, adjusting his glasses, and looking nervously around before scurrying down the corridor away from us.

Minutes later the door opened again and a tiny oriental girl sauntered out and across the hall, casually blowing smoke from her cigarette in front of her. She knocked on the door opposite and walked in without waiting for a reply. Rosie giggled, but stopped herself before I had to put my hand over her mouth.

So we knew where and the following day we got our pictures, with a little help from the oriental girl and a wonderful performance, so she told me, from Rosie, who acted as a potential third who got off on taking pictures of couples. The man bought it, and probably later, caught it from his soon to be ex-wife.

In the past I had to hide or burst in to get pictures that my client would believe, but Rosie had proved a useful and willing partner. I was wary of using her to imitate the oldest profession in the world, but she seemed happy to help and in the end she didn't have to have sex so I considered it part of her recuperation plan. If she could get so close without feeling the need to join in then she must be more and more on the way to being well and truly out of her old life and her old state of mind. And that, from her point of view, was only a good thing.

She had also put on a little weight over the week, stuffing herself with junk food as an antidote to her lack of drugs, but she looked better for it and I told her so. At first she didn't believe me, but after four or five days she began to give shy little smiles and accepted the compliments with good grace, even if she still didn't believe them.

The money from the job was useful and I gave her some for doing me a big favour. I'm not as quick as I used to be, and despite most couples being in a state of undress and therefore hampered in any possible pursuit, I was grateful for not having to test myself out.

I wouldn't say we were partners, but she had proved useful to have around. Plus she didn't say much, so she wasn't an irritant and she didn't cramp my style.

The main job was still at something of a standstill. The brief *tete a tete* with Firetti had proved only one thing; that he was serious about getting his money or his land back. Either way John was looking at the sharp end of a very big stick.

And I had no leads.

The mysteriously absent Cale had yet to make any sort of appearance, real or apparitional. And any details on Marello, which I had to see if only to get an accurate picture of what was going on, were not being made available. That didn't really even qualify as a line of enquiry, but it was all I currently had.

Perhaps, hopefully, it would be third time lucky.

We parked across the street. Rosie had wanted to come despite my telling her she couldn't and Daniel telling her she shouldn't but as is the way she got hers and sat with her feet on the dash, blowing bubbles from her gum, making them pop sharply, then unpicking the remains from her lip.

The red brick building in the dark leafy street, yes, dark even in mid-afternoon, looked strangely welcoming, and although I'd warned her that we may have to sit for hours

Rosie seemed prepared and excited by the prospect of a long uninvolved stakeout.

She had brought a couple of books and we'd picked up magazines and donuts, some candy. While she blew bubbles she was absorbed in a book, Grishams latest, turning the pages occasionally she ploughed on, utterly engrossed. I'm not sure where she'd got them all, I only had a handful scattered about the place, but I figured she'd got closer to Daniel than I knew. Something for which I was neither surprised nor sorry. He was an honest worker and an even more honest man, so if she was learning from him then she wouldn't go far wrong.

"Hey?"

She didn't look up, but did offer a vague grunt of acknowledgement in my direction.

"How you doing?"

She flipped her book shut, keeping her finger in place to keep her page.

"Whatja mean?"

"I mean that I've been with you for a week and you seem okay, I mean you're eating, you're reading, you get a buzz from my work more than I do which is great, but are you okay? Inside. I mean if you wanna talk, I'm here."

She smiled and knocked her head gently against my shoulder.

"I know."

She went back to reading about the latest southern lawyer in peril and I had to be content with watching the black front door of the red brick building.

For several hours nothing happened. Nobody, and I mean nobody went in or came out. Then at five and just after people started leaving, tying coats and saying 'see ya' to their friends and colleagues as they left and headed home for the evening.

But there was no Miss Baumann and there was no Mister Graziani amongst them.

For a while I wondered if we'd wasted a day watching them when they weren't there. I wondered with a scowl deep enough for Rosie to enquire if I was okay. I said yes and told her what I thought. She shrugged and offered to stay as long as I wanted. A good kid.

Dark descended and a few individuals wandered past, a few couples arm in arm, dashing past underneath the gloomy street lighting, huddling close as the rain started to fall, slowly at first, a few spots spattering the car, then a little heavier, then for five minutes an almighty deluge which sent mini rivers racing down the roads, before it all abated as rapidly as it had blown in and the odd spot returned to decorate the windscreen as we awaited something of more lasting and substantial interest.

There comes a point when you cannot sit any more. You cannot eat any more. You cannot watch nothing happening any more. I reached this point at just after eleven that evening.

We had been waiting in the car since lunchtime and seen hide nor hair of our two wanted figures, but we had not been despondent. Well I had, but Rosie had just carried on reading, eating and sleeping, which is the state she was in now as I opened the door of the car and crept out.

"Where you going?"

I sighed. I hadn't wanted to wake her. I had hoped that I would have been back before she had chance to wake up.

"I'm going in."

"Oh." It was the first time she hadn't wanted to come with me.

"You wanna come?"

"Sure, if you think..."

"No, Rosie. You stay there this time. Go back to sleep. I won't be long."

"Hey, how you getting in?"

"You don't wanna know."

I looked around and satisfied myself that I was the only one on this part of the street. I took a breath and marched across the street to the door, flicked out my lockpick and worked the lock till it clicked satisfyingly. I turned the handle and went in, looking back to see Rosie watching, eager to see me get in. I hoped it impressed her to see that I also had a few dubious talents.

Once inside I recognised the room and headed to the stairs. Hearing no voices, seeing no bodies I took a step, then another, looking above, behind, wherever, making sure I was alone. As I reached the elbow of the flight of steps a shaft of light darted down towards me and I crouched back into the shadow. A gentle, softly spoken voice, Italian definitely, floated down, saying goodnight, thanking someone for staying late. It was Graziani. I could tell with his first step out of the room. The body shape.

Sara must still be in the office. I shot like a bullet from a gun back down the stairs and opened the first door I found, closing just enough so I could see out, a lovely view of the entrance door.

Tony crossed and placed his hand on the handle, turning it a millimeter. Then he stopped.

My head pounded as the broom dug into my ribs.

Why had he hesitated? What had he forgotten? Please go home Tony, go, go.

Then I heard the rapid chatter of footsteps, bustling along down behind him.

"Mister Graziani, Mister Graziani."

"What? What is it?"

"You forgot your file for tomorrow morning." Sara caught up with him and handed over the slim red file. "It was under the Zipecki file on my desk." He took it. "Sorry."

"No problem. See you tomorrow."

"See you tomorrow."

He pulled at the door and stepped out onto the dark front steps, illuminated slightly from the low level light in the hallway, then closed the door behind him.

I started breathing again.

Rosie watched as a slim chink of light came and went. The door closed again and no-one appeared. If someone else was in there, then where was Midnight?

Then she froze. Her blood, gently warmed over the last few days, became icy as it coursed a route round her body, freezing, chilling, stopping the function. She jammed herself back into her seat, bringing her knees up to half hide her face as she peered down the street watching the familiar figure approach.

Luca.

As he reached the pathway he slipped his hand inside his jacket just as the door was pulled open, really open, and a figure filled the doorway.

"Midnight?" she squeaked, then clasped her hand over her mouth, hoping, praying her voice hadn't carried outside of where she sat. She held her breath as she waited for everything to stop, but it didn't.

As she looked again she didn't recognise the figure, but as Luca stretched his arm she knew what was coming.

The flash of light and the figure dropped to the floor.

As Sara turned away there was a bang and she stopped in midstep. I knew what it was. Too familiar. She knew as well, but instinctively. She turned and I could see she wanted to open the door, afraid of what she'd find on the other side.

I squeezed out of my hiding place and raced silently over to her, throwing my hand over her mouth. She jumped violently, but was quiet as she saw who it was. I held my finger over my lips to make sure she remained so, but there was no danger of her not being now.

I could tell she wanted to know why I was here, how I was here, but now was not the time.

We held the handle together and turned, crouching, peering out, concealing our presence as much as possible.

There was a body. Motionless, face down, dead.

As soon as the man hit the floor Luca pocketed the weapon and turned away, running from the scene, checking no-one saw, missing the wide eyed stare of his former plaything as she fought for breath as the bulky killer disappeared into the darkness.

She knew she should help, but she couldn't. She felt she ought to, but she daren't. Where was Midnight? If one man was shot, what about any others inside the building. She stayed and watched.

We looked for a few seconds, but there were no other bangs, no shots from anywhere and there was no-one else in sight. No-one on the steps, no-one on the street.

Sara whimpered a little as we waited for a minute longer. Not quite crying, but shocked and stunned.

Then I eased the door open further and stood a little higher, looking round a wider arc. I still saw nobody, but looked up at the car across the street. I raised my hand and saw Rosie reciprocate. She was okay.

The blood was doing a slinky down the steps, oozing darkly over one precipice after another, dripping stickily on the concrete, leaving a descriptive trail from the pool at the top as it moved inexorably to the sidewalk.

The body was heavy as I turned him. It was Tony and the void in his head was an obvious and horrific point of death. A hit. A palpable hit.

I went back inside. Sara just put the phone down as I reached her.

"Paramedics."

"He's dead, Sara. They won't be able to help."

We went back upstairs and sat down, not even talking, not saying anything. I poured a drink from the convenient bottle of brandy that was in the draw of her desk. She took it and drank it in one go. I poured another and she cradled it this time, rocking slightly as she held it.

"Mister...."

"I know Sara. Believe me I know."

The flashing lights outside alerted us to the paramedics and they soon had the body in the back and they were on their way. The police took statements and told us not to expect too much.

Sara and I went back inside and she curled up once more in the office, sipping the brandy and drifting in and out of sleep. When her eyes had been closed for a good five minutes without her jolting into consciousness every so often I stood and walked round the office, weighing up the cabinets and files, picking where wills were likely to be stored. I didn't plan to do anything tonight of course, not with Sara in the room, but I would be back, and hopefully with Tony out the way, she may prove to be more pliable.

I dragged Rosie in when I knew Sara would remain asleep, but she was equally tired, although a little wired from the events she witnessed.

She had hidden out of sight when the cops arrived, anxious not to get involved, and to be fair I couldn't blame her. I presume she'd seen everything though and might have an accurate description of who it was, but that could wait until the morning.

Which duly arrived. I was awake first having grabbed forty winks, closely followed by Rosie who was instantly alert and then Sara who was by turns pleased to see me, then confused, then wary as she noticed the girl by my side.

"Hey. Sleep well?"

She looked at me, then at Rosie, nodding as she did so, backing up into the chair, straightening her skirt, tying back her hair, making herself look presentable.

For whom? I wondered idly.

"Did I dream..."

"No honey. It was real. Tony's dead."

"Luca shot him." Rosie's sharp, solid voice made me turn.

"What?" Sara and I were together in the query.

Rosie looked hurt by the unintentional harshness, but repeated herself anyway.

"Luca shot him."

"Who is Luca?" was Sara's next, obvious question.

Rosie glanced at me, a touch of fear that she'd said something wrong playing in her look.

"He's a Mafia guy. Strange he came alone though."

"Not really. He often did jobs alone. Ever since Lorenzo was killed a couple of years ago he preferred to."

Sara was clearly astonished by the information that my feminine disciple was spouting, but I welcomed it. Suddenly

I had a bargaining chip. If Sara was scared by the information then she was scared by the people behind that. If she knew who she was dealing with, those who had killed, murdered Tony, then she might be more willing to deal with me. I hoped.

But now was not the time. Later when she'd settled down. If she took irrational decisions now, based on what she was feeling now, then she may be more reticent about changing her mind later on. If I didn't push it and presented her with facts later on when she'd had time to calm down, then I felt she'd be more receptive.

"Shall we grab a coffee?"

We headed down the street to a place Sara knew and sat contemplating rather than drinking the coffee.

I piled sugar into mine, much to the amusement of Rosie. Sara didn't seem to notice much of anything, so entranced by the hypnotic motion of the swirling brown liquid as she stirred it round and round and round.

I didn't know what she was thinking about, but I could have guessed.

When you see your first dead body, especially if you were so close as to hear and feel the last breath from that body, it's hard to think of anything else.

I took a sip and looked out the window. People hurried by, as people did when they lived in cities. It was a curiosity, but perhaps one you could justify. The buzz, the energy that you got from city life made you quicken your step, get there as soon as you can. Sometimes even then it wasn't fast enough. Being on time was regarded as a thing of fantasy when battling with traffic on the crowded streets.

"Why was Luca there?" whispered Rosie, anxious not to interrupt whatever was going on inside Sara's head. In fact she had beaten me to the punch. Why was Luca there? If Firetti was bothered to send him, and there was no other deal going on, then the men in suits were worried. Okay, maybe not worried exactly, but they knew something could be awry and they wanted it sewn up neatly. No loose ends. Famous for it.

"I don't know." Rosie slumped back into her seat and let out an audibly disgusted sigh. If I didn't know then how was anyone else going to know. After all I was the investigator.

"Why do you think he was there?" That was directly searching and I shot a glance to where she was sitting. She flickered a smile and dipped her gaze to the streets outside.

"Why do you think he was there?"

"I don't know your case."

This was true.

I took a deep breath and considered for a few seconds. If she was forcing me to think, then I had to think quickly.

"Okay then brainchild, let's go through it." I turned to face her, sliding my cup away from my elbow where, I have to admit, it was more than likely to be knocked over the floor, and jabbed my index finger onto the formica table top, making the point. "My client gets threatened, because of some land deal he did over a decade ago, by some very powerful people. The only lead is a dead guy who had connections with both parties, and the guy who ends up in a pool of blood is the dead guys lawyer." Even as I said it out loud it made no sense. Why kill a man without extracting information first if that is what you needed? And clearly that is what was needed, because there was no open and shut details that would make Firetti do otherwise.

"Revenge?" queried Rosie, sitting up, excited.

"For what?"

She actually thought for a minute or two, not letting the silence confuse her into a rushed answer.

"For the dead guy selling them down the river."

"It's okay, but it's light." That was the best I'd come up with so far as well. "But there should be something other than that. It's not strong enough for Firetti. Would Luca take the law into his own hands?"

"Possible. He did it once before but got pistol whipped for it. Fractured his jaw. He might think twice, but he's not the brightest."

"We'll say no then. I don't think he'd try again."

We dropped into thought once more. Rosie and me thinking and drinking. Sara... I couldn't say what Sara was doing. She could have been thinking. She certainly wasn't drinking. She was probably contemplating events. Events that had overtaken her and now faced her like a condemned man faces his guilt, or a frightened man faces his fears.

She looked serene, yet desperately unhappy. Turned to stone at the moment of deepest sadness.

I stood.

"Shall we go?" Rosie obliged and leapt to her feet, crashing her chair to the floor, making other coffee drinkers turn and stare at the metallic clatter.

"Sara?"

She looked up and shook herself.

"Sorry." She stood, dazed and confused.

"You wanna go home?"

"No, no. I can't." She spoke softly into her shoulder. "I should go back to the office. There'll be meetings to cancel."

Rosie almost tutted her disapproval, but I stopped her. This was no time to dictate matters. If Sara wanted to go back to the office, then I wasn't going to stop her.

Sara led the way out and I caught Rosie's arm.

"You okay with it?"

"Sure. I don't think she should go back in there, though. Do you?"

I had to admit I didn't, but I wasn't going to stop her. "No, but she's lost her boss, maybe her job and her lover."

Rosie's eyes glinted. "Really?"

"I think so. So, we have to take it easy, go with her flow. Okay?"

"Sure."

The street was fairly deserted, only a handful of cars and even fewer pedestrians. There was an ugly dark red stain on the steps and some surprisingly bright red blood contrasting on the dark green leaves of nearby plants; the horror of death and the beauty of nature highlighted with breathtaking clarity.

Sara carefully avoided the stain and hopped up the side of the steps, fumbling for her key then rushing inside, hardly stopping to open the door wide enough as she slipped in, snagging her jacket on the handle, tearing the pocket.

"Shit, shit, shit," she screamed at the hanging fabric, white against the black of her jacket. Then she could hold it in no longer and the tears came thick and fast, flowing over her face as she crumpled to the floor, sprawled ungainly, hands to her face, wailing loudly as her whole body shook with the effort as the emotion poured out.

"All my life," she blurted suddenly, pausing between great heaving sobs. "All my miserable life I've given to that bastard..." I knelt back on my heels, not quite sure how to take her comment. "...and now, now he's gone, I feel so free and alive and...and..." She paused, quiet now as she regained control of herself, querying what she was saying, realising what she was saying. She looked up at me, questioning as the words came out. "...alone."

For almost an hour we, or rather I, Rosie had wandered off somewhere, had the whole history.

She'd been born in Germany, but moved to America when she wasn't even a year old, being raised in New York, going to college at Berkely to study law, passing her bar exams, then applying to join every big firm she could think of and getting nowhere.

Then out of the blue came this job, advertised as a P.A with a keen interest in becoming a partner. She applied and got the job, joining Tony and his partner of the time Fredrik Tomes. Since then she'd basically done the same things; typing, filing, screwing the boss. Not great for a law graduate.

But she was in a secure profession, a steady job, and could afford an apartment that didn't come with rodent accompaniment. She'd stuck it out.

And now.

"I don't know. What can I do?"

"Sara, you're a law graduate, you can do anything, you're talented enough and probably prepared to work hard enough to do anything. What would you like to do?"

She considered me for a minute or two, looking round the room.

"I don't know," she whimpered. "I'd like to curl into a ball right here and go to sleep."

I tried hard to keep a straight face.

"Sara, that doesn't sound like the fiesty, attractive, confident woman who threw me out of here."

"It's not, I'm not."

We fell silent again. There were some limits, some lines that I had to cross eventually and thought about it now.

"What were you doing here, anyway?"

I looked blank, or tried to.

"What....I...I....wasn't. What?"

"When you almost scared me to death. What were you doing here? And who's the mine of information?" She nodded at Rosie who had sauntered back in, thumbs hooked loosely under her waistband, her jaw pursuing its lasting quest to destroy all remnants of gum that have ever existed.

"What?" She stared at us, questioning, using the word of the minute.

"I was looking for something."

"The will?"

"Sure, the will."

"Why?"

"It doesn't matter now. It really do...."

"Why?"

I had wanted to cross the line, not be dragged over it. But as I'd advised Rosie....

"I've got a case which needs me to look at it. Just for clarification."

"Yeh?"

"Sure."

"Midnight, as you've told me, I'm not stupid. I know what you want and I know why you want it." Her eyes had a touch of amused joy in them, not in keeping with her recent tears, more in touch with her self. I couldn't deny she was right. I needed to see it.

She stood and went across to a filing cabinet, flicking through some of the sheets inside before picking one out. She toyed with it as she crossed back to me, tapping it lightly against her thigh as she sat down and handed it to me.

I looked at Rosie as I took it, raising my eyebrows. Easy as pie.

The cover sheet was all lawyer-speak. I flicked it over. The second sheet contained the priceless piece of information that made the rest of the file so valuable, relevant and addictive. For the next hour there was no-one in the room, no-one in the world, no-one who mattered as I read through the dark hidden secrets that lurked in the crisp white sheets.

It was a strange experience being so involved in work. It had been a while.

But it felt good. Maybe cause I thought I was getting somewhere, maybe cause I felt I'd accomplished something in just getting the damn thing, and maybe cause I hadn't had a drink in almost twenty-four hours.

Relative Recovery.

The flight was too long and too hot and faintly disturbing when the pilot casually walked down the aisle handing out magazines to the first class passengers. Alix took one but didn't read it. She tried to sleep, but her eyes refused to close, responding to the maelstrom of thoughts that had dominated her dreaming hours since Tom's death.

She had thought of little else. Karen had to pack for her, purchase and collect her ticket and see her on to the plane, such was her catatonic state. Alix managed to walk and answer questions and respond to instructions, but anything else was currently beyond her. Tom, Tom and Tom.

The plane touched down at Athens International which looked a shoddy excuse for an international airport from the cramped comfort of the plane, but was welcoming enough in a dark deserted way as the passengers checked through customs at 5.30 a.m.

It was surprisingly cool as Alix slid into the back seat of a cab and instructed the driver to head for a small place marked on the map on the Peleppones. The driver made a small gesture of unwillingness, but Alix unfurled plenty of American dollars and threw them on the seat next to the eager cabbie.

Two hours later and Alix awoke to find her nose being assaulted by the worst smell she had ever had the misfortune to encounter.

"What the hell is that?"

The cabbie took no notice until Alix tapped him on the shoulder and held her nose.

"Ah, is the shit collection. Every day. Not last long. This your town."

He pulled over and swung across the street in a deft u-turn so he was facing the way he had just come in.

Alix got out and gave the delighted man a couple more US bills.

"Efcharisto." She thanked him as he sped away in the morning light.

Alix sat on her case and looked around her, trying not to breathe as the grubby dark red sewage truck passed her and disappeared round the corner, heading out of town.

The town was just breaking itself in for the day. Blinds were being drawn up or down depending on what side of the street the owners were on as the sun streamed down, low over the buildings. A few dark clouds drifted about way above the street, threatening rain.

Fruit was placed in front of shops, piled high in large baskets and boxes, but not so many postcards were on view as Alix imagined there would be in the summer months.

None of the many bars flickered with life, but a number of old men and women drifted in and out of the supermarket, entering with nothing and leaving with provisions for the day. Many wore black, constantly in mourning for their loved ones.

A stocky woman crossed the street further up away from Alix, a stranger just arrived, and disappeared down an alleyway.

A man threw open his front doors and sat at one of his tables, smoking a cigarette and drinking a glass of what Alix no doubted was freshly squeezed orange juice.

A couple of dusty mopeds zipped by, the drivers helmetless and smoking, stopping for a brief chat, a handful of purchases, before executing a tight turn and motoring back up the road.

Alix stood and picked up her case, leaning awkwardly as she hobbled to the man with the juice. He looked friendly enough, his dark moustache set on a perfect olive skinned face, his dark eyes scanning the street, as he smoked his way into the day.

"Good morning."

"Allo."

Alix looked at him warmly.

"Can I have one of those?"

The man stood and waved his arm towards the open door.

"Sure. Come, come."

Alix sat in the offered seat and blinked into the sun as a gust of wind whipped into her face, fluttering leaves and dust into the bar.

The man laughed.

"All the time it is wind here. Sun and wind." He looked at his guest as an old woman came out to join them carrying a pitcher of juice and a glass. She set them down on the table and left. "You are English?"

"Australian."

"Hostralian. We not get many of you here. I am sorry for my english it is not so good."

"It's fine. Better than my Greek."

"Ah, we change that while you here." He poured a glass for Alix and sat back, lighting another cigarette, offering one to Alix which he also lit as she nodded. "How long you here?"

"Dunno. I came to see a friend, so depends how long I'm welcome."

"You have friend here? In Tolo?"

"Sure. Mama Anna, I call her. She, or rather her family have a bar here."

"There are many bars here. What is the name of the bar?"

Alix shrugged and scrabbled around in her rucksack, dragging out a dogeared piece of paper on which she could just make out a name she had written there.

"Dionysos?"

"Ah, Dionysos. Manolis, he owns it. Anna is I think his aunt."

"Right."

"It is further along." He pointed down the road, obviously the only main road in the town and from his position on the corner of it he could see almost the whole length. "Come, I take you."

Tidying Up.

Fucking Daniel was hammering on the door again, hollering about a phone call, so I pulled myself away from the bed, and Rosie who had become a nightly inhabitant now, strangely comforting, and confronted my cheerful cousin.

"What is the matter with you?"

He smiled. He did that. I had a serious point to argue over and he smiles at me. Bastard.

"You got a call, man. Veeerrry distressed woman. What you been doing, man?"

I didn't know any distressed women, only the one who was less distressed and currently asleep in my bed.

"I don't know any."

"Sure man. Look...." He trundled down after me, making the stairway creak threateningly, "...I don't care man, but wass goin' on? I mean you got the girl, you got a distressed woman, man, and you got squat on your case. Is there a link here, Midnight, man? You got women and bitched up hangovers, but you got no work done."

"Daniel...Daniel, you are, forever have been and forever will be, no doubt, my conscience and my guardian angel all rolled right up in one mean spirited nigger package, but don't, don't fuck with me." I jabbed my finger against his chest.

He smiled.

He had got what he wanted. I had shown I cared. Cared about the girl, cared about the case. Cared about distressed women I knew nothing about. And that was, in his eyes, progress on the alcoholic apathy of recent days, weeks, months, years. I pulled a sneer and picked up the phone.

"Midnight Seyle?"

"Oh my god, Midnight, I'm in work and there is no work, I mean, I came to the office and there is no office, I mean, I'm here and there's paper, and drawers, and pens and....."

"Hey, woah, Sara, Sara?"

She was high as a whore and panicked as hell.

"I'm scared Midnight, I mean really scared."

And scared.

"Sara, Sara, sit tight, I'm comin' over."

"I don't wanna sit tight for fuck's sake, I wanna get out of here, just fucking pick me up, I'll be in the coffee house."

She dropped the receiver and I shot back up the stairs. Rosie was still asleep when I dressed so I scribbled a note and left it on the mirror. Bad choice. She never went near there. I stuck it to the door with some hastily chewed gum. She'd appreciate that. And probably eat the gum.

Sara was in a state, not helped by the little row of cups, empty cups, that sat giggling at her as she twitched nervously, examining every face, every car for familiarity, or unfamiliarity. She had her fingers screwed round a set of beads and her face was alive with worry. She sent her chair crashing as she stood to greet me, throwing her arms around my neck in a vice like grip and, worryingly, holding on.

"Sara, let go. Please."

She did and apologised as I picked up her chair. She sat as I got her another coffee. Decaff.

"So, what's up?"

"Bullshit Midnight, don't play games with me."

"Slow down, girl, just take a breath. You said come over and I came, but you didn't make much sense talking like you were. So tell me the story." I paused as she took a breath about to launch into whatever it was had given her such a shock. "Slowly."

She managed a half smile, but that was it as the lines returned to furrow her brow and her mouth twitched in anticipation of what she had to tell me. So much that for a second she hesitated, not knowing where to start.

"Last night?" I prompted.

"Sure, sure, okay. Last night. Well, last night was last night, I mean Tony and all...."

"Night before." I corrected.

"....sure, night before, whatever, and after being at the office you took me back to my place, dropped me off, had a drink and left with your...your..."

"Rosie."

"...sure, with your Rosie. Is she your Rosie?"

"Just looking after her."

"Right. After that I paced. I mean I walked hundreds of miles up and down the fucking carpet....do you have a cigarette?"

I didn't.

"Fine." She turned round the room and saw no-one who could help, so unwillingly turned back to me. "Okay, so I walked for like, ohhh, I don't know, hours, til about three, four maybe, then I just got tired and sat down and woke up this morning with the alarm to my building going in my head. It must have been like about seven." Her fingers flitted and flicked at the beads, pointing and waving demonstratively every so often. "So then I panic, cause I'm like normally in the office at seven thirty, so I shower, change, kill myself getting to the office on time, creep round The Stain....," as it had become known, "....and get inside." She looked at me, genuine fear in her eyes, written all over her face. "And there....there was just this mess. The hallway was fine, but the door was open. I didn't want to go in, but I had to. I couldn't hear anything... anybody...so I had to go in. And there was this mess. All over. There were papers everywhere, drawers pulled out, files turned over, the desk was empty, it was all over the floor, and I didn't know what to do. I couldn't cry, I was too scared, I should have left, but I didn't know where to go, I was just stuck in the room, stuck." She stopped and her fingers stopped and her hands stopped and her eyes stopped. "Then I called you." She looked up at me, wanting to know she did the right thing.

"You did the right thing."

She let the tension rush out of her shoulders and they dropped by about five inches, but then she started twisting and searching the room once more.

"Sara, Sara..." I placed my hand over hers, making her stop. "...It's okay. I'm here." This was laughable. Just by me being here it didn't make her safe and with the people I had met recently it probably made her less safe. But she appeared surprisingly comforted by me saying it. Maybe she just needed someone else to lean on. No Tony, nobody obviously in her life, maybe a kind word and a show of support was all she needed right now.

"I gotta go."

"What?"

I stood and she was on the verge of screaming at me. I smirked. I actually enjoyed winding people up. Usually it got me punched, but it was fun.

"You're coming too."
She stood and examined my face.
"Where?"
"Look, I have to make a call, then I wanna see the office, okay?"
"Do we...?"
"We do."

Daniel said that Rosie was up and about and helping him in the store. I almost blacked out. I had to ask if she was alright.

We sat and looked at the outside of the office. The lock had presumably been picked by an expert as there were no cops around. If there had been cops then someone else in the building would have been turned over or noticed the damaged door. But there were no cops. Everything looked normal from the outside.

But we sat anyway until Sara had enough and breathed deeply as we went inside.

My heart was pounding, but I had to appear calm. If I got panicked then there would be no controlling Sara, if I caught up with her as she disappeared over the horizon. But she was tightly attached to my arm. It didn't really help having her there. If someone was waiting for us then by the time she disentangled herself we'd be worse off than before. Dead or severely bruised.

But if it kept her calm then it was a risk worth putting up with.

I held my breath as I pushed open the door. I wasn't expecting trouble, but I guess I had learned never to expect anything. The trouble occurred anyway, whether you expected it or not.

The door swung open without a sound, merely setting the papers ruffling gently as they were crushed and blown by the gentle draft.

The scene was almost total devastation. The neat, ordered, ark of an office I had seen a couple of days previous was no more. It was as Sara had described. Papers were everywhere, making the room seem lighter, pens were scattered, the desktop was clear of anything. The computer lay broken. The screen smashed, the monitor blacked. The filing cabinets were bereft of contents, hollow and wanton. The drawers were bent and discarded, trampled and beaten then hurled aside in anger. Whatever they wanted they didn't find it.

"Midnight?"

I hadn't said anything as we picked our way through the debris. Sara was probably worried.

"Yeh?"

She said nothing. She had just needed reassurance that I was okay. Still with her.

I bent down and halfheartedley piled a handful of papers on the wide open space of the desk. Sara followed my lead and as I cleared the floor she tried to organise the sheets into some semblence of order, recovering the structure she lived by.

The papers were collected, the pens picked up and the damaged beyond repair stock placed outside of the door. I'd take them later.

I was somewhat confused that they, whoever they were although I had a fair idea, hadn't either toothcombed or torched the place.

If they hadn't found what they wanted, and they hadn't, believe me, then why leave anything? If they'd looked through everything and then trashed it then it would have taken hours. They knew where it was. And when it wasn't, then they trashed it. Angry, frustrated, scared of going back to their boss with nothing but a limp.

A couple of hours later I slumped in the corner by the window, the open window, letting some much needed fresh air float through the stale Tony'd environment that had been present here for too long, while Sara continued sorting things into piles.

She was good. Her hands flew over the pages, magically attracting the right ones with her sticky fingers and dropping them on the right pile in a blur of pale flesh and whiter pages. She concentrated hard and when she finally looked up she caught me looking at her, both of us surprised and embarrassed.

"What?"

"Just watching."

She looked at her hands as they straightened the piles in front of her as she blushed slightly.

"Do it in my sleep."

I jumped to my feet and came to perch on the only corner now vacant on the desk. I had to shift a carefully constructed pile slightly and almost died from the look I was given.

"Who did this Midnight?"

"Same guys."

"Sure?"

"Sure." I knew she had to know. "You going to sell this place?"

She looked around, walked a little, dragged her hands over the walls, the edges of desks, surfaces, remembering, knowing.

"Maybe."

"Well, you can't work here. You can't stay here. Seriously?"

"I know, I know," she offered wistfully. "But I have so much here. Though Tony's gone, I still have a lot here. I've never really worked anywhere else."

I couldn't argue with that.

"You'll always have memories, Sara."

"Thanks for the amateur philosophy."

I stood and changed the subject. Things were moving now. I had to move with them.

"You wanna take these?" I arced my arm over the piles of paper, a dozen of them.

"I need to. Except these." She picked up a pile and dumped it in the trash.

"Dead already."

We got some boxfiles, went back and collected the paper piles then loaded up and headed back to her place where we unloaded and Sara started organising once again.

I got a coffee and watched. She didn't want my help, didn't need my interruption. She had to have things how she wanted. After all she'd have to do the work now. I wondered if she'd realised and prepared herself for that prospect.

By the way she was meticulously sorting and arranging and rearranging she was well prepared for what was going to come in the next few weeks.

"Sara, I really should be going..."

"Don't."

I stopped. I wasn't sure I wanted her to be so dependant. I hadn't expected this much dependance. But I never expected anything anymore.

"I'll have to make a call."

She nodded.

"Sure."

The couch was comfortable.

Comfortable for a freshman, not for a middle aged recovering detective. I tossed and turned and flipped and spun right out all night, falling off twice, as noisily as I could just to make the point, before finally managing almost an hour of uninterrupted zee's.

That was destroyed by Sara crashing impressively around the kitchen. I flicked my eye half open for an instant and caught her looking at me as she prepared to drop a pan on the floor. She didn't see me and I closed my eyes. Her revenge had worked. I was awake. Now she could wait a little longer.

Normality.

The street was being hosed down from every angle, from every doorway as the stores began to open for the early morning trade. They would shut again at noon and open long into the evening, such was the Mediterranean style of doing things.

Alix followed a couple of steps behind, looking around her, taking in the sights and smells of the town. Her guide didn't talk much, just puffed away on his cigarette as he greeted a couple of people with a cheery wave, jabbering away in his native tongue of which Alix knew only thankyou and the ubiquitous *'ella'*, which seemed to mean all things and not actually mean any of them. Mama Anna had used it a lot.

Just as the pace slowed and Alix saw the angular Dionysos sign in gold print on a dark green plinth above the door there was a commotion behind them. Alix turned. There was an old woman with hands clasped to her face standing over a dropped bag of shopping, an errant melon rolling gently away as errant tears rolled gently down her face.

Simultaneously the two apparent strangers broke into beaming smiles and hurried to each other, embracing like the old friends they were and there standing in the middle of an uneven road in a town neither of them knew well one forgot about her shopping and the other forgot about her lover.

It was five minutes of car dodging later that they looked at each other. Manolis had appeared and was sitting outside his bar chatting to Alix's guide. The shopping had been retrieved and taken inside as Anna and Alix hugged, oblivious of the world carrying on around them.

Both were older and their looks betrayed this to the other, but Anna just burst into laughter as the corners of Alix's mouth turned into a warm, laughing smile.

"My dear child." For a few moments Alix stood as Anna stroked her hair, her face, held her shoulders. "My dear, dear child. I did not know you were coming to see me?"

"I thought I'd surprise you."

"You did, you did." She looked once more then turned her to face the bar. "Manolis, this is my beautiful Alice."

Manolis stood and came to greet his aunt's friend, shaking her hand and dropping a kiss on her cheek.

"Allo, very pleased to meet you. Anna talks so much of you, but she say you would never come here."

Anna shot him a look and playfully punched his shoulder, then took hold of Alix and marched her into the bar.

"Come, we gossip."

Meeting Cale; Moving On.

I had to leave at some point, but it didn't seem to make it any easier for Sara. She almost kept her fears in check, but still couldn't resist asking why I had to go, where I was going and when would I be back? I couldn't give her precision in my answers, but promised to return later. She smiled wearily, but she didn't look happy. She promised to sort through some papers and think about her future. What she was going to do now she had no Tony, no office, no job as such to command her attention day in day out. I knew she'd find something. She wasn't the type to sit and wait for something else to happen, especially now.

But, for the time being, I had to leave her.

I called in on Rosie and Daniel, both of whom were laughing like hyenas when I entered. Apparently Daniel's endless stream of stories-about-Midnight had been entertaining my young protege, and he had clearly been compelled to join in. Thanks man.

They wanted to know where I was going, so I told them I was going to see John.

Rosie wanted to come, but I took her aside and asked her to do something for me with the file Sara had given me. She seemed inordinately pleased at being given something to do which carried a hint of responsibility; accountable to me. Still, probably keep her out of harms way for the day.

They wished me luck as I left, Daniel on the verge of launching into yet another tale of defeat and embarrassment for yours truly. I was glad to leave.

Reasons for seeing John had multiplied enormously since the episodes at Sara's. I say Sara's when I imagine even she would refer to her place of work as Tony's. But somehow the macabre idea of a fat, ghostly Italian ruling his recently vacated roost was not something I wanted to contemplate for longer than absolutely necessary.

The file was one, with the valuable piece of information that John had to know, if he didn't know it already. I suspected he did, which then begged the question as to why he had been so reticent about garnering me the truth? If the piper wasn't being honest with me, then I ain't gonna follow him no more.

A progress report was another, but that largely depended on his response, or lack of, to the contents of the file. If nothing else then Tony's murder should be of interest to him. If people were starting to die, then John Barclay's cool, calm, businesslike exterior might yet be breached.

In the back of my mind there was a hint of an amoebic feeling that perhaps I didn't like Mister Barclay, but while he was paying my bills, especially now I was supporting two fully grown people, both of whom were requiring greater levels of consumer perishables due to the recent lifting of artificial substance dependence, that is we're eating junk to get over drink and drugs, but while he was paying my bills then any personal feelings were tucked away, determinedly hidden behind the new found solidity of my professional pride and the instant giant shoulder-like status that Sara and Rosie had bestowed on me.

His house was strangely gloomy as I pulled up outside, but my attention was grabbed and shaken around by the yellow 1980's Mercedes-Benz SL that sat brightly, lying low, its impressive, impassive teutonic visage wanting action, needing the buzz of acceleration on an open road to be fully appreciated and loved. For a brief second I felt its tug offering a viable alternative, but the red demon behind me swelled with anger at the appearance of the thought and I turned to appreciate the Mustang once more before passing an idle hand over the smooth paintjob and almost flat hood of the yellow Merc.

Gates waited and drifted me through to Johns office.

"Midnight, great to see you, sit, sit, I've got a surprise."

I sat and guessed it was to do with the car.

"What is it John? Oh, I like the new car. Although I figured you for a more modern model."

"The car? Oh hell no. But that is the surprise. Hold your fire."

He disappeared for a few moments, leaving Gates to hold the fort, guarding the door with a quiet that was threatening in the extreme. I wanted to tell a joke just to see him smile. But he wouldn't. I knew he wouldn't. I knew he.....

"Midnight, this is my wife, Cale. Cale, my protector, Midnight Seyle."

I had stopped talking not because of the surprise, but because of Cale. Cale Kline. I'd seen the pictures, but they didn't do justice to the real thing.

She was taller than I expected, her hair was thicker and more golden, her eyes, well they were hidden by the blackest of shades, her body had been surgically suctioned into the tightest fitting dress I think I had ever seen a grown women walk in. It was pale blue and she was perched on two inch heels, accentuating the shapely nature of her achingly long, wonderfully slender, sickeningly tanned legs.

My throat was crying out for a drink.

"Hi," I managed to croak, holding out my hand. She shook it, then turned to John and pecked him on the cheek.

"See you tomorrow honey."

She looked at me, at least I think she did. It was hard to tell, but her head certainly turned in my direction, then walked away, out of the door and gone. I looked at John, pointing to the door which now closed as Gates made his stealthy retreat, unaided by blaring trumpets or panicked calls from his Officer.

"John? I need to talk to her?"

"I know, I know, but she's....busy."

I was fuming. Not just because she'd walked out, but because he had paraded her then let her walk out, when he knew I... Oh it doesn't matter.

"To hell with that." I shot out of the door, quicker than even I expected, and almost quicker than Gates expected, but sure enough he was there like lightning at my neck, stretching my collar before I managed to shake him free and catch Cale as she reached the door of her yellow Mercedes.

"Mrs Kline?"

She turned sharply.

"Mrs Barclay, Miss Kline."

I was rocked back on my heels, but evaded the tone and ploughed on. Having finally got in the same building as her, I really needed to spend some time with her. Talking to her.

"I'm sorry, Miss Kline, Mrs Barclay, but I really need to talk to you. About your husband, about Mike Marello..."

"Stop right there Mister Seyle. As far as I can tell, and I'm a lot closer to John than you think you are, believe me, you've done him no favours so far. You've been on this case for, what two months, longer maybe, and I've seen squat of your work, and I know you've done nothing about helping him. So when you get something then you let me know."

"Miss Kline, Mrs Barclay..."

"One or the other," she interrupted testily.

"...I find myself in a no win position here. I am working on finding and solving the solution to your husband's problem, but I can only do it with co-operation from certain people, you being one of them. Mister Marello, if he were alive, would be another, but without him I'm being walked all over and I'm not getting anywhere."

"Well, when you do...you be sure to let me know."

She pulled on the handle of the door and curled her long legs inside. I politely slammed the door closed.

"Miss Kline...."

"Mister Seyle. I've spent less than five minutes in your company and I don't like you. You don't impress me. Now if you'll kindly get out of my way, I have to be somewhere else."

She spat the words and then floored the gas, spinning the wheels and leaving tell tale black lines on the driveway as she hurtled out onto the street.

I glared at the disappearing car, then at John who looked merely blank, Gates at his side, equally blank, but with an evil lurking beneath the surface.

I ran to my car.

There was something about the brevity of our meeting that further entranced me. Cale Kline was beautiful. She was brazen. And she was bitchy.

And she could drive.

I had to work hard on the wheel to keep in visual contact with the bright yellow sportscar, although being a bright yellow sportscar it meant that I could drop far enough behind and catch glimpses of her brake lights as she swerved in, out and round traffic knowing that she was still on the freeway heading....to the airport.

Of course. She had told John she'd see him tomorrow, therefore she must be going out of town. LA probably, auditions, shoots, something or other. I relaxed a little, now I thought I knew where she was headed.

I don't know if she looked in her rear view, but if she did then she'd see me soon enough. Hiding my red sports in a lane full of nondescript metal was like hiding her Merc. Impossible.

If she did see me then I guess she knew I was following her. And if she knew I was following her then she'd wonder why.

From my point of view there was nothing that I had gotten from what she said, or her reactions to anything I said, that helped. I was no clearer as to why she was so bad tempered. No nearer finding what she knew, if indeed she knew anything, cause John sure as hell thought she was an innocent in all of this. But if that was the case then why did she have to act like she did? There was no reason, unless that was the way she was with everybody. And being in the entertainment industry that was certainly not to be discounted.

She swerved suddenly and headed off the slipway towards the airport. I followed, several cars behind, but now it was where she was flying, not where she was driving.

I couldn't believe that John would have been suckered into marrying a nasty bitch like that though, no matter how good looking the damn woman was. I didn't believe it and I couldn't believe it.

Cause if I did, then why was I trying to kill myself by chasing her so hard?

If I did believe that what I'd seen was her normal self, then I had no need to talk to her as she probably wouldn't have given me the time of day let alone anything vaguely useful.

If I did believe that her fiery demeanor was how she reacted when confronted with everyday problems, then I would be feeling sorry for her, cause she'd be dead of high blood pressure before she was my age.

No, I was pulling up in the same car lot as her, and following the clicking of her stilettos because I knew, I had a hunch, that she was sweet as pie and she knew something. Maybe something about Marello, maybe something about John, maybe something about Firetti, maybe something about all three of them.

And maybe she knew nothing.

As I watched her check in I suddenly considered that she did know nothing.

It wasn't a good feeling. It wasn't an 'I win' feeling. It was a feeling of sudden desperation that, like so many TV detective shows, I was only going to get to the bottom of this case if somebody else died.

It was a feeling exacerbated by the stocky, bald man in a pinstripe black suit and RayBan shades with a bulge under his jacket that was neither bicep nor pectoral who I noticed casually, too casually, reading, or rather not reading the Tribune by the news-stand to my right.

As I watched him I knew where Cale was headed. I didn't have to look. Only when he looked back at his paper did I know she had stopped.

I looked up and picked her out, her blonde hair flourescent against the drab backdrop of La Guardia.

I saw her check in. I watched the goon watch her check in. Then he left.

Running to tell his boss, Gini Firetti, that she was flying to Florida.

"Florida!"
"Florida?"
"Yes. Florida."
Rosie and Sara had differing views on my announcement.
"Are you going?"
"Ooooh, Florida. Can I come?"
As I said, differing views.
"Sara, why would I be going? I don't know where she's gone, where she's going, and now I'm a couple of hours behind her already, no chance of catching her this time. But next time...."
"So you are going?"
I sighed what I hoped was a trying to be patient but you're really stretching it sort of sigh.
"Yes. Eventually. Eventually I'll have to go. That's where Marello is."
"Really? How d'ya know?"
I was beginning to enjoy the almost new Rosie's infectious bursts of enthusiasm. Sara clearly wasn't.
"Cause he's a detective," she snapped at an instantly quiet, unrepentant Rosie who stuck her tongue out as Sara turned back into the kitchen. I suppressed a smile.
"Cause he's alive, we know that, she's an actress, that's mainly LA, right, so why's she going to Florida now?"
"Audition, meeting, date..."
She shot me a look as she said it, wanting, maybe not but certainly looking for, a reaction. She didn't get one.
I shrugged in the merest of thoughts that she may have a point, but my heart was telling me no. My head was examining

the options, but my heart was pounding its rhythm and I knew not to ignore it.

"'Men who ignore their hearts are not worth wasting time on,'" was one of my Ma's favourite quotes when I was younger.

"'But Mom...,'" I had always countered, "'...he died on the way to America?'"

"'This is true, Midnight, but he was following his heart and he died a happy man, knowing that we loved him and knowing we would be content in following ours.'"

I never got further than that with my Mom. She had never explained how he died, and I never pushed to know. But some of her words made sense. Sometimes in weird ways.

"He's there."

Sara busied herself with something.

Rosie retreated to a chair and the comfort of a book, I didn't know which one.

They were waiting for me to say something.

"Look..."

"I don't want to hear it."

"Sara, I'm not going now, I'm not going this week, but I have to go. You know that. It's my job and until the unfortunate death of your boss, I wasn't getting very far with it. Now I have a lead or two and I need to pursue them, which means pursuing them, wherever." I looked at her, but she continued with whatever she was doing, tying knots in her cloth I guess. "You know that Sara."

Still she said nothing and still she didn't turn round.

I looked at Rosie who peered at me from behind the crinkled pages.

"Come on. We've gotta go."

Rosie was settled down in the store, trolling round giving Daniel a helping hand, so I disappeared upstairs and tried to read all the way through the file Sara had given me.

It was hard going, but finally I turned the last page, exhaling loudly and lengthily. It was dull for sure, but it wasn't anything that affected anybody I knew. So why was it important?

I could ask Sara, but I figured she wasn't the best to be talking to right now, and no-one else knew. John might have an idea what it meant, but if he really thought that Marello was dead, after he had been at the will reading an all, then he wasn't gonna be much use either.

Yet again, that left me nowhere.

I grabbed a shower, standing under the feeble jets of water for almost a half hour.

As I walked back into the bedroom, rubbing my hair with the towel, I didn't notice Rosie. Until she spoke.

"You're in good shape."

I switched the towel to round my waist and looked at her laughing face as I covered my embarassment.

"You shouldn't be looking."

"Yeh right, like I've never seen a naked guy before."

I had to give her that one. I figured she'd probably seen as many as me and certainly more recently.

"You still shouldn't be looking."

She just smirked into her book and looked incredibly grown up and incredibly young in the same instant.

I carried on drying and she was silent for a few moments.

"You really going to Florida?"

I glanced back at her trying to gauge whether she was upset by that.

"I'm gonna have to, sweetie. Why, you wanna come?"

She nodded, trying desperately not to look too keen in case I said no. I felt I should refuse her, but what harm could it do, and if she wanted to help, then I wasn't gonna stand in her way.

"Sure then. You gotta bag you can keep in the trunk, cause we gonna go at a minute's warning. We gotta be there, set already."

She nodded again, a huge beaming smile spreading warmly over her face, happy now she knew I wasn't abandoning her. She got off the bed and hugged me.

"You're great, man."

I was about to say that I wasn't, but felt that might just disillusion her. It would certainly disillusion me, so I shut up and enjoyed the adoration. For a change, it felt good.

The only problem with saying that I had to go to Florida was making sure I was on the case when I needed to be, and that meant sitting waiting for Cale to return the following day and then wait for her to take off again. A long haul sitting in Daniel's car was not my idea of fun, and certainly not his. He knew what I did to cars on stakeouts; they invariably came back looking more like trashcans.

Still Rosie offered to keep me company, so at least I might get some shuteye.

Okay, so I said the only problem. Problem one out of two maybe. Problem two came in the not unattractive form of Sara who was still bugging the crap out of me.

She was understandably jumpy, but I told her there was nothing to worry about. No-one knew she had been there the night of the killing, no-one knew she had seen the office after it had been turned over, no-one knew she was involved, and no-one knew where she lived anyway.

Of course none of this was accurate, but telling it to her calmed her down and made her aware that I wasn't just abandoning her either.

If they knew about Tony then they for sure knew about Sara. But that couldn't be a consideration right now. I had stuff to do, she had stuff to do, so if we both got on with our stuff then we could meet later in the week.

She was mollified, but I'm pretty sure she sulked anyway.

Stakeouts were a pain in the ass. They had to be done sometimes, but they were still a pain in the ass and not nearly so effective as cop shows like to make out. Sure, you get your target coming and going, and maybe if you're lucky enough to have the right equipment then you can hear them inside, but if you're just sitting, waiting, and waiting, for one individual to return and then wait some more until they decide to leave and even then you don't know if they'll be headed for the place you want them to be, then believe me, they're a pain in the goddam ass.

It had been several hours Rosie and I had been sitting there. Several hours of nothing. Now, I'm a patient person, and Rosie just tucks herself in with a book, as I'm learning, but there are limits. We had been there since just after dawn and it was now getting late in the afternoon.

John had gone out early and not yet returned. We had eaten junk and barely twenty sentences had passed between us.

I didn't mind, but there are times when, while sitting next to a person, you feel that perhaps you should be talking. Not even cause you want to, but just because you should and it might relieve the goddam boredom of sitting and waiting.

But what would we talk about. Rosie had to have her space whilst remaining in my protective cover, and she would make the move if and when she was ready to. I wasn't all that sure whether I wanted her to either. More pressure from her was something I didn't need while I was headlong into a real job for the first time in months, years even, and I wasn't convinced that I could give her the support she may be looking for.

I munched a yum-yum, feeling the sticky dough clog my arteries a millimetre smaller. Good stakout food and Rosie joined in which made it better, more acceptable.

I was amazed by her apparent lack of need for exercise. When I intermittently got out of the car to stretch my legs and do a little jog up and down the road, she sat and waited, content that her legs would work when the time came, despite curling them into strange positions inside the car. She laid her feet on the dash, then over my lap, then she sat cross legged on the seat. Sometimes she lay along the back, so I guess she stretched out a little, but basically she sat, read and ate. She was proving to be a wonderfully calming influence.

"There," she said suddenly from behind her book.

I hadn't seen her head move, but as I looked out the yellow Mercedes curled elegantly between the gates and retreated behind the safety of the high wall.

"Alright." I over-enthused with more elation than I felt. "Part one complete."

Rosie looked up at me and smiled then returned to her book. A restful influence and maybe a useful asset.

Half an hour later the Lord and Master returned bearing gifts, and was greeted by an ecstatic and from what I could see, and no I wasn't really looking other than to see who met him at the door, barely covered Cale, who embraced, kissed and dragged John inside and out of sight. I sighed and looked over at my female cohort. She had the faintest, sly looking grin on her face as her eyes scanned the words in front of her.

I sighed again and looked away. I wasn't going to dignify her thoughts with a denial. It wasn't worth it.

Almost an hour had gone by before the door twitched open once more and Cale, barely recognisable now with her hair swept under a headscarf, her eyes covered by huge dark shades and her body tucked neatly into jeans and a bubble jacket, despite the relative warmth of the pale evening that we all were slowly slipping into.

Once more on the road and feeling safer in the Mr Joe Public car. Safer that I wouldn't be spotted. Safer I could trail her to the airport without fear of discovery. At least from her.

I didn't know who else was out there watching her, watching me watch her, but I was sure there was somebody. Maybe not right now, but they would appear when I least wanted them to. I knew it.

"What ya thinking about?"

She'd mugged me again. Caught me off guard.

"What?"

"Yeh, what?"

"Oh stuff. You know."

"What stuff?"

I gave her a look. She shrugged it off and waited for an answer.

"You're suddenly very talkative?"

"Finished my book."

"Good?"

"Sure. Happy ending. Makes a change."

I smiled at her, what I hoped was an encouraging with a hint of sadness for empathetic value sort of smile.

"It does happen sometimes, you know?"

"Yeh, I'm working on it."

We sat for a minute, trailing the Merc, gazing at the traffic as it thundered into increasing darkness. Maybe this was the moment.

"I was thinking about what we were going to do in Florida. What do you fancy?"

"I thought we were working?"

I felt a little jolt of jealousy. She assumed that it was a we and not a you. Presumptuous, but on a second of reflection welcome.

"Sure we are, but who knows how long that's gonna last. We might only be there a night to get what we need. We could stay a day or so if you like. You think?"

She shrugged again, non-commital.

"Sure, if you like."

"You ever been to Florida?"

"No."

"You ever wanted to go to Florida?"

"Sure." She muttered her answer, barely audible over the hum of the car, but couldn't keep the flutter of excitement from permeating her voice.

"You know, I came here almost twenty years ago. I'd just started my detective firm, got my license, all that crap and then I got a job. Out of the blue, some folks called and before my feet had got used to the idea of having nothing to do all day I was chasing a case all the way down to Florida. I'd never been before, although having spent some time growing up in the South I had a bit of a mind as to what it would be like. But that was like before all the centres grew up, you know all the Disney stuff, Busch Gardens, all that, and Florida was just a sunny state with a number of Latinos living there. Sure there were bars, and hang outs, a handful of stuccoed buildings, but it wasn't like the millionaires second home it is now.

At first view I hated it, but I had to stay. I wasn't going to fail my first job, so I had to do some work. I walked miles, up and down, trawled bars by the dozen, picking up the trail of this guy, before eventually I just fell over him in a casino. He admitted what he was doing, and he offered me a lot of money to let him carry on. I asked him where he's got it and it worked out that while he'd been journeying down and while he was in Florida he'd been pulling deals, scams, whatever and had earned almost half a million in just over a month.

I stayed a few days before I called his parents and we had a fantastic time, drinking, getting scores, getting laid..." I looked at her to make sure I hadn't touched a nerve, but her face was impassive, just drinking it in. "...all that sort of stuff, and he showed me how he did it. He was a trader for anything. He'd buy something and then a hundred yards up the track he'd get rid of it, often for double what he'd just paid. It was amazingly simple, but he made it work in a big, big way, and he paid for us to stay there partying, basically, until I really had to turn him in.

At the end of his run he bought some stocks, shares, things like that. Just put all he'd earned into them. He told me a couple and I watched them over the next few years without ever really remembering why, and certainly not remembering him. But they rocketed. I figure by the time he was 25 he must have been a multi millionaire."

I shook my head in admiration. Rosie had said nothing and still she said nothing. Just looked ahead as the traffic thinned as exits were made and we followed the yellow sports off right.

We pulled into the lot and headed to check-in, got tickets and sat in the lounge, booked a hire car at the other end and boarded the plane, buckled in and waited.

"I'd like to go to Disneyland."

An Intriguing Man.

The Tolo beach was almost deserted. The narrow strip of pebbles and stones curled along with the buildings until it broadened into a swathe of sand at the far end from the main street. A few desultry umbrellas sheltered the handful of hardy souls from the pale sun as the wind whipped over the sea, shaping the waves and topping them with a white coating of surf before breaking them and running them up the sand, only to pull back, halting their progress and drawing them away once more, ocean debris marooned on the tide line like a symbolic artistic gesture concerning the end of the universe.

Alix slipped her feet into the cooling water as she walked, wondering where her urge to be by the sea came from, toying with the smooth pebbles beneath her soles, feeling her feet sink slightly into the soft patches of sand.

The beachside restaurants were beginning to open up, lighting candles to entice the hungry passers-by inside, clipping cloths to the tables to stop the infamous wind removing them. How so many could survive was a testament to...tourists probably.

A few more couples left for home. The whole beach was Alix's. As she reached the seats she took one, dropped the back and lay down, looking at the stars which could now be seen in the still blue heavens above, each one twinkling to its own rhythm, crumbling its existence into the history of the sky in full, exposed view of the galaxy, shedding the last vestiges of life from trillions of light years away.

The waves in front of her worked a little harder as the wind called for more effort, splashing under her chair now as her eyes closed and she released her senses to the ebb and flow of the slow tidal drift, the breeze flicking at her hair, whistling tunefully in her ear, hiding the sounds of the town in the powerful yet comforting blanket of Mother Nature.

Mama Anna had been wonderful, as she always was, knowing the things to say, the right things to talk about, the best advice, the most irreverent gossip and the worst keeper of secrets, but the gentlest listener and never eager to seek information if Alix wasn't quite ready to tell.

At first Alix had been puzzled by Anna's decision to leave Australia, but as she saw her in the homes and lives of her relatives she could only admire her decision to go to Oz in the first place. Anna worked in the bar and by all accounts had made a number of improvements without losing any of the natural charm and easy going nature that was prevalent whilst making it more profitable. Some of her husbands business skills had clearly rubbed off.

Only once, and that was all that had been needed, had they talked about Tom. Only once had Alix cried. She had sworn that she wouldn't, desperate to keep her feelings under control, but to hear someone else, someone else she loved, talk about him she couldn't help herself and her tears flowed into the wonderfully sweet melon vodka that she was now increasingly addicted to.

They had talked about her mother and the painful end to what had ultimately been a painful life, and Alix, through the truth serum of alcohol had to admit that she knew very little about her and even less about the mythical figure that had become her father. She had never seen a picture of him and never heard her mother talk about him. To all intents and purposes Mama Anna, the woman she shared her secrets with, the woman who had taken her to school, held her after her first heartbreak, celebrated when she won, commiserated when she lost, fed, clothed and looked after her until she was old enough, and now drank and talked like they were the best of friends, it was Anna who Alix remembered being there when she was growing up. Not the wiry, crinkled young, old looking woman who drifted in and out of consciousness. Not the once beautiful figure of Alix's formative years, a figure that had slipped from memory like sand through an hourglass.

Anna would never be her mother. She could never be her mother. But she was the closest Alix felt she would ever get.

"Excuse me?"

Alix peered up, away from her contemplation of the grains that scurried over her toes as she shifted her feet, but could only see the silhouette of a figure, a tall figure with broad shoulders as she squinted directly into the dipping sun. She held her hand up to shield her eyes.

"Yes?"

"You sit in my seat."

Alix jumped up and considered the place where she had been sitting, noticing for the first time the plain blue towel hung on the back and the black rucksack perched on a chair behind. She took a step back and to the side so she could see the man properly.

"I'm sorry, I didn't notice. Go ahead."

She turned to leave, an apology just reaching her ears as the wind picked it up and whipped it towards the town, safely away from the emotionally tormented ocean where it would get picked apart and swept away before it served its purpose.

Alix waved a hand and headed back the way she had come, dipping her sandy feet in the water, idly flicking stones a few yards out to sea, looking into restaurants, blinking the images of flickering candles from her eyes.

Looking back the man was sitting in his seat, head buried in a book, seemingly oblivious to the lack of anything or anybody around him in the gathering gloom. For a few moments she stood and watched him. He was so still, not moving any part of his body, barely moving just the one finger he used to turn the pages in front of him, braced against the wind, solid and still.

Later that evening as she put her glass to her lips she asked Anna if she knew him.

"I don't know everybody though, my sweet."

Although she hadn't described him well Alix was disappointed that Mama Anna didn't know who the man was, but she wasn't sure why. That night she slept restlessly, turning over and over under the single sheet, closing her eyes trying to will herself into sleep, contemplating the walls and the noises from outside, those she could hear above the plaintive moans of the low wind as it groaned through gaps and whistled through windows.

To no avail and when she woke the next day she was bleary eyed and obviously sleepy as she went to the store to get water and more melon vodka before breakfast.

By lunchtime, in the surprisingly warm midday sun, she found herself drifting towards the beach once more, casually wondering if the man would be there, almost, she worried herself slightly, hoping he would be there.

Why, why, why?

She turned off the road and walked down the plant covered path to the beach, pausing between concrete and sand to slip her shades on and survey the colourful scene as people played on the shoreline, swam in the sea and skipped over the blue surface on jetskis. She scanned the lines of white loungers to her right, occupied and otherwise, hoping if he was there he would have an available seat next to him. She saw neither, but she dragged a memory to the surface and contorted her face into a look of curiosity.

It had been his skin.

There had been something unusual about his skin.

It hadn't been wet.

And against the even tan there had been tell-tale lines, some pale, some much darker, on his shoulders and torso. Scars.

He couldn't have come from anywhere but the sea, could he? and then the marks, the scars. Alix felt a dangerous fascination creep through her body as she recalled the brief sight of him as she turned away.

His voice had been clipped, for the two sentences she had heard him speak, and not Greek, but not English either. More like the Euro-English which was becoming the first language of the un-unifiable continent and therefore not instantly distinguishable for someone like Alix, untrained in the linguistic vagaries of Europe.

Her feet disappeared into the soft sand as she walked along the beach, back towards the town, her hidden eyes constantly searching amongst the beach dwellers for the one man she had come to look for.

And there he was.

As if by magic he had appeared on a seat that Alix swore she'd been looking at, empty, just milliseconds earlier. She blinked, making sure she wasn't seeing things, but he remained, flicking his towel over his body before sitting and resuming his pose from the previous night.

Alix stood and watched, then saw a vacant place just behind and to the left and darted to it, scattering sand as she threw herself onto the seat arranging herself so she could watch without being seen. She leaned back, resting her head on the back rest and looking out from the bottom corner of her eyes as he took out a knife, delved in a bag and pulled out a peach, then searched for a bottle of water which he poured over the peach, making a dark patch of sand at his feet, before slicing the peach with his knife and eating the slices off the blade.

Alix watched him. Watched the precision, the obvious attention to what he was doing. And the way he did exactly the same four more times, not deviating at all from the routine.

He was tanned, darker now than in the gloom of last night, little lines showing on his body. His head was bald, shaved at the back as his hairline sat just forward of his crown, but smooth and brown. His eyes were dark, but to the fore, not hidden under the hoods of heavy eyebrows, his mouth was thin, but with a slightly fuller, gently curved top lip, his hands were huge plates, but they handled the knife so deftly. His body and legs were muscular without being so because he was too thin, and the overall effect made him look like he should have been hairier than he apparently was, thought Alix as she examined him more closely.

Then in the blink of an eye he was gone.

Alix shot upright and looked from his empty seat to the sea, to the left, to the right, not seeing him anywhere. She removed her shades and looked again, but he was nowhere. She had literally blinked and he had disappeared. She swore to herself.

"That is not ladylike."

Alix jumped up and turned, anger and fear burning in her look as she came face to face with the man.

"W-w-what?" She managed to stutter out, wishfully buying some time as her heart slowed down. But it didn't as she couldn't stop herself from staring at the scars which seemed more obvious now he was standing in the shade of the umbrella.

"May I ask what you do?"

"W-w-when?" She managed, her thoughts not working quickly enough to keep her up with what she was being asked. What did she do when? In life, or as she rocketed out of her relaxing seat?

"For the last twenty minutes, half hour? You look at me. Why?"

Alix's breath deserted her altogether. He had known she was there. He had known she was watching. He probably knew why, but was just being polite in giving her a chance to explain.

"W-w-what? H-h-how?"

He said nothing. He stood and watched her as she fumbled for an answer. His eyes never left hers, or tried to as she ducked away avoiding his gaze which searched inside her as he stood six feet away.

Alix shuffled her feet, continually looking at him then ducking away as he never moved. How had he moved so quickly, then arrived behind her so silently, and known that she had been spying on him all the time anyway?

The question was where she went now? She couldn't just launch into an inquisition of her own as he was currently the inquisitor, making her turn red uncomfortably under his stare. But equally she didn't want to just let him slip away as she had to admit to herself that she was utterly fascinated by him.

Back home in Australia she had seen men with scars, but they were usually from machinery or occasionally crocodiles. She had seen women with scars, often from machinery or occasionally boyfriends. But none of them resembled the motley collection that adorned the frame of the man in front of her. And she wanted to know how he'd got them.

"You interest me." She mentally kicked herself for not thinking of something more winning, but relieved that she had broken the silence.

The man nodded as if he had indeed known this was the reason and surprisingly he appeared to be satisfied, making a move back to his seat.

"But..." Alix made to stop him, but found she didn't really know what to say, although an idea thumped away at the back of her mind. "Where are you going?"

The man sat down and opened his arms. "I'm not going anywhere." He settled back, opened his book and resumed his relaxed position.

Alix felt her legs give way and she slumped back onto her own seat.

The Man was already engrossed in his book, flicking the pages with monotonous regularity, undoubtedly aware of the looks he was getting from an increasingly embarrassed and frustrated woman next to him. Alix intermittently ran her fingers through her hair, looked out to sea and scrambled her brain trying to think of something to say that didn't obviously sound like a come on. Phrases constantly popped into her head and she was on the verge of saying them out loud, but always stopped herself as she thought of a deviant connotation that could readily be attached.

The sand played round her feet as she squirmed them round in front of her. The wind played with her hair which she tried holding out of her face, but got fed up and just let it blow. The Man sat perfectly still, thoroughly unaware of the wind, and oblivious to the woman.

Alix stood, her mind made up to go.

"Sit down."

She whipped round. The man hadn't moved, but he'd definitely spoken.

"Pardon me?"

He said nothing, but closed his book patiently, looked up at her from behind the blackest of shades and motioned for her to sit back down. Alix did so without thinking.

For almost a minute they just sat, staring at each other, his intensity being matched by her discomfort.

"Alix..." Alix jumped to her feet feeling her skin crawl and the hairs she never really knew existed jump to attention on the back of her neck.

"How do you know my name? How do you know my name? How? Tell me?"

He motioned for her to sit down, but this time she was twisting and turning in front of him, unsure, excited and a little scared.

"Tell me how you know my name? Do you always go round town asking who people are, or, or, or are you psychic?" Alix could have kicked herself with the stupidity of the comment, but the man took no offence and removed his shades as he started to speak in his distinctive accent, crisp, to the point, but measured.

"Alix, sit down." He waited for a second, but she wasn't going to sit so he continued. "I ask one person. I don't ask the whole town."

"Hah! So you did ask."

He shrugged. "It is true. I am not psychic." He didn't smile. "Sit down, Alix."

It took a little time, but as he watched her she stopped jigging from one foot to the other like a lizard in the Sahara, she tensed her body from jittery confusion to controlled caution and she lowered herself down opposite him, making sure her eyes never left his.

"There you go. Now you are more relaxed."

"I wouldn't bet on it."

"But by definition you are more relaxed. Your body expends less energy when you are in a sitting position than when you are standing. So you see, you are more relaxed."

His words, his voice slithered over her and she felt her brain numb slightly.

"Are you a hypnotist?"

He shook his head.

"Do you teach meditation?"

He shook his head. His expression didn't alter.

"How did you know my name?"

"I ask. One person." He raised one finger to indicate.

"Who?"

"You do not need to know that. Why do you need to know that?"

She shrugged. "I don't, I guess." She paused for a minute, making her brain work by asking questions. He'd let something slip. Maybe. "Why?"

A hint of a smile played fleetingly over his lips.

"You interest me."

They had dinner at The Question Mark, a below the level of the road restaurant with views over the sea to the small island just off shore and the land further into the distance. He spoke in small sentences, neither revealing too much about himself nor appearing overly interested in her, and Alix went home that night feeling desperately deflated, knowing that although the evening had been nice it had been...well, nice.

He had given nothing, not even his name, nor what he did, what he was doing in Tolo, or in Greece for that matter for he wasn't a native. They, or rather she, had basically talked about her life and what she was planning for the next five years, give or take a detail or two.

As she drank with Mama Anna and hugged her warmly as she went to her bedroom Alix looked at the pale moon and suddenly felt that she would see him tomorrow. Somewhere without knowing, he would be there tomorrow. She curled herself under the single sheet, the fresh smell making her pull it tightly over her naked body. She closed her eyes and drifted off to sleep with an unfamiliar sensation coursing through her body as The Man haunted her dreams.

She didn't have to wait long. As she crossed the street to buy bread he was standing there, lazily slumped against the wall opposite, cigarette hanging loosely from his mouth, bottle of water hanging loosely from his fingers, his eyes hidden behind his shades. His crisp white shirt and his faded black shorts only made his dark tan darker. Alix felt her heart skip slightly as she caught sight of him, but put it down to her nightmares and the fact he appeared to be waiting for her. She hoped.

He uncreased himself from the wall as she approached, taking a step towards her, sliding his glasses half way down his romanly straight nose.

He nodded. She said hello.

"You want breakfast?"

"Sure. Where?"

He jerked his head back up the road.

"At the corner. Ten minutes."

"Okay."

As she said this he turned away and turned the corner, disappearing instantly as was his party piece.

Alix felt a little breathless, but content that his promise of the previous evening that he would answer some of her questions might come true a little sooner than she'd expected.

The bar was deserted, but for Alix and the Man and the bar owner sipping his orange juice, as he seemed to do every morning over gentle contemplation of the early morning traffic as it buzzed by.

Alix opted for coffee and an OJ while the Man tucked into what resembled a full English breakfast; sausages, bacon, eggs, beans, mushrooms and bread all fighting for space and cholesterol rights on the undersized plate. The litre of juice was soon emptied and refilled as neither spoke until all his eating had ended.

Alix tried not to look disgusted, but the man saw her face as he pushed his plate away and settled back into his chair.

He smiled.

"I don't know why you look like that. Breakfast is most important meal of day."

"Important for what, your dwindling cholesterol levels?"

He gestured dismissively to the oil-pooled plate.

"I don't have that normally. Eggs and toast. Cereal sometime. I only need fuel like that a couple of times a year."

"Fuel for what? I don't see you working twenty hour days?"

"You don't look hard enough."

Alix blushed and sought solace in her coffee, drinking quietly while she tried to think of a witty come back which by the time she thought of one she wouldn't be able to say cause it wouldn't be relevent, but she thought anyway, trying not to look at the Man as he looked at her.

"You'll answer some questions?"
"Maybe."
"You don't give much do you?"
"No."
"Touche."
He waved the minutiae away.

Alix wondered whether to dive right in or take it step by step. Her cautious side wanted the latter, while her heart was hammering her into submission for the former.

"Do you have a name?"
"Yes."
"Do I have to drag everything out of you?"
"Probably."
"What is your name?" She asked as if she was speaking to an idiot.
"Why do you get to ask me things and I don't get the same?"
"Cause I talk like a normal person."
"You say I'm not normal?"
"Do you think you're normal?"

He was into his answer when he stopped and actually sat back to consider what he was saying.

"Maybe not." He offered in a cloud of cigarette smoke. "Maybe I am not. Do you want to be associated with a guy who is not normal?"

Obviously not, screamed her conscience.

"Why not? Anyway, what's normal?"
"Well, not me apparently?"

Alix was on the point of following the bait, but knew she was getting nowhere fast.

"Do you have....What is your name?"

He leaned forward and pushed his head through the curtain of smoke that had remained in the remarkably still early morning air.

"Salvador."

"As in Dali?"

"As in El."

"You're from El?"

"Better the devil you know, eh?"

Alix couldn't keep the smirk off her face. He had obviously been through this spiel many times and one more wasn't going to make a difference.

"But I don't know you?"

"You ask many useless questions. You have ten left."

"That's not fair!"

"So?"

"Why only ten?"

"Cause I said so. Nine."

Alix shut up and ordered another coffee. The barman, amused by the lovers, as they were or soon would be he thought to himself, took his time at the bar, wanting to hear some more, but they didn't speak until he'd brought the coffee and left the room.

"Why are you in Greece?"

"I was working."

"Who for?"

"Me."

"Where are you from?"

"El Salvador."

"Oh." Alix blushed again, embarrassed that she'd missed the obvious give away minutes before. She dipped her head and frantically thought of some more questions, sifting the ones she wanted from those she wanted less, discarding and adding as she went.

"How do you know Tolo?"

"I didn't. A friend recommend it to me for peace and quiet."

Alix considered him for a minute before she asked her most wanted.

"Where are the scars from?"

He pointed at them as he went down his body.

"Bullet, knife, surgery, fire, surgery, bullet, alligator."

Alix's hand wanted to cover her mouth, but she clung to her leg beneath the table. She didn't want to appear either impressed or distressed.

"Wow. You really get shot a lot. What do you do, streetfight?"

"Was that a question?"

"No, no, it wasn't."

"You have four left."

She peered at the marks he had pointed at.

"You surgeon could have used smaller stitches, don't you think?"

"Maybe. Probably. Three."

"That wasn't one!"

"I think it was."

"God, you're awkward."

"I know, but being God and the devil at the same time puts a little pressure on."

"At least I know you have a sense of humour. Why are you so secretive?"

"Because I have to be."

"Why?"

"Because it's my job. If I'm not then people will know too much and one of these..." he pointed at the scars "...might just be the last one I get."

"And what is your job?"

"That is your last question, you know? Are you sure you want to ask that? Is there nothing else that you think of?"

Alix thought, but eventually shook her head.

"No. Come to think of it you're really evasive on this one, so I want to know. What are you in Greece for, what is your job, what is it that you do?"

The Man stood, dropped a handful of drachma on the table, picked up his bag, stubbed out his cigarette and looked Alix squarely in the eye.

"I'm an assassin."

He was almost a hundred yards away by the time Alix had stopped laughing and she had to run to catch him as he stalked towards the marina.

"You're not serious? People like you don't exist, only in movies. You can't just go round killing people, you don't just go round killing people do you? I mean you are joking right, you have got a sense of humour, we established that, so this is a joke, you made a joke, I laughed. I'm still laughing. I can't believe this." Alix stopped talking as she stopped walking, allowing him to pull ahead once again. She looked at but didn't see his long stride as it took him away. "Oh my God. Oh my God he's serious."

She ran her hands through her hair, looking round to make sure she was still in the real world. The town was still there, reflecting the sharp sunlight off its white walls, its trees bustling around in the wind that was beginning to pick up, cars and scooters zipped by, pedestrians shrugged past, not knowing what Alix had just found out and not knowing the man walking away from her could stop their heartbeat in an instant.

"Salvador? Salvador, wait up!" Alix pounded after him, catching his sleeve just he turned into the marina. She pulled him to a standstill.

"You ask questions I answer. Why you not believe this one? Cause you don't like the outcome? You don't like what I do? Believe me, I don't either, but I good. I very good. I retire tomorrow with money I have made, but there's always one more, one more who you think is perhaps worth it..."

"Worth it?! You kill people. Is that worth something? Does their life mean so little to you?!"

He shrugged.

"Sure, why not?" He watched the suspension of belief cross her face, the incredulity at what she was hearing.

"You don't value human life at all?"

"I get paid extremely well not to value human life. If there is a value on it, then I don't get paid nearly enough. To me and my life it is priceless, my survival instinct tell me so, but if others are not to live, then who am I? Fate is what it is, that is all. If they not meant to die, then wind change, I tread on branch, they wake up. If not then its their time to go, whether I get money for helping or not. And if its not me, then some other fucker do it. So, yes, I get paid to believe in what I do. It does not mean I don't value life. It is a job."

"But your job always ends with people getting killed."

"You make your point, Alix. It gets tiresome."

Alix drew her arm back in a flash to punch him, but her hand never made it more than halfway to his face. It was intercepted and pinned against the wall behind her before she knew what was happening. She looked from her hand to his face, his eyes bore into her as all her features showed panic. For the first time she had got beneath his icy exterior, what she had been trying to do for days, and she concluded she didn't like what she saw.

"Let go."

Her voice was shaky. He didn't release his grip.

"You wanted to know. You don't like it, you can leave me alone."

He held her arm pinioned behind her for a few seconds as he searched her face, but despite quivering like a jelly she remained impassive, her eyes darting all over, trying to escape from the tractor-beam stare she was locked in, but other than that she gave nothing away, no hint of whether she would see him again or not.

Finally he pulled her arm down, still in his huge hand. As Alix felt his grip weaken she jerked her hand away as she stepped back.

Salvador stared until he could do so no longer, then turned and Alix watched him disappear onto the richest looking boat that was moored in the harbour.

She rubbed her wrist, sensing rather than seeing his finger marks. For minutes she couldn't move, then finally some strength returned and she walked away.

Salvador watched her leave. He wanted her, but he knew it was in a different way than she wanted him.

Alix sat down as Anna poured glass after glass. They drank in silence until one of them had to speak.

"Alice, my baby, what is it? I know there is something. Is it about that man? The one you said about. It is always a man. Does this mean you are over your Tom?"

"No," slammed Alix emphatically gesturing for Anna to do the refills.

Anna obliged, watching the clear liquid as it teetered on the edge before pulling the bottle away just in time.

Anna joined her in the drink, but sipped as Alix bolted hers down in one burning mouthful.

"You can talk to me, you know, whatever it is, you are able to tell me."

Alix looked sadly at the older woman.

"I know, Mama Anna, I know." She burst into fitful sobs. "And you don't know how much that means."

Anna drew her friend close and comforted her, patting her head, stroking her hair, murmuring for the sake of it rather than anything coherent. Her sharp eyes warned away people who threatened to walk over and sit close by, her authoritarian air guarding and protecting the fragility of the sobbing Alix in her arms.

"It's....it's just....what...he...does."

Anna's eyes glinted, unafraid.

"What is that?"

"What...he...does... He...kills people." Her words were lost as she collapsed into more heaving sobs in Anna's lap, but Anna was close enough to make them out and she gave a hint of a smile to herself.

"Of course he does my dear, of course he does."

As Anna stroked and held her Alix drifted to sleep and didn't notice as Anna let go and watched as Manolis lifted her carefully up the stairs to bed, taking her shoes off and laying her down, closing the door quietly as he left her to her vodka induced dreams.

It was midnight by the time she felt well enough to venture out and she slipped quietly into a small seafood cafe where she ordered fried aubergine followed by swordfish and a bottle of water, despite Anna's suggestion that she should drink alcohol to nullify the pounding in her head.

Alix didn't hold with this theory and only really wanted food anyway, the water would probably chase what alcohol remained round her body making her feel ill again.

The aubergine was smooth and tasty and the swordfish succulent and stunningly grilled, its flavour making her tastebuds tingle with each bite.

She had a small bowl of ice cream which she had just begun when a dark shadow fell across her table.

"Hi."

Alix looked up and into the dark eyes of a killer.

She swallowed hard and took a sip of water as her fuzzy hungover mind creaked into action.

"May I sit?"

Alix wasn't sure whether she should agree or not, but Salvador had pulled up a chair before she could speak.

"I don't know..."

"I know, I know."

His voice was more mellow, perhaps more friendly and Alix felt herself soften in his presence, spooning ice-cream as he waited patiently for her to finish. She finally pushed the bowl away and picked up her glass as she sat back and regarded him with an inquisitive eye.

"I thought you said to leave you alone?"

"I did, but I can't."

"But you're a loner, you don't fall for people just like that."

"I know, but..."

"I'm different? I don't think so. You're too disciplined, too routine, too careful to let that happen."

"Maybe you don't know me as well as you think."

"Maybe not."

They sat in silence, neither looking at the other as both realised that there was an awkwardness between them now. Probably because Alix had found out something she didn't want and didn't expect, but also something deeper, more destructive.

In the end Salvador stood and left, leaving Alix alone with her Evian, staring at the bottom of her glass in time honoured contemplation.

"She doesn't want one."
"She does. Tomorrow. Here." Salvador took another half a million drachma and shot a look that was met with the most blank eyes he'd ever come across, apart from looking in a mirror.
"It better had be. Or I'm gone."
He turned and went.

"Alice, come and sit. Manny's got his special ouzo, here have one."
Alix took a glass and sipped the liquid, pulling a face as it kicked back after she swallowed.
"Nice," she choked, spluttering and coughing into her hand.
"I knew you'd like it." Anna patted her back, smiling broadly at Manolis, laughing as Alix raised her head, eyes streaming, face laughing at her own plight as Anna and Manny watched her recover opposite them.
"Is good, yes?"
Alix glared plastic daggers at Manny, her mouth twitching in appreciation.
"Yes, it's good. Very good," she added as the warmth hit her stomach, adding to the residue of earlier and making her head swim excitedly, even if the feeling in her throat was more bile than ouzo. The food had lined her stomach, and she hoped that would last until she managed to drag herself to bed.

Which was looking increasingly unlikely as Anna and Manny looked as if they'd been drinking all night and were ready to carry on for an hour or two yet. Alix glanced at her watch. One thirty a.m.

Anna and Manny talked around her for a while, casually filling her glass every so often, making sure she was included without being included as they spoke in Greek to each other, knowing Alix would only be able to catch the odd word.

Alix looked round the busy bar. Even now as the early hours broke their way into the morning there was not an empty seat to be found, groups stood by the bar chatting, gesturing, drinking, served competently, prettily by the local bar girls who knew Manolis, despite his drunken appearance and his head to head with Anna, was watching them like a hawk, making sure they smiled occasionally as they dipped in and out of the tills for change, handing over lagers and ouzo and retsina to the locals and the tourists without prejudice. If they had money and they weren't there to cause trouble, and you learned to spot the troublemakers soon enough, then the service was sharp, efficient and pleasently carried out.

The atmosphere in the bar was the same. Occasionally fights occured, but they were mainly between drunk locals and drunk tourists and swiftly dealt with by Manny and Anna who was so surprisingly strong allied with her visual ferocity that the brawlers found themselves on their backsides in the street before they had a chance to retaliate. Not that many of them would against a woman.

Manolis stood and quickly scouted the tables, picking up handfuls of glasses and depositing them on the bar with a wink to Peta and Helena who winked back, but swore under their breaths. He of the wandering hands would be obeyed so long as he stayed a distance away.

Anna watched her nephew as he toured the room, stopping and chatting as he removed glasses, making the customers evening go with that extra little swing. With the locals it was fine, a nudge, a nod, how's your day was sufficient. With the tourists it was the language, Manolis spoke five excluding Greek, and enquiries about their holiday, suggestions for what to drink, where to eat, where they were going after Tolo. Making them feel at home, make their holiday go smoothly.

Manny looked back at Anna and held his hand up. Anna smiled and raised her glass.

"Alice, are you okay? You are quiet."

Alix squirmed as she thought of whether to mention her evenings meeting.

"I'm fine."

"What are you thinking about?"

"Nothing. Really."

"Come on sweetie. Is it Tolo?"

"No, no, God no. I love this place."

"Really? I only like it sometimes. Tomorrow I take you to the house I'm having built. Then you fall for a place, no."

"You're building a house? Where?"

"Up the coast. You'll like it."

"You never told me. Anna, I can't believe you never told me."

"Alice, I didn't think you would be here long enough. But you are, so you can come see." Alix was utterly thrilled by the development, feeling Anna deserved something for herself rather than working all the time for no end. "Are you thinking of leaving?"

"I don't know Mama Anna. Maybe. Do you think I should?"

"You are welcome to stay here as long as you want, you know that. I would be delighted to have you, but sometimes I feel you have another life, your own life, that is your own and nothing to do with me. A life that you should return to before you get bored, get, what is it, solid?"

"Stale."

"Okay, stale. Wherever you go, back to Australia, wherever, maybe you should do it while you have the urge. Before we blunt you."

"Anna, you'd never blunt me." She looked at Anna, seeing a hint of sadness in the expression on her face. "See, you don't want me to go."

"I know."

"But maybe I should?"

"Maybe you should."

They sat holding hands, sipping ouzo, both knowing Alix would be leaving soon.

"Where would you go?"

"America," stated Alix firmly. There was an instant edge to her voice.

"Why there? It is a long way away from your home here and your home in Australia?"

"I know it is Anna, but there are things I want from my life and America is the place I have to go to get them." She caught the inquisitive look. "Things even you don't know about Anna. Mom's last coherent wish." There was now a steel to her blue eyes.

"Alice, what is it? You're scaring me a little. Your face has gone so hard."

"Just something. But I've had a thought which might be helpful."

"Oh."

"Oh Anna, it's okay, don't worry. I'll take care of myself. I always have, you know that."

"I do my angel, but I was there to pick up the pieces if anything went wrong. If you're in the middle of a country you don't know, then who's going to be there for you?"

"You'll always be there for me, I know that. Won't you?"

"Of course I will."

Their hands squeezed together. Alix felt suddenly sober at the thoughts that raced through her head. She shook slightly. Anna noticed the change, but said nothing. Alix was capable of making the right decision on her own.

She was up early and headed first for the marina, the large boat, the expensive boat she had seen him on. She called his name but he didn't reply. She knocked on the hull, first with her hand then with her shoe, but still no answer.

Alix walked back through the town disconsolately, looking into bars, hoping she would see him, knowing he had to be here somewhere if his boat was still here. For a fleeting second she wondered if it was actually his boat. If he could kill then stealing would be no problem. She pushed the thought to the back of her mind, praying that it wasn't true, although after his most telling revelation she felt she could put up with anything.

The street was bustling to life, but Salvador was nowhere. Alix passed Dionysos and Anna watched her from the shuttered window, hiding herself behind the wood and the netting. Anna nodded and sighed. Another day.

Alix trudged on, knowing the beach would be the last place she could look before going with Anna to the new house. If she was to leave in the next couple of days then she'd have to sort a few things out.

The beach was also just coming to life, but she saw a dark blue towel on a chair and an accompanying black bag. Her heart gave a little leap, but her mind was coldly in control this morning. All business.

She sat down and waited.

This time she saw him as he appeared from the sea, a giant form rising from the surf, his broad shoulders and athletic figure with its littering of linear trademarks appearing more imposing than ever as he approached her.

"Good morning."

"Hi."

"You are sitting on my seat."

"I know. I wanted to make sure you saw me."

"Okay?"

Alix waited until he'd towelled down and slipped a shirt on. He turned to walk along the beach. Alix hesitated.

"I have to get back to the marina. You come, we talk."

Sounds like perfect sex to me, considered Alix, but returned his request blankly and followed a pace behind.

"I'm leaving."

"Aaaahhh," grunted Salvador knowingly.

"I'm going to America."

He didn't reply.

"I want you to come with me."

This time he stopped.

"Why? You don't like me much, and if you don't have a job for me, then why need I come with you?"

"I do have a job for you."

"Ooohhh, you have a job for me now. The lady has a job for me. Am I to be your boyfriend or your bodyguard?"

"Neither." She made herself say although she wanted both. "I may need help."

"You may need help? May?"

"I don't know how things'll pan out, but I need someone to be there to bat for me. To shoot for me."

"To shoot at you?"

"No, no, to shoot for me, on my behalf. I hire you to shoot for me."

Salvador face broke into a smile, but Alix didn't see the funny side.

"Okay. I got to go over there anyway, so you in luck. I'll come with you."

"Good." Alix stayed calm although she wanted to leap up and down and wave her arms about.

She gave him a time to meet her at the airport and shook his hand formally as she left.

A business deal was a business deal.

As the road curved among the vines and the olive groves the lush greenery, the parched earth and the bluest Ionion sea made a perfect Mediterranean tableau for the brilliant white half-house which rose up from the small fruit trees that surrounded it. From above it, from the road, it looked almost square, the two completed levels sitting widely and emptily in the middle of the green groves with the blue beyond.

"Oh Anna, it's stunning. What a view!"

"Wait till you see it finished my dear. You'll come back won't you?"

"Try and stop me." She looked at the vines and then back at Anna. "Are all these yours?"

"No, no. I paid a great deal of money for the strip down to the sea. Greeks are very protective of their property, taking their time to complete it, one level at a time, only when they can afford it do they move on. These vines, this land belongs to Fannasis Pirodou, and now because I persuade him to accept my overly generous offer, he can tend the vines when he likes, build his house when he likes, retire when he likes. He has worked hard, and now he has some comfort and I have a big house with a path to the sea." Anna smiled a conspirational, winning smile which Alix joined. "It will be spectacular when it is finished. Then you must come."

"I will, I promise."

They took one final look at the house then got back in the car and headed for Athens.

Athens International was small and stuffy. Sweat poured from officials and frequent flyers alike. Alix sat on her upturned bag and fanned herself with a magazine, checking her watch against the clock on the wall behind check-in.

He was late. Very late.

She walked to the desk and planted her passport and ticket in front of the dark skinned boy with slicked back black hair. He greeted her, asked her all the usual questions and wished her a pleasent flight. As she turned to go he beckoned her back.

"Miss Mercer?"

"Yes." She said wearily, wondering what he could have missed.

"There is a message for you, from a..." He checked the name on the front of the telegram style note. "...Mr Dali." He handed the note out to her.

Alix gritted her teeth and snatched the piece of paper.

"Thankyou," she spat out at the unfortunate boy who shrivelled behind the desk and concentrated earnestly on the next in line.

Alix walked away before tearing at the paper and scanning the words.

'Alix - sorry but left earlier - find you at Dulles.'

She read it twice feeling startlingly out of control again.

"Bastard," she muttered to herself as she waited in the cramped departure area, causing the bad case of body odour on her right to get up and move to another seat with his small child in tow, muttering to himself about the language of young women these days.

Alix wanted to make a comment on the personal hygeine of some men, but stopped herself and tapped her feet impatiently.

In America she'd be in control. She'd have to be in control.

Time Spent.

"What size is that?" screamed Rosie in delight as I staggered back under the weight of two large colas and a kilo of popcorn.

"Almost your size," I laughed back, amazed and relieved to see her smiling and enjoying herself. Maybe it was just Florida, being away from the city, being bathed in sunshine, meeting Mickey and Goofy, being swung upside down at high speeds, being assailed by pre-pubescent voices declaiming the below average girth of the globe, or eating and drinking like she, or I, had ever done before. Ever. But whatever it was it had put a smile on her face and allowed the pursuit of information to take a back seat for a day or two.

Sara it seemed, and I was loathed to admit it, but Rosie knew it too, had been right. Cale had had meeting after meeting, an audition here and there, and we had trailed her up and down all day for the last three days. Apart from today, our visit to the Magic Kingdom, when I had trusted to luck that she wasn't going anywhere after seeing John arrive at dawn and hearing them discuss their carnal plans for the day. The wonders of tiny little bugs. With John saying he was jetting out late in the evening, Rosie and I had plenty of time to amuse ourselves.

And we did, riding the rides, seeing the sights, meeting the people, well characters, and eating extensively, dropping trash and timing the men-with-claws to see how long it took them to locate and destroy. Not long. We had a ten dollar tip to the quickest of the day. If we could find him of course.

Coming to America.

For the second time in what seemed like a very short space of time, although the flight from Athens to America had taken ten hours, Alix sat slumped on her bags waiting for Salvador who was, yet again, late.

She scanned the faces as they crowded past her. He wasn't among this latest group. She sighed and sat back, leaning against the wall, resting her head back and for a second letting her eyelids drop closed. Alix casually wrestled with her bag and dug out a melted Snickers, peeling the wrapper and licking the chocolate that was stuck to it. It always made her feel sick, melted chocolate, but she couldn't resist the taste and the stickiness that went with it, especially Snickers. She finished the bar and screwed the paper, turning and flicking her wrist so it flew into the trashcan five feet away. She smiled to herself.

"Good shot."

Alix jumped to her feet and met the steely, yet strangely friendly gaze of her hitman.

"How long have you been there?"

"Oh, only a couple of minutes. You enjoyed the chocolate?"

Alix gave what she hoped was a sarcastic smile as she frantically banished the image of her getting delicious pleasure from running her tongue over the sticky paper.

"Can we go? It'll be a nightmare getting a cab."

"No problem. I have a car."

"Of course you do. Of course you have a car. Why wouldn't you, I mean you leave Greece early so you can make me look stupid by getting a car, a job, a fancy apartment on Fifth Avenue." Alix mumbled to herself as she swung her bag onto her shoulder and followed Salvador outside.

"What are you saying?"

"Nothing. Really nothing."

He threw her bags in the trunk and opened the door for her. Alix slid inside the low slung silver sportscar and wanted one immediately.

"Great car."

"Isn't it? I had to get something cool if I'm going to be cool, you think?"

"For once I agree with you."

They both slipped on shades as Salvador revved the engine and screeched the car out of the airport and into the traffic on the freeway.

"I'd like to go...."

"I take you to our place."

"Our place? What do you mean our place?"

"I figured you'd need a place to stay, so I rented an apartment. It's big. You'll love it." He smiled a beaming smile as Alix sulked.

"I might not be there a great deal as I'm going to have to be moving between here and LA if I'm going to break Hollywood quickly."

"Sure. Whatever. But you'll still need a base here. And I'll be staying here, so I need a place. Makes sense?"

Alix shrugged, still sulking.

"S'pose."

"Good. You will like it."

"Anyway, what do you mean you're staying here? I hired you and if I need you then you'll have to come with me."

"Maybe. I am not so far. By plane."

"Sal, I have hired you for a job..."

"But I haven't seen any money yet, and until I do then I am free agent, no?"

Alix's mouth dropped open and she was left speechless. After asking him to come to America he then takes over and gets a car, a wonderful apartment she thought later as she followed him inside, and a life away from the job she had potentially got him over the Pond to do.

"I have to take care of myself. You understand?"

"Sure I understand, but I had given you a job, so what are you planning to do when I'm not around?"

"You are not the only one who needs my help."

Alix fell silent, thoughts racing through her mind, not stopping to be analysed, just flying into the vortex of her cortex.

"You're more talkative in America?"

"The land of the free speech."

Feeling she was getting nowhere, feeling like she wasn't yet in control, Alix looked at the buildings as they drove through the city.

Finally she was here, where she wanted to be. Where she had to be.

Man in a Wheelchair.

It was dark by the time we left the characters to their beds and headed for our own, although Rosie wanted to stop in every bar on the way back to the motel. We didn't, but we sat in the motel room and drank some cheap beer I'd picked up from a liquor store, getting steadily drunk until we passed out, through sleep or alcohol or maybe a mixture.

I woke and found Rosie gone. I couldn't hear the shower running and for a dark moment I panicked. My sense told me she couldn't, wouldn't, shouldn't have gone far, but then I thought of Luca and what they were capable of, and I'm sure they were in Florida, just as I was, following Cale.

Which is where I should have been right now.

I stuck my head out of the door and looked, but didn't see her or hear her. I went back in, splashed some water on my face and threw on yesterday's clothes, before dashing outside and leaning on the trunk of the car and waiting.

I knew it was dangerous bringing her with me, especially as I knew that her ex employers were becoming more and more involved, but I couldn't resist, and the previous day had only highlighted that as she had laughed and smiled like a regular kid, instead of the nervy, semi-adult, semi-streetwise, doped up punching bag I'd met weeks before.

I was sure that while I had done some good, it was of her own making that she was now more hooked on McDonalds than cocaine, and although some days I caught the haunted wanting look of her past as we drove by dealers and pimps, she knew and I knew that she was better off without them. But the cravings of an addict were hard to eliminate altogether.

But where was she. The lady in reception hadn't seen her, nor anyone else that morning. I looked at my beat up watch that slipped round my wrist. God, it was early.

A cup of coffee was a good wake up call as I returned to the room and sat on the unmade bed, savouring the taste and smell as I could do little else. Eventually I scribbled a note and left it on the bed, grabbed my jacket and headed out. I had to do something and trust she was okay. If she wasn't, and I shivered as I thought it, then I'd find out soon enough.

Traffic was still light in the early part of the rush hour and the hire car mingled easily with the rest on the freeway. I mentally checked the electronics in the trunk, making sure I had what I probably wouldn't need.

I switched the sound on and heard the early morning nothingness I partially expected but hadn't really wanted. If I could hear Cale then I'd know I wasn't late. But I couldn't. There was no snoring, not that I thought she did of course, and no clinks of cutlery on china, or cups on tables, so she wasn't breakfasting. I didn't know whether I would be able to hear the shower, but I couldn't right now anyway, so that rather defeated that theory. I left it on out of boredom, hoping some little sound might give me a clue.

"Midnight?"

Several horns blared warnings as I slithered the car across all three lines as I reacted, badly, to the voice.

"Yes?"

Why was I talking? It was a one way system.

"Midnight, if you can hear me, then it's me, Rosie. Cale's in the shower. Don't worry, she hasn't been anywhere yet, but I think she might be heading out quite early, so if you are listening in then put the pedal to the metal man. Catch you later."

Then it all went quiet again. I turned up the volume, but just got louder fuzz.

How? And how?

There was coming along for the ride and then there was driving the damn thing yourself. We would have words.

But mainly good ones.

As I arrived Rosie dived into the car and told me to head round to the back of the smart hotel.

I didn't ask. I guessed it was probably Cale, and after Rosie had been busy already she undoubtedly knew more about what was going on than I did.

Sure enough the fair haired woman was noticeable as she pulled out of the lot in her rented car. I didn't think she noticed me and we stayed a ways back as we trailed her through the Sunshine State, Rosie grinning broadly in self congratulation.

"How?"

"I have my ways."

She might tell me when she thought it best, but I wasn't going to hold my breath. She clearly enjoyed this little secret.

I concentrated hard on Cale as she shot down sidestreets in the blink of an eye. Maybe she had spotted us and was trying to shake us off, but my driving wasn't that bad, and Rosie kept a close eye on the car in front, despite it being more obvious as the roads narrowed that we were the only car going in the same direction.

Finally she pulled up to a gate, spoke into the intercom and slid the car through the space as the gates opened desperately slowly. There would have been enough time for me to follow, but that would have been asking for trouble and besides there were other ways of getting in.

"So Mister Drela, how can I help you?"

I resisted the temptation to shuffle my feet, but only just. Lying and using false names wasn't my usual plan of action, but spurred on by Rosie I was trying something a bit different.

"I'm looking for a place for my mom. She's eighty, just turned and really she's not capable of looking after herself. I mean she's mobile an' all, but it's the little things and she's not getting any better."

"Oh, that's a shame. I'm sorry to hear that. Of course, we don't generally provide one to one care so if she needs that then I..."

"Oh no, she's nowhere near that stage, and I hope she never will be, but somewhere more comfortable, like this...," I gestured expansively, making the right impression, "...would suit her down to her aching feet."

My eyes followed the slender figure that swayed past me.

"Okay Mister Drela, if I could take some details...."

"Damn, sorry I left them in the car. I'll be back in a little while."

"But..."

"Right back."

Cale had reached her car by the time I reached her.

"Miss Kline?"

She looked up, her face tensed and her hand tugged at the door.

I placed my leg against it, preventing her from opening it. If I'd turned round I would have seen Rosie jigging up and down excitedly at my belated bravery.

"Mister Seyle..."

"Miss Kline."

We held each others gaze for the briefest of milliseconds, before I couldn't hold it any longer.

"Miss Kline, how is Mister Marello?"

"Who? I don't know who you're talking about?"

"The gentleman you just this second visited. Mister Marello? I didn't realise your memory was so bad. How can you be an actress if you can't remember just two minutes ago. It must take a helluva lot of takes."

She dropped her head, slid her shades off her nose and then fixed me with a steely glare, her eyes, emerald green in the light, searing into me. I felt like I should melt, but I obviously didn't.

"Mister Seyle, I don't know how you found me here and I don't particularly care because you just return to wherever it is you happen to have come from and leave me alone. I know you're meant to be working for my husband, but you're not working for me, as my bodyguard, as my personal assistant, as my protector in chief or even as my hired help. So the less I see of you, the better."

"Does John know Mike is alive?"

"What do you think?"

"So he is alive?"

Her eyes flashed for an instant, then she shook her head, a look of disgust crossing her beautiful features as she replaced her shades and jerked the door open, carefully curling her shapely legs into the leather interior.

I closed the door after her. She scowled.

"Drive carefully."

I stood and watched as she left, wondering if she knew what I was going to do next. I waved towards Rosie. She gave me a thumbs up then buried her head back in her book.

"Mister Drela?"

"Hi. I'm real sorry, I thought I'd put them in, but I can't find them, so I'll have to head off and come back later."

It worked as a moment of panic crossed the girls face as she thought she might lose a sale.

"Well, seeing as you're here can I give you the tour? Save you coming back later?"

I hesitated, trying to look as though I was wavering.

I shrugged, looked at my watch just for effect and agreed.

Angelica showed me everything from treatment rooms to bedrooms, from the kitchens to the washrooms and eventually we drifted outside. It was warm, but not the stifling heat of midday as the sun had yet to hit that mark. There were a few elderly bodies dotted around amongst the greenery of the landscaped acres, some talking, two blokes playing checkers, a man and woman talking about the fearful crimewave in sleepy Indiana that was front page news, a gaggle of women chewing over the Hollywood news laughing and giggling and pointing at a broad shouldered man resting by the perimeter of lawn.

I paused and switched Angelicas voice off inside my head, instead tuning in to the women a few feet away.

"Mikeys fancy woman....." "...with Tom Cruise..." "...never hear the end of it..."

"Mister Drela?"

"Absolutely."

"Angel? Angel? Can I borrow you? Mary again."

Angelica touched my arm lightly.

"I'm sorry. I'll be right back."

She bounced lightly over the lawn with the step of a fitness addict.

I smiled at the women and headed over to see Mikey.

He dropped to the seat as I approached, shaking his head sadly, resting his hands on the stick that was planted firmly into the earth between his feet.

When I was within a couple of meters he lifted his head and regarded me with a stern intensity.

"Hi."

"What can I do for you?"

I sat down, making him turn and regard me with something approaching suspicion.

"I'm..."

"You're not from round here are you? I don't recognise you. Are you a relative?"

"No, no. I hope to bring my mom here soon."

He nodded as if that were a believable scenario.

"Sure. Why not? It's a good place."

"Yeh. You been here a while?"

"A few years."

"You like it?"

"You don't like places like these, but I guess it's tolerable." He looked past me. "Of course it's not so bad for me. I got a friend who stops by every so often. For others....If they got no-one...."

He left the image hanging in the space between us.

"Sure. Sure."

"You'd visit, right?"

"What?"

"Your Mom?"

"Right. Sure."

"You don't sound sure?"

"No I am. It's just you never imagine getting to a moment like this. It's begining to kick in."

We sat in silence for a while, both thinking of other things. I would never be in the position that I was playing now, but neither could I imagine sitting where Mike was and saying the same words.

"So how did you end up here?"

"Illness. Cancer. I was old and didn't want to fight it anymore. Officially I'm in remission, but the chemo knocked the life out of me. I'm here cause I want to be. Plus it's safer than me trying to live out there." He shrugged his head to the fences that surrounded the gardens. "I get food, warmth, some company, pretty girls walking round. At my time of life there are precious few things that keep a man wanting to wake up." He looked sad, then looked up at me and smiled before I realised he was looking at something else.

"Hey Mikey, you okay? Mister Drela, your god-daughter wants to know if she should wait..."

"Bring her in, bring her in." Mike waved his arm and Angelica looked at me for confirmation.

"If that's okay with you?"

"Sure it is. Angel's a softy really. Besides it does us good to have some youth round here. How old is she?"

"Sixteen."

"My daughter's twenty something, I forget, but it does me the world of good when she stops by. She's the friend I mentioned." He huddled in conspirationally. "She's an actress. Just got a part opposite that Tom Cruiser fella. She's gonna be a star, I'll tell ya."

I smiled along with him as Rosie bounded up and perched herself inbetween us.

"So this is...?"

"Rosie. Hi."

She held her hand out and he took it, shaking it softly.

"Pretty, pretty." He muttered almost to himself.

"So what's your daughter like?" I asked, embarrassed that I probably knew already.

"She's wonderful." He began absentmindedly, staring at Rosie as he spoke. "She's tall, wonderful girl, talented, friendly, and wonderful."

"What's her name?"

He considered this for a minute. A minute longer than necessary.

"Kate."

A Team.

Salvador was laughing! And not just a polite I'm sorry, but I'm going to have to kill you now laugh, but a laugh at the end of a really good joke. Alix waited for the door to open, imagining who he was with hoping it wasn't, no was, a woman.

It wasn't.

With him, arms around shoulders, broad grins lining their faces, was a man of similar stature, the same seemingly trademark shades and the same lean slender body hidden beneath jeans and plain, simple t-shirt. A scar cut through his right eyebrow and his head had the merest covering of stubbly hair on top, but a dark goatee - moustache combination made him look sinister and sexy. The newcomer removed his shades and Alix noticed his soft gray eyes as they slid up and down her body.

"Alix, this is Francis Zitelli. Francis, Alix Mercer."
"Hi."
"Hi, pleased to meet you."
"You two know each other?"
"From way back. We each took a shot at a VIP. Apparently they found the bullets so close together that they could have been siamese."

"Out of such things...."

"What?"

"Oh nothing."

"Anyway, this is your number two guy. He's good. Not as good as me, but he's good."

Much good natured backslapping ensued which Alix felt she could quite happily live without, but she wasn't going to rock the recent accord that she had found with Salvador so she stayed silent until the boys had stopped being boys.

"So we leave for LA tomorrow morning?"

"Excellent. What time?"

"Nine."

"Okay. In which case, my friend, we have time to hit the town." More backslapping followed by the retreat of the the two men towards the door.

"Hey, where you going?"

"To get drunk."

"But..."

"You wanna come?"

Alix fought for a minute with her conscience. Of course she did, but not out of a pity ask. She squirmed a little.

"No."

Salvador and Francis looked at each other and shrugged before laughing their way out of the door.

Alix watched the door as it swung shut. She stamped her foot.

"Shit."

Tales to Tell.

I had left, reluctantly, and with promises of returning tomorrow to pick up where we'd left off. He'd seemed pleased and said he was looking forward to it. I hoped he was, cause then he might be more forthcoming.

The day was too hot and Rosie and I found Mike in his room. He had the TV on and was watching baseball with an almost reverential look on his tanned, lined face. We stood for a few seconds and watched him. He didn't look across at us, but kept his eyes firmly on the screen, his muscles twitching as he hit each hit, ran the bases, threw batters out and cheered with the crowd. Occasionally he made to raise his arms, but they got to shoulder height and then he stopped, dropping them slowly back to his lap.

I knocked.

He glanced over and beckoned us in.

"Bottom of the ninth, sit down."

We sat and watched the final plays of the game which gave the Marlins a 3-1 victory.

"Alright, way to go Brewster, alright." He clapped his hands together and watched as the coverage flipped to commercials, then reached for the remote and flicked it off so the picture flared and disappeared to black.

"Not a Yankee then?"

"Not any more. Support your home side and this is my home." He took a sip of water and struggled to the window, parting the curtain and looking down at the view below, whatever it was. "Too hot right now."

"Sure is, a real hot one."

He turned back to us just as Rosie picked up a photo of Mike with Cale. Mike struggled back to the chair, reaching forward and sinking into it.

"What's she like?" I turned and shot Rosie a look for asking the first, impertinent question.

"She's wonderful. I don't know how she's mine. She's too good, a heart of gold. I don't know what I'd do without her."

I took a deep breath. If I was going to get anywhere, then today I didn't have time for subtlety.

"She might be in trouble?"

Mike turned, shock covering his face, swiftly followed by confusion as his eyes flicked from me to Rosie, who just nodded as we'd agreed.

"What? What do you mean? In trouble with who? What sort of trouble? How do you know?"

"It's okay Mike, really. I'm working for her husband, John Barclay, and he's had some threats made against him. So far they've just been about him, but I think it might escalate."

"Who is it?"

"Gini Firetti."

His face never flickered, but slowly took on a resigned look.

"Do you have a copy of it?"

I dug in my pocket and pulled out a variety of pieces of paper, one of which I handed over. Mike took it and held it at arms length to read it. He finished and handed it back.

He stood, a little shakily and hobbled to the dresser, leaning heavily on his stick, reaching in and pulling out a box.

"Here, can you..."

Rosie jumped up and carried the box back to the bed, setting it down and going back to her seat.

Mike dropped off the lid and put his hand inside, pulling out papers and looking at them one by one, tears filling his eyes then dribbling steadily down his face. He wiped them away and after a few minutes of repeating the same procedure he seemed composed and flicked through a few more of the papers he held in his hand.

I watched and couldn't help but watch, it was compelling viewing. There was a change in his demeanor, his body had sagged and become more worn before my eyes, his eyes had lost what little spark there had been evident the day previously, and his hands shook as he passed whatever it was through them.

"Can...can you help her?" He didn't look up. He just stared at what I think was a picture, a black and white photo of what looked like a man holding a little girl. I looked at Rosie. She was non-comittal and looked as upset as Mike.

"Yes." I spoke definitely, feeling more sure than I had any reason to.

For a while he remained unsure, staring at the picture, replaying the moments of the picture, maybe wanting to return to the picture, a bygone black and white age where he wasn't old, Cale, Kate was innocently growing up and there were problems that he was capable of fixing by himself instead of relying on a black man and his 'goddaughter'.

He reached over and handed me a scruffy piece of paper, torn and lined from years of being folded.

I took it and pulled it gently open. It didn't fight as new paper would have done, but unfurled it's tired corners and lay flat, the hinges of the folds as effective as the age of the paper.

A birth certificate. And a style I didn't recognise. I looked at the top of the page and saw a lion and a unicorn.

England. England? Why had he given me a birth certificate from England for a boy or girl....girl I didn't know. Katherine Clare Sutcliffe.

"I don't....?"

"Kate." Rosie's voice drifted weakly over me.

"Kate?"

All this time Mike had been watching me. Now he spoke.

"I've never been to England."

"Kate? She's not...." Suddenly a whole load of pennies dropped and I sat straight with the realisation. "Then who?"

No-one said anything and I wondered why. I looked back at the certificate and the other names that were there. Gordon and Mary Sutcliffe.

"Then how?"

Mike stood and went to the window once more. Rosie sniffed and wiped her sleeve across her face. I sat, shocked and waiting.

She didn't look like him, but I figured she'd taken after her mother, and they seemed close, must be close if she flew down to Florida to visit regularly. I felt like I was missing something, but I had no idea of what it was going to be.

"I was coming over from Italy. We stopped to pick up in England. There was me and a gang of others, Carlo, Guiseppe, Mila, a few more, I forget. We were coming to America. Coming to the greatest country on earth where Lady Liberty would welcome us in and feed us, get us jobs and make our lives better. Carlo had an uncle here or something, and I had my brother who had left two years before me. We were coming to make money and enjoy ourselves. We could stay with relatives and treat it as an extended vacation."

He continued to look outside, his voice more steady but heavy with unburdened knowledge.

"It was a large boat, you know, filled with people from all over, Italy, Spain, France, Americans, English, and generally people mixed with their own."

He stopped and came back to sit down, levering himself into the chair with great effort, sighing heavily as he settled.

"We, the Italian guys, had regular card games. I mean there wasn't a whole lot else to do so we bet and played cards. One night Carlo arrived, drunk, and with him was another guy..."

"Sutcliffe?"

"Right. They were drunk, smashed out of their faces, hardly stand up straight, but they want to play, so we let them play, thinking hey, easy money. But this other guy had a bag with him, open, and he carried it real careful and set it down real easy, even though he was drunk and had no idea of what else he was doing, he was taking real good care of this bag.

We thought nothing of it and carried on playing. We played and played that night taking this guy and Carlo for more and more money. I mean we played all night pretty much. Taking from Carlo was okay, cause he was one of us and you know, we weren't gonna let him down. But this other guy. We just took and took all night and he got more drunk until finally he had no money left."

Tears began appearing again and touching his cheeks as his memory played over.

"You okay?" I enquired, anxious for him to keep going, but not wanting to force him to.

He held up a hand, telling me to hang on, to wait for him to compose himself. He did.

"This guy jumped up and turned the table over. Money, cards, bottles, the lot, everything went over. He was real angry, mouthing off, swearing, shouting, 'where's my money, where's my money you bastards, you fucking bastards, where's my money'. I was the eldest, by about two weeks, but still the eldest, so I square up to him, hoping he might get scared, realise he was drunk and back off. But he didn't. He squared up to me, swung a punch which missed by a mile and almost sent him to the floor with the effort. Then he stood, and we did the walking round each other thing. I didn't want to hit him, cause, you know, he was out of it, I was taller and younger and it just wouldn't have been a fair fight. But he swung again and his fist flashed in front of my face. I just swung back on instinct. One to the stomach, upper to the jaw, and he fell backwards."

Marello broke down again, this time holding his head in his hands as his sobs made his body shake. Rosie went round and put her arm round his heaving shoulders, whispering something to him. It was still some time before he continued, before he could continue. Rosie sat with him as he carried on.

"His head...his head...smacked...smacked on the side of the table...broke his neck." He sobbed into the room. Then he seemed to calm down, taking deep breaths, as if having said it made it okay.

"We stood, stunned, felt for a pulse, and sat back, looking at him. I mean none of us had killed anyone before, we didn't know what to do. We just sat and looked for hours, what seemed like hours. Then I decided we had to get rid of him. It was still dark, no-one was gonna be round, so I picked him up, no-one else would till I bullied Carlo into it, and we carried him to the back and pitched him over. We sat and waited with him forever before we actually got the courage to do it, pretending he was asleep to the solitary person who was walking round the boat at like four in the morning. Just as we let go there was a shout from behind us and it was Guiseppe holding this guys bag, holding it at arms length, away from him like it was poison, or a bomb. 'Look, take a look' he shouted at us. We went over, we ran over and opened the bag. There was a baby and his room key. I had emptied his pockets and had his passport and shit like that, a bit of cash he had held onto. But now we had a baby."

"Cale, sorry Kate?"

Marello nodded. Rosie rolled her eyes to the skies as if to say 'who else could it have been?'.

"We argued. We argued like Italians have never argued about anything, about what to do with her. Everyone blamed me, 'cept Carlo, and said I should take it. I blamed myself too, but like hell was I gonna take a kid. In the end I went up to his cabin with the idea of leaving the baby there and hoping her crying alerted someone she was there. But I couldn't do it. I sat on the bed with her and you know she was so small, and she was so warm, and she smiled at me and she stopped crying when I picked her up. She was perfect. I couldn't do it. I slept there with her cradled up with me, and I woke up the next day and I cleaned out his clothes all his belongings, took 'em downstairs with me and took little Kate as well."

Love had replaced the tears in Marello and it was as jolting as the latter had been initially. There was genuine feeling for the tiny little girl he had orphaned then taken home.

"Of course, everyone now said I was mad for keeping her, but what was I gonna do? Anyway, I did and she grew up as mine. She is mine."

"And she doesn't know?"

He shook his head. "She doesn't know. Any of this." He gestured to the box he held in his lap, suggesting there was more in there, more revelations that no-one knew but him.

I wanted to know it all. It may not have had anything to do with John Barclay or indeed much to do with the present day Cale Kline, but there were things in there that were important enough for him to have kept them all these years.

"What else?"

"I think, Mister Drela, you need to ask why?"

Did I? I asked.

"Because if you are here, helping Kate, and you are helping John and he is being hunted by Firetti then Firetti will be here and I won't, if you get me."

"But..."

"No buts Mister Drela. I know why Firetti is after John, after all I did the deal, and Firetti will get his compensation, but he will kill me first. He's like that. I had to tell you so you could help Kate."

"I don't know if...."

"We will Mister Marello." Rosie - again.

"My lawyer has copies of some of these documents and my will."

"Graziani?"

"That schmuk!? You are joking. No, my lawyer down here, works for Hanson and Grettel, good guy. But you have it all. My entire history is in that box and I give it to you so you can protect Kate."

"I..."

"She mustn't know."

I looked at the wealth of papers in the box.

"What, all of it?"

"The important bits."

I digested that and hoped I'd know which were important. When the time came. Not that I thought it would as Cale and I weren't exactly on the friendliest of speaking terms.

"Sure. Important bits."

Rosie would know. Female intuition.

"Now I need my rest, for what little time I have left." He smiled warmly, not a the sad smile I half expected. "Take the box. And help Katy."

I picked up the box and nodded, giving an encouraging smile.

"Great to meet you, and thanks. I'll look after Cal... Kate."

We didn't say goodbye.

I was breathing heavily by the time we hit the ground floor, and all I could do was to look at Rosie, who looked back and offered nothing. Nothing.

I slipped on my shades as we stepped outside into the bright harshness of sunlit Florida. Rosie stayed a foot or so behind me. I cradled the box. The gate opened and we were relieved to make it back across the street to the car.

For a long time we sat and contemplated the box. We didn't even remove the lid, but just looked at it and wondered. Well, I wondered, I couldn't say what Rosie was thinking. She didn't say anything so I figured she was contemplating too.

"What do you think?"

She looked up at me and shrugged.

"Open it." I went to, but she clasped her hand over mine. "But not here."

I was about to pull away when a familiar car pulled up.

Plans.

"Guys, do whatever, I've gotta go." Alix crashed the door closed, raced down the stairs, drove the ten minutes to the studio and ran to the building she had been given for the audition.

Damian met her at the door.

"Alix, honey, you're cutting it fine." He glanced at his watch, a new Tag Heuer he had decided to afford. "You've got about five, okay. Now remember this is on the back of Making A Move so be sassy, you dig? Be you, babe. Be great." He dropped a kiss on her cheek.

"Sure Damo. You think I can do this?"

"I know you can do this. You know you can do this." He looked at his latest leading lady and saw a glimmer of uncertainty still hovering round the corners of her eyes. He rubbed his hand over her shoulder, up and down her upper arm, then caught her gaze again. "For Tom."

The uncertainty turned to outright terror as Alix walked with a confidence she didn't feel into the building, crossing her fingers and refusing to look back at Damian, who she knew would just be standing looking like a proud parent on graduation day.

She was ushered in and told to take a seat by a small bespectacled woman with a large cleavage. Alix sat and thought that the small woman could probably type 1000 words per minute and speak six languages. She suddenly felt inadequate.

The door opened and out walked a beautiful blonde with incredibly long legs. Alix shrank into the cavernous chair and felt more inadequate.

"Thanks Cale, great, we'll be in touch."

The door closed with murmuring voices behind it.

Cale smiled at the small genius.

"Thanks Betsy, say hi to Mo for me."

"Sure thing Cale honey. Take care y'hear."

Alix jumped to her feet and faced Betsy.

"That was Cale Kline?"

"Sure was darling, and if you want my opinion she's got the role."

But Alix was out of the door and watching Cale as she swished into Damian's arms, kissing the air by his cheeks, then swished on, curling her legs into a golf cart which zipped off in another direction down one of the many Famous Name Boulevards that made up the backlot.

"Miss Mercer? They'll see you now."

Alix turned and forgot Cale instantly, ignored the smug you're-wasting-your-time-dearie look that sat unpleasantly on Betsy's face, and marched into the room.

"Ah, Miss Mercer, great, this is Scott Neill, Elisha Johanssen and Owen Brock. You'll read with Owen. I'll give you a couple of minutes." He handed her a handful of paper with a brief backstory and lines of dialogue. Alix scanned it for a few minutes, then said she was ready.

"Okay, it's Owen first from page one....and go."

Owen walked across and took her hand in his, dropping his head to hers and pushing his lips against hers. His breath smelled of cigarettes. Alix pushed him away.

"What the hell you think you're doing?"

"Honey, I saw you watching me. Whatcha think I'm doing?"

"You think you can just walk over and lay one on me? Think again buster. Back off." She pushed him again and turned to go.

"Besides..." Came the deep, menacing voice from behind her. "...I think I got what you want."

"I very much doubt..." She stopped at the piece of paper he twirled in his fingers. She stepped gently back to him and made to take the paper. His hand jerked it away and he looked down his nose at her, sneering slightly and the desire on her face for the scrap in his hand.

"So what's on the paper that you want, and you don't want me, sugar. You gonna tell me, or do I have to beat it out of ya?" He grabbed her and hurled her to the floor, face down. He sat on her back, pinning her there. She wriggled round so she was on her back.

"Alright baby, I knew you wanted it." He looked down to unzip his trousers. Alix pushed him off and followed him as he stumbled backwards, finally collapsing on his butt. Alix was there in an instant and straddled him, leaning over him, her breasts swinging gently inside her shirt, enticingly over his mouth as she slammed his wrists against the floor, making him drop the paper.

"Oh I want it, I want it bad." She stood in a flash and brought her foot down into his groin, making him curl up in agony. She casually picked up the paper, slid it into her pocket. "But not right now. Thanks."

Thirty minutes and a couple more scenes later Alix left the room to the same words she'd heard earlier... "Thanks. We'll be in touch."

She didn't wait to hear any of the murmured words, but scooted out of the building with a hurried goodbye from Betsy lost on the breeze behind her.

Alix charged to her car, jumped in and headed out of the lot, only to be brought to a screeching halt as a man walked straight in front of her.

"Asshole," she screamed. The man removed his shades. It was Francis.

"I'm on a plane," Salvador shouted again.

"Where to?" Alix shouted back. For the third time Salvador replied he was going to Florida.

The connection cut and Alix was left holding a dead phone. "Shit." She turned to her accomplice who was leaning up against her car looking as though he hadn't a care in the world, pulling lightly on a cigarette, his eyes hidden behind dark shades. "Francis, what's he doing?"

"He's following your mark."

"I know that you jerk. Why's he doing it without me. He wasn't meant to go without me."

"I guess he didn't want to lose her. Relax already. We'll be right behind them, then you can be with them both."

"What's that supposed to mean?"

"Hey, nothing alright. I'm just saying. You wanna be there, you gonna be there, just a little after Sal, that's all. Don't get your panties in a pickle."

Alix shot him a look of loathing and hoped he'd get bugs in his dinner as she slammed into the car and roared away, leaving Francis in a rather larger cloud of smoke than provided by his Marlboro.

One Mess After Another.

"Shit."

"Who is it?"

I peered into the darkness. We had been waiting for a couple hours after the car arrived and now it was dark.

"I didn't think Firetti went anywhere?"

"He don't normally."

"Well he do now."

I watched the man walk through the gates, a right hand goon with him. Rosie rested her chin on my shoulder. I hoped she wasn't scared. I was.

If Firetti never went anywhere and he'd come here, then it must be important. Important enough for him to take a trip outside his heartland. They wanted something. And they wanted it bad enough to take a holiday.

John had heard nothing recently and I hoped that Firetti had switched his focus to Marello, who of course I didn't want to see lying on his back in a pool of blood, but let's face it, he wasn't the one paying me.

And as Marello had prophesised earlier if Firetti knew I was helping John then he knew I was here and so Marello wouldn't be, if I knew what he meant. I was beginning to understand.

I hadn't thought of bugging Marello's room. It would have been useful, up to a point, as I figured I knew what was going on in the building across the street.

"Hey Michaelangelo. I thought you were dead."

"Antognini. It's been a while. How are you?"

"Well, well. And you?"

"Not so good. They say I'm in remission, but hey..." He threw his arms in disgust. "You never get better."

Silence permeated the room for a minute. The goon stood beside the door, which was closed, his hands together in front of him, watching the two men in the centre of the room.

"So what is it that you want, Gini?"

"You mean you don't know? I come down here and you don't know? I'm shocked. Really." He paused as Marello managed a weak smile. "I want what's mine."

"Well, actually, at the time it wasn't..."

"I want what's mine. I want what you took from me. What you took from me."

"Gini, at the time..."

"At the time, at the time. Bullshit, Mikey, bullshit. This is now. I don't care about then. Sure we had problems, but I was still in line and you took over with no authority. So I want what's mine."

Marello sighed and stood, shuffling slowly to the desk and removing a small book.

"Gini, even if I had anything, and I don't right now, then why should I give it to you? I mean you're not exactly into good causes, now are you? I could leave it to cancer research, which would be far more personal to me, or AIDS research, or a hospital, even this place. I don't think you need money, and if you do then something has gone wrong in the business and you're not making it work. And what will your family say about that?" Marello flipped open the book and held it in his lap. "And besides, what do you want it in, land or money? Cause I have neither one nor the other for you today." The man now back in the chair looked up at the passively angry features on the face of the man who stood over him. "Why do you need it Gini? What are you doing with it?"

"Come on Marello, you know the score. This is how it's played. We collect on unpaid debts. None of this pussyfooting around, waiting for things to arrive, we go and get what's owed to us. And this is owed to us. So either you pay us or we put a bullet in your brain."

Marello just smiled as he wrote on a piece of paper in the book.

"Oh I think we both know you're gonna do that anyways, whether or not I give you anything you want. So if you shoot me, sorry, when you shoot me, then you can ransack my room and find...." He gestured round the sparsely decorated room. "....nothing. Either way you lose. I'm gone, but so is the money, your money."

Gini pulled his piece out from under his jacket and held it firmly against the temple of Mike Marello.

"So be it Mikey. You wanna play it this way, I can play it this way. Ricardo here is very adept at breaking bones with the minimum of fuss, so if you want to go to the next world piece by fucking insolent piece, then fine. I have no compunction against doing that."

"Gini, Gini, look at me, I'm dying here. I'm actually dying here and you're threatening me with broken bones? What is the matter with you? I'm an ill man. A getting old, ill man. I'm not scared of you, and the reason you're here already tells you that anyway. When I die you'll see the truth and get what's owed to you."

The click of the hammer was barely a noise and the exhalating pop from the silencer similarly faint. Only the streaks of red that ran onto the white sheets, that dripped onto the floor and that splatter-patterned the wall behind him told the story.

Firetti reached over and plucked the book from his dead hand, reading the note, the place to go, the man to see, what would be waiting in box number 213.

"Shit."

"What is it?"

A momentary sense of deja vu.

"Firetti. In a hurry."

I waited for a few minutes until their car disppeared from view, then waited a few minutes more to make sure they weren't trawling the streets, then I got out.

"Come on."

"Sure?"

"Yeh sure. But there might be blood."

Rosie hesitated but still clambered out and followed me over the road. We climbed the gates and went inside. With the night staff on the place was quieter, less busy, and we slipped upstairs easily and found what I had been dreading.

The door was unlocked.

Blood covered everything, or so it seemed. There was white and red contrasting all over the room. Splattered on the walls, in rivers to the floor, in pools on it. It was strangely poetic and coupled with the peaceful look on Marello's face, even more so. He had a violent death, but he had been at peace with something; himself, Firetti, the world in general.

Footsteps.

Rosie and I looked at each other as they approached, then round the room. Shit.

The door opened, the nurse screamed and Cale ran to the cold, lifeless, bloodless body that sat rigid in the chair.

"Oh my God, oh my God, shit, shit."

"Cale it's..."

She spun round, her eyes blazing that someone else was here.

"What the hell do you think you're doing here? Get out, get out," she yelled and brought the nurse running back with reinforcments.

"Cale it was..."

"I don't care. In fact I do care, and I hope it was you. You, you, miserable piece of crap. You have been nothing, nothing but trouble for me since you started protecting, allegedley, my husband, and I will see you fry for this, you fucking bastard."

"It wasn't...."

"Really? Then what the fuck are you doing here? Get out, get out, get out."

"There are things..."

"Get out before I kill you myself." I caught her gaze and saw there was no arguing with her. I had to talk to her, but hoped she would calm down first.

"Don't do anything stupid." She shot me a look that warned me off and I pulled Rosie after me, actually glad to be out of the building before the cops showed up. That's when things usually get interesting.

Cale held the phone to her ear.
"Hey Link, I need a favour."

As one car pulled away another slid carefully into it's space, the occupant already with his mobile glued to his ear.

"I'm here."

"Where?"

"Outside some building. Big place, gated entry. Holy shit."

"What, what, what?"

There was silence at one end of the line.

"Fuck me, a whole load of cops showed up, paramedics. Looks like someone got roasted."

"Salvador?"

"I'm telling you already. Call you later."

The line clicked off.

"If passengers would like to buckle up, we'll be landing in a few minutes. The time is coming up for midnight and it is hot and humid down there tonight. Thankyou for flying with AmericanAirlines, we hope you enjoy your stay."

Alix looked anxiously at Francis who looked blankly, tiredly back.

"Relax Ali. It'll come."

"Okay Cale?"

"Sure, I'm overwhelmed, thank you so much. I'm just in the middle of something right now, but I'll talk to you more tomorrow."

"But you're saying yes, right?"

"Sure, sure Scotty. Talk to you tomorrow."

In LA Scott Neill dialled another number from his memory.

"Hi Elisha. She said yes. Start spreading the news."

Alix sat up front watching the building as the police milled around. The wailing sirens of the ambulance drifted into the distance. Salvador closed his eyes and listened to the news report on the radio. Francis flipped peanuts into his mouth and watched the nurses.

"...and finally tonight it has just been announced that Cale Kline will star in the new Howard Martin movie set to start shooting early next month. This ends the lengthy search for a relatively unknown leading lady to star with Owen Brock in the movie. Kline will play the part of Brock's new partner in the hard hitting cop thriller provisionally titled Thicker Than Blood. Now the weather with Ken Graham...."

The motel room seemed smaller by the piles of paper that now decorated it. Gone were the threadbare carpets and bug invested sheets, to be replaced by a man's history. Well, that's what he told us.

Rosie was reading something, I didn't know what, but she'd tell me soon enough. I was reading from the diary of one Gordon Sutcliffe, feeling intrusive and morbidly fascinated by the writings of a dead guy I had neither never met nor had heard of. Okay if he was famous, then he was public property. But he wasn't, hadn't been and now never would be. Not in the global sense of fame that we understand at the end of the century.

He had apparently been famous in his home region in England. A wealthy landowner with fingers in many sidelines which he dipped in and out of with regular profit making moves. He wasn't popular, according to his own words and the numerous news clippings, but he appeared not to mind, preferring to concentrate on his work and making money rather than spending it or spending time with his wife, Mary and their new baby girl Kate.

His journal said much, strange for a man in his prime in the sexist Sixties and Seventies, and yet revealed very little. There were details from work, from his various sidelines, brief mentions of Mary and Kate, various accounts with other women for which he seemed oddly proud and desperately unhappy, and then his final entry.

Rosie flipped me a beer which I fizzed open and put to my lips, letting the cold liquid slide down my parched throat. It tasted good.

'There are things that I wished had never happened, but they have and there comes a time when standing up and being counted is all that's left. I am sure Mary knows, if only cause her bloody mother keeps dropping hints. I want to smother the old hag. She'll have to wait. There are things to do at the factory in Preston. Norman needs sacking. She's not leaving without me or my darling Katy.....'

It went on about businesses I had never heard of from then on, technical details, people called Norman and Walter, Fred and Smithy, Pasty and Potter.

The pages after that were blank, the journal ended by his death on his way to America.

Why was he coming to America?

Rosie and I spent hours flicking through scraps of letters, diagrams that meant nothing, letters from England, photos of baseball players, box numbers, bank names, all the lifetime of little things that Marello had kept to see him through his final years.

"Hey Midnight, take a look."

Rosie leaned over and handed me a picture of a baseball team. The caption read 'New York Yankees Season 1972'. It was covered in faded scrawls; signatures of each player. I turned it over and found the players names like a roll call on the back.

Top Row: Louis Perkins, Dave Johnson, Mack McNeill, Silvito Georgio, the names read on and on. I came to the bottom end of the bottom row and flipped the picture back to look at the photo. It was hard to tell, hard to pick him out at the end, away from the focal point, faded over the twenty plus years of sitting in a box just like this, not being looked at, not being shown to friends, relatives, surviving the sticky fingered infants, but losing it's sheen to years of dust.

But it was Marello.

"I never knew he was a ball player," I whispered to the world in general, not wanting an answer, but just acknowledging the fact that I was sifting through the most important aspects of this man's life and I barely knew his name.

I drank some more.

There was a reason behind it. A reason why he gave me the box. Was it cause I just happened to be there, or maybe something else?

"Cause you happened to be there, happened to tell him what he feared would happen, and cause you said you could help Cale."

I looked across at Rosie.

"Are you psychic?"

The following day I hit the library and found his playing record. Short and sweet. He had been a catcher, '72 was his one and only season in the Majors and even then he was forced to give up before the play-offs due to injuries sustained in a street brawl. He was well liked and respected for his perseverence in playing for years in the Minors before getting his break, and was given a big send off by the Yankee crowd as he stood in the middle of the diamond on crutches waving his farewells. Apparently he never went back.

Rosie wandered in with coffee and donuts and we were quickly ushered outside, where the books couldn't get damaged. Yeh right.

That afternoon we spent locked in the motel, surrounded by papers, struggling with it all, hoping I'd absorb the important bits. Hoping Rosie would recognise the important bits.

The car pulled up across the street and Link switched the engine off, chewing noisily on gum, his eyes hidden behind dark shades, his arm resting idly on the open window. He could watch all day 'til she said otherwise.

"So what you want to do?"
Alix looked up from biting her already desperately short nails.
"How the hell do I know. I'm thinking."
Francis flipped cards into an upturned cap. Salvador sat back on his chair watching Alix.
"We have to wait."

A Step Ahead.

The law firm of Hanson and Grettel had a flash looking entrance hall and a smart looking PA on the front desk. She was dark haired, wore glasses and peered at us over them as we approached, probably wondering what we could posibly want with her respectable law firm. I had jeans and a sweat-top, Rosie, overlong cargo's and a hooded top, both gray, twirling gum round her finger as she walked.

"Good morning." She managed not to sneer. "Can I help you?"

I took the card, nicely dog-eared, from my pocket, uncrumpled it for greater effect and read the name from it.

"Jason Bornville. We're here to see Jason Bornville."

"Do you have a time?"

"No, no we don't, but if you say it's regarding a box I got from Mister Marello, I'm sure he'll be expecting us."

"Okay. I'll just try for you." She picked up a phone, punched a number and turned away slightly as she spoke. It was a couple of minutes in which Rosie twirled and fell over as she looked up at the high roof above us and I took in the surely fake marble pillars and the calming fountain in the lobby. "Excuse me, can I take your name?"

"Seyle. Midnight Seyle and Rosie...." I couldn't recall her last name. "...and Rosie."

The girl looked confused, but relayed the names in all their abbreviated glory.

"Okay, Mister Seyle, if you'd like to go to the sixth floor, Mister Bornville will meet you out of the elevator."

"Thankyou, Miss..."

"Keri. Keri Stephens."

"Thankyou Keri Stephens." Rosie smiled and waved as we slipped inside the silent, carpeted elevator, half expecting a cappucino machine to flip out from one of the walls and pour coffee for us while a techno-voice seduced us from the ground floor upwards.

Instead Rosie trampled the carpet as best she could and an uninspired 'bing' signalled the end of the ride as the doors swished open to an indoor-palm tree'd haven of opulence and sobriety. A man in a dark blue suit with a blue and red tie, which frankly looked pink, stepped forward.

"Mister Seyle?" He extended his hand. I shook it as I looked around.

"And you must be Rosie." He held his hand up and Rosie obligingly high-fived it. "Alright. Attagirl." He stood, straightening, reaching his full 6'2".

"Shall we go into my office." He lead the way. We followed.

Jason had short dark hair, highlighted into a lighter brown on the top by natural or unnatural means - I didn't know - and he seemed to know all about me.

"Working for John Barclay? Is he as tough as his business suggests? He works hard for his money, right?"

I agreed with a wry smile. "He sure does."

Last Train to Midnight

"So Mister Seyle, it is Mister Seyle isn't it? Mister Marello said you were using the name Drela, but Seyle is right, yes?" Again I nodded, not even bothering to question from where he had got my real name, apart from the receptionist downstairs. "Okay, Mister Seyle. Mister Marello, as I've intimated, informed me that you'd probably be coming to see me, sooner rather than later and probably after his death. Is that right?"

"That I would come or I would come after his death?"

"Both."

"Yes. I guess. He gave me your name, not directly of course, it was in some of his personal papers which he gave me shortly before he died. I didn't know then, but I guess he only gave me the box because he knew that he wasn't going to live much longer." I lied. "Your name was in his numbers book and I knew that this was where he had trusted the remainder of his assets."

"Of course, of course. Again he told me as much just the other day, about you I mean, and he also said that I was to help you in any way I could. I was to show you anything you wanted to see. Anything at all Mister Seyle."

I looked from him to Rosie to the window and back to him.

"What is there?"

"Well, what we have is mainly paperwork, but we also have information concerning deposits in other institutions, which may be of more interest to you."

"Maybe, maybe not."

We had a hit a juncture where I had to decide if I wanted to see what Marello had hidden away. Of course I wanted to, but if it subsequently got me killed then I guess I didn't.

But life lived in fear is a life half lived.

"Okay Mister Bornville, if we could start with what you have...."

"Sure, sure." He stood and buttoned his single breasted jacket. "If you'd like to follow me, we can give you some privacy to look over the papers at your leisure. If you need help with anything or don't understand anything just holler. Oh, and there's tea, coffee, chocolate, water, juice just to the left of the elevator. Just help yourselves."

Rosie helped me as we began yet more sifting. I don't think she knew what we were looking for, but then again neither did I. I was praying for something to jump out and hit me 'tween the eyes, making me scream with the obviousness of it.

A large portion of what we had on the table in front of us was lawyer stuff.

Long sentences with long words that meant nothing. Dull as shit.

Although I was technically on the right side of the law it didn't mean I had to embrace all aspects of it.

But slowly we managed to pick out three items that piqued our interest out from its dormancy.

Two that Rosie found were related to banks; one a box number and key and the other an account number in the name of Bornville J, but interestingly had two signatories.

One I found was another box number in Antigua in another familiar name.

Jason was as friendly when we left as he had been when we arrived, telling us not to hesitate to call if we needed anything.

I had to go away and think about what I was going to do.

But first I had a strange urge to call Sara.

"No, Link, don't do anything. Just keep watching where he goes, who he sees. I want something on this guy."

"Apart from sex with a minor?"

"Really?"

"I don't know, but his chick friend isn't old enough if they are."

"Don't assume Link. Facts. If I'm going to get rid of him then I need him to go away permanently."

"Exactly. Can't I just pop him?"

Cale thought for a minute, wondering if that would just be the best plan, the easiest solution all round. He had already cost her one man she loved, she wasn't sure she'd be able to cope if he cost her the other.

"No. I need more. Just keep watching."

"Sure thing babe. Your money."

"Sal?"

"She's still on the damn phone. She never gets off it. One minute it's her agent, then some bloke, then some women, now some other guy. She needs to have her mobile implanted into her ear to save her fingers from RSI"

"Okay. Keep listening."

"Sure. That I can do."

New York was getting warmer when Rosie and I touched down. We had decided to come back, even though I still wanted to do some searching in Florida. But Sara had almost finished sorting out the remains of Tony's business and for a couple of days grace in the Big Apple I could wait.

I went to see John to tell him about the latest developments, but Gates ever so politely informed me that John had gone to Seattle for some work deal he was grinding on and would be out of town for a week or so. Even better. That meant I didn't have to report my tale of no news.

Jason called on the Sunday morning and told me that in answer to my question of Marello's will, nobody was allowed to be present and only the beneficiaries would be informed. I thanked him for getting back to me, but slammed the phone down.

That had been one of my best opportunites to find out just what Marello had hidden away and who he was giving it to. Not any more.

"So where are we going then?" Sara came back into the room and shooting a glance at the curled up Rosie, sat down next to me with her best j'accuse face on.

"Florida, just for a coupla days, then down to the Caribbean for a few days."

Her face softened at that and because Rosie didn't jump up and get all excited, mainly cause I'd told her the previous day, Sara smiled and dropped her head to my shoulder.

"It's work isn't it?"

"'Fraid so. Sorry."

She looked up. "Oh well, can't be helped. Neat to get away, I guess."

"Sure is and nothing like doing it on a freebie to Antigua."

"A freebie?"

"Sure. You don't think I'm paying for y'all? Daniel knows a guy who owns one of the smart villas on the beach and we're getting it for nothing, just the cost of the flights."

I hadn't told Rosie that part so it was a good feeling to have both her and Sara wrap their arms round me without fighting each other for once. Long may it continue.

Florida was brief and not so special. Sara was bored, but managed to help with Bornville as she knew more of the terminology he used. Still it wasn't anything we could do until his last will and testament had been read.

So Antigua it was.

It was hot. Damn hot. The island looked magnificent as we touched down and it was equally magnificent as we were driven at breakneck speed, but by the most laid back cabbie who spun the wheel with one hand as the other played bass on the door or the roof, tapping the beat of the stereo, tapping Marley to the masses. In fact I don't think it was Marley. Just one of the many imitators. But the rhythms were similar, and as the cab was hurled round corners on fewer wheels than it should have had in contact with the ground we slid from side to side, unconstrained by belts. The faint, aromatic, relaxing smell of ganja hit our nostrils as we slowed to our destination, smoked with the uniformity and equanimity that Americans chew gum. One for all and all for one.

I heard a rumour that the Jamaican soccer players had half time drags and scored more goals in the second half than any other team. I have no evidence of that.

Our home was white, surrounded by parched grass at the front and side, open to the track that passed for a road, and a large blue pool at the rear, with the sand and ocean just yards away. Sara just looked open mouthed, probably wondering if places like this really existed. Rosie was on the sand in seconds and paddling in the surf seconds after that; happy as a sandboy.

I watched them both and opened up, moving into the cool interior, fans spinning already, shutters keeping the sun out, tiled floor cold under my bare feet. I don't know how Danny met these people, but I hoped he knew a few more.

I threw the bags in the rooms; Sara and Rosie in the double, me in the single, and went out to join them.

Sara was sitting flirting with the water of the pool; dipping her toes in, dragging her fingers through it making it ripple across the otherwise calm surface. She hid her eyes behind dark shades, but moved her head to look at me as I came out on the deck. She smiled, but said nothing. I smiled back and turned to look at Rosie as she danced her way through the breakers, turning cartwheels, doing handstands in the water, until she saw me watching and ran back, dripping saltwater all the way.

"Man this is awesome. Come down the beach, man, come on." She took my hand and dragged me away. I offered my hand to a reluctant Sara who looked at it, but refused to move. She played her fingers in the water and looked to the bottom, seeing things that perhaps she'd hoped to leave in New York.

The following day I left them at the house and went into St Johns to find the Antiguan bank with a certain deposit box I wanted to get my hands on.

I found it on the main street and entered. It was deliciously cool inside, but still warm enough for the employees to be wearing shirtsleeves.

"Good morning sir. And how can we help you?"

"Hi. I'd like to get at my safety deposit box."

"Sir, alright. Have you got the number and i.d?"

"Sure." I handed them over.

"It's a pleasure to see you Mister Barclay. I don't think we've ever had you down here before, is that right?"

"Sure is. I thought I'd better take a look before I get too old, you know?" The girl had the grace to laugh with me and took me through to a room where she asked me to wait while she retrieved the box.

A few minutes later she returned, a silver rectangle under her arm as she pushed the door closed.

"Okay sir, I had to contact Mister Bornville to verify your application to get access, but he's out of town so a lovely woman called Sara said she knew you were down here, so here you go." The girl put the box on the table, removed a key from her pocket and opened one of the locks. She moved away. "Your key opens the other one."

"Great. Thanks."

I waited until she'd gone before I breathed a sigh of relief that the phone intercept had worked and took out my own key.

It turned smoothly. My heart was strangely normal, beating out it's steady duh-thump in my chest as I lifted the lid, expecting more papers and being somewhat disappointed by just one item.

I took it out, placed the box on the floor and looked inside the envelope.

It was a Dear John letter.

'Dear John, If you are reading this then I am dead. But don't worry I enjoyed my life and hope that you have too. There are more things in heaven and earth Horatio.

This is not to reminisce though, but to outline a few things for you.

Cale is a very special woman. You wonder how I know? Well, I know her as Kate, but she is Cale to you and to most of the world, so I will keep it easy for you. You never knew that she lived with me, that to all intents and purposes I am her father. I am not her natural father, but I brought her up. The story is long and probably you'd skip it anyway, so I won't bore you. Anyway, I kept her away from everything I ever did, as much as I could at least, which is why you never met her prior to marrying her. She never knew you either, so don't worry about it being a set up from my side; she never knew. By the time she was old enough to know what was going on in my life I was a legitimate businessman so she knew nothing of the Family side of my previous existence. Just as well otherwise she might be dead as well.

Anyway, what with you marrying her this box is all but useless as it outlines her life before she did meet the love of her life, and the fortune she is worth.

These days I don't know the ins and outs of her money, you'll have to ask Jason Bornville, but she had a rich English industrialist for a father who left all his estate to her and I have invested it since. It was worth a couple of million then, so now, who knows. Ask Jason.

Well, that sums it up really as far as you and I are concerned. I would have left you money from the deal, you know, but hey......

Besides, I left you Cale. Look after her Johnny.
Your willing accomplice and one time friend,
Mike Marello.'

I was speechless. I looked for secret compartments in the box but found nothing. This was all? This was all that John would have to fly down for? One letter? Okay, so Cale was rich, so why hide it?

I left and went back to the beach house, not wanting to tell the girls we had to go, but knowing we had to. All too soon we'd be back in New York.

A Step Behind.

Jason Bornville was not generally a nervous man, but surrounded, as he was, by men with guns nerves were shaking him into a sweat. It was not even that the guns were pointed at him, cause they weren't, but as they were held loosely in front of each bearer or as they offered a tell-tale bulge beneath the jackets of the others Jason knew they were there. And they knew he knew.

"Okay guys. Mister Firetti, I guess you know about box 213 already. Mike said something like this might happen. He didn't mention your entire family would come down to see me." Jason tried to laugh, but only succeeded in a high pitched squeak. "Okay, okay, hmm, let's get on with it. 213. Two-one-three. Okay." Reaching in Jason pulled out the box, turning and placing it on the table in front of Gini Firetti.

"Mister Bornville. I'm a reasonable man, but I would like some privacy. It's a personal thing, you understand?"

"Of course, Mister Firetti, of course I do, but it's just that...." A couple more guns were slipped obviously out from under jackets. Jason gulped audibly. "Mister Firetti, you have to understand that I have a job to do as well...." The man on his right and the man on his left took a pace each towards him. He felt under his collar where it was getting suddenly incredibly hot. "Okay, okay. I'll leave you to it."

Firetti opened his arms in a gesture of thanks as Jason backed out of the room, his eyes flicking from one gun to the next. Once out of the door he slumped against the door and exhaled loudly, moving away from the door in case they heard him and thought he was listening.

A few seconds later as Jason leaned on a desk just away from the door, it opened again and most of the men from inside the room came out. Jason hadn't counted how many were in there, he thought about seven, but five were certainly no longer inside the room.

Inside Firetti opened the box and looked at almost $5 million. He said nothing. He did nothing, but calmly took the bag from Luca and began placing the money into it. As the last bundle was packed in and the zipper closed he motioned for Luca to open the door, then he followed him out, leading the way out of the building with a startled, but relieved, Jason Bornville one of many watching them go. Jason waited until the cars had moved out of sight then he went into the room. The box was open, the key still in the lock, a $100 bill sitting alongside, a solitary clue to what had been in there.

Everybody Watching.

John had gone out of town. I didn't know where, but I had a wild guess and called Bornville. He confirmed that the last will and testament had been read, the beneficiaries informed and the subsequent bequests bestowed on those lucky enough to be included in Michaelangelo Marello's final thoughts.

I didn't know, and to be honest at the time I didn't really care what John had been given, apart from the letter. Of course I assumed that John had been left something other than the letter. If he hadn't then I wondered just how close he and Marello had actually been. Business partners; sure. Friends; maybe not.

The letter had been a puzzle for a while.

Why had it been left? Why had it been left so far away from where Marello and Barclay had known each other? And was it true? Did Cale and John really not know about each other prior to their 'accidental' meeting? Was Marello in fact the architect of lifetime security for the adopted daughter he so clearly and dearly loved?

I had left the letter in the box, pretty certain that John would be directed there somehow, someday. Of course after my deception he may have trouble getting to see it now, but that, I considered with a definite rationale, was no longer really my problem.

I had seen it. So what? If John saw it, then so what? He would know some of the backstory, finally.

As I, or rather we as I kept reminding myself, discovered there were another two pieces of information of interest. Jason Bornville controlled one. The other, the box, could have been anything. It could have been for John. It could have been for Cale. It could have been for the Cat Protection League.

Bornville, therefore, was still high up on my list.

But Cale was first.

I knew she was at home. For a change a hurried stakeout had worked and pinned her down to the marital home where Barclay was not. Cale and Gates the Mysterious, or Downright Creepy if you want, were home and as she had not left the house for a couple of days I figured she was staying for a while.

I had insisted that this was one job I had to do by myself. I couldn't be doing with distractions, though Rosie was often helpful. But Sara still interrupted in the most plaintive ways and at the most incongruous moments.

I don't know why, but I found myself thinking of her a great deal.

Anyway...

Gates buzzed me in without threats of strange underworld deaths, for which I was thankful, but Cale was true to form and unreceptive. Creepy and Bitchy in the same house. The All New Seven Dwarfs. They needed a Rottweiler called Snow White and the whole Disney/Addams Family crossover would be complete.

Fortunately Gates looked less inclined to kick me out than I thought he might be. Still, I didn't want to waste my obviously brief time with Mrs Barclay.

"Miss Kline....."

Last Train to Midnight

"Are you still here?"

"Miss Kline..." I repeated in a firmer tone, hoping to make some sort of impression. She turned to look vaguely in my direction.

"Mister Seyle, you should know that I am holding you directly responsible for the death of my father, and I am not responsible for anything that may happen to you as a result of your involvement. If you continue with this bizarre and frankly futile exercise in protection, for which I have seen little evidence of success or in fact effort, then I will have a restraining order placed upon you. Does this make my position clearer for your strained resources and intellect?"

Gates may not have wanted a fight, but I did.

"Cale, you don't seem to realise what is going on here. Your husband is in serious danger of being killed by the same people who shot your father, the contents of whose will may hold the key to whether or not the contract gets carried out or not. The contents of whose will may also point to and clarify other aspects of your life, John's life, and which in turn may help my job. If you know anything about anybody who is involved, if you think you know anybody who is involved then telling me would be a good option, an option you should be looking to take." I paused. "Now." I hated raising my voice, but there were times and situations when, as a last resort, it became pretty much necessary.

Cale though seemed unmoved. She stood and flicked the ash from her smouldering cigarette into a flat metal tray beside her. She looked straight through me. Slowly she swayed her seductive way towards me, stopping as her toes touched mine, her face millimeters away from mine.

"The only person who I know is involved is you Mister Seyle." She dropped her cigarette so that it bounced between us on its way to the floor. She didn't even glance down, but crushed it into a pulpy mess on the marble floor. "It's been anything but a pleasure knowing you Mister Seyle. Goodbye."

Gates was gentlemanly in showing me out, again. I suspected that he had had more than one run in with Mrs Barclay, and I liked to think that made him a little sympathetic.

I wasn't convinced though that sympathy formed part of the enigmatic butler's repertoire.

The first two steps he took down the landscaped driveway were accompanied by the jabbing of fingers onto numbers and the dialling tones of two local calls.

"Link, when I'm in LA for rehearsals next week. Then."

"There's this black guy been in there ten minutes. He's just leaving."
"Okay Sal, you take him, I'll stick with the woman."
"Fran, we should flip for it. Why do you get the better looking option?"
"Cause you are the better man at this, so you get the harder job. Watching the woman is easy. She's not going anywhere."

Sal grunted and turned the ignition. Leave the Queen of Hearts and follow the Spades.

Trouble in Paradise.

The bank was on the main street, wonderfully cool inside, but John Barclay was a man who took aircon for granted and besides, this was a day he had waited a long time for.

The goddam dick, Seyle, had almost found out about Marello before, but not now. Marello was gone. Gone, gone, gone and hopefully forgotten. If he had been true to his word then the problems involving Firetti were about to come to an end.

"Morning sir, how can I help you?"

"Hi. My name is John Barclay and I'd like to get my deposit box please."

"Mister Barclay?"

"Yes."

"Okay Mister Barclay. If you'd like to take a seat, then someone will be right with you."

"Thankyou." John turned and sat in one of the pale cream couches that adorned the bankhall, picking up a paper, The New York Times, and flicking to the business pages.

A few minutes passed before a man approached him.

"Mister Barclay, would you come this way please."

John stood and followed the man into an ante-room. Both men sat down.

"Mister Barclay..."

"Is there a problem?"

The man shifted uncomfortably in his seat, not quite meeting John's look.

"There may be."

"How? Is my identification not good enough for you?"

"No, no, it's fine."

"Then what?"

"Mister Barclay came in just last week."

"Pardon me?"

"A Mister Barclay came in last week and asked to look at his deposit box, the same one you now request. He also had i.d, and the key, like you, and he also got clearence from Mister Bornvilles office."

"Well call him then." John was almost on his feet, his temple pulsing with indignation, his veins throbbing in outrage. "Call him, call him." He stopped and waited. "I am not a liar, Mister Tarker. Call Mister Bornville and we can get this straightened out."

Collis Tarker left the room and picked up the nearest phone, dialling a number he had on a sheet in front of him.

"Hanson and Grettel, I'm Erin, how can I help you?"

"Jason Bornville please."

"Okay. Can I say who's calling?"

"Collis Tarker."

"Hi Mister Tarker, how are you? Just hold and I'll put you through?"

The line burst into some little known attempt at classical Muzak before a man's voice interrupted.

"Jason Bornville?"

"Hi Jason, it's Collis Tarker."

"Hi man, how you doing? We'll have to catch up sometime. I just need an invite to the Caribbean."

"Sure man, anytime you down here, give me a call." Both men laughed and accepted they would probably never meet each other.

"Alright, what can I do for you?"

"Jason, I've got a man in here asking to see a box. A Mister Barclay."

"Sure, John Barclay. He was here for a will and said he was going down there. I would have called ahead for you guys, but it's just been so busy. No time to stop and smell the roses, you know what I mean."

"Right. You know him then?"

"John? Hell yeh."

"Okay, then we have a problem. I had a guy in here last week saying the same thing, Mister Barclay, wanting to see the same box. We called your office they said you were out of town, but they knew Mister Barclay, described him real well."

"Who was it and what was the description? The Barclay I know's about 180 tall, graying hair, 85-86 kilos."

"Black or white?"

"What?"

"Is the man a negro or a caucasian?

"You're kidding right?" The silence told him otherwise. "He's white."

"Okay. You've just described our guy. Last week from a girl called Sara we had a guy of similar height, bit heavier, but black. Someone got it very wrong somewhere, and I don't think it was my girls."

"Well buddy I got news for you. We don't have a Sara."

For a few seconds there was nothing worthwhile that either one of them could say, so all they said was so long and catch you later before putting the phone down.

One went back to confront his customer, the other redialled and wanted answers.

John unlocked the box, not knowing what he might find. They swore nothing had been removed from the box, but John wasn't convinced they could be certain.

Inside was an envelope, unsealed.

He took it out, looked round it before sliding the letter out and unfolding it.

He started reading.

Trouble at Home.

"Jason, I have no idea what you're talking about."

"If I find out it was you then you are going to be in a huge vat of trouble, buddy. You could have ruined my career if anyone had found out."

"Then why are you so keen to know? If you don't know then you can't be lying about anything that may or may not have taken place, can you?"

"Don't try and be technical with me Seyle. If I find out..."

He left a threat hanging in the empty wires. I ignored it.

'But there's nothing to find." I figured there was no point in even planting a seed. "I swear I wasn't there." I left it there. No need to clarify something that I didn't want to exist.

Bornville slammed the phone down.

He knew it was me. I knew he knew but couldn't prove it. So I wasn't going to let him know. I had what I wanted.

The other account had to be the investment of Cale's money.

The box.....

Sadly of the two men who I knew who knew what it was, one was dead and the other had just scratched my name off his Christmas card list.

Which yet again seemed to leave me with nowhere to go, but home.

Down Time.

Rosie had actually gone out someplace with Daniel, a respite for which I was thankful. I slumped on the bed and flipped open a cola, taking in the sugar hit as my head hit the pillow.

I didn't want to sleep. Probably couldn't if I wanted to. My eyes drifted over the ceiling, vaguely thinking to myself that it needed a lick of paint. I wondered where Rosie had gone with Daniel. I guessed it was to the wholesalers as that was where Daniel often went at strange times of the day, but it could have been for ice-cream. Rosie loved her ice-cream.

My cellphone buzzed inside my pocket and bleeped annoyingly as I took it out.

"Midnight Seyle?"

"Hey Midnight, how you doing?"

It was Sara. She sounded conciliatory. I didn't know why.

"I'm chilling. You?"

"Chilling too."

"On the roof?"

"Sure am. Watching the clouds float by."

"You'll be catching pneumonia up there. Too chilled."

There was silence. I wondered what she was thinking. I stood and went to the window, looking up, idly hoping the clouds above her were rolling by me.

"You wanna coffee?"

"Gimme ten."

"Sure."

The guy following me stopped on the opposite corner, then rolled slowly over the street as I caught his glance before I pressed the buzzer.

It had startled me for an instant as the vague recollection of the feelings I had first come across many years previously crossed my mind and infiltrated my train of thought.

Being followed, I mean really followed, is unnerving, even if you think you're used to it. Just knowing that somebody is so interested in you as to make your business their business, and knowing that any business you undertake will more than likely be relayed to some higher power who then has the say-so on what to do next. A bullet could be lodged in my body depending on what I did today, or indeed what I had done last week. The car disappeared out of view.

I pressed the buzzer.

Link raced the car round and pulled back to the junction just as the door closed. He jammed his fist against the wheel and swore under his breath. He wasn't totally sure, but he thought the black guy had seen him. Oh well, wouldn't matter beyond Tuesday.

Across the street Salvador saw the black guy go inside with some white chick. Good looking girl he thought to himself. He also saw a guy in a car banging his hand on the dash with his eyes firmly on the very same door. In fact the car looked really familiar.

Sara was curled up in jeans and a shirt, sipping the richest, darkest coffee I think I had ever tasted. Along with the cola my caffiene high was really kicking in.

"You okay?"

She nodded. She looked tired, a faraway tired, despite the coffee. Her hair was loose, resting on her shoulders, shaping her face. Her naturally dark skin still darker from the Caribbean sun, the tan being shown off to hypnotic effect by the pale blue shirt, her brown arms snaking across her body as she drank, her neck falling into enticing shadows on her chest as the loose shirt offered to reveal more, but wherever she moved never did.

"I just needed some company."

We just sat for a while. I flicked through the channels on the TV, pausing for some sport every once in a while, catching up on the latest news stories. We didn't talk much. Sara seemed happy enough to do just that.

At some point she got up and went to the bathroom. I called to check in with Daniel and I guess Rosie. They were good, so I shut off the phone and carried on channel surfing.

"You want some take out?"

"Sure. What you having?"

She shrugged.

"Dunno. Pizza?"

"Sounds good."

She called, I opened a coupla beers, one of which she took as she came back to sit down.

"Twenty minutes."

"Cool."

We drank beer and waited with the screenstars doing our talking.

Link watched the building, smoking, blowing smoke rings out into the air, watching a delivery bike pull up and get paid by the white chick for the pizza he left. Link's stomach rumbled. Christ he was hungry. He flicked the smouldering butt onto the pavement and revved the car into life. They could live without him for ten while he got food.

Salvador ripped open a plastic-packed sandwich and took a large bite, chewing slowly as he watched the car opposite roll away. He drank some coke and settled back, listening to his favourite opera play on the car stereo. There was nothing to compare with the real classics and whoever invented the car stereo needed thanking. A lot.

"What are we going to do?," mumbled Sara questioningly to me through a mouthful of good pizza. She struggled to keep a straight face as she struggled to keep the crumbs in her mouth. I smiled calmly back at her and asked her what she meant.
"I mean, what are you going to do? I mean, well, you know, about the money?"
"What money?"
"The money. Marello's money."
I ate, thinking of an answer to a question that had been on my mind for days. "I don't know." That was honestly the best I could come up with. Sara just scowled at me, disbelievingly as well. "What?"
"You really don't know?"
I had to shrug and admit that I was currently at a loss as to what to do and where to go next.

She placed her slice of pizza back in the box, licking her fingers and wiping them on her jeans as she sat up on her heels, fixing me with something akin to an 'I have a plan' stare.

"We know there are two other places of interest, and we know that one of them at least contains a great deal of money."

"Potentially."

"Whatever. But the other must as well. The box."

"The box, the box, I know the box." I looked at her. She was eager to know, keen to do something positive, but I really didn't know what we could do. Maybe I was missing something. But I didn't think so. Still, I made an effort and followed suit by placing my slice back in the box, licking my fingers and shifting my position to a more comfortable one for me, and hopefully one that seemed to show I was more interested in what Sara was saying. She leaned forward as I looked up.

"Okay, okay. We know what John's letter said so we know there should be money somewhere."

"In the account."

"In the account."

"Controlled by Bornville, who does not have me high on his list of favouite people right now."

"A minor point. And the box."

"Must be money, and I guess for someone else, and if it's not John or Cale, then....."

We both thought for a minute, licking invisible pizza sauce off our fingers which hinted at the taste, frowning in tandem, puzzling over something simple.

"If not John and if not Cale then who? It has to be someone. His wife? Did he have a wife? Friends from way back?" She looked at me as if I wasn't trying. "Come on, Mister Detective, help me out a little."

"Okay, he had no wife, friends is possible, but unlikely I think. Whatever was in the box was a secret. Why keep gifts to friends a secret? No, I think it was something bigger, maybe a pay-off of some kind..." I left the thought right there and jumped up to get another beer.

"But that would seem to be Barclay?"

I nodded. I had to agree.

"I know. But that would seem to be wrong, unless Marello was playing games and creating a paperchase for Barclay."

"But why would he do that?"

"Dead people often do. They like to feel thay have an influence even after they've been scattered off the George Washington bridge. Could be playing games."

We fell into a thoughtful silence again, picking up on the pizza where we left off. I was missing something.

Salvador carried on eating as the door opened and the man came out. Link woke up and slid his shades back over his eyes, immediately alert.

Salvador calmly placed the remainder of his sandwich in his mouth, wiped his hands on the passenger seat and turned the ignition. Pulling across the street as Link also moved off, both in slow, careful pursuit of the same target.

"Salvador?"

"Hey man, how's it going?"

"It's going well Fran. And you? How's the girl?"

"Still at home, still going nowhere fast. Hey, I had a call from our boss lady. She says she wants us to pick the blonde girl up next week once she hits the set. The boss is gonna be someplace else, so it's up to us I guess."

"Sure no problem. Cool Francis. I'll catch up with you later."

"Sure man. Have fun."

Last Train to Midnight

The trio of cars slipped through the darkening night, lights blazing, giving no cover from the glare they threw over the tarmac. Salvador watched both his front and back, keeping close tabs on his mark and the suspicious guy behind him, a guy who was an increasingly impatient driver as he swerved out to overtake on a busy stretch of road. Salvador let him, slowing slightly to let the car pull in front, in between him and the red Mustang. Sal sat back and lit a cigarette, dropping back away from the other two cars. He could feel it. Nothing would happen tonight.

Absent.

John was conspicuously absent for the rest of the week. Gates wouldn't tell me where he was and Cale didn't even bother with a denial. She just glared at me as if I was a nothing on the atom of life. A real charming lady.

Not that seeing John was high on my list of priorities. I had guessed he wasn't around because he'd been to the Caribbean. Equally he probably didn't really want to catch up on what I'd been doing on the case of the threatening letters. In fact, if he'd asked me I don't know whether I could have told him anything anyway. After all I had seen a few things I wasn't meant to, and although it helped me, it didn't make it any easier for me to explain the lack of actual evidence I had. Bummer.

I had decided that there was something going on beyond the threats on John Barclay. Unfortunately I had no firm idea of what it was.

In amongst the papers from Marello and from what the letter had said, I had been adding two and two and making four, five, twelve and twenty-two. Many options. No answers.

Sara had hit a rut of some kind. She suddenly had lost all her get up and go, all the verve and drive and passion she'd felt since I'd met her. Well since the shooting. Sara had always been on the edge of her seat about stuff, but now it was all she could do to flick the channels or make some coffee. She wasn't bored or depressed. Just resigned.

We were spending some time together, doing nothing, just sitting, talking occasionally. She said she wanted to go to Hawaii. I said I wanted to see the world. She asked me why. I couldn't answer her. I always thought it would be great, just to see other places, meet other people, but increasingly I had become to see that perhaps all I was missing was something in my life at home. Something I looked forward to, other than getting blasted every night and waking up with a heavy metal thrash band jamming in my head, a frozen shoulder, a stiff neck and blurred ideas of where I'd been and what time I crawled into bed. Something, and I hesitate to slip into psychobabble, real.

It was actually Rosie who told me I'd matured since she'd known me. I had smiled and stuck my tongue out at her, but Sara had agreed and after I looked in the mirror and liked the shaved, close cropped image that stared back, free from large black trash bags dragging my eyes to my chin, I conceded that they may have a point. I hadn't sought Daniels opinion. There are limits to my belief system.

The weekend passed by in a hazy smell of pizza and ice cream. Sara and Rosie were teaching me well and as Sunday rolled into Monday rolled into Tuesday thoughts of a normal life had planted seeds and run headlong into the desert to watch what happened.

Tactics.

Los Angeles was bathed in warm smog, hazy sunshine filtering through to tempt the Angelinos out from an unlikely fortnight when they had been forced inside from the ceaseless rain.

Cale Kline stepped out of the airport and immediately hid behind her shades. She scoured the cabs for one which looked like it should be for her, but saw none. Instead she picked one and marched towards it.

"Hey, hey miss, that's mine. It's my cab."

She shot her most icy glare at the stranger who had just appeared, but it was lost behind the dark spectacles and as she looked the man up and down she was glad it had been.

"Really, does it have your name on it?" She couldn't resist from striking a blow.

The guy laughed, his face creasing gently as he did so.

"No, no it doesn't. But it does have my case in the boot. Sorry trunk."

"You're not American."

"No. English." Cale picked her glasses off and looked him up and down once more, this time with an obviousness even a Limey couldn't miss.

She held out her hand.

"Cale Kline."

"Francis Wilmott. A pleasure."

"Where you going?"

"Beverly Wilshire."

"Cool. On my way. Wanna share?"

"Excellent. Thank you."

The cabbie packed the trunk and shot Francis a look which Cale missed as she curled into the backseat of the cab, letting her skirt ride up her thighs as the Englishman climbed in beside her. No harm flirting.

Twenty minutes later and the bumpy street they were on was not one Cale recognised from any she had bene on in LA before.

"Hey buddy, hey, where you going?"

"Short cut."

"Really. Well, could you get us back to the highway, cause this is like no short cut to anywhere I now."

"Well, maybe you don't know many places lady."

The driver spoke in a clipped foreign accent. European, but not English. Maybe Russian if the movies were to be believed at all.

"Look...," she started, but was halted by the cold metal pressed against her neck. "What the fuck is going on?" Cale shouted with as much force as she could.

"Don't scream and we ain't gonna hurt you, okay? We gonna take a ride to have us a bit of a talk. We'd like some answers and we think you'd be able to help us out with them. So don't worry, baby, it's gonna be fun." The English guy was talking like a Latino now, something that didn't really match his clean shaven complexion. Cale shivered. An involuntary shot of ice darted up and down her spine, making her neck tingle and her whole body tense. The driver, she could see in the mirror, was impassive, concentrating on the road ahead.

"Look, I have to be somewhere."

"Yeh, we know. But not today, hey? Maybe we let you go tomorrow. If you're a good girl." His smile was lecherous as his pale gray eyes caressed her body. Cale wished she'd tugged her skirt down over her legs, but now it would be too obvious and she didn't want to draw any more attention to herself. She dropped into silence which seemed to suit the men, one who drove, the other watched as they took turn after turn, making sure she didn't know where they were before pulling into a lot full of lock-ups and coming to a stop.

"This is it? We're stopping?"

"Sure are babe." Francis waited while Cale willingly got out of the car, not bothering to struggle as she felt sure the gun in his hand would be used in an instant. Francis looked around as the driver opened one of the lock-ups and then threw him the keys. "Cheers man. I owe you." The cab pulled away and Francis ushered Cale inside.

The walls were bare. There were hockey sticks, a football, a baseball bat, some tins of paint lying round the floor. And a chair.

Francis smiled. "Home sweet home."

Salvador looked aghast at his boss as she shook her head and blatantly refused to see his point of view.

"No. If this guy has been following Cale then I want one of you on him."

"But Francis is going to need a break. I should be in LA with him."

"But you aren't. Doesn't that tell you something? If your instincts are so good, and up until now you've never listened to me at all, then why are you here? You must know something's dodgy. This guy has been after Cale…"

"I don't think he's been after her. I think he's been to see her a couple of times, but I don't think it's her otherwise he's had no luck."

"I don't care about her at the moment. She'll be useful in time. This guy worries me." She thought for a minute. "I need to talk to him."

"Fine. I go get him."

"Salvador, wait. I can't do it now, I have to be in LA. Keep an eye on him. I want to talk to him." She said it firmly and looked him in the eye as she said it, making sure he knew what she meant. Not that it was hard to follow, even for a Russian.

As Alix took off for the other side of the country Salvador took to his car and found the guy playing chess and drinking coffee with his girlfriend in a cafe near her home. He cut the engine and watched for a while, taking in every detail of the surroundings so that if anything changed he would know instantly what it was.

The guy was older than the girl by maybe ten years, and the other girl who sat with them was just a teenager. She looked bored and as he watched she got up and went to the counter, bringing back a cup of something, probably coffee, it was all these people seemed to drink, and a plate of donuts.

Salvador's stomach rumbled reminding him that he had missed breakfast for the first time in months. He checked his watch, checked the area, checked his piece was safely tucked in his shoulder holster and took a calculated risk.

The older of the two women looked up as he walked in. He smiled an awkward smile and went to the counter, getting hot water and some toasted bagels before taking a seat away from anyone. He reached inside his jacket and pulled out a book, American Psycho, and flipped to his marked page.

It was a decent book, weirdly grotesque in a down to earth way that was at once horrifyingly sick and as natural as going for groceries.

The chess game finished with a single clap and a squeak of delight from the woman and a grudging headshake from the man. The teenager, sugar covering her lips, looked up and acknowledged the result, then returned to her book. Salvador craned his neck to see what she was reading, but was frustrated by the girls knee as she curled up once more. The pieces were set up once more and battle commenced again.

Shooting Match.

'*...There should be nobody like you, nobody like you, nobody, nobody, nobody who's like you...*' Link murmured in vague time to the music on his headphones as he turned the corner, feeling the bulge in his pocket, cocking it, making it sure it was primed, ready for action. He put his shades back on and took the gun from his pocket, holding it in his hand, flexing his fingers as he settled one of them on the trigger.

'*High upon the goodstuff, on the road to Santa Fe...*'

His mind swirled with a hundred thoughts as he focused on the sign above the store where he was going. He paused outside, breathing steadily, gun back in his pocket as he leaned on the window watching the pathetic tableau of coffee house bliss he was about to....

'*...Could be on the downslope, watching raindrops hit the floor...*'

I saw him standing, but thought nothing of it. I didn't recognise him. Maybe I thought he was out of breath as he just leaned on the window, but nothing more. Besides it was my move.

Salvador looked up as the door opened and his hand was inside his jacket instantly, flipping the piece from it's pouch in one swift, slick, well practised movement, firing the moment his finger made contact with the trigger.

'...Give in to it and it can show the path to take, give in to it and it will show the lines to take...'

Link had his gun out and pointed at his target as he entered. He heard a shot and for a second faltered, not sure whether it had been him or not.

After he fired the other guy hesitated and before he had time to pull off a shot Salvador's first bullet ripped into him and jerked his right arm back, making him lose the gun which fell to the floor with a metallic crack.

The pain! The searing pain which tore through his arm was followed by a thud into his chest which sent him back against the wall. The startled faces swam before him, followed by his mother, that touchdown he scored in his sophomore year at high school, Leslie in her parents bed, his first jail time, then it all faded into a bright light before blackness covered it all. Covered it all.

Salvador's third and final shot buried itself neatly alongside the second in the bloody hole that was, seconds earlier, the guys chest. By now the women were screaming and people were shouting for police and paramedics. Salvador looked at the blood, replaced his gun under his arm, dipped his head and walked out of the building, across the street to his car. LA suddenly seemed inviting.

Last Train to Midnight

I looked as the guy slumped against the wall, not seeing as the door opened and closed, only making sure that the flecks of red on the board and on my clothes and on the floor belonged to the dead guy and not to Sara or Rosie. Sara was screaming, mouth wide, rubbing anxiously at her face, leaving streaks of blood as her fingers pulled over her skin, making her look like a badly made-up native American. I was by her side in a flash, arm round her shoulders, rocking gently with her, wiping her face clean with tissues, calming her down till she just cried loudly. Better than screaming.

Rosie had curled into a tighter ball as soon as the first shot echoed across the room, shielding her face with her book, and only now did she emerge, fear etched into her features, fortunately free from any spatters of blood. Her jeans had spots of red on them, but she looked at the man on the floor, then at me for reassurance. I nodded and she came over and joined in the hug. I slipped out of it and left Rosie hanging tightly off Sara's neck.

The door was open frequently now as people ran out and others, passing by, stopped and stared in at the growing pool of blood.

I kicked the gun across the floor, and locked eyes with the store manager as he leapt over the counter and stood beside me by the body.

"Cops on the way?"

He nodded grimly.

"Know him?"

He shook his head, his gaze never leaving the dead guy.

"Who popped him?"

I shrugged. I didn't know. I saw who it was, but I didn't know him.

"Some guy. Some guy in the right place at the right time. For us at least. Not for this poor bastard."

295

I gently kicked the guys foot.

Rosie and Sara brushed past as Rosie took Sara outside.

"You okay?"

The man in the white shirt next to me looked up at me for the first time.

"Sure. Sure, I'm fine. Hey, just glad it wasn't me on the end of a bullet."

I knocked his shoulder.

"Sure man."

I went outside and waited until the police arrived.

Alix sat in a vaguely familiar office and waited. The plan had been set and now she was smack in the middle of executing it. It was only when Howard Martin walked into the room that she felt nervous.

"What?"

"Mister Martin I...."

"I don't have time. I have an absent leading lady and I don't have time." He turned to the petite woman who had followed him in. "Linda, what is this?"

"Howie, she said..."

"Did she? Oh well then, that's okay. I mean if Hannibal Lecter walked in and said something, you'd believe him too I guess?"

"Well, you know he'd probably be coming to see me, so no."

Martin shot Linda a look of distaste and then fixed his steely stare back on Alix.

"Mister Martin I was passing by and wanted to see if you'd decided on the casting for Thicker Than Blood. You know I tried out for you a couple of weeks ago and you never got back to me, but you also said call in as you might need some extras. So I was passing." Alix shrugged and smiled as she registered the confusion on Howie Martin's face as he struggled to remember if he had said anything of the sort.

"Sit down."

Alix sat and watched as Howie called in his PA to pull a tape out for him, slide it into the VCR and press play. Linda perched on the desk. Howie stood directly in front of Alix so she had to lean out and crane her neck to watch her own audition tape.

The foursome watched for five minutes and then Howie turned round to Alix.

"You're hired. I can't be doing with all this starry crap of not turning up when they feel like it. Honey, you got lucky. You'll save me time and money. I like that. Let's go."

Alix was tired already and didn't need the interruption from Salvador.

"What do you mean you shot him?"

"Alix, how many times do I have to spell it out to you. The guy came in to shoot the black guy. He had his weapon out. I just fired. I'm sorry if this ruins your plans, but it had to be done or part of your plan would be on a coroners slab by now."

"Well, why didn't you stay there? I thought you were watching the black guy? What's his name by the way?"

"Midnight Seyle. And I couldn't stay there in case I got recognised. I figured next best. At least I can help Francis."

Alix pushed her hands through her hair and sighed heavily. It had been a long day and was likely to be a gruelling shoot as they were on a tight schedule.

"Fine. Fine." She waved Sal away and turned to go back to bed.

"I go now then."

"Fine. Go."

Salvador shut the door and joined Francis in the car.

Complications.

Sara was traumatised. Having witnessed the aftermath of a killing she had now been right next to one. Close enough to feel the blood. And understandably she was in no position to cope. Even those trained to deal with death at close quarters are not always able to maintain the icy cool exterior of detachment that has to go with their job to some extent. Yes it's sad and depressing and a waste, especially in the young, but if for one minute you spent time contemplating these things then your job would be impossible. The belief in a reason was, it appeared to me, important for sanity.

Rosie seemed little changed. For a couple of nights she wanted to sleep close to someone, but apart from that she just carried on reading and doing the things she wanted to do. Daniel gave her stuff to do which gave me time for Sara.

I took her for walks and we drank lots of coffee. We ate out a few times, but that first week just passed in a blur, an oasis of flashbacks which all had blood stains in them, making the memories stagnate into the awkward clarity that makes them what we imagine them to be and often not what they actually were.

It didn't help that in the middle of the week I got a message to go see John.

In the weeks I hadn't seen him, or maybe just in the last few days, John must have lost twenty pounds and seen several ghosts. He was thin and white. Not the tanned, muscular man I had first met. He was visibly shaken and the normally impervious Gates was also obviously distressed by his boss' condition.

"What's up John?" I tried to sound calm and as if he had cut into my most important, most busy week, but inside I was hollering for him to tell me.

"Cale's missing."

News indeed.

"When did you last hear from her?"

"She called me from the airport in LA when she got there. But since then, nothing."

"What was she in LA for?"

"She was starting working on a movie, some Howard Martin thing, can't recall the name. Not sure she even told me." He bit his nails and ran his chewed fingers through his ragged, starkly gray hair. When he looked up his eyes pleaded with me before he had time to utter the accompanying words. "Find her Midnight. Please find her."

Salvador took the list and as Alix drove away he opened the lock up and approached Francis who stood over the quivering, dirty figure that was Cale Kline as she shook within her restraints, tied, as she was, to the chair.

"Okay mate?"

Francis nodded and took a bite from the sandwich in his hand. Cale's eyes bulged as Salvador stood over her.

"So, you not talking today?" He smiled an evil looking smile which made Cale lean further away from him and squeal behind her gag. Salvador reached forward, behind her head, his face close to hers as his fingers worked the knot and pulled the rag away from her face. A scream got caught at the back of her throat as her captors hand slapped over her mouth.

"Now honey, you gonna be quiet, right, cause if you not then we might have to start being nasty. And believe me, you don't want that to happen." There was a stealthy menace in his voice that made Cale tense and send the scream back to where it started from.

As his hand came away she swallowed and licked her lips, trying to moisten them back to life after they'd been left out to dry either side of the gag.

"What do you want?" She stuttered nervously, her voice croaking with disuse. Sal bent down and offered her some water which she drank thirstily, gulping loudly and swallowing hard. Cale took what she could and dribbled some down her shirt hoping it might cool her. It didn't.

"We would like some truthful answers to some questions. We have plenty of time, although I guess by now some people will be missing you. But then again maybe not." Cale let an involuntary squeak escape which brought a threatening look and a raised hand, but no violence. A tear squeezed itself out of her eye and trickled down her cheek. She flicked her tongue out and caught it as it edged passed the corner of her mouth.

Francis scraped another chair forward and sat down, crunching on an apple now.

Salvador circled round behind Cale, predatory, cautious, playing with his victim.

"I have a list of questions which we have to have the answers, but first there are some things that we have to ask in order to make sure you will be telling us the truth, yes?"

Cale nodded, unsure and scared as to whether she could or should speak.

"Okay...," Sal continued, "...firstly is your name..." Cale heard the click of a tape recorder but didn't dare take her eyes from the man now back in front of her.

"C-C-Cale K-K-Kline."

Sal leaned in and faced her eyeball to eyeball.

"Try your real name?"

Cale's eyes flicked around, searching for something else, maybe some hidden meaning that she'd missed. But she couldn't think straight and that was her real name.

"That is m-m-my real name."

Her head jerked back as the flat hand slapped across her face.

"Wrong. Your real name is not Cale Kline. What is it?"

Cale's face was now covered in tears and her cheek was reddening from the blow.

"It is it is it is." She wailed and tried to escape the hand that backhanded the other side of her face.

Sal let her recover then squatted down in front of her.

"I hate to hit women, especially beautiful women..." He let a finger drift down her neck and over one breast before pulling it away. "...But if you don't play the game then I am afraid I have to keep doing it." Cale shied away and bent her head to her chest, sniffing and hiding her face from Sal.

A few minutes passed as Cale sniffed and cried and Sal and Francis watched her.

"Okay, we try another one. Where were you born?"

Again Cale looked confused.

"N-N-New York. I was born in New York."

Once more Sal's flat hand connected with her beautifully grubby face.

"Wrong."

"I was I was I was. It's not fair, that's the truth." She shrank back in her chair expecting another smack, but it didn't come. Instead she felt something being poured onto the back of her hand. As her head turned to see what it was she heard the flick of a lighter and the flare of flame as her hand caught fire. She screamed, but only into the palm of Salvador as his huge hand covered her mouth. The flame died quickly leaving her hand feeling hot, but otherwise unaffected.

"Next time we don't use meths."

I realised that LA was going to be the place to start, but that meant leaving Sara once more. And I really didn't want to.

So New York it was and something of an old friend.

"My husband is John Barclay."
Sal nodded and offered her some water as a reward.
"Good, good, now maybe we get somewhere."
Cale drank most of the pint offered to her, gasping for air when she finished, savouring the run of cool water as it raced to her stomach.
"Okay, what about your father? Who is your father?"
Cale sighed, thankful she was being asked questions she knew the answers to.
"Mike Marello."
Her weak smile of triumph was despatched off her face with another vicious belt from Salvador's open hand.
"No. No. I thought we had finally got to some answers, but no. He is not your father."
"But..." She shrivelled into silence as his hand was raised again. This time it stayed in the air and didn't descend against her face.

"Okay, we are not getting anywhere. We will try again tomorrow." Salvador motioned to Fran who stepped forward and gently fed some sandwich and water to Cale who ate and drank hungrily, as though each bite could be her last meal.

When that was done Fran replaced the gag with some difficulty as Cale squirmed against having it tied back in place and then she was left in the dark once more as the two men opened the lock up and disappeared into the night.

A few meters down the street Sal spoke into his mobile.

"She knows nothing."

I sipped a club soda and tried to concentrate on what Sara was saying and not on the club that was giving me shivers across the street. I was thankful for rescuing Rosie and also for not bringing her with me. Hopefully, and this was a vain hope borne out of desperation, nobody would recognise me and I could get in and out without hassle. But knowing this was unlikely I had emptied my pockets of any identification and told Daniel to look after Sara and Rosie. Just in case.

"Midnight, are you listening?"

"Sorry. Miles away across the street."

Sara glanced nervously to the door I had pointed out to her earlier on.

"You don't have to do this, you know? We can leave right now."

"Thanks, but I'm paid to do a job and this could be of benefit to two at the moment, so unfortunately I do have to do this." I looked at her. "Sorry."

Sara reached across the table and covered my hand with hers.

"Don't worry, I'm here."

"And you better stay here. Otherwise we could both be in crap up to our necks."

We held hands for a few moments before I stood up and announced my intention to leave.

"You okay?"

"I need a scotch."

I struggled with the door and felt like my legs were going to give way with every step across the street. I hoped that to the goons on the door I just looked drunk and not scared shitless.

"Hey man." I waved a hand about in the air as I passed by and into the nauseatingly familiar surroundings. They laughed and didn't block my way. Must have looked harmless to them. Thank God. Phase One complete.

In the bar Sara watched without breathing and then as the broad back of her friend disappeared inside she went to the bathroom and threw up. On her way back she ordered a large gin and returned to her window seat. She waited and watched.

The room was as I remembered. Unsubtle red lighting and an atmosphere that was knowingly uncomfortable, warm by the bar, cool by the stage. Warm to encourage drinking, cool to encourage hard nipples. Pleasure all round for the punters.

I glanced around and saw no-one I recognised from my previous time here which was something of a relief. I looked up to the balcony and saw Luca staring right back at me. I froze. For a few seconds he looked straight at me before pointing in my direction and turning his head to issue instructions to whoever else was up there.

There was just time for me to get a drink, a much needed shot of Mister Daniels courage, before I felt a heavy hand on my shoulder and a whispered voice in my ear offering me the chance to meet with Mister Firetti.

They could have just asked.

Firetti was sitting in exactly the same seat as I guessed he must do every night, flanked by the bruisers in his employment, or his family, which ever it was these days. I was thankful for the iron grip on my arm otherwise I'm sure my legs would have failed me.

"Mister Firetti...."

"Shut up. Shut the fuck up."

"I'm looking for Cale Kline and...."

Blood filled my mouth and I'm sure I felt a broken tooth slide down my throat.

"Listen to me. Listen to me. Are you listening to me?"

I nodded and swallowed hard, feeling nauseus instantly.

"Are you listening to me? I don't have Cale Kline. I don't have Cale Kline. I don't have her. I don't know where she is, but I know I don't have her. Are you listening to me?"

I nodded again, sending drops of blood to the floor

"I don't have her, but you have something of mine. Now, I don't want her back. I mean, I'm a generous man, you can keep her. But for taking her... That's wrong Mister Seyle. That is wrong. And you can't take from me. You cannot take from me. People learn this, and they only get told once. You cannot take from me. So now, I have to tell you and hope that you learn fast." He had stood and was now in front of me as I tried to stand straight and face him, which I couldn't do.

Especially after a quick one-two combination to my stomach and then my face. I hit the deck and wanted to stay there, but was hauled to my feet and half carried half dragged outside.

Sara sipped at her drink intermittently, glancing across the street and picking at her nails as well as she sat nervously waiting for Midnight to return.

She couldn't help wanting him to be safe and for odd moments as she watched and waited she wished she'd gone in with him, just to be another body, someone to walk him out of there. She drank again, noticing her glass was now empty as she inhaled air. She looked at the bottom of the glass and instinctively raised it, catching the barman's eye as she did so. She raised an eyebrow and waggled the glass. He gave her a thumbs up and a smile and a wink as he reached under the bar for a glass.

Sara played with her empty glass, anxiously flicking it round within her palms, her fingers roaming over the smooth surface as her face searched for signs of movement from the door opposite.

I had given up thinking anything but self preservation as punch after punch and fist after fist crunched into my ribs or smacked into my jaw and cheek. One of them held me up as the other two, though it felt like a hundred or more, took rapid turns in pummelling me to death, for that was for sure where I was going to end up. Still I thought of nothing but trying to curl into a ball to hide from the fight. Run away and live to fight, no, just live, another day.

The pumping beat from the bar room and the wolf whistles and calls from the drunken barflies mixed with her own fears as the minutes ticked by and Midnight showed no sign of returning. Still she sat tight, not wanting to move, knowing he had said he might be longer than the twenty minutes he had originally quoted at her. She drank. Damn, empty again.

"Leave him." One more fist, fortunately a tired one, slammed into my torso, knocking the last vestige of breath from my bruised body.

Correction. As the guy let me go and I crumpled to the floor the impact knocked the last breath from my bruised body. I dribbled blood onto the cold concrete, I caught a glimpse of a rat eyeing me up cautiously from the other side of the alley, I felt the hint of a breeze against my face.

It must have been minutes that I lay like that, but it seemed like a lifetime, and not a comfortable lifetime either. A lifetime in which hallucinations and blood had become the staple diet and movement was no longer required by the sedentary human body. And rats multiplied by the second.

I didn't like rats.

My arms worked, although pain made me shiver as I struggled to claw my way up the wall. My legs were like jelly, but the solid brickwork was a welcome comfort that I leaned against. I slumped along for maybe a meter then stopped through sheer agony. I couldn't see as my eyes had both closed up, swollen beyond recognition, no doubt blacker than my own skin. I held my arms across my chest and I'm sure I could feel the dried blood underneath my sodden and slowly encrusting shirt. Another meter along and I collapsed to the floor. The lights from the street were a blur just out of reach and sight. I could feel a wall of rodents just waiting for me to slip into unconsciousness. My legs were no longer up to the task and pulling myself along with my arms threatened to break the odd rib I had left intact. I sat and concentrated on pulling small lungfuls of air into the heady mix of blood and bile that raced up and down from my lungs to my stomach and then back up again all the way to the sidewalk in front of me.

A couple walked out of the club and passed some comment about fucking drunks as they walked by. I held up a finger. I hope it was the middle one. They all felt numb.

Once more minutes felt like days and as the cold evening air drifted inside my clothes I shivered more and more. I'm sure I heard bones cracking with the effort, but I knew I had to sacrifice more of them if I was to get into view of.... somebody. Anybody. Anybody with an ounce of sense and a mobile phone.

"Hey, you lonely lady? I can keep you some gooooood company."

Sara took one look at the gold jewellery which adorned the Latino's hand and said no, turning back in time to see a man slide awkwardly, carefully and ungraciously to the sidewalk.

"Holy shit."

"Hey, come on lady. I know to show you good time, no?"

But Sara was out of the door and dodging cabs as she hurtled across the street.

"Midnight, Midnight, oh my God, are you alright?"

The man on the ground would have laughed but bone breaking was no longer a viable option.

"Oh my god, oh my god, oh my god. What have you done, oh my god, what am I going to do, where shall I take you, Midnight, where?"

The voice in his head was screaming something about a hospital, but his lips couldn't move and his eyes couldn't see.

After making sure he was still alive, he was still breathing, just, Sara finally pulled out her phone and dialled 911. The paramedics were there within twenty minutes and within thirty the ambulance was on its way.

Last Train to Midnight

The hospital was heaving with desperados; some there for the warmth, others who were actually ill. They all fought for limited bed space and with the security guard. Sporadic fights broke out amongst them, mostly those who were too high or too stoned or just too plain drunk to care or know. Everyone was yelling, none of them were heard.

"You ain't goin' in there, man. You ain't, coz I say you ain't, so back off and git your face outta mine." The security guard was a tall African-American who answered to the name of Bones. No-one really knew why, but the way his eyes flashed and the fierce regularity he removed people bodily from the ER suggested breaking them had come into it at some point. And not his own.

"Hey Bones, how's it hangin' man." The paramedic high fived Bones as he passed, moving sharply through the open door that led to Nurse Wendy.

Nurse Wendy was small, petite, with a voice like a foghorn and a right hook to match. If anyone managed to squeeze past Bones then they didn't make it past Wendy Brook.

"Whatchya got, Tweenie?"

Simeon Tween had a name that came from Harvard, fixed with a mind from Berkeley, but both lived in the body of a pro-wrestler. He and Wendy lifted the sick black guy onto the table.

"Guy, badly beaten up, pulse at five-five and weak, broken all over, bp ninety over forty and on its way down, and as you can see, he can't. Not much of a talker either. Girlfriend says his name's Midnight. And now it's twelve-o-one. Ironic. I like that."

"Get outta here, go on. Bring me one I can save for a change."

Alex Baldock

Tweenie and partner left, Bones stopped Sara getting too close and Wendy was joined by Doctor Hal Noonan and they went to work.

It was light when I managed to prise open an eye and look out on the world around me. A world I didn't recognise.

I felt I looked bad. One of those feelings that you just know without having to look in the mirror. My legs were heavy, my arms weak, my face ached, my head pounded and my body, the parts that weren't numb, were sore to the point of me having them surgically removed. I peered down to watch my feet and noticed why my legs were heavy.

Sara was fast asleep, head rested on my thigh, her face turned to mine. I reached out to stroke her hair, but had to stop as my shoulder socket threatened to disconnect.

"Sara? Sara?"

Her eyes flicked open.

"My god Midnight, you're awake. I hoped... I mean I wanted... I wished..." She sat up and pushed her hands through her hair. "Shit I must look like crap."

I tried to smile.

"Don't matter. Can't see you anyways."

"The doc said it was touch and go. You had like so many broken bones. I don't think you've got a rib left."

"Can you spare one?"

She half laughed and half sobbed, gently caressing my hand, looking at me without wanting to, seeing I don't know what. A body encased in a white cast I guessed.

"Where's the doc?"

"What, what is it? Are you in pain? I'll get a nurse."

"No, no. I need to know when I can get out of here."

"Midnight, you ain't goin' anywhere for a while. You have no ribs, you have a broken arm, a broken collar bone, a cracked pelvis, a face that looks like it went twelve with Holyfield. It's not pretty. You need rest. You stayin'"

"Honey, that's great, but I have to go."

"You can't. I mean what if this happens again. They can patch you up for only so long. Once you're in bits then it's harder to do."

"Sara, listen to me." She made as though she was going to butt in and start talking again. "Listen. You know I've got to get out as soon as I can. Cale is missing, Firetti hasn't got her, she must be somewhere and I need to know where she is, for her safety, for John's safety and in order to finish this damn job."

"This damn job is why you were within an inch of...of... you know, last night. Quit it Midnight. You have to stay."

"No, I have to go."

We glared at each other, neither giving in, both secretly knowing that the other had a point. I had to get out to finish what I had taken on, but doing so could easily end up with me back in hospital or on a coroners slab. But I had to try.

Cale's hair was no longer the golden wave of wealth it had been a fortnight before. Instead it was dark and greasy and looked more dirty brown than anything else. She walked round the tiny lock-up rubbing her wrists, bending and stretching as she kept one eye on her captors who stood by the door and talked to each other in whispered tones as they in turn kept one eye on Cale. The same ritual had been followed every day since early on in her captivity. They had even brought in a multi gym for her which she had used occasionally. Generally she was still tied up and these times of exercise were thoroughly guarded. She was never allowed to be by herself once the ropes had been released and she had never tried to make a break for it. She knew it was somewhere between unlikely and impossible for her to overpower one of them let alone both. Sure she was quick and strong and powerful, but they seemed like pros and she wasn't anxious to test them or push them into a position where they had to react. It didn't stop her thinking about it though.

"What did she say?"

"We going to release her soon, a few days."

"Then what?"

Sal shrugged.

"I don't know. Alix has her own agenda on this one. She is taken up with the movie right now, so I guess we just do as she say. I imagine that one of us follow Cale and maybe the other go back to the black man, probably you cause he may remember me."

Fran nodded his agreement and watched Cale as she lay back and pushed the bar above her head.

"Shame though."

Searching History: England.

The cane added to my image, but interrupted my training for the Boston Marathon. But at least I was out of the hospital.

My ribs were bound but not plastered, my arm had a cast and a sling and my pelvis, well I just had to be careful and not bump into anything. The bruises had pretty much gone, but one or two scars reminded me, just in case it slipped my mind, of what had happened. I figured there was enough to remind me though, not least the fact that I had been released into Sara's care and she was clearly not going to let me out of her sight. She had even given up her bed for me.

Rosie was impressed and concerned and happy with Daniel and she'd come up with something new that I was about to unimpress Sara with.

"I have to go to England."

"England? I don't think so. New England would have been a maybe, England is a no."

"Sara, you can come as well."

She seemed placated by this.

"Still no."

"Sara, come on. You know as well as I do that I should still be in hospital, but I'm not and I'm not for a reason. I have to figure this out and now I have to go to England to do it."

"You can't, you just can't." She thought for a second as her face pleaded with me to reconsider. My face was still painful enough for me to remain impassive without trying.

"I am going and I'd love you to come. In fact I need you to come. I'm still in pain, I can barely dress myself and it would help if you could come with me. Please."

"But what if you get into trouble over there?"

"I won't, I promise."

"You don't know that." She slapped my good arm.

"Hey, careful I need that one." I took her hand with mine and pulled her close to me. "We'll be real quick. A weekend, a long weekend. We're going to see someone called Granny Riley. How dangerous is she going to be? She may have information, but she's gonna be a little old lady, a bit deaf, grey hair, walking cane. In fact I'll probably get on really well with her." Sara smiled. "But I'm serious. I have to go and I have to see this woman and I need you to be there. I want you to be there."

The flight to England was uncomfortable, despite managing to abuse John's wealth by travelling first class. I couldn't sit still for longer than ten minutes at a time, which in turn drove Sara nuts and made us both irritable and annoyed by the time we got through baggage claim at Heathrow and on the connector up to Manchester, which, thankfully, was only a forty-five minute hop up the island. I feigned sleep, anxious to distance myself from over indulging in any more food that was forced upon us at regular intervals.

Sara also slept, resting her head on my shoulder. She looked at peace and I half wished she hadn't come. While I was ninety percent sure that Granny Riley would turn out to be a benign old woman there was a niggling feeling that the face behind the name was attached to a hulk of a psychopath who had garnered his nickname from caring for injured birds with a love and tenderness that so obviously belied his bulk and otherwise violent tendencies, British irony being what it was. I think.

Manchester was wet, but the hotel, again at John's expense, was warm and Sara and I crashed out for the night in adjoining rooms.

The morning was equally wet, but the forecaster suggested we were in for brighter spells as the day progressed, so as we set out for the heart of Liverpool and a place called Garston, I was quietly positive. Sara was just quiet.

"Midnight, I'm scared."

"Don't be. We'll be fine."

"How do you know that?"

"I have a cast on my arm which is in a sling, I have a walking cane and a face that still doesn't look or feel quite right. I know that in America this may be an invitation to add to it, but I think some forms of primitive civilizations still exist where they respect injured people."

"Oh ha ha. Sarcasm, as you well know is the lowest form of wit."

I smiled as she slumped into a silent fit of pique. She would think of other things hopefully as she drove through streets where there were more houses boarded up than had drapes hanging in the window, following the signs that seemed to be everywhere and often pointing us in entirely opposite directions.

Finally, after what seemed like an eternity of wrong turns later, we stumbled across Garston station, parked the car and asked for directions. After some translation we worked out it was just down the hill from the station. A couple of blocks in other words, make a left and there it should be.

And there it indeed was.

The red brick building was shiny with the recent rain, the grass a little greener and our hopes a little brighter.

The house number I had was a row house, terraced, with an iron gate that creaked when I pushed at it with my cane and a solid looking wooden door. The sills and windows looked new though and the buzzer chimed welcomingly.

Sara clutched my arm in a final scared good luck gesture and we shared a quick look, catching each others eye and holding the gaze until we heard the door open.

"Hello, can I help you?"

The woman was old, or certainly older than me. Graying of hair, a frail appearance but a voice that was made for the theatre or the army, strong and forthright, there to be counted and not to be taken lightly.

"Hi. Are you Mrs Riley?"

"That I am young man and who might you be?"

"Oh, I'm sorry, my name is Midnight Seyle and this is Sara Baumann."

"Hi."

"Oh I see. Well, pleased to meet you. Is there something I can help you with? After all you seem to have me at a loss. You know me, but I don't know you."

"Okay, sure, erm, do you think we could come in?"

"I don't think so. You don't look like a man an old woman should trust. There are a lot of male/female con artists working together these days. And I'm not saying that you are, but we don't get an awful lot of Americans round here, so you'll understand if I appear unwilling."

"Sure, sure." She spoke without an accent of any sort, only a hint of anything on certain words, the flattening of vowels here and there giving away her roots, other than a member of the British Empire.

She gauged us quizzically.

"What is it that you want from me?"

I stumbled over my thoughts, not quite knowing where to start.

"We've come about your grand-daughter." Sara jumped in and added a glowing smile, full of empathy and sorrow and understanding. We were in.

Cups of tea, coffee or something stronger were offered. Sara and I had coffee. Mrs Riley had a brandy.

"Purely medicinal." She offered us some. Sara declined. I agreed. I could use some painkilling. "What happened to you, young man?"

"Oh, a brawl, streetfight. Some thugs mugged me and I made the mistake of fighting back."

"Oh dear. I hope the police found them."

I grimaced. "Unlikely."

"Oh I'm sorry. I didn't mean to be nosey, but if you don't ask then you'd never find out anything, would you? My mother always used to tell me that." She took a gulp of brandy and swallowed it down, not even flinching at the taste. "Well, are you going to ask me what you came here to ask?" Both of us paused and looked at the elderly woman wondering where to begin.

"Okay, here goes. Mrs Riley are you called Granny Riley?"

She sat up and nursed her brandy closer to her chest, her eyes dancing at the recognition of the name.

"I have been. Where did you get that information?"

"Your grand-daughter's father, your son, recently passed away and he left us some, what you might call momentos. Your name came up."

"I seriously doubt that. I never had a son. My son-in-law died many years ago. About twenty, maybe twenty-one now. So I believe you're mistaken."

"But there were letters from you to this man. If he isn't your son, then how did you know him?"

"Mister Seyle I do believe you've outstayed your welcome. If that will be all I have to call my bookmaker and feed my birds." She stood and peered down at us.

"Your grand-daughter is missing," I blurted out before I could stop it. That wasn't what I wanted to say, but it was an instant shock that might get her to talk a bit more freely. "And we're trying to find her. Your name did come up in some letters from this man, a Michael Marello, and so anything that you can tell us could be vital in helping us find her. In fact we hoped she might be here." I looked around and saw no evidence of anyone approaching Cale Kline. "She isn't is she?" I added weakly.

Granny Riley sat down again, filling her glass once more as she did so. She looked more frail now. Sara jumped up and went to crouch beside her, stroking her arm and muttering soothing words like a mother does to a baby who's been stung.

"Not Katy, please not Katy."

A few minutes passed with Granny Riley in a semi state of shock, me sitting there like a spare part with nothing to do and Sara playing nursemaid and confidante as the woman began to speak.

"I made him go you know. I wanted to hurt him for what he did, how he made Mary suffer. My darling Mary. I loved my grand-daughter more than anything, perhaps even more than my daughter, which I know was probably wrong but I couldn't help it. I drove her away by telling her to make it up with him and he punished me by taking Katy."

"Who Granny Riley? Who was this?"

She looked up and saw Sara's kind eyes.

"Why do you call me Granny Riley?"

"It suits you."

Both women smiled. I watched from across the room. Sara knelt down beside the chair as Granny Riley finished her brandy and held her glass a fractionally unsteadily as Sara poured her another. I wanted to reach across and tell her not to fill it too full in case it got the old lady too drunk. But I didn't.

"They'd been fighting a lot, just shouting mainly, but once he'd hit her."

"Who hit who?"

"Gordon of course. Gordon hit Mary." She looked at us incredulously as though we were meant to know this already. She sighed realising she'd have to start from the beginning.

"Mary is my daughter. Gordon was her husband. They'd been fighting, most couples do at some point. I know I did with Gregory. Anyway, one week it had been really awful and Mary had come to me and asked to stay. I of course let her, but tried ever so hard to make her go back to him. I didn't want her to be one of those modern marriages that split up and ended in divorce and recrimination and a mess for everybody and a nightmare for the children. But while I told her to go back to him she wept and wept and said she couldn't and she wouldn't and she was going to leave him and me and go to Australia on one of the last subsidised ships.

Of course I didn't believe her, I didn't want to believe her, but the way she screamed at him I suppose I couldn't blame her. I don't think I could have put up with it every day, every week.

Anyway, this one day he came home from work at lunchtime fuming about something. He stormed round the house slamming things here and there, breaking cups, plates, throwing things and screaming at Mary. I was next door with old Mrs Bewes, but I could hear every word they yelled. I remember just turning scarlet. I mean what must the old woman have thought. Actually she was quite deaf so I don't think she heard a word, but anyway.

Then it went all quiet, and I could hear Mary sobbing and pleading with him, then I heard a muffled thump and then it went quiet again until I heard the door slam and then Gordon drove away some ten minutes later.

I went home immediately and Mary was there curled in a corner weeping silently. She just looked at me, almost in terror, then she ran past me and upstairs only to return a few minutes later with a bag over her shoulder.

She told me she was going to Australia and if I loved her at all not to tell Gordon where she'd gone. She kissed me on the cheek and walked out.

I didn't even go to the door. That was the last I saw of my daughter."

Sara was almost in tears at the story, wiping her eyes carefully so as not to smudge her mascara. The old woman looked excited and saddened as she finished, staring into the middle distance more and more and talking to us less and less.

As she began again she turned her face back to Sara.

"Of course Gordon came home that night ready for war....."

"Where is she, where is my wife? Where is she?"
Granny Riley sat serenely at the kitchen table.
"I don't know."
"Yes, you bloody do. Where is she?"

Last Train to Midnight

His face was angry and red and pressed very close to hers.

"I don't know." She managed to eke out with slightly less conviction.

"You evil interfering bitch. Where has she gone? And if you don't tell me I'll do to you what I did to her? Where is she?"

"She's gone."
"Where?"
"I can't..."
"Where?"
"A....."
"America?"

Granny Riley felt a small smile of satisfaction creep between her fears as she nodded her assent.

"I knew it. I knew she was up to something and you probably put her up to it, didn't you? Didn't you? America, eh? Well, fine she can run away, but I'll find her, and you can watch while I destroy her as well. I'm not finished with you." Gordon slammed the door only to reappear seconds later. "Where's Katy?" Granny Riley sat up, suddenly aware that she had not noticed whether Mary had Katy with her or not. If she had then the baby was in the bag. If not then darling Katy was still upstairs, hopefully fast asleep.

Her eyes flicked to the stairs to be met with a brief cry which wafted hauntingly down to them.

"Still here then? And you didn't know? Well, we'll see how she likes this. We'll see how you like this." Gordon raced up and came back holding a baby in his arms. "I'm taking Katy with me."

"No, Gordon, please, no, not Katy, not my darling Katy."

"Yes, old woman, your darling Katy. This might make you think twice before messing with me again."

The house shook as he slammed the door.

"I never saw him again either, or Katy. I never heard from either him or my daughter again. But I did get two letters. One from Australia and one from America from people I had never heard of.

The one from America said that a girl called Katy Sutcliffe was alive and well and living with this man, Michael, and his family, but as he was not making any more trips to England then if I wanted her back I was to go to America. I couldn't go, but I kept in touch. It was probably for the best.

From Australia I received a letter from a lady called Anna which said a woman named Mary Sutcliffe was alive and well and working on a farm in a small township on the western side of the country. Again I wrote back and said there was bad blood, but could I stay in touch with this Anna lady. So I did. Indeed I do."

Granny Riley had seemingly recovered her strength and had not touched any more of her brandy. She was more composed than Sara even, but then she had apparently come to the end.

"Weren't you concerned what had happened to Gordon?"

"Not initially. He was very wealthy. He had money and I'm sure he did love Katy so whatever had happened to him he would have managed to get out of it. So long as Katy was well. Besides Michael told me everything about how Gordon had become suicidally morose on the ship and jumped overboard."

I think my jaw hit the floor at that point.

"Of course I didn't believe him. Gordon was too stubborn and arrogant for that. He got in a fight and lost. Michael was good enough to pick up the human pieces."

"But what about Katy being brought up in a strange land, by strange people?"

"She was too young to know and I saw it as an adventure for her, even if only I knew about it."

"Did you tell Michael about your daughter?"

"Not really. He wasn't a great writer."

"Did you tell Anna about your grand-daughter?"

"Of course. And she told me about mine. Anna and I are the closest of friends without having actually ever met each other."

"Woah, back up a pace. This Anna told you about your grand-daughter? How is that possible?"

Granny Riley's eyes were wide.

"You mean you didn't know about Mary?"

"No, what about her? We've only seen the American side of things."

"Oh good lord. Mary got on the boat to Australia knowing she was pregnant. At least hoping she still was pregnant after he had raped her that afternoon. That was why she left Katy. She knew that Gordon loved his daughter like a real father does and because she knew she was pregnant she left Katy for him. It wasn't that she didn't love Katy, but just that she didn't want Gordon to follow her and she was a fair person. If he had something he loved and it was after all his daughter as well then he would be less prepared to chase her. She had no faith in me holding out for very long."

"So Cale has a sister?"

"Who?"

"Sorry, Kate."

"Yes."

"Do they know about each other?"

"I don't know. I never told Michael about her, as I said he wasn't a great writer and I wasn't in the habit of gossiping for the sake of it, but Anna knew about Kate. Whether Anna mentioned Kate, that I don't know."

"What is her sister called?"

Searching History: Greece.

The name had meant nothing to me, but the whereabouts of Anna was a useful piece of information that could prove of some benefit, although as we left and headed back to the car I sensed that Sara was itching to say no. I remained silent and didn't give her the option, pretending to think hard about our next move.

"The mysterious disappearence of up and coming movie star Cale Kline has only just come to light after the studio involved in producing what was to be her latest movie contacted Los Angeles police after almost two weeks without any word from her. Miss Kline was due to start shooting at the beginning of last week, but when she didn't show up on day one a replacement was swiftly moved in in order to cope with the tight shooting schedule. So far the police have no leads...."

Sal pressed the volume down and turned to the other two people in the room.

"Alix, we have to let her go."

Alix scowled at him, but nodded in a conciliatory gesture.

"I know, I know. We sure she knows nothing?"

"Yes. She thinks Marello is her father, she thinks she is an American, she thinks she now has no family, apart from Barclay."

Alix screwed up her face, registering something which could have been defeat.

"Okay. I'm not shooting tomorrow, they're doing other stuff so I've got an audition in the morning. If you drop her outside the studio then I'll see what I can do."

As I had predicted Sara was less than happy about my next arrangements, but she didn't shout for too long and finally gave in gracefully after I told her to treat it as a holiday to a part of the world she'd never been before.

I obviously hadn't planned to stay in Europe much longer than I had to, but after Granny Riley had been willing to talk and help us out then I had to go and find out the rest, just to satisfy my curiosity.

The hotels carried MTV and CNN so we managed to keep up with the breaking news on the newly discovered missing starlet that I was looking for. And I was having no luck.

I knew that Cale wouldn't be in Greece as she knew nothing about that side of her family, but Anna was going to enlighten me before I flew home.

The old lady perched her bifocals on the end of her nose and flicked through the book. She could never remember the code. Finally she found it, dialled and waited an eternity whilst she was connected. The lines were not great at the best of times. Eventually the call clicked through and immediately there was someone on the other end.

"Anna?"

Last Train to Midnight

The address that the Englishwoman had given us was correct, but Anna was not there. We were given other directions and headed out into the sunlit Greek countryside. Sara slept a lot, I guess some of the jet lag catching up with her, which was fine by me. It had been almost a week since we left the States. As much as I'd tried to persuade her she'd like Greece and to treat it as a break she wasn't pleased by us having to come here. I don't think that she was the adventurous sort.

In between watching the empty roads ahead of me, the green and grey mountains to the right and the ocean to the left, I watched her.

Her dark hair blew bewitchingly round her face as she slept, making her more angelic, her lips were slightly parted and her hands lay in her lap, clasped together gently. I couldn't say when I'd first really fallen for her, but now I found it hard to be without her. I had needed her to come on this trip with me because I was still very fragile with bones healing all over the place, but I had actually wanted her to come as well. I enjoyed the time I spent with her and I sensed that she felt the same way, although being a guy this could just as equally be wrong. I wasn't great at judging the fairer sex.

She breathed into life and caught me watching her. She smiled a warm encouraging smile which I returned.

"You okay?"

She nodded. "Watch the road."

We came to the house and as we stepped out of the car we both held our breath and looked at the pure white palace we had stumbled across.

It looked huge from the road at least, deceptively large I thought as we drove up to it, set in amongst the vineyards, looking over the sea. It's three levels rose into the blue sky, the walls whiter than white, newly erected and yet to be weatherbeaten.

We got no anwer at the front and walked round to the back. Here the middle and top floors had large balconies and the ground opened out onto a deck which then had a path running down some steps to a pool some twenty yards away, again surrounded by terrace with loungers strewn round under the only trees for miles that didn't grow olives or grapes.

The pool was paler than the sea beyond, but just as still, apart from a few ripples caused by the brown body which swam up and down.

Sara and I shared looks and picked our way down to the poolside.

We stood until the woman swam back to our end and noticed us. If she was surprised she didn't show it, but floated back to the steps and climbed out. She wrapped herself in a towel and padded over to us.

She eyed me up and down and did the same with Sara as she approached, then held out her hand.

"Hello. I am Anna. You must be Mister Seyle and Miss Baumann. Can I get you a drink? Carlos should be back in a short time, he's just gone into town, but I'm sure we can find something. Come."

The inside was simple, terracotta tiles virtually throughout, simple wooden based furniture, mosquito nets over all the beds in all the bedrooms. The refrigerator was packed with food and drinks, many drinks, bottles of water, fruit juice, wine. Anna poured three glasses of juice and we went to sit on the deck immediately outside of the back door.

"What is it that I can do for you?" I must have looked shocked because she continued. "I don't believe in wasting time Mister Seyle. You have come for information on Katy's sister and their mother. I know that. What can I tell you?"

"Erm, Anna, I don't know what Mrs Riley..."

"Granny Riley. No-one ever called her Mrs."

"Sure, okay. I don't know what Granny Riley told you, but if you're willing then we'd like to clarify a few points concerning the girl and her mother."

"Certainly. Granny said that the sister, Katy, is currently missing."

Sara coughed.

"Yes, that's true."

"Well, Mister Seyle, I will try to give you help."

"Erm, thankyou."

I tried to organise my thoughts in an instant of a second, but they were still swirling from the fact Anna was expecting us. I wasn't sure though in amongst everything that I was surprised. If Anna and Granny Riley spoke over the years concerning the girls then of course they were going to alert one another if anyone came snooping round digging for information. Although to be fair I hadn't had to do a lot of digging.

"Okay, then I guess I'll start with how you came to know them?"

"When they arrived in Australia, well, I should say when Mary, God rest her, arrived in Australia, she knew she was pregnant, but she wasn't expecting for a few months, so she managed to buy a farm, money taken from her husband I think, and she set herself up with some help from locals who were only too willing to help put their ailing community back together.

Anyway, when she have the baby she puts an advert in local paper for a nanny to help. Shortly before she arrive in Australia my husband die and leave me a wealthy woman. He ran restaurants.

Anyway, I am doing nothing and at the time I was on the edge of moving back here to what family I have. But I decide to stay and help. So while Mary was running herself into grave by running farm, I look after baby and watch her grow up and love her almost like my own.

Of course I do not blame Mary, I could see that she love doing her own thing, but it mean that I grew perhaps too much in love with the child."

She dabbed at her eyes and took a moment before finishing. "I think that is it really. The rest are details for which I don't think you have any need. Am I wrong?"

"No. No I don't think so. Mary died you say?"

"Yes, when the girl was, oh I don't know, not so long ago twenty I think."

"And you returned here?"

"A couple of years before."

I was making mental notes, knowing Sara was doing the same so we could compare later.

"Have you seen her recently?"

"Yes, a month or two ago. She was on her way to America."

I sat up and knocked the table, making the drinks sway precariously in the glasses.

"I'm sorry. Did you say Alice was on her way to America?"

"Alice? Why did you call her that?"

"I'm sorry, what?"

"Alice? You called her Alice."

I looked at Sara hoping I hadn't made a horrible mistake.

"Yes. That is her name, isn't it?"

Once more Anna looked saddened by the revelation, although if she had brought her up then why was she so upset by me using her name?

"Yes, yes, it is her name. But I am the only one who still calls her that."

"Why?" I was clearly missing something.

Anna fixed me with a hard glare, searching my face to be sure I wasn't trying to take her on in any way. Her eyes seemed strangely empty even when filled with tears. I felt a shiver run down my spine.

"She has changed her name. I knew her and will always know her as Alice, but now she has changed into Alix."

Explanations.

Alix watched as the cab pulled up alongside the sidewalk, and the bedraggled blonde with an unwashed face and greasy hair was pushed, blinfold, onto the concrete. She waited until the cab pulled away then came out from behind the gate of the company next door and walked along as if she was just out for a stroll.

As Alix approached Cale pulled the material away from her face, took stock of her whereabouts and stood up.

"Oh my god, it is isn't it? I mean you are aren't you? Oh I'm a big fan. Oh my god, you're not auditioning too are you? Oh that would be so cool."

Alix took hold of Cale's shoulders and looked into a frightened, bewildered, familiar set of eyes.

"W-what?"

"Auditioning? Reading? Why, what do you call it?"

"W-what?"

"Come on. I mean though, I have to say, and don't take offence, but you don't look too great. Can I help you get cleaned up? We've got a few minutes. Here." They pushed through the revolving door and dived into the nearest washroom, Alix pushing Cale ahead of her. Cale went with it, not knowing where she was, but thinking that anywhere would be great right now instead of that lock up.

"Here, drop your head. That's right." Alix pushed the water on full blast and soaked Cale's hair before squeezing a handful of soap from the dispenser. "I know it's not ideal, but it might just get some of that grime out. What have you been doing? Here, take your jacket off." Cale was tugged out of her clothes and Alix washed her as thoroughly as Cale would allow. "You okay? I mean you don't say much? Wow, you're in great shape. I wish I was a gym bunny, but it costs and I don't have time, trying to hold down a job and audition in between an' all, but one day. Did you ever find that? I bet with a rich husband though you've not really had a problem like that."

"You think?"

"Oh god you speak. I was beginning to think you'd gone mute there for a while. You okay now?" Alix handed her some paper towels with an 'I know' shrug.

Cale nodded and brushed her hair out, pulling at the knots and tangles that had accumulated. She slipped awkwardly back into her clothes, knowing they looked filthy and probably smelled the same, but having no choice.

"Thanks."

"Hey no problem."

"No really, thanks a lot." Cale shook Alix's hand as she felt her composure coming back with each droplet of water that dripped off her hair.

"Are you auditioning? I mean if you are then you know, if we could do it together, then it might make more of an impact, you know?"

Cale hesitated, not feeling like doing anything but going home and having a long relaxing soak, but looking at the face in front of her she agreed.

"Sure. Remind me what the part is again?"

"Oh excellent, I know we'll nail it. Okay, the story is about these two best friends since like forever, who fall for the same guy...."

Sara was delighted as we touched down back on American soil, or rather tarmac. I was perturbed, but relieved that everything had gone so smoothly, worried that it had gone too smoothly, but hoping that I could now piece all the bits together and find Cale and go back to being a dead beat private dick with no money and a drinking problem.

Okay, maybe not.

"And the breaking entertainment story at the top of the hour is the reappearence of starlet Cale Kline. Miss Kline disappeared from the set of Thicker Than Blood over two weeks ago with no explanation and no message. The FBI were called in earlier this week, but now they are expected to leave the investigation. Miss Kline was seen this morning with, amazingly, the actress who is rumoured to have taken her place on Thicker Than Blood, young Australian Alix Mercer, going into Paramount studios almost arm in arm. Sources inside the studio will not confirm why they were there but it is acknowledged that the director, Steve Leibowitz, and his producers including the Pape/Casey team responsible for last years smash hit Cool as Ice, have been in the studio putting finishing touches to the cast and script for My Guy, their next collaboration. Kline and Mercer looked friendly, but if they're going head to head then don't expect to see them together much in the next few days.

Moving on now....."

Rosie was delighted to see us and threw her arms round both of us as we walked through the door into Daniels store.

Sara, finally, was accepting Rosie and hugged her back, making sure she had one arm round my waist, just to feel reassured.

"Hey Rosie, how's life in the store? Where's Daniel?"

"Gone out. He went a while ago. Not come back yet."

"Are you here by yourself then?"

"Sure am." She lifted her sweatshirt to show me her tee underneath. Across it the message 'I'm in charge' was emblazoned in bright red letters. She seemed insanely proud.

We chatted round for a bit, or at least I did. Sara dived upstairs for a shower. Rosie was enjoying herself and was learning a lot real quick, so Daniel told me when he came back from wherever he'd been.

"Hey Dan, I'm not sure about leaving her by herself, you know?"

"Hey, back off Midnight. You ain't here. You know nothin' man. She cool, an' she good dammit. She real quick and she help me more'an you never did."

I took the point and quit while I was vaguely ahead.

I said my farewells, shouted one to Sara, and headed off to see John.

Who, I'm pleased to say, was looking more like his own self. Still a little pale and a little lacking in bulk than when I first met him, but he had more color to his cheeks and he had more of the go get em attitude back in his walk and talk.

"Ah, Midnight Seyle, where have you been?" His voice had an edge to it.

"I have been to London, but the Queen ain't there."

He didn't get the joke. Don't blame him.

"Want to know where I've been?"

I shrugged. "Sure."

"Well, first I was in the Caribbean..." I looked up sharply. Gates had a smug grin on his face. John saw the look of discomfort that shot across my face and continued, warming to his theme. "...lovely part of the world, full of secrets and surprises that you just don't expect. Ones from your best friend, ones from your wife and even ones from your employees who are actually paid to tell you things. Really fascinating part of the world.

Then, you know I came back here, to the loving arms of my lying wife and find that she's disappeared without trace. No-one seen her, no-one knows where she is. Employees promise to find her. Why would she be in England? I wondered to myself, but hey, they know best.

And finally I go to LA to try and find her myself, only for her to reappear, mysteriously, without any warning, without anyone seeing her walk back into society, and carry on as if nothing had happened. So I come home, the Feds go home and nobody is apparently any the wiser because nobody in this fucking world has seen her for the past three weeks."

His face was red, his veins throbbing in his forehead and I could see them close up as his face was only an inch away from mine.

"What happened to your face?" He looked me up and down. "And your arm?"

I thought he was going to go through my entire body, but he didn't and seemed to slip back into shouting mode. "So? Say something?"

"Erm....."

"Erm is right Mister Seyle. Erm is very, very accurate. I pay you to do a job. Like I pay Gates, like I pay my employees at the office, at the restaurants. I pay you. I do not pay you to shoot off to Europe when you feel like it."

"John...?"

He turned and walked away. "What? I suppose you have some sort of prissy explanation for all this, huh? Go on then, try me."

I stood up straight and put a bit of distance between us. Gates hadn't moved a muscle while John was losing it, but now he did and left the room silently.

"Okay, okay…" I breathed out heavily, trying to make it sound like I was calming down, but inside I felt like running at high speed in the same direction as Gates. "…John…" Saying his name gave the whole situation a friendlier aspect. I hoped. "…I'm sorry about the Caribbean. But I had to be there and I had to see the letter, or rather I had to see what was in the box.

You see after Marello, and after being so close to Marello when he was killed, I had certain documents that pointed to details which nobody knew about. Certain things which only a few people knew. Marello knew what was going on as soon as I found him, and he knew that Firetti was going to come after him in the same way that he came after you. But with one difference. Firetti was never going to kill you."

"Yeh right, tell that to the judge."

"Seriously. He was threatening you and he may have used a bit of violence, but I don't believe he was ever really going to kill you. He wanted Marello."

"Why?"

"Because Marello was Family."

"Family?"

"Yes. Not like blood relations an all, but you know Italian Families." John nodded. "Marello had let them down, Firetti thought he'd stolen from him and that was ultimately unacceptable to Firetti and Marello knew it."

"So he killed himself?"

"In a way. He had you and a few others fooled into thinking he was dead, Graziani was another, but something didn't quite add up. Remember when I asked you about him there was a slight hesitation. You weren't convinced. And so it worked. Marello changed his name and checked into a retirement complex in the sun, away from most of the New York life he'd known. But his daughter, or the girl who believed she was his daughter wouldn't leave him and he found he couldn't live without her either.

Which is sort of where I come in. When you thought Cale was having an affair some of the time she was away on auditions and some of the time she was meeting her Pops in Florida. She may or may not have known that you and Marello had been involved, but that doesn't matter one way or the other, except maybe in your mind, but it really doesn't."

The look on John's face showed he wasn't quite ready to believe everything just yet.

"So getting back to my original question, why were you in England?"

"Hang on, hang on, I'm getting there. The point now is what Marello has concocted with his will and the monies he left here there and everywhere.

Obviously the box was for you, and I don't know if you were actually at the reading or not..."

"No, I wasn't."

"...okay, but I know that there were other accounts. I don't know who for, though I could guess, and I don't know where, but that's sort of irrelevant."

"Who are they for Midnight?"

I agonised for a while, but it wasn't going to make any odds one way or the other. John's letter had told him that Cale had money somewhere and the other was the only other piece in the puzzle.

"Cale and Firetti."

"Why? Okay, maybe Cale, if she was his daughter..."

"She wasn't his daughter."

"What? Whatever. Anyway, okay maybe Cale, but why Firetti? If the son of a bitch was going to kill him anyway why did he leave him some money?"

"I think because ultimately he felt guilty about how he'd made his money. He took the land when he was in temporary charge of the Family, made millions off it through you and when the day came he planned to give it all back."

"But why wait? Why couldn't he just write Firetti a check?"

"Because he also didn't want Cale involved. If he paid Firetti off too early then he risked being pumped for more, maybe with Cale as an unwanted bait. By waiting until Firetti needed it, until Firetti was so eaten up by what Marello did however many years ago, Marello made sure that Cale didn't become a factor. Firetti was gunning for Marello. Marello knew it and accepted it. He was playing everybody for a long time John."

"Okay, whatever you say. But was he then going to hand over his life story to some random person like yourself who just happened to be in the room at the right time, or was he going to leave it to Cale or me or Firetti to work out after he died?"

I shrugged. "I guess we'll never know."

John went and sat behind his desk, playing with his pen, tapping it on the top impatiently.

"Okay, so why were you in England again?"

"Alright. Oh, where is Cale by the way?"

"I have no idea other than in LA. It was on the news a couple of hours ago. She just walked into Paramount this morning, large as life. She hasn't even called me yet." There was a definite edge of bitterness and anger lingering around his words.

"Really? And you have no idea where she's been for the last however long it's been?"

"No I don't. I don't know, the FBI don't know, LA cops don't know. No-one fucking knows. It's an absolute shambles and when she gets in touch or home, if she ever does, then she'd better have a damn good excuse."

"Or what John?"

He shot me a look that would surely have killed me on the spot if such things were possible.

I glanced at my watch.

"Shit, sorry John got to fly. I promised Sara...sorry."

I turned on my heel and left quickly, too quick for Gates who closed the door serenely after he had stopped me slamming it.

I hadn't promised Sara anything, but I didn't want to reveal everything just yet and I had other stuff to chew over.

And I had to see Jason Bornville once more. If, of course, he would see me after the, erm, misunderstanding over the Caribbean. He really had to.

Sara and Rosie and Daniel were all in the store and doing various things. Daniel and Sara were talking, Rosie serving the one or two customers who were lined up by the counter.

"Hey Midnight, how was it?" Sara came forward, anxiously looking for further signs of physical violence, then relieved as she found none she took my arm and just held it as I stopped in the middle of the aisleway.

"He was fine. A little over the top about Cale and the whole Caribbean thing, but he seemed to listen and take on board what I tried to explain to him. At least he was prepared to do that, I guess." Sara and Daniel nodded as if they completely understood. Rosie giggled. "I'm not sure where that leaves Cale now she's returned, or us. I figure John's not going to hear from Firetti again so then that part is done. Cale will have some explaining to do, but apart from that then she is in the clear and a very rich woman in her own right."

"What about Alix?"

I looked at Sara and shrugged. Alix was the joker in the pack. I knew she was in America, but not why. I didn't know where. But she was not top of my list.

"I think Jason can help us."

"How Midnight? He's not going to see you for one thing and even if he does then he's not going to be the most receptive or giving audience. He's done his job, so he's got nothing left to give that someone somewhere doesn't know."

I sighed and looked at my shoes. This was all true. This was all true in the very real sense that my trip would be wasted and my job had come to an end. "Cale doesn't know." I offered more in hope than in anything else.

"Midnight you're clutching at straws cuz. You have run out of work and you're clutching with a very tiny hand at a very small straw. You have finished. You can go back to your liquor and your headaches and your hangover cures." Daniel turned away chuckling to himself.

"He's right Midnight, come on leave it. Get on with something else. When Barclay spreads the word you'll be swamped with work, too much that you just can't handle it." She paused and looked up into my eyes. "By yourself," she added, holding my arm a little tighter. I smiled down at her.

"We'll see. We'll see."

Firetti's mouth was screwed into a knot of anger as the frown he had worn all morning turned into a grimace and finally exploded into rage as he stood and hurled the chair across the room, closely followed by the table. The papers that were on it fluttered to the thick carpet and were blown around from the open window on the seventeenth floor accountants.

The man in charge looked at those around him and waited, gathering his composure and his breath as he threatened each and every one with a look that carried nuclear missiles from under his eyebrows.

"Who is this woman? How does she know what I have lost? And why now do I have to go and get it back?" Nobody spoke and nobody dared to move. "Well? Nothing. Not a thing from each one of you. That is pathetic. Five million dollars is what Marello gave to us for what was rightfully ours anyway, the Family's. Five million. A fair price? I thought so. Luca, you thought so. Bernie, you thought so. Five million. It's okay and it is what Marello offered us, as is his right, God rest his soul. Until this arrives in Freddie's hands saying that the land is worth ten times that from someone I've never heard of." He glared at them again. Each man shuffled his feet and stared at the most interesting bit of carpet he could find. "Why is this woman doing your jobs? Why is it she who is telling me what I should be hearing from the likes of you and you and you?" He accentuated the point by jabbing an irate finger at the chest of every man. "But now I look like a laughing stock. The other bosses are laughing out loud at me for accepting five million for something worth fifty. I've gone soft. I'm small time if I can't get a dead man to pay up." Still no-one made a sound as they endured the tirade. "So now I have to go and get my entitlement. My entitlement." He walked to the door and turned as he got there. "And hopefully one of you ignorant rent boys will come up with some way of doing it."

Alix and Cale squealed over the bubbles as they went in all the wrong places. The celebratory champagne for nailing the two lead roles in the audition was going down well although Alix was convinced Cale was still on autopilot. She had performed superbly, but it had been just like switching on a light. Once the scene got underway Cale had been transformed and sparks had flown between them. But before and after she was almost zombie like in her approach and appearance. She jumped at any little sound, she was constantly looking around her and picking at her clothes. The champagne had had some effect and Cale was now acting as though she'd been drinking all day, but something was not right.

Alix was desperate for her to snap out of it. Sal and Fran had circled the block a couple of times, but Alix had waved them on again. She didn't want to leave Cale and she didn't want Cale to see her with Sal and Fran for obvious reasons. Maybe if she got her completely drunk then she wouldn't notice, but that might take too long and involve money Alix didn't really have to hand. Thank god for visa.

"No."

Jason Bornville looked directly at me and uttered the word I knew he would.

"Jason…"

"Which part of no don't you understand?"

"Now there's no need to resort to kindergarten humor."

His face went red, with rage or embarrassment I couldn't and wouldn't say.

"Mister Seyle, I think I've made my position perfectly clear."

"You have, Jason, but I think you should know that your actions could put people in grave danger."

He paused and turned back to me.

He studied me for a few seconds, evaluating if I was serious or not. He decided not.

"I don't believe you."

"I am very serious. If you don't tell me..."

"I can't tell you."

"You don't know what I'm asking."

"I still can't tell you."

I sighed heavily. The death threat option may have come too early.

"Jason, we are in a soundproof room, only me and you and all I want to know is figures. You don't have to tell me who gets what, but I need to know how much is involved. And I meant what I said about putting lives in danger."

He sat down and stood up again. He paced the room scratching his face. He looked at me, out of the window and back at me.

"I could be jailed."

"Who's going to tell? Not you and not me. Who's to know? I only want the figures. One in the box and one in the account."

"I don't know the one in the box."

"Sure you do."

"No I don't. We take them in, but they're private. We don't know, we're not meant to know. And the account is only part of the final figure. There are investments, share options. A total can't be precise. I can give you a ballpark?"

I had to cut my losses.

"Sure?"

He ummed and aaahed and tortured himself unnecessarily for a few more minutes before giving me a figure which was on the high side of my estimate. The very high side.

"And the box?"

He shrugged.

"I really don't know, but from what he left and the size of the box, three, maybe four." He threw me a half smile, offering grudging defeat, before slumping into a chair and holding his head in his hands. I patted him on the shoulder.

"No-one knows Jason. No-one knows. You don't tell, I don't tell."

Alix held the phone for Cale as she drunkenly fumbled with the numbers, pressing them with the dexterity of an elephant. She was doing it from memory and as Alix waited, phone in hand, frustration on her face, as Cale made the call Salvador and Francis stood outside and made their own call.

"John darling, there you are. Where are you? No don't tell me, you're on the phone." Cale giggled and almost fell over. Alix pulled her back up and Cale steadied herself once more. "John, I'm fine, I really am. I met a lovely woman, a lovely friend called..." The name was lost as Alix snatched the phone away, returning it immediately as Cale rambled on. "...but I'm fine and I'm in Los Angeles and I got another part in another movie. Isn't that great?"

"Cale, where are you?"

"I'm in Los Angeles sweetie."

"I know that, but why are you there and where have you been for the last month?"

Cale looked confused and a little alarmed by the demandingly cold tone from the other end of the line.

"I've been here John. I mean you knew that I've been here, I mean I told you I've been here...in Los Angeles. John, I'm in Los...Los...Los...oh god I'm gonna throw up."

"Well call me when you've decided where you've been and when you're sober."

"Salvador, how are things? It is good to hear from you."

"Things are well. Alix is fine and holed up inside right now. How are you?"

"You should know better than to ask, but I can see your concern is sourced by a desire for your money. Don't worry you will get it. In fact I may get someone to deliver it personally. Don't worry."

"I am not worried madam, but I just like to make sure we are working on the same, how you say, playing pitch."

"Oh we are. But I have something else for you...."

The line died and Sal looked at it with a smile of satisfaction.

The motel room was small and it smelled. I could have afforded something better on my expenses, but I figured that after blowing Europe on John then the least I could do was show his credit card some respect. Better late than never.

ESPN was on showing some college basketball. I had a box of pizza which was going down smoothly, washed down with some cheap scotch which was going straight to my senses. How quickly you get unused.

Bornville had put some numbers on what I basically had worked out.

Marello had left money and investments and god knows what else to Cale, his daughter. She was a multi millionairess many times over now, in her own right without John's considerable help.

Also to Firetti there had been a substantial amount which, from the sound of it was similar to what Marello had invested in the land initially.

And nothing for John. Except the letter which had blown his personal relationship into small pieces and stuck them all over his life. Extreme, but cost and actually effective.

Duaine Corness made a three pointer and high fived his way back down the court. He would go number one in the draft and was expected to earn upwards of $2 million for his rookie season. Much more with endorsements.

Now I had to find Alix.

I figured Cale was still in LA and would probably remain there until she made up with John, which from the way he had been talking may not be as soon as she thought.

John would be busy doing whatever he was doing. He may go to Cale, but after trailing over to the other side of the country once only to find nothing then I didn't think he was the sort of man to try again. Especially as Cale had materialised, apparently unharmed.

Firetti was gone.

And that only left me. Well, me and Sara. Well, me and Sara and Rosie.

I didn't know how it was going to work, but I had a feeling in my body for Sara that hadn't happened too often in my life. If she felt the same then I hoped that we could perhaps make something work. For a while at least.

Rosie I cared for, only because I felt I perhaps owed her some sort of stability after getting her out of Firetti's hands, but also because I think she cared for me. I had been a sad lonely drunk when we met, but now, partly due to how she had made me go for ice cream rather than beer, I was not a drunk. Twelve baby steps, one day at a time is how the program teaches it, but I'd done 'em all and now faced alcohol with the sort of indifference you usually reserve for TV shows which fill the time before your favourite show comes on. If it was there I took it, but I didn't look for it or even want it any more.

I had an urge to call Sara.

The phone rang a couple of times before it was answered.

"Midnight?"

"How'd you know?"

"Turn on Entertainment Tonight."

"What? Sara, what are you..."

"Midnight, turn on Entertainment tonight, come on. You have to see this. You'll want to see this."

"Okay, okay." I flipped over and got a Cheetos commercial. "You want me to watch a Cheetos ad? Sara, what's going on?"

"Wait, wait."

The line stayed silent until the commercials faded and the smiley faced presenter came back to haunt the viewers.

"Welcome back. Now after weeks of mystery, no word on her whereabouts Cale Kline finally emerged yesterday into the LA sunshine. Seen walking into Paramount with a friend it was announced earlier today, exclusively to Entertainment Tonight, that she had been given a lead role in the next Steven Soderbergh movie, as yet untitled. Equally mysterious is the fact that her friend was none other than Alix Mercer, the relatively unknown Australian who took Klines role in the currently shooting Thicker than Blood, and who has, extraordinarily, also been offered a major role by Soderbergh and Paramount executives. Mercer is taking Hollywood by storm after her debut in Damian Cross' Australian hit Making A Move recently wowed audiences at the Sundance Film Festival. Her star would certainly seem to be in the ascendent. Martin, any further word?"

The camera cut to a still of Cale and what I presumed was Alix in a bar. It was grainy and it could have been anyone, but the voiceover from Martin suggested it was Cale Kline and Alix Mercer celebrating.

I flicked the mute.

"Sara, I'm going to LA."

"I'll meet you there."

LA was steamingly hot and unrelentingly busy. Cars and cabs were nose to tail from International to downtown as seemingly everybody hit LaLaLand.

Sara pulled me through check-in and we both collapsed as we finally hit the beds in the only room left in the block. A twin with no shower and a view of the fire escape across the street.

I couldn't sleep much, but instead listened to the night-time music of sirens and shouts that drifted in on the warm breeze which fluttered the net at the open window. Sara in the other bed a few feet away seemed to take no notice, occasionally adjusting her position, once plunging her head under the pillow. Maybe she did hear, but chose to ignore.

I slipped out from under the sheet and stood at the window. A blue siren swept down the street below me, wheels screeching at the corner as it struggled to make the turn, then dimmed in volume as it raced down the next street.

Thoughts fogged my brain. If I found Alix and she knew, what then? Only Cale and her could affect some sort of relationship. If they wanted to. Alix and Cale looked friendly enough in the pictures from TV, but the camera always tells half truths, leaving the real stories for those that bought tickets for the live performance. And there was no reason for Cale to suspect Alix as anything other than an acting adversary. Names have been changed to protect the relatives.

Alix knew. There was no doubt about that and clearly she was in America, Los Angeles, Hollywood to further her ambitions, but if getting close to Cale was one of them then she had succeeded already. But my mind played on and on that there was more to it. There was no reason, but I couldn't get rid of the thought.

Sara turned over again and hummed as she did so. A warm contented hmmm of deep sleep wrapped up and closeted away from the cold world outside. Safe and warm in bed.

I watched her for a while, first from by the window and then sitting on the edge of my bed. I just sat and watched her chest rise and fall under her white t-shirt as she lay on her back. Then she turned to face me, her lashes on her cheek, eyes closed tightly, lips slightly parted as she breathed shallowly, head resting on her forearm. She curled her legs up under the covers letting one foot drift into view. She frowned slightly in sleep and for a few moments her breathing became deeper, her eyelids fluttering as she worked her way through her dreamstate.

Her tousled hair contrasted with the white of the linen, tendrils escaped and draped themselves over her face, now at peace again. I heard my stomach rumble, trying to hide the first stirrings of lust from just below.

Sara's eyes crawled open and she stared at me without confusion, without fear, but with something else. Then her face didn't flicker at all, but she pulled the cover back.

I slid in beside her, my arm round her, feeling her bare legs against mine as we both drifted into peaceful sleep.

Despite my best intentions to get out of bed and sort my life out, or rather the lives of those involved in my life, or something similar, I stayed and held Sara and she held me and that was it. We just took turns in lying with our backs to each other and draping our arms over and round each other, just savouring the warmth and the comfort and the smoothness of skin against skin until there was no way to get around it, but I had to pee.

This seemed to break the spell. I came out and made coffee while Sara disappeared into the bathroom. Seconds later I heard her running a bath.

The coffee was not good, but it gave a little kick to the day which would have been otherwise absent.

I peeked out of the window at the shadows and the sunlit haze over the buildings that didn't reach into the dark depths of our room.

"Hey Midnight?"

"Wass up?"

"I used all the hot water."

"Shit Sara." I began, but decided it wasn't her fault. "Hey don't worry. I'll get washed up in the sink."

It went quiet. I hoped she was suffering uncontrollable guilt for making me wash in a tiny sink with lukewarm at best water.

"Hey Midnight?"

"What?" I splurged water all over the mirror, the floor, me.

"Erm...you wanna get in here?"

"Why? What's wrong? You got a spider in there?"

"No, erm, I mean you wanna get in the water?"

I wasn't sure I'd heard her right, but chanced it anyway.

"With you?"

She hesistated before answering.

"If you wanna?"

I looked at the sink and the soap resting on the surface. It wasn't even close to being a contest.

"Okay. But if I ain't looking then you ain't looking? You got a deal?"

"Sure, sure."

I walked through the door with my eyes closed and my arms outstretched and kicked the john.

"Holy shit, oh my god that fucking hurt." I hopped and held my toe, steadying myself against the wall as I rubbed some life back into my toe. I heard stifled laughter.

"I'm sorry Midnight you just looked so funny."

"You ain't s'posed to be looking."

"I'm sorry, I'm sorry."

But she couldn't help but laugh and neither could I. I opened my eyes and slumped on the floor, holding my toe and laughing until tears ran down my face in a mixture of mirth and pain. I looked up and Sara was looking right back at me, leaning on the side of the tub, chin resting on her hands. Her hair was slicked back and her face was flushed from laughing and the remnants of hot water that lapped round her body.

"You ain't supposed to be looking."

I hauled myself up and crawled over to her.

"I know, but I can't help it." She knelt up to meet me as I took her face in my hands and brought her lips to mine.

We rocked together until the water went cold, then dried ourselves on the sheets as we made love until it went dark.

"Productive day, huh?"

"I would say so."

"Me too."

Loose Ends.

Salvador stood in the middle of the room talking into his cellphone.

"He's in town with his girlfriend. Yeh, her. Okay."

Alix wandered in and threw her purse on the chair.

"Who's in town?"

For a millisecond Salvador faltered, but remembered a by line he'd caught sight of in Variety that morning.

"John Barclay. With Cale."

"Who were you talking to then?"

"Francis."

"Where is he?"

"Out in the car. Anyway what's with the questions? You had a bad day on set?"

"No, no it was cool. Just curious that's all. You always seem to be talking to people and yet you never seem to know anybody if we're out someplace."

"People I know don't go to someplace."

"Figures."

Alix slumped in a chair with a coke to her mouth.

"What is it Alix?"

She thought for a moment.

"Cale. I mean now I'm here what do I want her for? What am I after?"

"I thought money. Is this not it?"

"Yeh, I guess. But what with Making A Move doing so well and Thicker Than Blood and this other one which I'm doing with Cale for god's sake, I mean am I going to need this money?"

"But it's also for your pride, for your family, for your mother. You were made to struggle for your life and this woman got all of which half was yours. That counts for something and if you didn't believe it then you wouldn't have come to America, you wouldn't have asked me to come with you and you wouldn't be here now. You want this woman to pay for what she has which is yours."

Alix was sitting up rage and hurt blazing in her eyes.

"You're right. You are so right. When?"

"I cannot say. But the time will come and you will know it is right and you will be ready for it."

"Cale, what do you mean you can't tell me? I'm your husband, of course you can tell me?" John stood screaming at his wife who for once was cowering in a corner and not answering him back. "Or is this another of your little secrets which I won't know about until somebody leaves me a note in his will?"

"What?"

"Oh forget it. I just want to know where you've been for the last three weeks. You can tell me. I think I have a right to know. If you've been with another guy then fine, but so long as you're up front with me and you're not going behind my back and lying to me. Cale, honey, I just need to know you're not lying to me?"

"John, I'm not. I'm really not. I just can't tell you, cause I'm not really sure. I mean it seemed real, but now I think about it, oh god I don't know. If it was then fine, but it's over and I don't want to think about it."

"Well I do."

"And I said I don't." Cale stood and finally fought back in a way John was used to. Despite her still refusing at least now she was returning to normal and fighting back rather than letting the emotion wash over her. "John, you have to leave it. Just leave it alone."

"Cale, it's because I care."

"If you care, John, then leave it and me alone."

Her voice was dropped almost to a whisper. John turned on his heel and walked out.

"Seyle, where are you?"

"I'm in LA, John, where are you?

"I'm in LA also. What are you doing here?"

"I have to catch up with Alix Mercer."

"Oh right. Oh okay. Any luck already?"

"Not yet, but I'm working on it."

"Give me twenty minutes. I'll find her."

"John?"

"Yes?"

"What did you call me for?"

"Oh hell, nothing. Just wanted to let off some steam about Cale and you were the first number. I'll call you back."

Sure enough twenty minutes later my phone Beethoven'd into life.

"John?"

"Hey Midnight, how you doing? Well, doesn't matter. Alix Mercer on set at Universal tomorrow, ten a.m. Don't miss it. Gotta go."

I didn't have time to ask him how or, well, how, and part of me didn't want to know, but being a rich well connected businessmen must enable you to pull some strings. I didn't question. I rolled over and kissed Sara.

The morning was bright and for once I was up with it. Mainly, I admit, because Sara was up and in the tub early so that the hot water didn't run out. Not that it would have mattered.

But since we were up we made it to the Universal lot on time and were ushered through to where cameras, lights and people scrapped for space. It was noisy, noisier than I expected and there were people everywhere. Literally.

I stood for five minutes and watched as Alix and Owen Brock, I recognised him, stood waiting for the lights to be right, then reset after they did a take. It was amazing how quiet the set was whilst actual shooting was taking place, in total contrast to the noise and chatter when the cameras weren't rolling.

We were slightly early and even when my watch said ten-thirty and we were late I didn't care. I had only seen a couple of movie sets and it was an experience I always enjoyed. I guess not being involved made it easier to appreciate what was going on, but I think I would have enjoyed it whatever. Sara stood jammed next to me, holding my arm, in equal awe of what was going on around her.

"How can they do that with so many people watching?"

"It's not real. That's the way they look at it. It's not real."

I couldn't tell whether this satisfied her curiosity or not, but she seemed to accept it and didn't whisper anything else to me. This may have been due to the look she got from some short, scary looking bloke with a stopwatch in his hand and headphones hanging round his neck. But I didn't dare ask.

It was gone eleven when the director called a halt and asked for the next set up and we were able to get to see Alix.

Her trailer was small compared to Owen Brock's parked right next door, but it was lavish inside with everything you could want and then some.

"Hey, come on in. I'm Alix Mercer. Who do you work for?"

"I'm a private investigator. I work for myself."

"Sure. What can I help you with Mister...?"

"Seyle. Midnight Seyle. Call me Midnight."

"Okay, Midnight. And you are?"

"Sara Baumann. Pleased to meet you."

"Likewise. Anyway, what can I help you with? My agent didn't say much, something about a John Barclay?"

"Yes, yes, I'm currently...Well, that doesn't matter. But do you know Mister Barclay at all?"

"Can't say I do. But then I've not been in the country long. Is he someone I should know?"

"Well, that entirely depends..."

"Coffee?"

"Thanks."

"Depends on what?"

"Well, what line of work you're in. He's a big shot in New York, Wall Street, finance. I guess being on the other side of the country and being in movies then you probably wouldn't have run into him that often."

"Guess not."

Alix handed two coffees over.

"Unless you knew his wife?"

"He's married? Damn. Sounded like a guy a girl oughtta know, right?"

"Sure, why not." I drank some coffee and sat down next to Sara as Alix offered us seats. She sat down opposite sipping evian. "Do you know his wife?"

"Who is she?"

"Cale Kline?"

I thought that she might drop the cup for a second as she let herself be shocked by the name, but she recovered and held on to her drink.

"Yeh, sure I know Cale. Met her the other day at some audition. Seems like a nice girl. Didn't know she was married to John Barclay though."

"Learn something new, right?"

"Right."

"How well do you know her?"

"Not very. As I said I only met her last week."

"But you know about her?"

She shook her head. "How do you mean?"

I looked at Sara. This was obviously going to be hard work.

"Come on Alix, I..." Unfortunately Beethoven got in the way. "Excuse me." I climbed out of the trailer and answered the call.

"They've got Cale."

"John? What did you say?"

"They've got Cale."

"John, who's got Cale? What do you mean they've got Cale? Where?"

"Firetti. I just got a call. They want me to meet them."

"Where?"

"He wants me to pick a place. Where?"

"He's just playing with you. Let me think."

"We don't have time to think, dammit Midnight."

"Okay, okay. I know a place. There's a disused station to the south, rail link, tram link something like that. I used it years ago on some case, anyway, head out there, I'll meet you."

"Fine. You'd better be there."

I switched off and went back inside.

"We gotta go."

Sara stood. Alix didn't.

"You too."

"Me? Why me?"

"It's about Cale and John and Marello and Anna and your parents. You'll want to be there."

She stood and followed.

"Who's Marello?"

Endgame.

"They're going. Where are you?"
"With Firetti. He's on his way too."
"Stay close. Catch you later."
"He is going?"
"Yeh, he's going."
"Good. Good."

"He's going boss."
"Okay, stay well back. He doesn't need to know we are right behind him. All in good time."

"Hey, you there Fran?"
"Yeh, what's up?"
"I have a procession here."
"How many?"
"Three cars, six people."

We arrived first and took up central positions on the platform. I checked to make sure my gun was loaded, anxious it didn't come to that.
"You okay?"

Sara nodded into my chest.

"You won't get hurt will you?"

"I hope not."

"You do this a lot then?"

"No Miss Mercer, I don't. In fact this is my first time for a while, so all I can say is try to relax and it'll all be over soon enough." I didn't believe what I said and I didn't sound convincing, but maybe the words were enough. If Firetti had Cale he obviously wanted something, probably money, off John. I hoped he wouldn't freak when he realised we were all here.

I heard a car pull up.

"Okay sweetheart, here's where it ends. This is your last train, your last stop. If you wanna see tomorrow, you better hope your husband's in a generous mood." Cale's arm was pulled sharply and she stumbled into the station.

First in was Cale, shoved roughly from behind by Luca. Then Firetti.

"Where's Barclay?"

"He's on his way."

"Why are you here?"

"Protection."

"I thought you were dead?"

I waved my cane at him and held up my arm in a cast.

"Not nearly."

"I shoulda fucking killed you for Rosie you nigger son of a bitch."

"Get a life you dago wimp."

Luca was straining to be let off the leash, but Firetti shook his head almost imperceptibly, gesturing for him to plonk Cale in a dirty broken chair that sat by the tracks.

"We'll wait."

"We sure will."

Alix and Sara were sat against the wall behind me, the entrance to our right, Cale, Luca and Firetti opposite us with the tracks behind them. I leaned heavily on my stick watching Luca fidget with the gun in his belt. Firetti was motionless stood behind them.

"Firetti, you bastard, let her go!"

John half ran half staggered onto the platform away to Firetti's left, stopping as he saw who was here and the situation we were in. Luca was itching to whip his gun out, but once more Firetti placed a calming hand on his shoulder.

"No time for pleasentaries John? I thought we could get to know each other. Not as friends you understand, but more business associates."

"Whatever you want Firetti, just let her go. She has no part of this."

"Oh no no no. That's where you're wrong, John. You see she is married to you. Connection by association. Just as Mister Marello was unfortunate enough to do business deals with you so his debt passes to you, and your debt to your wife and so on."

"No, Firetti. This ends now. Let her go."

"I quite agree that this should end now. It is tiresome on my part also. But I can't let her go without some recompense." John sighed and reached into his pocket.

"Slowly, slowly. You understand our caution."

John nodded. He was only feet away from both our little camps, but bang in the middle, his back to the entrance and the serene figures who now walked in.

"Anna?"

"Mama Anna? What are you doing here?"

Alix stood and ran to her, hugging her hard.

"Patience child, patience."

John shot across to the other side, Firetti was open mouthed at the interruption, but still managed to keep Luca's trigger finger under control.

"What is the meaning of this? Who are these people?"

For some reason he looked at me. I was only too happy to oblige.

"Mister Firetti, this is Mama Anna and Mister Jason Bornville."

"Aaaah. Mama Anna I know, only through a certain letter. Mister Bornville, I believe I've had the pleasure." Firetti stepped forward and shook a shell shocked and frankly pale Jason by the hand.

"This is unreal," murmured John, now on my left. He was right though.

"Okay, now we can all sit down and tell ghost stories."

No-one laughed.

Bornville was clearly in shock and fearing for his life, Anna and Firetti were eyeing each other with looks of wrestlers as they circled the canvas waiting for the other to strike. Alix clung to Anna's arm and John and Sara watched in fascination. I tried to keep an eye on everybody, but failed miserably and Cale squirmed in her seat, held there by an increasingly agitated Luca.

"Shall we get down to some business?"

"I was trying to before you interrupted. What business do you have with any one in this rat trap?"

"You Mister Firetti and you Mister Barclay. Not for my personal gain you understand, for I am not a greedy woman, but purely for expenses."

"Expenses for what?," queried John, anxious to know who else was being paid for this little charade.

"For many years of my life."

John started laughing. "For what? For what? For many years of your life doing what? Nobody here has ever seen you before, so how can any of us owe you anything?"

Anna said nothing. Or if she did it was drowned out by two pairs of running footsteps that echoed round the concrete walls. Two athletic men hurtled into view, but pulled up in time and took up a fifth point in a now unequally sided pentagon in between Jason and myself.

Cale leapt off her seat.

"You and you!" She pointed at the two men.

"Cale, darling, you know these men?" John asked sympathetically, hoping the answer was one he didn't think it was.

"Yes. These two bastards were the ones who held me captive for three weeks."

"Did they do anything to you? Did they hurt you?"

Cale looked up at John, tears filling her eyes. "A little."

She was about to run to him when Luca slammed her back into the chair.

"I'm Francis, this is Salvador and we were only acting on our orders," piped up the smaller of the two newcomers.

"From who? Was it you Firetti?"

"No."

Everyone looked round the room and all eyes rested on Alix.

I knew why. Anna knew why and Alix knew why. Salvador and Francis had just acted on orders and Firetti and Luca didn't care much.

Cale and John traded glances and then both turned on Alix.

"Why? What the hell are you doing? Why?"

"Because she ruined my life." The room was stunned into silence. Alix burst into tears suddenly and let go of Anna's arm. She pointed at Cale. "You ruined my life."

Cale was open mouthed. So was John. Jason had just turned a shade of white I had never seen before.

"How? I've known you for a week. How could I possibly have ruined your life?"

"You took my father away from me and left me with an ill and depressed mother who could never escape what he did to her and punished herself to the day she died for it. I lived with her for so long having to hear the stories. It wasn't me screaming at night when I was two, it was her. As soon as I could walk and talk I had to take care of her. For almost twenty years I lived in the back of beyond looking after a sick woman who loved a girl I never knew existed as much as she loved the girl she could hold in her arms, and I never knew why. You took her from me better than you could have done if you'd been there." Alix wiped the tears away with her sleeve. "And you owe me."

Anna reached out for her, but Alix pulled away, standing alone now, staring at her sister.

"I never knew. I never knew," Cale repeated, "Alix, I swear I never knew."

Alix snapped.

"Well I knew about you, you bitch, I had to hear about you from the day I was born and all I've ever wanted was to be in this position and to make sure that that could never happen again."

In a blur of speed Alix pulled out a tiny pistol from under her shirt and managed to squeeze a shot off towards Cale. Instantly Luca had seen the gun he tipped Cale off the seat and pulled his gun out ready to fire back, but Salvador had got there first and wrestled the gun away from a distraught Alix.

As Alix slumped to the ground and a bullet nestled in the plastic chair guns appeared from everywhere and were pointed in a variety of directions.

Luca had one trained on Alix, Salvador on Luca, Firetti on John, Francis on Luca, John on Firetti, Anna on John, Bornville on me for gods sake. As we waited Luca eased another out from his belt and pointed it at me. Sal cocked Alix's and handed it back to her. She pointed it at Cale.

Sara was sobbing quietly behind me. I reached round and took my pistol out, looked round the faces and held it in front of me pointed to the floor.

"This won't solve anything."

"It would solve a lot of things."

"No, Firetti, it wouldn't. All it would do is end up with a lot of dead people. Look, me, you, Luca, Cale, John, Alix. I hate to say it, but if it wasn't for Luca we'd already be picking one body off the floor. This won't sort anything."

Luca shrugged and looked to Firetti for support.

"I'd give it a try."

"No," I almost screamed at him. This was already way out of control. "How about we put the guns down?" I replaced mine behind my back, tucked into my belt.

"I don't think so." Luca shook his head and adjusted his grip slightly. "I don't think so. I owe you for Rosie."

"What do you owe me? You were killing her?"

"She was mine to kill."

The room was silent at the statement. There was just nothing that could do justice to its ridiculousness. Sal adjusted his position and raised his aim slightly. I guessed he was ready to put a bullet right between Luca's eyes. I looked around. Luca was in trouble with both of Alix's guys aimed at him. Both John and I were facing two barrels. The situation wasn't looking great.

"You owe me man."

"Shut up Luca," Firetti snapped. Luca opened his mouth to argue, but thought better of it and went back to concentrating on where his arm was pointing.

"Firetti?"

The oldest man in the room shrugged and lifted his gun to the ceiling before uncocking it and sliding it back into his shoulder holster. John breathed an audible sigh of relief and turned slightly to his right so he and Anna were trading targets.

I figured Luca and the other two guys were capable enough of reading the situation so Alix was my next shot. Excuse the joke.

"Alix?"

"No." She didn't turn her head, but Sal shook his and opened his hand for me to see bullets resting there.

"Anna?"

"I want compensation."

"John?"

"I have no idea what's going down here Midnight, but I am not used to this. I mean really, shooting at each other, this kinda thing doesn't happen, does it? I'm not used to this, but until she stops aiming for me then I'm honour bound to aim right back."

"Jason, put the gun down." He scared me more than anybody cause I imagined him being a real loose cannon. One twitch and he could be off, spraying the place with bullets. And being first on his hit list I wasn't anxious to have that happen.

"No way man. You screwed me over big time. People will find out and I'll lose my job, my girlfriend, my career, my life. This is going to happen man."

"No, it's not. Put the gun down."

"No way man. You can't make me."

"Jason, you think that if you put a bullet in me then you're going to get out of here alive anyway? Look around you. There are half a dozen other people just as desperate in here to do something that they'll regret later. Most of them don't even know you, so wouldn't think for a second before putting you away. You get where I'm going, man?"

"You can't make me, this is going to happen." He was almost screaming at me now, hanging on to his last vestige of self respect as he tried to face me down in front of the gallery.

Just then Francis turned slightly to his right and placed the barrel of his gun firmly and squarely against Jason's temple. I wasn't sure about the smell of urine, but Jason dropped his gun to the floor with a metallic clatter. Fran kicked it into the centre of the group where I stepped forward, picked it up and threw it onto the tracks between Cale and John.

Cale had her gaze fixed on John, occasionally flicking her eyes to check that Alix still had her in her sights.

"Go on Cale."

Cale edged forward on the floor, causing John and Alix both to yell at her to stop. Sensibly she did. Luca edged over to her, putting one big foot next to her as a barrier so she couldn't go any further. He licked a film of sweat from his top lip.

"You touch her again man and you're dead." Salvador spoke clearly so everybody heard him and no-one was left in any doubt as to what he was going to do.

Jason dropped back and slid to the floor against a concrete pillar behind Anna. Francis turned and aimed for Luca once more. Luca's eyes were darting now, from Sal to Fran to me to Alix. A drop of sweat dripped from his brow and hit the floor.

"Boss?" Firetti said nothing.

"Alix?" She still shook her head.
"She owes me."
"A life?"
"Yes, a life."
"No, Alix, that's not true. I didn't know, I was one for fuck's sake. I was a baby, I didn't know, I didn't know."
"You think that's an excuse? It happened and I lived with the fallout. You may have been a baby but I've got no-one else to blame so you're it, sis. I'm sorry, but you are it."
"I'm sorry, I'm sorry, I'm sorry," Cale blurted out as she dissolved into tears, distracting John from Anna. John knelt down and laid his gun on the floor beside him, taking Cale in his arms.

As Cale reached up to John Luca reached down for Cale and didn't even get there. A hail of bullets threaded past each other, some ricocheting off walls as the intended targets fell leaving empty space and screams to fill the void.

Cale knelt over John wailing as she held him close, her hands covered in his blood which was flowing from a fatal head wound.

Luca lay on his back on the tracks, a bloody hole where his chest had been.

Anna lay slumped on her side, a single shot in the left side of her head.

Jason lay curled up on the floor jibbering pathetically. He would never get his suit clean.

Alix just sat watching grief flood over her sister. She was too numb to do anything.

Francis and Salvador still had their guns out, covering everybody in case there were other shots to be found and fired, sweeping the room for targets constantly.

Firetti had gone. Francis told me later that along with himself and Salvador it had been Firetti who disposed of Luca.

I was on my back trying to comfort Sara who was having trouble stopping the bleeding from my shoulder as she couldn't see through a curtain of tears. Once I was sure the shooting had stopped I passed out.

Epilogue: Six Months Later.

The shoulder, my shoulder, was still uncomfortable, but I would live. Although tying a bow-tie was proving remarkably difficult.

"Midnight, you ready yet?"

"I'm right there."

The limousine was waiting outside and already held Cale and Rosie, both dressed in stunning new designer dresses, fresh from their afternoon shopping trip. Daniel had moaned to begin with, but then found out that Cale was springing for both so encouraged them to go spend, spend, spend. "After all, you wanna look good for the premiere."

And that's where we were headed. Thicker Than Blood's premiere starring Owen Brock and Alix Mercer in a new Howard Martin film from Universal studios. Much of the subsequent box office depended on such nights.

I'm not sure why Alix had invited us, but I wasn't going to pass up the opportunity of getting dressed up and spending an evening with those more famous than myself. Okay, I could go to San Diego zoo and do that, but you catch my drift on that one....

Rosie was all smiles. I had given her my old place after I moved in with Sara. It was over the store and Daniel could keep an eye on her. She had complained for a bit, but then realised she'd have her own space and a little bit of money from my cousin. I had gone back once or twice, but she hadn't gotten round to changing it much. A lick of paint and a damn good clean, but it made all the difference.

So she said.

Cale was quiet, had been since the shoot out, but she was getting better all the time and Alix always mentioned that on set she was a totally different person. Once there was a camera in her face she just seemed to switch on. But if she wanted she would never have to work again. John had left her most of his fortune, Gates got some of course and I got a decent amount which meant my life was a lot easier, but Cale got the bulk and together with her own fortune which Jason, once he fully recovered after his ordeal, managed to sort out she became one of the richest women in America.

Alix was heartbroken about Anna's death, but hid it well as she threw herself into her work. She rarely spoke to or about Cale, but acknowledged her sister as just that and after Cale had generously written her a million dollar check she gave up any feelings of retaliation for the perceived loss of her childhood rights and inheritance. The secret remained between the few of us who knew.

And Sara and I decided after I was released from hospital that we should find a place together. We looked for a couple of weeks, but there was nothing we liked so I moved in with her.

Of course I asked if she'd like to move into my place, but she seemed unwilling. Don't ask me why....

About the Author

Alex Baldock left university in 1996 with an Honours degree and no idea of what to do. He worked in retail and a bank, spent a year in Australia, found wine, fell in love, got married and through it all occasionally sat down and wrote or went out and played golf.

He lives with his gorgeous wife, Bonnie, and beautiful daughter, Robyn, in a Leicestershire village.

Printed in the United Kingdom
by Lightning Source UK Ltd.
121369UK00001B/1-39/A